Bruar's Rest

Jess Smith

was raised in a large family of Scottish travellers. She is the bestselling author of *Jessie's Journey: Autobiography of a Traveller Girl* and its sequels, *Tales from the Tent* and *Tears for a Tinker*. This is her first novel. As a traditional storyteller, Jess is in great demand for live performances throughout Scotland and beyond. More information can be found on her website, www.jesssmith.co.uk.

Bruar's Rest

JESS SMITH

my 'first novel'

hope you enjoy

Jess Smith

MERCAT PRESS

First published in 2006 by Mercat Press Ltd
10 Coates Crescent, Edinburgh EH3 7AL
www.mercatpress.com

ISBN-10: 1-84183-105-0
ISBN-13: 978-1-84183-105-3

The publisher acknowledges subsidy from the Scottish Arts Council
owards the publication of this volume.

Set in Goudy Old Style at Mercat Press

Printed and bound in Great Britain by Bell & Bain Ltd

ACKNOWLEDGEMENTS

To all my family and friends

To Michelle Iona Melville

To Shirley, a fine poet, songwriter and singer

To my mate, Sheila Stewart MBE

To Mercat

DEDICATION

I dedicate this story to Spook: co-editor of my life

INTRODUCTION

*M*y seed for writing was planted twenty years ago, when I set off to pick the brains of Mary, a tradition-bearer and relative who lived in the coastal area of Aberdeenshire.

I half-joked about writing a book, told her I'd been toying with the idea of telling the world my life story, with several old ghostie tales thrown in. She knew cracking spook stories, I wanted inspiration and if ever there was a tinker tale-teller, it was her.

'This book,' I told her, 'is in its wishful stages, an array of handwritten bits and pieces about my childhood on the road in our bus-home.'

'You mean life as a human sardine, with seven sisters, parents and some mangy dog.' She grinned and slapped her thigh, at the memories of Daddy manoeuvring the bus alongside her wee cottage, engine revving, us tumbling over each other to cuddle the life from her, escaping like kennelled pups from the narrow door of our bus-home.

'Not much of a life though,' her smile gave way to a frown, 'to write a book about, I mean. Are you sure it would work?'

'Of course it would, I have memories galore. For instance, like you said, living like sardines—in deep winter, when Jack Frost clung to eyebrows and toes, our closeness kept away his icy stings. Or that incident that had travellers the country over in awe—you know, that time when Daddy took on four drunkards who would have murdered us all on yon dark moor up Dalwhinnie way. Wee gladiator he was that night, beating them to pulp. What a braw story, don't you think?'

1

A blank look told me she wasn't impressed, nor believed in the feat of my five-and-a-half-foot father; so I tried the academic approach by saying, 'Surely, as part of Scotland's travelling community, you think it's important to preserve a lifestyle, one which has been in place for two thousand years; wouldn't you say?'

'Ach, who cares about our kind? Nobody jumps through hoops to preserve a rat, my girl, and in society's eyes we're no better. You'll be hard pressed to sell a book about tinkers, they're next door to an ape; sub-humans, little else, surely you know we're nothing more.'

She sank into a floral patterned armchair, leant forward with her arm on a bent knee, threw a sour look in my direction, then went back to ponder fond memories. 'Do you mind how each year you'd rush in here, wee face all red and rosy, full of excitement to share your latest epic tale of shroud-washing banshees and fierce werewolves? I told your folks at the time, even as a wee lassie, there was a gift in that head of yours. But never mind ghost-shockers and bus-dwelling, I know a story that would make a great book, one tailor-made for you: listen!'

⎯

So while I sipped hot tea with my host, who was a sort of cousin of my father's (to explain connections would take far too long and prove a novel in itself) she began to recount a saga of epic proportions. About someone called Megan who searched the country for her husband, the strangely named Bruar—one single casualty amongst the millions of the First World War.

World War One is definitely not my favourite period in history; those were dark times when souls were lost to pride and greed. Nations with guns for brains slaughtering each other at the raising of an old general's finger. World War Two was just as bad, it took my daddy away, leaving mammy to go it alone with four children for six tortuous years. No, wars weren't my thing.

Mary, though, was on a roll, galloping out words of past times, and only by clanking the kettle against the kitchen sink and turning the tap full on did I manage to halt her charge. I hadn't the heart to tell her that those kinds of events didn't hold me one bit. Innocent people dead, the guilty left to gloat. It was disrespectful of me, yes, but I could only see war as a game of winners and losers; and what was it all for in the end? We have tongues! Surely, if they were used truthfully, the wise of all nations could find common ground.

I'm a placid kind of body, whereas Mary could skin a cat without touching the poor thing, so while we were discussing her tale I asked out of curiosity, rather than any real interest, were the characters real people?

That didn't matter, it wasn't important, it was a grand tale and she continued pressing me to write it down.

Yet it was a monster epic and it terrified me. My brain at that time couldn't contemplate a paragraph, never mind thousands upon thousands of words. If I realised my dream of writing a book, it would have to be my past, not Mary's murderers and lost souls, that would fill its pages. Hers was a story for another day. Hell, I didn't even know if I could write.

Yet, in the years that followed, like a running stream I made my mark on the world through, not one, but three books. A trilogy about a Scottish traveller and her dying culture!

I had been uncaged; I was a free creature once more. The words of Charlotte Bronte's Jane Eyre spring to mind: 'I am no bird; no net ensnares me: I am a free human being with an independent will.'

It was after publication of my first book, while I was gathering ghosts and folklore characters to fill future books, my phone rang. It was Mary. I did keep reminding myself at times of her tale and wondered what negative response she'd had to my writings. On the contrary, she'd really enjoyed my stuff, especially when it used her contribution of ghosts and witch tales. I was astounded, though, at how quickly she pressed the case of Bruar and Megan's tale. If determination could win a prize, in my mind she'd won a high honour.

'I knew fine the days on the road would make good reading,' she said. At first I thought she'd changed her tune, then came—'but have you given any more thought to that lassie with the lost husband?' The forthright, I would even say furious tone took me a little by surprise.

'No, I've been researching the old ways, Mary. The origins of gypsies need researching for another project I'm toying with, and to tell the truth, I'm still not convinced I could do that story justice.'

Instantly a stuttering apology followed. One book in the bestseller list and I was awarding little respect to my dear old mate, brushing her aside with a lame excuse. I felt her silence on the end of the phone and knew I'd been far too harsh. Thankfully, though, an answer came from her that sounded quite light-hearted; it even afforded me a laugh, albeit a kind of goblin-like shriek followed by a low hiss.

'You can look at my craggy face and find all the details of an old gypsy, if that's what tickles you, lassie. Come up and see me. I'm not at all well these days, old age ye ken, and any road, I could do with a bit company.'

———

Not blessed with children, her husband long dead, she was quite alone apart from her Tam, a nippy West Highland terrier. So off I went to visit Mary and nippy Tam in their tiny low-roofed cottage, nestling in a cove on the Aberdeenshire coast. Clear blue sky went as far as the eye could see, marked with tiny wisps of white cloud. If it hadn't been for a covering of frost on roof-tiles one might have imagined it early summer, not March.

Holding a mug of steaming tea, one arm curled around my knees, I stared into the teller's eyes while heat from the coal fire warmed my body. Strangely, perhaps now that my own story had been told, I found Mary's World War tale attractive in a way I couldn't explain. Hearing the characters come to life once more, I needed to get closer to them: what made them tick? Until now they had remained patiently silent, waiting on a pen that could give them an eager rebirth.

She sensed my eagerness and took the story further back, this time into Bruar's past, telling of his mother's demise which, to be honest, dug into my marrow.

But whether it was a lack of belief in my slender abilities or fear of taking on such a massive storyline I don't know, but my excuse was on cue. 'I'll write it as a short story, I'm no use at the novel, me. Those long story writers are gifted, I'm not!'

'Aye, right,' she said, smiling through a gap-toothed grin. There was for a minute a cooling of the atmosphere, I saw the eyes narrowing, nose twitching, and thought, 'here we go again, another argument.' I was wrong, however.

Stretching her cardigan across the narrowest of shoulders to keep the grey sea haar rolling in from the ocean from chilling her bones, she stared into my soul, as old folks seem able to do. 'Can you put the neck of a giraffe onto a rabbit, or push rain back inside its cloud?' she asked, then added, 'It was man who invented the pen.'

I wondered if my old relative was reaching an age when, instead of going through life with added intelligence, she was slipping back into childhood. But maybe it was I who, with all my individual characters catalogued for future books, was slightly off balance.

I didn't know at the time what she meant, but later, while mulling over my visit, it became clear to me: she was simply implying that 'to a writer, outer galaxies are reachable.'

'Getting a wee bit senile,' was the last thought I had of her standing on the red doorstep of her spotless cottage, smiling, one hand waving, the other folded over just as spotless an apron, her dog, wee Tam, tight against those tartan-slippered feet.

As I looked in my rear-view mirror, that image of her waving, dog barking, seagulls diving for biscuit-crumbs scattered onto paving stones to the front of the house, was the last I saw of her. My last look drifted into the mouth of sea mist that swallowed all in its path. What I witnessed that day was old Mary's preparation for death; two months later she fell foul of a massive heart attack. The best ghost story teller in all of Scotland had left the earth a sadder place, as far as I was concerned. A great tragedy, and in my hands rested her dirge tune; could I play it?

A mound of research, the adornments of fiction and Mary's facts (lodged methodically in my head) were merged to produce the story and journey which you, my dear reader, are about to embark upon now. I cannot enlighten those of you who ask, of my characters, 'Were they real people?' because, as is the way of many mist-folk, nobody like Mary tells a story with proven, documented facts. However, I may go some way in answer to you at this early point by saying, a blood-red vein does trickle in and out of a certain beating heart.

Mary had informed me that the main players in her story were part travelling stock, and maybe that's a reason why I found myself leaning towards this tale. If at times you find it difficult to grasp their culture, don't worry, I'll guide you through. However not all the players are mist-folk; like squares in a patchwork, in this story many different cultures are fastened together.

Perhaps you're at home, sat in that favourite armchair, G&T just so, or fingers warmed around a nice cup of what you fancy; maybe you're lying in bed, cocoa at hand; maybe you are in a train or plane surrounded by strangers. Wherever you find yourself, come with me, I'll tell you a story of how one lone young woman followed a flame of devoted loyalty through fear, murder and forbidden love.

Bruar's Rest

'Run lassie, find your man, he sleeps above the earth, not below, fast go your way, like the stream, winding forth blindly, yet always aware of treacherous waterfalls cascading over sharp rock. Mind how you flow, wild child of Nature: go on until the great tide frees your tired limbs and the hidden sun shines for you once more. Embrace the warmth of he who waits in the shadows.'

THE BEGINNING

Our tale opens in 1892.

Rory Stewart, a young Highlander, wild and far too fond of the drink, was the only son of a peat-cutter who'd passed away many years ago. His mother had also answered death's call, leaving him and his older sister Helen. She was a staid and stern young woman, whose only ambition was to join a nunnery and live in quiet servitude to her faith. When parents were gone, she opted instead to take care of her wayward brother. A choice that brought constant regret.

She did her best, but his love of drink and raising trouble in the quiet village of Durness, the northernmost point of Sutherland, caused her hours of torment. However, when a tinker man and his niece came passing through the village, his eye fell upon the bonny lassie. She had a power of beauty that crept into his sleep; if there is such a thing as love at first sight then surely it happened when he saw her. She had no liking, though, for men held under the power of alcohol, and for a while refused to look at him, still less would she share frivolous words.

She was to his eyes a rare beauty, serene and charming. It was hard to believe she'd been a walker of the road, living under stars, washing in freezing burn water and laying her head wherever the feather fell. To him there would be no other: this had captured him, his dream woman. He'd not fallen in love with a lesser being as many might have considered such a match with a tinker; he'd fallen for an angel, who would prove his very own salvation. Down on one knee he went, but not until he had proved there was no longer any love of demon drink in him would she so much as afford a smile.

So day followed day of sobriety and his wild nights were forgotten. She had tamed the tiger.

Under the roof of an ancient chapel, along with her only relative, an old uncle, and his sister Helen as witnesses, Rory married his lassie.

His wild ways seemed behind him, and he would only ever raise his kilt on rare occasions like New Year and birthdays. Helen saw little of him, since he took on his wife's occupation of wandering Scottish by-ways. His wife showed him how to cut bracken, snare rabbits and make brooms. Money made wasn't thrown away on a night's boozing, but went instead into a small wooden box; winter sustenance would come from that container. Once, for a brief time, the couple appeared at Helen's door to say a baby was due.

Rory's lassie loved the north, where his roots were. She wanted to rear a family and stop travelling, and after Bruar, their first child, was born life could not have been better. The uncle, who had been forced to care for her after her parents were killed in a flood that washed away their campsite, left her in the capable care of Rory and headed west.

A second child was nearing its time when Rory gained possession of a derelict cottage. It was in dire need of major rebuilding, but he was determined to complete the task. It would take a lot of hard work, but she was worth it. They pitched a tent next to the ruin and both worked hard.

From their clifftop vantage point, gulls, guillemots and puffins watched as the young couple, each filled with dreams, built, with loving devotion, their new home. She thought it a lovely spot overlooking the sea, ideal for chasing sea breezes and telling her many forthcoming children stories of her people of the mist.

They had lain under the stars, making love and promising each other they would fill the village nearby with a whole clan of wee Stewarts. Girls would be like their mother; boys like him. All that life could offer lay at their feet. They even joked with Helen when she came to help with toddler Bruar, freeing them for longer hours of eager toil, that she should turn her home into a nunnery to teach her nieces and nephews the ways of her God.

Helen was fond of her brother's wife, even though she'd not much time for mist-wanderers or the summer walkers, names that Highland people gave the tinkers. Oh, some gossip had gone around, but it soon dispersed when folks saw how much the young lassie had changed the wild Rory. Her brother now had purpose in life, he was happy, what more could she ask.

ONE

*H*er labour began with tiny twinges. At first she sang through the pains, playing gently with wee Bruar and a wooden train his father had made for him from odd pieces of wood.

'Do you need anything, my pet?' Rory asked, handing her a stone jar of milky tea, and seeing to his young son. His gaze went through the cramped tent, already showing a few holes at its base, where on a torn mattress stuffed with crushed bracken his lassie would give him another child. He'd voiced concern at how uncomfortable she might be, but in her usual way she assured him that a tent was where her mother brought her into the world, and her grandmother had given birth there also.

He knelt, kissed her and ran a cool hand over her warm brow.

'I'm doing away nae bother, my love,' she said. 'Now, you get on with rebuilding that house of ours, little Bruar will keep me company.'

She worked through her pain without obvious complications, yet deep inside the situation was far from normal. As each hour passed, she grew more stressed than the last. As an added anxiety, the baby was showing no signs of response, and now each pain riveted through her back with dire severity. As her womb grew stiff she began to claw at the stretched skin.

'Oh my God, the baby has breeched!'

Terror rose, gripped itself onto her thumping heart as she felt the concealed infant lodge itself tightly in the birth canal. It needed help—it had to be assisted, if not it would die.

Rory, thinking all was in hand, popped his head in the tent door.

'Go get your sister, fetch Helen!' Her hot, clammy hand found his arm, fingernails sank deep into flesh.

Like a hissing poker, fear burnt through him. His wife's exposed breast heaved in deep waves. 'For the love of God, what's wrong?'

With arched spine she raised herself onto two reddened elbows and gasped, 'It's closed, the way out; my bairn panics. Oh God, Rory, run like the deer, fetch help—Helen—run, man!'

'I won't leave you, not like this.' He knelt, cradled her through each excruciating push, feeling as useless as a hermit crab without its shell.

'I'll not see this baby alive if I don't get help! Go now!' Again her attempts to move the infant failed, as she arched her spine and screamed: 'Please, please, man, it's not coming. I feel sick and faint, I need help, get Helen.' She clenched her teeth and her breath hissed through each nerve-ripping surge of agony, beads of sweat bursting from every inch of stretched skin.

Little Bruar crept, like a terror-struck rabbit, under a corner of blanket and tunnelled deep. His mother never normally shouted or screamed, so he'd be best to stay hidden until she stopped making frightening sounds.

—

Rory in his panic pulled on broken leather boots. It would take him half an hour to reach his sister's house, but there was a closer neighbour. Not far away, just along the beach, in a cave, lived an old man. A strange creature, and it was said he could see future events. People living in that area relied on 'the Gifted One' for that. But not Rory: even as a child he did not like the man and would avoid the dreadful dingy cave in which he dwelt. Only people seeking word of their future went near him.

But now Rory was desperate. Stumbling over grass clumps, sinking into mounds of wind-blown sand, splashing through the incoming tide he called out, 'Balnakiel, old man, my lassie needs help!' He kicked off his seaweed-tangled boots; broken shells and sharp stones cut into his bare feet, blood oozed. Bounding over rocky, rye-grassed banks, he found the cloaked seer hunched over a low-burning fire, his hooded head adding to the mystery of the man.

'Did you hear me? I need help; my wife is in her child hour; can you go fetch my sister, or stay with my family in the tent, while I fetch her?'

Silence followed. The man showed little sign of concern at his young wife's threatened predicament; he just muttered, eyeballs rolling in an oval-shaped head. Then, as if possessed, he rose up onto unsteady legs, thrust an arm skyward and prophesied: 'No use! No use!'

Rory dropped on his knees and begged. 'For God's sake, old man, my lassie will die!'

But to his horror, Balnakiel fell back in his chair of knotted drift-wood, the hood draped over his lowered head, and with a shaking arm he pointed to a circle of pebbles at his feet.

'See, Stewart; see how the stones never lie! She will meet a cold dawn!'

Rory grabbed the old skeletal creature, kicked the seer stones sending them in every direction, and shook him violently; but over and over Balnakiel repeated, 'Cold dawn, no use, I see the *Ban Nigh*, the washer of the ford—she covers your woman in her shroud. The baby lives, it lives...'

Rory didn't feel his fist thud into the old man's lantern jaw, nor hear his wispy red-haired skull crack against rock, or see blood spurt from his eye; he was already running and stumbling back to help his lassie.

Crawling under the closed tent door he called out, 'He wouldn't help me—God curse that evil old bastard, he wouldn't...'

The sight that met him as he rushed into the tent halted all words. A new baby, coiled around its birth-cord, mouthing silent cries like a fish lying on a stone, weakly punched the dank air from within its mother's pale, twisted form. His precious wife had, with her last ounce of strength, delivered him another son.

Opening wide eyes too young to understand reality or feel death's sting, Bruar had awakened from a sleep to the sounds of his father's deep sobs. He sat staring at his mother's twisted face and lifeless body. Was he dreaming? From his corner of woollen blankets and damp feather pillow he shivered, lost in the turmoil of frightening pictures and the weird sounds whistling outside around his tent. If older he might have dived for cover, fearing unearthly horrors, but he was only three years old. Nothing made sense to him, just a mother's cuddle and a father's smile.

Rory cupped his dead wife's face in his big hands, apologising profusely for his failure, crying and sobbing; all the while rocking back and forth: 'don't leave me lassie, I can't do it without you, oh please...'

He sat for ages, head sunk in shaking hands, mumbling incoherently. Then a faint cry came from the new-born, uncomfortable at the sensation of blood congealing and tightening on his gossamer skin.

Clumsily the new father, now half insane with grief, raked in his pockets. From one he took a small penknife and cut the cord, finding a piece of dirty string among rusty nails and a soiled flannel in his other pocket; he rolled the string around the end of birth cord nearest the tiny belly to which it was attached and tied it tight. The baby winced, wriggled and uncurled matchstick fingers of pink and mottled red, opened wide the small mouth and filled new lungs with virgin air.

Going through his actions automatically now, Rory dipped a cloth into the basin of cold water by his wife's bed and wiped the child. It winced again as he laid the small bundle, wrapped in a torn sheet, next to Bruar. He said to the traumatised boy, uncaringly as if his children were nothing more than unwanted mongrel pups, 'Here lad—a brother for you.'

All that mattered was dead: their mother, his partner for life, the woman who promised to love him forever, was gone. What could he do with the children? His job would have been to provide food for their bellies, not to offer the love for their souls that only a mother could give.

Little Bruar pushed away the small bundle of life and huddled into his father's side. What was a brother anyway? He was more concerned by mother's silence. With fear and curiosity he tugged at the damp sheet covering her porcelain face. Questions tripped off his tongue to fall like silent ash around his grieving father's ears: why was she messy? Why cold and grey-coloured? She didn't touch his face and run her fingers through his tousled hair—why? Daddy was crying, he'd never known his father to do this—why? One small candle flickered by the tent door, not the big oil lamp—why? And who left this baby? Innocent eyes stared at Rory, waiting on one touch, a simple nod just to reassure the little lost child, but there was nothing. Angry in his confusion, he shouted, 'Daddy, you're squeezing Mammy, you'll hurt her. Can I have a cuddle, Daddy?'

There was no place for his son, only for loss and pain. The whistling ocean wind blew cold through the tent; Bruar felt its bite, he wiped

14

away tears from his father's face with his small hand and tried with his body to push a wedge between his shaking father and dead mother in a futile attempt to find warmth.

The baby opened his mouth with a sucking motion, searching for milk, and when none came started crying. No one had told him who this baby was, yet nature had linked them together, and Bruar felt the blood ties. Gently the youngster turned his father's face in its direction. Rory uncurled his arms from around the limp body of his wife and carefully laid her down. He felt for and touched the toddler's head. 'I know, I know, lad, I hear, he has good strong lungs. We'll get down to Auntie Helen's, she'll find us milk.'

Scared and confused, little Bruar pulled at his mother's arm. There was no response, so he turned once more to his grief-stricken father: 'Make my Mammy get up on her legs and open her eyes, cause me scared. She's lost her tongue, Daddy, has a cat got it?' His tiny shoulders shook, bottom lip trembled.

In grief his father had no answers for one so small. How could this fledgling gain the slightest understanding of his mother's still form? Rory made an attempt at explaining why Mammy was sleeping forever, but was interrupted by sounds from outside the canvas dwelling. A slender arm wrenched back the tent door; there stood Helen, head and shoulders covered by a green, woollen shawl. Her face was grave and furious.

'Rory, I'm right disappointed, surely the drink isn't in you at a time like this, when another baby is due? Folks are looking for you, and man they are as angry as a sea-monster scouring the waves. You had no right hitting the Balnakiel! They say it was the fuel of wild drink that made you. God, man, he's lost an eye!'

'Shut up, woman, I have no stomach for your biting tongue, or anyone's, leave me alone.'

'Leave you alone!' She hit him hard across the face with her shawl. 'I'll flog you for bringing shame on the family name. Will you never learn?'

Slowly he moved aside. His young wife was becoming rigid, her flesh marble-hued; the skin of her eyelids was tightening, exposing half-opened eyes. He turned to gaze upon her, then fell in a crumpled heap at his sister's feet, unable to stand the sight.

Helen's tongue tightened, a lump spread from her breast bone and froze in her throat when she saw her sister-in-law's body covered by the sheet. 'Oh, God help us, she's not—I, brother, had no idea she was in labour—why did you not send for help? The bairn is...?'

'Aye, bless her, she did it without help, brought that wee one into the world.' He pointed at the infant lying behind Bruar. 'But tell me, sister, who could I have sent for help? Little Bruar here? My lassie thought we'd manage, and I promise you we were fine until her back arched and the fear took hold. She asked for you! I only wanted Balnakiel to sit with her and the wee lad. I begged on my knees, pleaded with him in that stinking, slime-walled cave. He just stared with those bead eyes, head rolled on narrow shoulders, prophesying. The last thing I needed was that mad swaying and muttering, on and on about death coming for my lassie. God help me, sister, it was all that I could do not to hurl the beast head-first into the sea. He kept repeating those sick words: 'she would die and meet a cold dawn'. I had to shut him up. Curse that pig who's in league with the Devil, for she is stone dead! It wasn't drink that made me hit—what would anyone do? I meant to shut his mouth; and if the chance comes again, I will, I'll swing for him! He should be glad I didn't kill him. Look at my lassie, an hour ago she was as healthy as any woman having a baby, still fresh, a mere girl. And what does this wee man know of death? How can I tell him that his mother is not coming back to cuddle and kiss him anymore?'

Helen put an arm around his shoulder and whispered in his ear, 'It wasn't the drink, you were sober; people will understand it was the grief that made you hit the Seer, and not the fuel of alcohol. Stop fretting about this little chap, sure infants heal fast.' She was trying hard to help her brother, but the sound of angry voices grew nearer.

Several crofters had found the Seer limping and bleeding heavily from a gash on his head. Now they were seeking vengeance, heading toward the tent. She ran to meet them, shaking her head and warning them not to approach Rory in his present state. One old woman shouted that her brother should take what was coming to him for injuring their Voice of Prophecy.

Helen stopped them, pointing to the tent. 'You could not make his pain any the worse. See.' She opened the tent door for all eyes to see what lay inside. 'My brother's wife has died in childbirth. See if you don't believe me.' She gently lifted the cover, exposing the pathetic scene. 'Now, surely, you can show a bit compassion for this young family.'

Two or three people stooped inside, and then quickly drew back with hands covering mouths. Yet even though the sight of death was shocking, some hard-hearted souls still found words of condemnation. 'Rory Stewart, bury your woman and take yourself away from these parts, and heaven help you if we ever see you again.'

The fisherfolk and peat-cutters whom he had been part of before marrying the travelling lassie took leave and were soon gone, quickly distancing themselves from the visitation of death.

Over the sand dunes of Durness point where he had promised to build a picturesque croft, a grey cloud spread to meet a cold sea breeze. All Rory's hopes of future and family lay on the bracken under that soiled sheet. His oath never to touch alcohol now meant as little to him as the vapour from the lid of a whiskey vat—the 'angel's share'.

'Margaret Mackay has just this past hour delivered a blue bairn,' Helen said. 'Poor wee mite, her man is burying it as we speak. She has fullness of breast milk. Now come, brother, gather what you can, I'll manage both bairns. There's no time to spare, the fisherfolk might change their minds and come searching for your blood. Hitting the Seer was a terrible thing, no matter what the reasons. And if this infant's not fed soon, he'll be joining his mother.'

Taking a firm hold of her slim shoulders, he rested his sad eyes on the children and pleaded, 'Look after them for me. I'll stay with their mother for a while, make my peace. I'm in no fit state to father a rat, never mind these two. I'll come for them when I'm able to be a provider.'

She wanted to tell him the cottage could still be built, to be a home where he could rear his sons, but she'd enough knowledge of her brother to know her words would fall on deaf ears, his pain-etched face said it all

It was the little ones who needed attention now. She dashed home to her small croft not more than half a mile away, stopping at Margaret Mackay's to ask her to spare some of her breast milk; it would be sufficient until she was able to milk her cow.

⎯

That night and the following day she busied herself with her new charges. She had no way of knowing whether her brother had buried their mother, or, more to the point, fallen foul of the angry coastal dwellers who looked to the Seer for guidance. In their ignorance, they would think a one-eyed seer could only part-see their future, and what good was that?

But the lack of news brought her little peace. Still worried, and feeling in his state of dire mourning that Rory might do himself an injury, or worse, she wrapped the baby in a shawl, tied him to her front, and with wee Bruar at her side went back to the place that not so long ago held nothing but the promise of new life and a future teeming with happy times.

Turning the bend in the road before walking through the sand-dunes she saw a spiral of thick, black smoke. 'Stay here, Bruar,' she said, motioning the child to sit in a patch of long grass. Down she went, hoping the burning heap wasn't what she thought. A distinctive smell intermingled with ash and flame and was gently carried skyward by a soft breeze. As the odour found her nostrils she covered her mouth with one hand, tripping fingers of her other hand through a string of rosary beads and muttering prayer after prayer.

A stick hung loosely from his hand as he pushed pieces of burning garments into the eager flame, tears flowing freely from swollen red eyes. As her shadow fell across the sun's light, he looked up and croaked, 'I know you think it bad what I've done, but sister, it was her way, that if ever she went before me I had to burn everything.'

'It's blasphemous, brother, to burn flesh. Jesus will come back at Judgement Day, and he won't find her. Think of it when your time comes: she will not be waiting, but eternity waits for you beyond the furthest star.'

'Oh, sister, can't you see my life is here and now? She was my heavenly star, now gone forever. What care I of eternity, your Jesus or anything else? However, if you go back to the ruined cottage you'll find I've buried her in the ground—this is our tent and belongings. What you smell is the blood-soaked bed covers.'

'You have two fine boys who need a father. Now what kind of a man puts his own feelings before those of his children?'

'I am no use to them. Please, Helen, can you see to them until...?'

He didn't finish. Already fisherfolk, smelling the burning clothes, were coming over the dunes. He kissed the new infant's spotlessly clean face, smelling his freshness. Wiping tears from Helen's cheeks, he said, 'Kiss my wee Bruar, and when you tell them of me, don't mention the drink. And if you can, forgive me.'

He pulled a canvas haversack over his arms, positioned a cloth cap over a thick head of curly hair. A crooked stick lay half hidden in the sand, he lifted it and was soon striding along the beach.

'Rory Stewart,' a voice called, from over by the highest sand brae.

Fists curled into granite-hard knots at the sound of that voice. Slowly he turned to see Balnakiel, his tormentor, leaning on a crutch, face half-smothered by a dirty, blood-soaked bandage. 'Come here, young man, I have to tell you something.'

'I've no mind to apologise to the like of you,' said Rory, walking off faster now than he'd intended.

'If the boot was on my foot, lad, I'd have done the same thing.'

Rory stopped in his tracks. His wife's dead body was still a vivid picture in his mind and he shouted, 'Why?'

Old Balnakiel looked to the heavens and said, 'what's before you, boy, will not go by you. I saw your woman, surrounded she was, by the *Ban Sidh*,* they were lowering her shroud and singing her death song.' He hobbled closer to where Rory stood, and partly whispered with a soft growl, 'Just as crystal clear as I see them lower yours!'

From head to heel Rory felt the shiver of a hidden terror, a terror that had dogged him from childhood to manhood. His awe of the sea prophet was now apparent; he feared his own end. In his head he heard himself shout 'when, and by whose hand?' but the words would not come out. His tent was now a flicker of ash, already lifting into the breeze; his spirit was broken and he needed a drink.

Without waiting for an answer he ran faster than a stalked deer, and soon disappeared into a sea haar that was crawling over the beach with shroud-like stealth. Rain fell from the heavens to douse the

---

*Author's note: *in Highland communities superstitions abound. Feared among all shore dwellers was hearing, and God forbid, witnessing, the haunting sight and sound of a* Ban Sidh. *This was a creature supposed to be of wispy thin appearance, with long, grey-white hair that danced from head to feet, a skull face and no eyes; it heralded a coming death. Fishermen who were late home from a trip at sea would cause great worry within households, until their boat was spotted far out on the horizon. Women would enquire of each other if a foreboding was in the air. The wisdom of older females would be sought to see if anyone had experienced anything strange, for instance whistling winds or howling dogs. Rory had been reared on such tales—he'd a deep inner fear, and perhaps that was part of the reason he left his sons. Shakespeare fashioned Macbeth's witches on the model of the* Ban Sidh *(pronounced Banshee).*

funeral pyre, sending curious onlookers scurrying home. Helen took a long corner of the baby's shawl, covered her head and retraced her steps to where Bruar stood waiting obediently. Rain ran down his red cheeks from a head of curly blond hair. With one hand he pulled a torn jersey closer under a shivering chin, and with the other he waved in the direction where he saw father running.

The final spiral of dingy smoke that was all there was left of a happy home danced among the now heavy raindrops. A lost boy wondered if Aunt Helen would feed him some of her chunky vegetable soup, he'd liked the taste. The feel of her soft bed, with its wooden headboard, had been great fun when she took him in once after mammy and daddy had been rained out of the tent. She could do anything, could Auntie. Maybe one day she could bring mammy back and daddy too; one day.

From that day, Helen, who once harboured dreams of serving her Jesus as a nun within a high-walled convent, was, for the foreseeable future, a full-time mother. Neighbours, who were few, came by to remind her often that his children were welcome, but they hoped that Rory had disappeared like a sea fog, and he'd better not come back.

So life along the costal domain of Durness, with peat bog to its rear and the ocean swell to its front, went on without a hair of his head being seen in those parts. Helen knew her brother's fondness for drink would make any journey he took troublesome. His sons filled her days with responsibility, yet at night when the lamp was extinguished, the boys tucked up safely in their beds, she'd listen for those heavy-booted feet upon her doorstep, and the gentle tap- tapping of his clumsy fist on her cottar door.

It was seven long, happy years later, when thoughts of her brother seldom entered her mind any more, that he did indeed come home.

It was a lovely spring morning, lambs bleated and gambolled on the nearby braeside. She'd been busy with the annual spring clean-ing. The boys wrestled playfully on the green at the back of the house before running towards two hill ponies, grazing amidst heather and rock. Bruar, well-made, big for his ten years, was as strong as any good-sized teenager, and a power of help to her. Jimmy though on the contrary a slip of a lad, could cut the peat alongside his older brother, working a full day.

Helen sang softly to herself without the slightest inkling that someone was watching her every move.

Not wishing to disturb her, Rory went round the other side of the house to admire the fine job she'd made of rearing his sons. He rested his back against an old fence-post, rotted by the wind-blown sea spray.

Bruar held himself well, 'a lot like me,' he thought, proudly. The other lad, small like his mother, yet had strength in him, seldom seen in a seven-year-old. He watched and wondered what name she'd given him; no doubt some biblical tag, knowing her.

His feet were blistered, his back weary with travelling open drove-roads for weeks on end, yet it was a journey well spent; it was worth it just to see them—his very own sons. He could have forgotten about them, given up any claim he had to them. But like a wounded deer scoured from the herd, his way was hard. He'd been wandering for years, reasoning and arguing with himself, whether he should go home and be with the boys, or trek aimlessly until his body aged and broke, until it succumbed to the harsh elements of a freezing winter.

One day, after a night plagued with dreams of his lost lassie and who she'd want to be raising their sons, he rose from under a torn canvas hap and headed northwards. It was as if his late wife had made the decision for him: 'go back and reunite with our sons'.

Her mouth parched, Helen stopped to make some tea and check the boys, and then came the shock. She saw him, cap in hand, hair showing an appearance of time-ravaged grey. His rugged looks, with a prominent scar running down his right cheek, told her that her brother would have fared better staying hidden in the fog. Yet there he stood, back from wherever he'd hidden himself, and he was there for only one thing—to collect his sons.

Her ears filled with heart-beats pounding in her chest like deafening drums. She had poured natural devotion as powerful as that of the most loving mother into those youngsters as if they were her own. They were known for miles around as her little orphans. The fisherfolk had said that with his wild temper, surely Rory would have met his match and would now be dead; that father of theirs, who took the eye from the Seer.

No words were exchanged as she walked stiffly into the house; he followed at a safe distance, shutting the door at his back. Her inner fury reeled her round to face him, she met his eyes from a vortex of anger, her emotional state deepened with disgust and fear. He was subdued, exhausted and ashamed. After a long pause, she asked coldly and straight to the point, 'You come for the boys, Rory?'

'I do, sister,' he muttered, as he laid a bag next to the bread-board on the kitchen table. 'There is money—enough for the years of feeding you done. If you pack their clothes, we'll be away.'

A rage swelled in her beating breast, she gathered the money bag in her hand and threw the meagre offering off her table. 'You saunter back into their lives, all this time not a word, nothing to say one way or other if you're dead or alive, nothing!' Her fury rose as she fumbled for a heavy iron pot that sat, half-filled with boiling water on the stove. Holding it level with his face she hissed through the cloud of steam, 'Those boys are better off without knowing their drunkard father. Now get the hell out of here, and don't bother coming back.'

He showed no fear, leaned down to retrieve the bag and said, 'Look, sister a lot of flowing water has passed below the bridge since those days when I'd spend hard-earned peat money on drink, but since my lassie died I've changed. I've been working every hour, how do you think I made this?'

'For all I know, you battered some poor soul and stole it. But it's not about money. It's about Jimmy's first wobbling steps, his little mouth never able to say the words mama or dada. His first words were "dog" and "cat" and "Bubs" for Bruar. And as for me—' she put down the pot and rubbed away tears flowing over her thin face: 'My name was "Hell". Me with my Bible being called that—do you know how much laughter that brought to this house? Oh no, how could you. You were away some place wallowing in self pity. Always about you, wasn't it, Rory? All about my big useless brother.'

He made a futile attempt to hold and comfort her, but his hands were pushed aside as she went on, 'and then the sickness that would worry me onto my knees and make me pray through the fever, nights and nights with my sweet little sons—they are not yours, they are mine! Now get out, get out!'

It was then he saw the full pain his sister had endured; what he'd put her through. He slumped down on his knees on the stone floor, his arms clumsily circled her thin frame. 'Forgive me, Helen, I never meant you hurt. Please see it in your heart to understand.'

She quickly composed herself and took his hands away. She

brushed back and then ran trembling fingers through the loose hair that had escaped from a cotton hair band. 'Where did that scar on your face come from then?' she asked, calmer yet still filled with hurt and anger.

Before he could answer, Bruar, followed by his brother, came panting into the house. When he saw the stranger he ran across and held her hand. 'Is this big man bothering you, auntie?' he asked.

'Och, not at all, son.' She gathered him into her arms and squeezed the youngster tightly.

In her quiet way she was never one to frill an explanation with unnecessary words, so rather than waste time, she brought the boys around her aproned knees. 'Bruar, Jimmy,' she fidgeted with their collars, running her hands over their shoulders, flicking dead grass from their tousled hair, took a long pause, then said quickly, 'this is your father! He's come back for you, and thinks nothing of taking you from me.'

For a minute of uncomfortable silence the boys looked from Helen to Rory, children trying to make sense of the awkward situation.

Rory sat down heavily in a tattered, cushioned armchair, taking warmth from the welcome fire. He studied Bruar's face, searching it in the hope that he might remember him from that last night when his mother died. Such traumatic events—surely something had left its mark in his mind. 'Son, I know you were only three, but do you have no memory of me?'

Bruar said nothing and turned his back. Apart from one or two fishermen handing in a basket of herring now and then, men seldom sat in that chair. His aunt had a rule about allowing them into her house; men were strictly doorstep visitors. Yet there he was, sitting in that chair as if he knew it was her knitting chair and not used unless she allowed it.

Helen's legs began to shake. Overcome by events she sat upon a wooden chair. The boys, like pint-sized soldiers, took up position like sentries at each side. Jimmy held her hand while Bruar draped an arm, sleeve rolled up like a real working man, around her shoulder to assure her that *he* was the man of the house. Oh yes, many times he had thought that if father should dare to show his face, he'd have plenty to say. Yet as he examined this stranger's appearance, his watery blue eyes and square, broad shoulders, he felt drawn to him in a way he could not explain.

As he looked from his aunt to the stranger he found a change on her face never before seen. Her jaw was firm, blue eyes staring and filled with fire. She was holding a handkerchief between her hands and tying it into knots. He'd heard her muttering many times under her breath, when he and Jimmy got too much for her: 'God help me, I love the two o' you, but I hate that big useless father of yours for leaving me this burden.' Yes, there wasn't another man who could cause that expression, so through clenched teeth he said, 'He's back then.'

Rory smiled, and could not stop the lone tear that escaped and ran over his cheek. He pushed out a shabbily dressed arm and touched his eldest son on the shoulder. He so wanted to hold him; to kiss that young red cheek, so vibrant and fresh. But no words came forth, a lump of emotion blocked up his throat like a hard lump of solid oak. He turned to his younger son and whispered instead, 'James is a good name, lad, that was our father's name. I'm pleased you have it. It's better than Abraham or Jeremiah.'

The boys gazed at each other bewildered by the remark, but it brought a thin, wry smile to Helen's stern face. She remembered how as a child she had named new lambs born to a neighbour's ewes after biblical characters, and was for a moment touched by her brother's memories of days when they were closer.

For a moment silence in the low-roofed cottage thickened as no one uttered a word. Rory patted an old black collie dog lying curled in a ball at his feet.

There was a power of explaining to do, convincing his children to accept him. It was not easy, he knew that; but first Helen deserved an explanation as to why he had come home out of the blue. He had positive plans and wanted them all to share in them; to be a family.

'I've worked my back sore just to bring money here. I had to let you see I'd keep my promise. I've been feeing with farmers in Perthshire and Angus. Work comes by way of harvest and grouse-beating. Oh, I can turn my hand to many things. And I happen to think it's a better place to bring up a family further down the country.'

Helen kept silent. Bruar asked him why he'd taken so long to come home.

'Son, I don't know. Time just seemed to drift by, working, paying my keep, there never was much left over. It's taken a long time to get this money here; and losing your mother like that. You do remember, son, how Mammy died?'

Bruar dropped his head, shuffled uncomfortably from foot to foot. 'No, I don't. But Auntie, she told us how you took the eye from Balnakeil and how you ran away. Yes, we know all about you.'

His father moved closer and said, 'Aye, and no doubt you've heard about me being the wild drunkard? Well yes, I hold my hand up, I might at times have let drink make memories fade. But that was a long time past; I've not so much as smelt the stuff for more than two years or so.' He took his son's hand and slipped the bag of money into it. 'I'm clean now, son, and ready to take on the responsibility of caring for you and Jimmy.'

Helen wanted to ignore the sincerity in her brother's face, he'd surely forfeited all rights to his children. Why, after all this time, had he come back to haunt them, disrupt their peace? He'd no rights at all. She hated him, at that moment she wished he'd been murdered, destroyed.

He saw it all, the anger and pain in her face, and without a word fell upon his knees for a second time, sobbing for forgiveness. 'Sister, please,' was all he could say, as like a baby he laid his heavy head on her lap.

Her heart was weeping, the reason why a sweet spring day had changed into a horrible nightmare eluded her. Yet what had years of bad dreams been preparing her for, if not for this day—his return. She ran her hand over his head, and with each stroke her sisterly love was born again. She didn't hate him or want him dead, she wanted to see him happy, with his children. They weren't hers, she'd no rights. 'In God's path we walk the bends and the straight,' she told herself, 'all I've done is keep these little boys on the right road.'

She pushed away his head from off her lap, stood up, gave the smouldering embers in the fire a poke and said in a subdued tone, 'I'm feeling the effects of age'. Holding back tears welling in her eyes she continued, 'Boys, you should be with your father...' Never in all her life did she think she would hand over her charges to him in so meek a fashion. Nights she'd lain in bed cursing him, swearing he'd take them over her dead body, but here she was dismissing the only things in the entire world she loved, as if they were nothing more than her neighbour's full-grown lambs ready for market. Yet again another phrase from her book of simple teaching came to mind: 'The meek shall inherit the earth'. Yes, they were ready to be given back. Then her thoughts lifted: what if her brother would stay home—here in Durness?

Her brother had other plans, though, and they didn't include taking the boys from her. He threw up his arms, beamed with new vigour, shouting his offer into every corner of the cottage. A small moth fluttering in a corner flew out through an inch of open window, obviously unused to such loudness.

'I want us to go south where we'd all get work, you too, Helen. There's no need for you not to move with us, be a solid family again?'

She had the opposite view. Her hope was that instead of living on the road as his wife, the boys' mother had done, they'd stay at home cutting peat, and in time would all be one big happy Highland family. This, she thought, would be the best solution.

She rose from her chair, lifted a broom and began brushing up the dried grass which she'd picked off the boys. Then she laid her broom against a window frame, lifted a blue vase of wilting flowers and said, 'I'll go and throw these out while you three discuss going on the road and things.' With these quiet words, she lowered her head and walked outside.

—

If her charges had felt anger towards Rory, it was soon dispelled. It was if he'd never left them, and they each fought to hold his attention, asking eager questions about what he'd done and where he'd been.

Helen wouldn't up sticks and move away though, there was no point. Sure, her heart would break and for a while be empty, but she was a Durness spinster, not a wandering traveller. No, she'd stay in her secure little home and bear a lonely existence.

With formality forgotten, Bruar, gingerly at first, walked around Rory as he sat by the fire, staring for ages at his scarred face, big broad shoulders and thick mane of grey hair. With his rugged and worn appearance his father looked older than his thirty-five years.

He sat by him and asked, 'Auntie Helen told us mammy was a tinker. Is that true, Rory—sorry, father?'

'As wild and as beautiful as a gentle roe deer. She smelt like flowers, and her hair was as black as the shiny wings of a raven,' he said, closing his eyes to see the precious vision clearer in his memory.

'She sounds right bonny. I'm going to marry a beautiful girl one day, father, you know?'

'Oh, you are, are you?' He laughed then added, 'She might be a beauty, but there will never be another to match your mother.'

'Will we live in a house, father?' enquired Jimmy. 'It's just I knew some travellers who came by from Caithness, they said the winters in tents were killers.'

Rory drew a hand across his younger son's shoulder, and sat back in his chair, 'We've got a good long summer ahead, and it's the tent I have, but don't worry. When winter comes I should have managed to secure a house from a factor, providing we get winter work. But listen, your mother, she was born and reared in a tent, and it didn't do her any harm at all. It's how you build one, that's the secret. I'll show you soon.'

Bruar asked if, like him, they'd also have to work.

'Hard work is good for young lads, but only if you want to. I'll do the providing,' he assured them with the full weight of his conviction.

For a while Jimmy and Bruar talked things over, then Bruar, being the oldest, said, 'Daddy, me and Jimmy think before you get much older, you'll need us to see to you.'

Helen could hear this from the compost heap where she had loosely tossed the withered flowers, and knew then she'd lost the two most precious people in her life. Aware that on this day her chapter of surrogacy was closing, she had to speak with Bruar alone, certain things had to be said. Going inside she called him, Jimmy went with his father at her request. Rory took his younger son's hand and walked outside to give them time together. He knew she was going to tell Bruar about the 'promise'; though he was aware of it, it was not his place to speak about it.

'Son,' she told Bruar, 'listen to what I say and never forget it. In time I was going tell you of the "promise", but I hadn't planned it so soon. Your father is the last of our family's line. In the ancient burial ground by the Parbh below the lighthouse there is one plot. It was destined for him, but because he laid a hand in anger upon the Balnakiel Seer he has forfeited it to you, his eldest. Whoever you marry she must see that you are buried in that old graveyard. You know where it is, for I have taken both of you many times. That is how it must be. And another thing, although he's promised the drink hasn't passed his lips for years, watch for its lure. Not even a priest of the church has enough will-power to resist it when the desire for it is strong. Drinking is like cleaning a cloudy mirror; suddenly a grand image will appear, but it only exists in the drinker's head. The image looks dull again when the drink is gone. That's why many fall victim to its charms.'

The youngster understood little of these words at the time, nor did his immature thoughts rest on anything beyond the excitement of a wide, open road that was waiting for them. He wanted to see and breathe the newness of the southern Highlands, a prospect that was so much fun to one who'd been no further than the few miles either side of his auntie's croft.

But how different would be the sting of reality. They were used to a warm bed within the sheltered walls of that low-roofed croft, with the sea winds to its back and mountains to the front. These were to be denied to them; from then on they would live the ancient ways of their late mother, a hard and bitter life in which the elements would take their toll on two pampered boys. That was how it had to be; their father had decided, and from that day on his word would be the rule of the family.

One final conversation between sister and brother was about that scar. He said he'd fallen over a clump of heather upon a sharp rock which missed his throat by an inch, striking his exposed cheek instead. He leaned forward, planted a warm kiss on her cold brow and whispered, 'I was sober at the time.' She just shook her head in disbelief, reminding him, 'A tiger keeps its stripes, brother.'

Next day after breakfast, the boys said their farewells to the only mother they knew. After saying goodbye also to Heather the cow and running from the nipping beak of an old red cockerel, they set off with a father who had until then been like a ghost from some recurring nightmare. Would he prove to be a hero, or maybe like that spirit from a bad dream come back to haunt them?

TWO

*T*he next ten years saw them constantly wandering from place to place, living under canvas and eating from hand to mouth. They slept beneath summer skies, filled with stars or rain clouds, and they were familiar only with Mother Nature's goods, her fish from the streams, fowl and rabbit from the heather moors. She filled their bellies and covered their bones with strong muscles. So into manhood grew the once petted boys, who became expert in all ways of survival. No thanks to their wayward father, though. One thing did turn out to be true; those wise words from Aunt Helen when she warned of their father's fondness for alcohol. Its lure at times became too strong for him; he'd slip away, find a dingy drinking den and be without reason for weeks. If not for his sons, God alone knows in what state he'd have ended up.

In lieu of pay for work they'd be offered a derelict building, un-roofed but with four walls to keep out the bitter chill of winter winds. They regarded this as a godsend. But this was only while work was available. More often they made do with a bracken-stuffed mattress and rough tent for cover, little else. Life hardened the young men. Sometimes they'd seek out their father from some flea-ridden den and drag him home semi-conscious, simply to add body warmth to a midwinter bed. Otherwise they might have forgotten his existence, rolled up their bundles and headed north.

If Helen could have foreseen the way her brother would drag the boys from place to place without so much as a thought to their well-being, she'd surely have murdered and buried him deep in bogs of peat.

In the areas of thick forest around remote glens in Angus, by moorlands teeming with grouse overlooked by snow-capped mountains they found enough work to sustain them for several months. For many years past Rory had camped there; being sober at the time he lingered for a peaceful summer, but did not stay for winter. Now he had brought his family into its bosom, severe and harsh, at the coldest time of year. If it were not for the rows of dense conifer trees and a high stone dyke circling their campsite, nature's ferocity would have taken no prisoners.

Rory was curled up in the darkest corner of the tent, growling at the snowstorm ravaging through the glen. He'd found a drinking buddy by the name of O'Connor, a big Irish tinker wandering through the area, and had asked him to pitch his tent next to theirs. Both men had earlier drained a bottle of potcheen distilled by the Irishman out of devil knows what. They'd planned to visit Kirriemor, the nearest town. Down there was a drinking den where local men, ploughmen of the land, gathered, and some others—low women, the kind O'Connor desired. The local men were notorious both for their hard working and their drinking. The women, wild and without scruples, filled their beds; there were more than enough reasons for the nomadic men to linger.

'Curse that blasted snow,' bellowed Rory. 'Is there no food? I'm at death's door with the hunger!'

Bruar answered, 'I'll skin a rabbit in the morning, but for now shut your mouth, father, and give us all peace.'

From a boiling kettle Jimmy poured his father some tea, which was gratefully accepted. 'Thanks, my boy, you're a fine son, not like that bugger there who spits on his own father.' Jimmy shook his head. 'You deserve all you get, craving drink; no wonder Bruar scolds you.'

'You remind me of your mother—a gentle-spirited angel, never raised her voice, not once. But him,' he stared at Bruar, 'too much of me, that's your problem.'

'Heaven help me then, eh Jimmy?' Both boys smiled at the comment as each strained their eyes, trying to play a card game around a flickering candle to while away the storm, ignoring Rory's simmering disgust at the dreary, storm-filled night.

As the hours ran by the storm intensified. Rory, wide awake and cold sober, called to O'Connor. 'Hey, in the next tent, how do you fare?'

His neighbour, obviously unable to sleep for fear of his tent taking off into the snow-heavy sky, called back, 'Well now, I have never felt such a force of wind in all me life. May the Holy Mother keep a watch on any poor soul out in this, they'll be stone dead if they're not sheltered, to be sure. The ground will be well buried when that stops, and we'll see a few lean days in its wake.' The Irishman muttered on incoherently, and in time fell silent. Rory called out to ask him if he wanted to join them in their tent, in case the howling wind stole his.

Silence followed. This bothered Rory, so he moved clumsily past Bruar's feet to get closer to his neighbour's canvas home; his son shoved him back. 'God, man, can't you go to sleep? Leave him where he is, there's enough rank smells in here already. O'Connor's fine.'

'Mind your tongue, boy, I'm still your father and I'll have a bit of respect. Are you alright, man?'

There was something wrong, because if anything the Irishman was renowned for his runaway mouth. His voice was usually a match for the best of storms, but now not a murmur came from his abode. Rory raised his voice, but still nothing.

'Maybe he's swallowed his Irish tongue,' Jimmy joked.

Bruar laughed loudly and said, 'With a bit of luck, eh, brother?'

'I swear you two buggers have no shame. Now get out of my way, I'll have to see if he's alright.'

'Oh, sit where you are, I'll check him.' Bruar stretched a woollen balaclava over his head, slipped one foot outside the tent-flap, but before he took another breath he felt something slump against the tent and slide down the canvas.

'What, in God's name, is that? Hell, I'm staying put. That must be a ghost, for no living thing could survive this night!'

Rory buttoned up his jacket. 'Stupid lad, there's no such things. Now get out of my way. I'm more concerned that a bough of that creaking oak that hangs over us has just dropped its load of snow, and maybe the whole bloody tree will be next to come down! Or have you considered that it might be a lame deer; one that could feed us for a month.'

Before another word left his mouth there was another thump against the tent; a weight dented the canvas, then rolled down. All three now darted outside. Snow, powered by a high northerly wind, blinded them. Hands groped in the pitch dark and soon found, not a broken branch, but a body! In a flash it was dragged inside. Bruar quickly brushed clogged snow from the blue nostrils of the small figure, while Jimmy removed frozen, ice-matted gloves, and began rubbing life back into thin hands. The three of them pulled off a sodden wool coat to see that their intruder was a young female. Instinctively, Bruar began rubbing furiously at her shivering flesh with warm hands. 'Come on, lassie, open your eyes. No, don't sleep, there's a brave lass, tell us your name.' Over and over he rubbed, and kept prompting: 'Good lass, what was that you said? Speak now... tell us who are you are...'

With sudden jerks of her body, followed by fists thumping the air, the lassie's small frame jumped back to life. Her frightened head turned to her rescuer; eyes staring wide, her hands found his warm face. 'Mammy and Rachel, where, where is Mammy and Rachel?' she screamed.

They stared at each other in horror. Somewhere out there, where the murderous storm ruled the night, were two others. The young woman fell back into Bruar's arms and slipped back into unconsciousness; instinctively he tore off his clothes and covered her with his warm body, while Rory and Jimmy donned every article of warm clothing they had and set out to find the girl's family.

Each footstep sank helplessly into drifts as they called out to the strangers, who by now were probably frozen solid by the stone dyke, which was their only guide. Rory's hunger for drink was striking and gnawing into his cold innards, which helped convince him their rescue was a futile bid. He was about to signal that they should turn back when a voice, weak and shivering, gasped out the words, 'Over here!'

Jimmy pushed his father towards some gale-lashed trees, 'There they are, come on!'

Sinking into deep drifts of snow, panting with the effort, they dragged themselves and struggled until they found the two small winter travellers huddled together. Whoever the girl was who'd braved the storm to find help, she was certainly endowed with the bravery and heart of a wolf. Before setting off, she'd built around her mother and sister a house of snow. The rescuers, their determination renewed, gathered the frozen pair and made for home quickly.

It took a lot of rubbing frozen limbs and the devouring of gallons of hot tea before a new dawn brought an end to the storm. Thanks to the brave efforts of the rescuers through a long night, a mother, Annie, and her two daughters, Megan and Rachel, had survived.

That morning, once the initial shock at being among strangers had subsided, and thankful to be alive, Annie began to tell the sad tale of why she and her daughters had left a good wintering ground and were forced on the road.

Rory declared that it was a stupid act, heading out onto the roads with winter coming, but he soon discovered it wasn't through their choice. Annie's man, John Macdonald, the head of the family, had suffered a fatal back injury while leading a string of horses off the mountain. It had been a successful day of deer shooting and the ponies were heavily laden with deer when one horse reared. John tried to stop the beast, but it bolted, dragging him from the narrow path. Both man and horse plummeted down, striking a rocky outcrop below before tumbling another hundred feet. No one could have survived such a fall—it was a terrible death. His employer, a stern, hard-hearted man, reacted to the accident without sympathy. He simply declared that without a strong male to help with the work on the estate, they had to leave the Glen Coe campsite.

Megan, trustful of the one who'd saved her life, snuggled close to Bruar. Through the night his body had given her warmth, and that comfort helped her. She'd curled her arms tightly around his neck, refusing to part from him, until the moment when she heard her mother's shaky voice telling the reason why they had left a good wintering camp site. She rose from her warm bed, still angered by the memory of their previous landlord. Trembling on wobbly knees, and with hands curled into fists, she hissed, 'We'd already a strong tent erected to face a long winter in, but he insisted, that stout-bellied pork pig of a laird. He said that without Daddy we were just useless women, and to make sure we went, he put fire to our tent!' Her green eyes stared in anger as she went on, 'That bastard will be dead now, because I piled the curses on him! He never even left us to mourn our loss!'

Annie, small and frail, hushed her daughter and leaned over to touch Rory's big hands as they were folded across his chest. 'We owe you and your boys here a debt of gratitude. All I had, apart from what we buried back at the dyke side, were just little family trinkets, and I left these in Glen Coe. But I'll pay you back—I'll work for you, do a bit of cooking or whatever.'

'No need, woman, we'd have done the same for any poor soul trapped in a snow storm.'

His coldness saw her draw away her hands. Embarrassed, she turned to Rachel. 'Will you go back and fetch our bits and pieces, my lassie.' She spoke also to Megan about gathering sticks for a fire, but could see that her eyes were fixed on Bruar's face and she hadn't heard a word. Before she had time to repeat her request, a gasp came from young Jimmy. 'Father, we clean forgot the Irishman—do you think he's alive?'

'Lord, so we did! Hell, boy, I don't know.' They threw open O'Connor's tent doors, which flapped wetly at each side of the tent as they dived inside. 'What a smell in here! I feel it's a cold dawn for him, father,' said Jimmy, covering his mouth and nose with both hands.

A filthy mound of grey blankets parted to show the red, bleary-eyed face of O'Connor. 'That, my dear young fella, is no the smell o' rotting flesh, it's the aroma o' me socks—I burnt the buggers on me stove. I was about to join youse last night an thought I'd heat me tootsies first, but wit me feet cosy I fell into a deep sleep. I woke two minutes ago from a lovely dream where I was rescuing damsels in distress from a high tower, and God, did I not nearly burn me tent down—the bloody tings were smouldering and it's a blessing they didn't fire the place.'

Jimmy lifted his eyebrows as he turned his head away from the foul-smelling place and said, 'Your dream had a hint of truth to it, because see what we have in our tent.'

O'Connor crawled inside, and what a shock he got seeing the three females huddled together like little rabbits. 'Well now, wid ye look at this? If I'd been awake, all you women could have shared me bed.'

'With that stink not one would have survived—they'd be gassed!' For that remark, Bruar got a slap across the head with a wet bonnet.

Throughout the day, everybody was busy trekking the path back and forth and building a proper tent for Annie and her daughters. By the day's end they'd a fine abode erected close by, yet not too near; Annie insisted that a little distance would allow privacy.

For whatever reasons, Rory had little time for the newcomers to the campsite and kept to himself. He was unlike his eldest son, who could not keep away from them, and had already bonded with fifteen-year-old Megan. He loved the way she said things, her way with words;

silly turns of phrases that made him smile. For the first time in his life he had found a friend, one with sea-green eyes that flashed amber when caught by the winter sun, a girl with a slender frame yet already blossoming into womanhood.

Rachel, her older sibling, cleaved to Annie, and although grateful to her rescuers, offered little in way of conversation. Yet it could be noticed she did soften in Jimmy's company.

The winter continued; Annie, not a well woman, spent most of her time inside her tent or huddled close by her fire. Rachel was not as vibrant as her younger sister, who told tales of monsters and banshee demons, entertaining all who listened around the fire when night brought its giant shadows. The older sister had a dislike for the culture of her birth, and spent long hours nagging her mother to find a proper home. Megan, on the other hand, was as wild as the fox and just as cunning. Bruar was aware that from that first night when she had lain frozen in his arms a deep attraction was drawing them closer; her nomadic beauty filled his dreams and daily thoughts.

Rory too noticed his son's attraction for the fiery Megan and voiced his disapproval, but when he was asked why, the answers were sparsely given. 'She's too young... untrained... she has a bad tongue...' The young man put his father's negativity down to nothing more than his distrust for anyone unless they shared his ways with the booze. But then Rory said, 'Those Macdonalds are uncouth—your mother who knew of them told me that.' Bruar cornered his father, asking why his mother would say such things, and demanded to know. But Rory refused to say anything, and soon Bruar, filled with his attraction to the raven-haired beauty, forgot about his father's remarks. A warm spring soon cleared the frost from the dykes and pushed out buds on the waiting trees, adding to the tide of emotion growing between the young pair.

Time on the small campside ran onwards uneventfully. Rory and O'Connor continued drinking when spare money came to them by way of odd jobs from farmers. At times no one would see them for days, then loud intoxicated voices would herald their return from wherever they had been drinking.

The highlander's sons resented his behaviour, but it had been a long time since they, as children, waved goodbye to Aunt Helen. Her wisdom had indeed proved to be accurate, yet in their own way they hoped that sooner or later their father would realise the errors of his path.

Annie's health slipped forever on a downward spiral. Rachel fussed as Megan tried to bring laughter to her mother's life, making faces as she recounted how certain people in Kirriemor would lecture her on how not to be a tinker as she hawked there.

When not running through heather moorland with Bruar, she made grand brooms and heather pot-scourers that she could hawk. These handy kitchen implements were made by tying bundles of heather at the base and hacking off the branches lower down; this would expose the rough edges used by country wives for scrubbing stubborn grease and burnt food from iron pots.

It was while hawking in the town one day she met a non-tinker who would prove to be their greatest friend. A saviour in every sense of the word was the local doctor, Doctor Mackenzie. He was a small-set man with a reddened face, flowing moustache and greying hair. A clay pipe seemed to live between his teeth, being plucked out and popped into the pocket of a worn brown waistcoat when he was unhobbling his constant companion, an ancient grey mare.

Megan was heading home after selling a handful of pot-scourers when she accidentally slipped on wet leaves scattered about the doctor's gate. He'd been trimming a trailing ivy when down she went, grazing both elbow and knee. Taking her to his surgery, an annexe of his parlour, he quickly cleaned and bandaged the injured parts. At first few words were exchanged between them; her kind seldom spoke to strangers. Yet he had soft hands and a friendly face, and soon she warmed to him. A friendship was born from that day on between the campsite dwellers and the elderly medical man who one day would prove more than just a healer.

Doctor Mackenzie was kind to his nomadic neighbours, and he frequently took a morning ride along the winding dirt track road to check them for ill health. To Annie he proved a godsend on more than one day or fevered night.

—

It was a beautiful day as Megan rose earlier than the rest to fetch some pheasant eggs. Treading softly in bare feet, shoes in one hand, basket for eggs in the other, she whispered through the thin canvas of Bruar's tent for him to come with her. Hurriedly he dressed, saying to his half-sleeping father and brother that firewood was needed, he wouldn't be long. Rory was asleep, or at least pretended to be. Jimmy lifted a limp hand in response as he rolled over to claim his brother's vacant space in the bed.

Soon the young couple were running through the heather-filled moor side. Several times they chased the grouse from their warm nests, making them stretch their wings and reach for the sky. Tiring of that, the pair fell laughing onto the coarse heather. With all the wonder of youth before them, they stared up into the cottonwool sky of that perfect spring day.

Bruar, who had never forgotten his Highland home, threw back his head and said, 'Oh lassie, what would I give just to be standing with you on my own soil. Aunt Helen would just love you to bits, I know it.'

'Tell me of this land of yours, then, lad, so that I too can fill my mind with pictures.'

'I have told you a dozen times before, surely you tire of hearing it?'

'Never!'

'Into the northern county o' Sutherland, where I was born, you'll find a cotter village, Durness. There, rugged cliffs hold back northern ocean swells that would surely swallow Scotland if it were not for their mighty heights. Once, centuries ago, wild Norsemen tried to conquer that land, but all they achieved was to claim watery peat graves for their lost warriors. Do know you why Cape Wrath is so called?'

Megan gathered her skirt into a bundle and sat down upon a rock, green eyes growing wider with every exciting word. 'No, no, tell it me quickly.'

'Those very Vikings gave it that name. It means "the turning point". No further south would they dare venture in their terror, that's where they discovered that our peat bogs show no mercy. The Pentland waters north by Orkney and Shetland and across to Norway saw them fill their long boats and flee like scared crows. The place they fled from was to them the land of the South. It was why they called it Sutherland. High puffin-nested cliffs and deep as hell peat bogs frightened them off, tails tight between their legs. You see, Megan, they had the evil intent in them to rape our women, burn the Highlands, and claim the very land, but the inhospitable marshes where Hell-Nick himself dwells claimed their wiry limbs instead. My aunt Helen swore that when she and Dad were youngsters, they unearthed their thick-necked swords and shields once while cutting deep into the peat.'

He was like an excited youngster as he proudly shared with her his story, face lit up as he remembered how wonderful it was on cold blizzard nights when he and Jimmy would huddle around Helen's knees. The flames of a roasting fire shot up the chimney as they listened to her tell tales of Red Eric, the Dane who scoured around the coastline screaming that one day he would defeat the peat bogs—but he never did.

'Oh lass, I can feel in my blood how my ancestors would have felt, watching from the peaks o' Reay. All the way to John o' Groats slithered a stream of longboats full of terror-stricken warriors dripping brown and black with the bog water.'

'You're a vivid teller, Bruar, almost like you were there yourself. I too have a piece of history regarding boggy ground. In Glen Coe a vast expanse of moorland, where they say a whole garrison of Roman soldiers disappeared, spreads itself for as far as any eye can see—Rannoch Moor, it's called—and I can say with hand on heart, there's many a night I sat in fear listening to witches and warlocks getting drunk on human blood!'

'Now you're pulling my leg.'

'Yes, but its worth it to see the look on your face.'

They walked on, laughing and sharing tales of a homeland that had been lost in the mists of childhood.

'What are you thinking now, my love?' she asked, as he failed to respond and she saw a serious frown replace his earlier smile.

'Look, if I ask a promise, will you—' his brow lined deeply beneath his shock of blonde hair. 'On second thoughts, it's far over great a request, best I don't burden you with it.'

'Ask whatever you want, Bruar. You must know how I care for you. If the power is in me, I'll do it.' She searched his solemn face for a response.

He sat down upon a solitary rock seat and for a space of time fell silent. Obviously thoughts of great depth were swimming round his young head. They placed a distance between them. Then he held out his hand to her. 'Megan, you know that I am the oldest, and that gives me a position among the Stewarts? Now, I am being serious, so listen. Do you know anything of ancient burial sites?'

'Aye, my late father's older brother William, who passed on last year, lies over at Glen Coe next to him, in a quiet spot within the Lost Valley. Great brute of a man he was, nobody thought his heart would stop beating, but it did. Now, hurry up and spit it out, what is it?'

'Well, in our burial ground, which lies on Parbh, there is one place left. It was meant for my father, but he can't take it because he forfeited it to me.'

'And why not?' She seemed surprised. 'Surely big Rory has more claim than you?'

'I thought that too, but my father took the right eye from a Seer while filled with anger. It was a terrible thing. It happened because mother was in danger of losing her life during Jimmy's birth, but you know how important a Seer's eyes are. There is an unspoken rule in Highland parts: one must never do battle with a foresight man.'

'My God, I never would have put your Dad down as such a fool—a drinking one, aye, but not as mad as that he would do damage to a seer.'

'He wasn't right in mind at the time. I won't say anything else on the matter.'

'Oh yes, you will! You started the story, now finish!' Megan rose to her feet, only to be pulled back down with a forceful tug on her arm.

She kissed his cheek, brushing his hair with moist lips and asked softly, 'Is the Seer you talk of the one who dwelt in a cave beyond Balnakeil, him with a beard of red flame?'

'His beard was of red hair, not flames; yes, that's him.'

'Gosh, I've heard folks from the north who wandered through Glen Coe mention his powers. Some say that in his day he could predict an end to the world.'

'He predicted my mother's end, and that's all I know.'

Gently she played with his thick blonde hair, asking quietly, 'Did that mean she was dying?'

'It seems the birth of my young brother Jimmy was too much for her tender frame.'

'But surely then the Seer was telling the truth?'

'Yes, but folks thought my father meant to kill the Seer, because with him being a drinking man and the Seer dead against strong alcohol, they thought my father harboured a grudge. It was desperation at his failure to help. He begged the foresight man to bring assistance for mother, but he refused, saying she was dying. Father belted the Seer so hard he knocked the eye clean out of his head. Who could blame him? Mother was dying with the labour.'

'People can be forced into doing terrible things when worry and fear fills them.'

'He cursed father, and let mother die!'

'Oh, don't torture yourself, my lad. I'm certain big Rory gave the pig exactly what he deserved.' Her words were for his benefit, but her inner fears went deep, and she felt shivers running through her bones. She'd been warned by her mother that the power of the Seer can bring about the events he foresees, whether good fortune or bad fortune. She whispered to her silent companion, 'May it be that the red Seer put a curse on your father, and it will pass down to you?'

'Ha, I don't believe in rubbish talk like that.' Shrugging his broad shoulders and changing the topic of conversation, he said, 'In all of this country there's no prouder man than me.'

'And tell me now, why is that?'

'You, Megan, because I have met you. So if I'm cursed, then that's fine.'

'Look,' she asked, 'what is this promise that you ask of me?'

He rose from the rock seat they'd shared and held her close until she could feel his heart thumping in his chest. 'Megan,' he said, 'I know at fifteen you're a mite too young to share my bed, yet surely you feel I'll love none other. You'll be my bride when the time is right, because we are meant. But it's about the future I want to ask of you. In later years, if Death shortens my lifeline, will you make certain I am laid in the ancient burial ground at Parbh? My Aunt Helen will tell you where it is.'

She felt that cold shiver return to run the whole length of her slender spine. It made her push him away, turn without a word and run off into the purple heather.

He darted after her, and soon was holding her again, brushing aside her windswept hair.

'Lassie, promise me.' His repeated request grew louder, his jaw rigid, face stern.

'Bruar, talk like that frightens me. I'll be your woman when time says, even have a dozen wee bairns, the spit of you. But this talk of death—it pulls a black shadow over us, stop it.'

But he kept on at her, and soon, if only just to hear no more on the morbid subject, she made the promise he asked for.

'All right, if you die first and there's breath in me, I'll take you back to the place on a grand charger. If I haven't got one of those, then the hind end of a wee cross-backed donkey will have to do. Failing that,

I'll carry you on my back. There now, are you happy? Will you put an end to this serious talk so you can get on with gathering firewood?'

'That's all I will ever ask of you, Megan,'

Hands clasped together, in the fullness of youth they skipped and jaunted back down the braeside where their families were stirring from a long night's sleep. Feeling a wispy breeze lift her skirt and with the previous conversation dead and buried, she pulled him to her, closer then she'd ever dared do before. Now he'd shared his secrets, her promises were given, it was only right from then on, she knew their fates were sealed. 'Kiss me before we reach the campsite—go on, kiss my body!'

He tried to laugh at her show of lusty affection, as her lungs filled with fresh air, and the buttons missing from the neckline of her dress exposed the swell of youthful breasts. He wanted to touch, to kiss her, but men don't do that kind of thing until marriage. Aunt Helen had told him once that when he found her, the right woman for him, he had to mind and be a gentleman. With this in mind, he jumped onto a rock, stretched out his strong arms and proclaimed, 'You will have a tent fit for a tinker queen!' then added, 'I'll build the strongest cart in all Scotia, and have it pulled along with a wild Palomino stallion. That's when we're married.'

He'd rejected her advances, and it stung her. 'Now, what makes you think I will spend the rest of my good days with the likes of you, Bruar Stewart? I've changed my mind. I think all that talk of seers, caves and Vikings has made me think twice.' She tossed back a head of jet-black, curly hair, stared upward at a wood pigeon high above and shouted, 'This laddie thinks I am in his pocket, and he hasn't even kissed me full on the lips yet.'

She was inviting him, teasing even as she ran off.

If only she knew how difficult it was for him, the mere smell of those freckled breasts, the pulsations of lust tearing at his loins as the odour from her warm underarms filled his nostrils. It was all he could do not to rip off her dress, run his tongue over all her body's beauty and be like a wolf, taking his chosen bitch, lost in bestial wildness. But as a man he had something else to prove, not just to her but her sister and mother. The distance between them afforded him one final look as she skipped through the heather, the roundness of her thighs, so smooth, now silhouetted by the fully risen sun. Its rays played like music around her bouncing curves. Suddenly a voice in his head penetrated through

41

his passion. 'Respect her,' it whispered over and over again, until the lust subsided and his eyes saw the girl, not the woman.

'What has our love life got to do with a bird anyway, wee feisty woman?'

'Well, he's up in the sky yonder, and until you do the proper thing, then that is where you might as well be.'

They both knew they would join together: it was fate, nothing could change that. Yet she also knew she yearned for him now, so tried again with teasing and playful caresses.

This time he was having none of it. He pushed away her small wandering hands and calmly mused, 'Come now, my little virgin, where is the shame in you?'

'Since when was kissing a sin?' She gave him a long lingering stare, her sea-green eyes flashed; a wink followed, she kicked up her heels and ran off through the heather. He called after her that he was away into the forest for wood, and was certain he'd heard the sound from the campsite earlier of her Mammy whistling. 'And you've not even gathered a single pheasant's egg neither,' he added, tousling his blonde hair, grateful all the more to the quiet voice that had broken through his lustful thoughts and calmed a brewing sexual storm deep down.

'Good God, Bruar's right, I clean forgot to gather the breakfast! What a fool I can be sometimes.'

Annie's shrill whistle sent her scurrying back empty-handed, little knowing how much self control she had cost him.

He mopped his sweating brow after the trial of his willpower and clumsily began to build piles of firewood gathered from the forest floor. Soon two large bundles sat comfortably on his broad shoulders. Heading homeward, he heard Megan's older sister Rachel laying into her.

'You hussy, have you been working the pants of yourself with Bruar Stewart and forgot the eggs?'

'I have not! What a bitch. I swear, Rachel, the devil himself forged your tongue. Mammy, this she-cat is saying evil things! Anyway you're just a jealous cow—I bet there's not a male within a hundred miles who'd look twice at that pale lifeless face.'

Rachel grabbed at her young sister, screaming that she'd rather live in a rat-infested dungeon than take off at an unearthly hour of the morning to fornicate with a man.

Shaking her head at the disgraceful conduct of her girls, Annie scolded them. 'Stop that, the both of you. Rachel, fetch water for tea.

Megan, I hope the heart's in the fire, you've been gone the best part of an hour. I heard you whispering on that Stewart lad, I hope there has been no nonsense. I'm in no mood for you two fighting neither, so put an end to it or I'll switch the pair of you.'

Annie, still weak, tried hard to stretch her bones and rise from the tent, but the pain in her body turned her stiff instead. She winced at the aches now passing like waves throughout her body; only forty years had she been on the earth, yet she felt so very old. Megan had always been a step ahead of her clutches, uncontrollable. By the age of four she'd sat on a horse's back; Annie smiled through her pain, remembering how her man had made longer reins for the little arms to reach. 'She was taking the deer off the hill with him by the age of six. Now the child is growing up and will soon be a wife; she's chosen a man already, by the sounds of it.' A look at the girl's legs also brought a smile. 'It wasn't all that long ago two twiglets carried her growing frame in great leaps, and now they are so pretty and shapely. Yes, she'll be a woman soon, and thank God, because I won't be around to help her. Better that she's coping. Rachel has always been steady, I'll not have any problems worrying about her. Old before her time, never enjoyed the joy of youth, my plain Jane.'

Megan forgot the petty argument with her sister; she was more worried that their mother was in pain. She lied that there wasn't a single pheasant egg to be seen, saying 'The bloody birds are becoming more cunning, it's harder to seek out their nests,' then went on to blame hedgehogs.

'Gosh, mammy, are those bones of yours tightening again? I'll do the chores today if you want another hour or two in bed. Doctor Mackenzie will come if I fetch him,' she said, putting an arm around her mother. More quietly, she whispered, 'Mother of mine, Bruar is far too much the gent to take my maidenhead, even though I would offer it on a plate, so don't fret yourself on that. I'll keep it a while yet.'

Annie loved both her daughters, but without a father, controlling them was no easy task, especially Megan. She patted her wayward daughter gently on the hand and said, 'That's not necessary, pet, I'll be fine after a cup of hot sweet tea.' She stroked her face and added, 'I know you, lassie, and there's a rising in that woman-to-be body, yet with the Stewart I feel you will be sensible. And Rachel, well, she was only looking out for her wee sister.'

Bruar walked over and dropped the large bundle of firewood at their camp, putting light to their fire before going over to his own camp and doing the same.

Annie thanked him. 'You are a good boy, and I hope I can trust my lassie in your hands.' He lifted a hand in reassurance that Megan would be safe, before going into his own camp to waken his father and brother.

Rory, the worse for supping forbidden liquid the night before, half-opened his eyes at the opening of his tent door as the sun's rays entered and brought life to a million particles of dust. He called to Bruar, 'have you any tea laddie?' Then added that he'd heard that Macdonald lassie hooting on him, further remarking that she'd a flame in her belly wanting on a man. 'You'd do well to keep a grip on yourself, or that wee fire demon will have you roped and branded.' Bruar hushed him. 'She is the one I have chosen, and nothing you say to bring her down will change things.'

His father grunted as he pushed his arms into a damp jacket. Then, muttering to himself in a low gruff voice he wandered off to the forest. He'd wash in the burn, and probably find a secluded spot to do what he'd been doing a lot of lately—bringing up the green contents of his gut.

Within an hour all the camp dwellers were up and about their business. Bruar, Rory and Jimmy (who, incidentally, had more than a fancy for Rachel if she but knew it) took a day working on vermin control on the scattered farms round about. As there was never a lack of rabbits, moles and rats, they were regarded favourably by the local farmers, and with plenty of rabbits to eat, their bellies were filled. Megan and Rachel hawked round the tiny villages nestling in and near the Angus glens, selling their pot scourers and brooms. A cool gloaming brought the foot-weary workers home.

After supper, both boys shared Annie and her daughters' fire. Bruar wondered where the Irishman was, and called over to Rory lying resting in his tent. There'd been no sign of him for several days.

Jimmy hoped he'd slung his hook, but just as he scraped a final drop of gravy from his supper plate, a course, rough voice could be heard coming round the bend in the lane, singing out 'Danny Boy.'

'Lord, why does the earth bring that useless bastard in among us?' said Bruar. 'Could he not start walking away and forget his way home?' Jimmy scolded Bruar for his sharp tongue, and asked the bearded ruffian where he'd been.

He'd been drinking with a few rough Irishers living up at the farm in a shed. 'They were going back to the old country,' he said, 'and we was supping a goodbye drink. Where's the wrong in that?'

Nobody answered; they hoped he would collapse into his tent, but instead he rammed a hand into his torn coat pocket, retrieving a large green bottle. 'Well, me auld highlander, do yez want a sup?'

Rory was not sober for long, as both men gulped and sang until a full moon and drunken sleep brought silence to the night.

Annie still wasn't well and so Megan went off to bed, sharing soft tales with her mother until she too slept. As Megan lay listening to a hedgehog digging in the rough heather at the rear of her tent, her mother slept fitfully.

As the last embers of fire crackled, Jimmy and Rachel felt themselves growing closer. Each of them could see in the other similar qualities and ways.

Next day, when work was over and the fires gently smouldering again, Doctor Mackenzie came trotting along the path. Hobbling his old horse to a gnarled oak, he called out, 'Are you folks in good health? For a sharing of your tea I'll give you all a wee bit look-over.'

Megan and Bruar, who were away somewhere over the high hills checking rabbit snares, would have been sorry not to see and blether awhile with the good doctor. Annie had been sore and thanked God for his visit. 'I have a pain worse than bairn-labour, doctor, could you give me something to help me sleep? Rachel, pour him a mug of good strong tea, and if you and your sister haven't eaten them all, a scone to go with it.'

The doctor knelt and lifted a feather pillow, fluffed it and gently laid her back onto it.

'Is the big world still turning, doctor?' asked Rachel, gladly pouring him a strong mug of tea from the blackened kettle suspended over the campfire. She buttered a few scones as her mother asked, then added, 'You see, sir, I sometimes wonder if we are the only folks left alive. We never see a soul unless we go hawking, or buy butter and milk from the good farm wives.'

'Apart from the village folk and the screeching curlews I have no knowledge of the outside world myself, Rachel.' He winked; she blushed, bowing slightly as if he were royalty and made an excuse to leave.

'She's a lady, is that lass of yours, Annie,' he said, watching the way she moved and thinking that if her rags were replaced with fine clothes one could easily see her fitting into a world of finery.

'Aye, she'd be pleased to hear you say such things, for all she moans about is getting free of this life. But is my lassie as near as would be able to hear me? I have to speak serious with you, sir.'

He was concerned at her tone of voice, detected her fear. Casting an eye at Rachel and seeing her speaking with Jimmy, he replied, 'I must say they make a fine pair, where are the other two?'

'Never mind them. Listen, doctor, there's these awful searing pains in my chest, like a hot poker piercing at my heart. Promise me you won't tell the girls, now will you, because if there's a bad thing wrong with me I don't want them worrying.'

He knew enough about tinker folk to tell that when a pain was admitted it was serious. He could see by looking at the woman that she was anxious, and so whispered, 'You have been too long caring for these lassies. Stop concerning yourself about them so much. Now let's have a listen to these innards of yours.' Ushering her to a secluded place at the back of the tent he gently pressed a large stethoscope at her chest. 'Where exactly is this pain you speak of, my dear?'

Never having seen a stethoscope before, she at first drew back from its cold touch. The old man smiled and gently persuaded her. 'Come now, lass, this only tells me what's going on in there.' He ran a hand across her upper chest and under her chin.

The beats sounded faint and solemn. Mackenzie was long enough in the tooth to know a weakening heart when he heard one. Her face also told a story, with greyish lips, yellowed eyes and cold, clammy skin. 'Annie, you tinker folk doesn't like untruths, so I hope you listen to me and take life easy from now on.'

Cupping her face in work-gnarled fingers she gazed into his eyes, looking for an honest answer to her next question. 'How long, doctor?'

'Now, lass, only the Lord himself can say for sure. But you have two grand lassies who will see to your every whim.'

'Please don't tell them. I can't bear the thought of them hovering about with tear-streaked faces. It's only months since their father met an untimely end. No, I'll keep this strictly with your good self. Now I can hear that big highlander Rory Stewart calling on you, best you take a look at him too. He doesn't half cry out in the nights.'

Doctor Mackenzie crept out from the tent, wishing he'd a magic wand to turn Annie's thin canvas abode into a warm wee cottage with a fire, and a bed that would at least keep her off the damp ground. He could easily have offered her a death-bed in the local hospital, or, better still, a bed in his house, but he knew that tinkers desire only to wait on death in the embrace of mother earth.

As he stood up, the sight of Rory approaching took thoughts of Annie from his mind. 'Hello, big Stewart my man, what can I do for you?' he asked.

'Well, good doctor, my stomach has been rejecting every morsel of food these days.'

'I bet it has no problem with the cratur? The whisky will be the reason for your gut being a bother. Stop supping and I bet within a month the stomach will be back to normal.'

'You're a hard man for one who is supposed to heal, I can tell you. The water of life hasn't passed my tonsils for months—if you don't believe me, then ask Jimmy over there.'

Young Jimmy, who had gone back to weaving a basket after Rachel answered her mother's call, smiled at the doctor, said nothing and continued with his work. The doctor went over to him. 'Can you swear your father hasn't touched the drink, Jimmy?'

The young man lowered his dried reeds to the ground, stood up and whispered, 'If you smell my father's breath, then you'll see that not weeks but hours have passed since he was filled with stuff O'Connor the Irishman brewed.'

Rory had no problem in hearing his son's whispering, and raised his fist. 'You lying toad, I'll switch the hide off you for that! The drink doesn't affect my ears.'

'Rory, I never thought you a violent man towards your sons. I'd lay off the demon drink for more reasons than a sore belly if I was you.' He handed him a bottle of stomach chalk, saying, 'Take a spoonful every four hours.'

'God love you, man, this'll cure the gnawing.' Rory thanked him once more, before crawling inside his tent, probably to drink half the contents before O' Connor slipped him another bottle of homemade, hellfire brew.

Round the bend in the road, in a quiet spot another family of tinkers had found refuge. Before heading home, the doctor popped his head inside the tent of the McAllisters, who were anxiously awaiting the arrival of their first baby. A quiet couple, they kept to themselves, bothering no one, and never joined the campfires of the others.

They were private and shy, nothing like Megan, who came singing and laughing with Bruar over the high hill above the campsite. When they saw the doctor unhobble his horse, they hurried to see him before he left.

'Hey, Doctor Mackenzie, wait on us, see what we have for supper,' she called at the top of her voice, holding aloft and waving a brace of cock pheasants and two large buck rabbits; but he was already trotting away and didn't hear her.

'Would you take a look at that,' she said to Bruar, 'the only visitor we get, and we miss him.'

'You'll see him next time,' he told her, adding, 'I think the lassie McAllister is due her baby soon.'

'Yes, I suppose so. But I'll tell you something, I didn't like the colour of Mammy this morning. I think she is not letting on about her illness. She says it's her bones that ache, but I think it might be far more serious a problem. Do you know I got up in the night and heard her whispering to Daddy's memory? I hope we don't have to fetch the doctor sooner.'

However, when the summer's solstice came, Megan's words echoed with an uncanny truth as Annie awakened in the dead of night, screaming and fighting for breath. Her screams roused everybody from their beds. 'Death stands on the forest edge waiting with his scythe, can you see him lassies? Look, his head is hooded and he hovers like a dragonfly.' Rachel was crying, unable to ease her mother's suffering. Megan gripped Rachel and said, 'You and Jimmy go fetch Doctor Mackenzie; I'll stay with Mammy until you come back.' In no time Rachel and Jimmy were gone along the old drove road to bring the doctor, while she and Bruar comforted the dying woman. 'Mammy, you look at me and ignore old Death, for sure I'll cut him in bits with his bloody scythe if he so much as winks at you.'

Minute by minute Annie's breathing became less erratic, but this was replaced by a rasping sound from within her throat. This frightened Megan—she'd heard older folks speak of 'the death rattle', and if their words had any truth then there was certainly no mistaking the sound. Tears flowed down her cheeks and gently landed on her mother's face. 'Mammy, please, don't die! Rachel's coming with Doctor

Mackenzie, he'll make you better. Oh mother, I love you so much. Don't leave us so soon after Daddy, we need you!'

'Megan, you're making it hard for her to let go,' whispered Bruar. 'Look, her eyes are glazing over, she wants to join your father. Let her be, my love.' He prised apart both her hands that were tightly clasping Annie's and moved closer to the dying woman. Suddenly she arched a rigid spine, drew in one last breath, then slumped back lifeless on her horsehair mattress.

'Say goodbye now, your mother's gone. See how peaceful she looks.'

Megan could not gaze upon her mother's dead face, and ran out into the night. The moon was spreading gentle rays throughout the forest; she threw herself down on the rain-moistened moss to empty her mind of everything apart from the thought of her mother's silent, dead frame. 'Oh Mammy, Mammy! What will we do, now you've joined Daddy?'

Far up on the high hills a solitary eagle lowered his churk-churk call as if out of respect for the death on the moss-covered ground below him. A lapwing gently ceased its flight and bobbed upon the earth inches from Megan's mournful figure. Perhaps a fox or weasel had killed its chicks, and in some strange bond of nature the bird sensed the girl's grief as being akin to its own.

Bruar left her in peace, to break on her own the invisible birth cord between a mother and her child. When she'd cried herself sore, he brought her back to see to the duties that must be carried out for any dead soul.

By the time Rachel and Jimmy arrived back with Dr Mackenzie, Megan had composed herself and had Annie's small, lifeless body laid out. After certifying the time and cause of death, the doctor stayed a while. He offered his condolences before slowly walking off alongside his horse, saying he'd send the priest if they wished it. But there was no need, the girls informed him; they had their own ways of burial.

Throughout the next day, refusing help from other hands, they prepared their dear mother for her rest. Moistened flax was carefully inserted in her ears and nostrils to keep out evil spirits; to prevent demons from looking into her soul, her eyes were covered by two small river pebbles. And finally, every inch of her body was wound round with muslin cloth. When their trembling hands had finished this last duty, only the ground awaited. Jimmy had nailed up an oblong box with whatever materials he could find, and it was into this narrow vessel that the girls very gently placed Annie.

Bruar watched them from among the nearby willows. He felt a silent pride that there was no longer any sign of the girl in Megan, just a strong, controlled woman doing her duties with a firm resolve. As they covered Annie's coffin with a blanket to await her burial on the next day, he was astonished at the precision and respect of their ritual. Then, as was the way of the Macdonalds of Glen Coe, they covered their faces and fell silent.

O'Connor tried in vain to coax them to have a wake—'In my part of the world they do,' he told them.

All through the night they sat by their mother's remains. No talking and no moving, rigid and silent they watched, until far upon the hillside a black hooded crow screeched to herald the dawn. A thin smirr of rain had changed to heavy mist as the tiny band of silent mourners lowered Annie down to her place of slumber in the middle of the moss-carpeted forest floor. It would have been a blessing to put her across beside her husband in Glen Coe, but that was not possible. However, Annie had had no belief in burials, saying to her daughters many times, 'When I go, just pop me in any old place and I'll find my way to your Daddy.' So here they were, laying her down in a secluded, gentle glade, where small roe deer wandered by and brightly coloured jaybirds rested. Here the red squirrels darted and chased each other's tails, and here all around tiny sparkling dewdrops would fall from the moist trees and water the roots of the bluebells and wild primroses to carpet their mother's grave. 'Yes, Mother,' whispered Megan, arm entwining Rachel's, 'here you will be well cared for. Mother Nature herself will see to that.'

Rory ushered his two sons out of the glade to allow the lassies their last moments with Annie. Minutes later, just as they too left their mother's graveside, a small cry pierced the air. The secretive McAllisters gave the world a new life, a boy.

'As one life goes below another comes up,' said the Irishman, sticking his drunken head out from his tent and calling on Rory to join him. Strangely enough, the highlander, dependent as he was on the demon of alcohol, declined, opting instead to take himself off into the forest. Perhaps to remember his own wife's demise many misty years ago, or perhaps it was just that he'd not the stomach for drinking that day.

THREE

*A*s the rest of the summer drifted by, it was not only Bruar and Megan who grew closer, but a feeling of companionship had touched Rachel and Jimmy. They spent days walking and talking, growing more dependant on one another. Rachel's wasn't the same as her sister's relationship, not as passionate, more comfortable.

Rory spent less time drinking, and his sons hoped and prayed that he had changed for the better. He'd even taken to rising first, lighting a fire and starting breakfast. Perhaps it was Annie's parting that made him see how precious a good family was. He never said so out loud, but it was a far happier camp when the Highlander was a sober man.

Not so O'Connor! If he'd staggered home cut and bleeding once, then he'd done it a dozen times. He'd found a drinking den in Kirriemor, one usually frequented by burly ploughmen who joined in quarrelsome debates about Ireland and its history.

'One of these days, man, you'll take a battering from the ploughmen you won't walk away from,' Rory warned him, genuinely worried. 'Why don't you go back to Ireland and find some family to share time with?'

If there was a family somewhere O'Connor never let on, he cared not what happened as long as he could pay for and enjoy the pleasure of alcohol. 'Tomorrow and its worries can take care of themselves,' he was heard saying many times, as he slugged the final dregs from an emptied bottle.

By autumn's end Megan had at last reached the age of consent. She decided to ask her future father-in-law what were his thoughts on his son mixing with a tinker Macdonald? Bruar was busy in the depth of the forest cutting firewood; she'd voiced her anxiety about speaking with his father, so he left them together to give her time to bond with big Rory. Gingerly she went over to his fire, and sat uncomfortably down on a large log. Now, for the first time, she was going to speak about her innermost thoughts and worries.

'You know that now I'm sixteen, your lad and me will be wed?' She was surprised at the loudness of her voice, and blushed red. This made him smile and he answered in soft tones.

'Aye, lassie, that I am; and I'll say this for you, I never thought you good enough for Bruar but there are ways in you that are strong and honest. You've a depth to yourself, I've seldom seen one so young with a spirit like yours. I'm sure the lad will do no better. His mother was a tinker you know, aye, just like you. Her folks came from the west coast, although I only knew her uncle. My Lassie—that's what I called her—was abandoned into the care of the uncle after her parents were killed by a deluge that washed their camp site away. It was a blessing she had been playing on the hillside at the time. Poor thing, she used to wake up in the night screaming, I think she was remembering her drowned relatives. She had a heart that loved everybody. Even wee robin redbreasts with broken wings brought tears to her bonny eyes, and God she had the most beautiful eyes.'

That was the first time he had taken her into his trust, she felt warmed with words she'd never thought to hear from this once drink-filled excuse for a man. His words brought a sense of pride. It felt right to be taking on his name, and within no time the pair were relaxed and comfortable as they chatted on.

Yet there was a clearing to be done. The resentment he harboured towards the Macdonalds had bothered her—why did he feel so strongly? Before another word passed between them she had to know. His easy flow of conversation made her think that while in this mood she would be able to question him further.

For a moment he dropped his head, ran a hand through his thick grey hair, and looked quite sheepishly at her. He said, 'It's not you. It's a story I was raised on that was told by wandering tinker folk who used to come up to the far north, about the feuding MacIan Macdonalds—that was the proper clan name, you know, lass.'

Yes, she did know.

'Well, there's an old tale was brought to our ears about the Glencoe massacre. Campbell of Glen Lyon, who had been given instructions by the English King William to kill all of the Glencoe Macdonalds, had been secretly having relations with a Macdonald lassie. She was already promised to her cousin Alister MacIan. Now to get rid of him, Campbell, along with a certain powerful Edinburgh man by the name of Dalrymple, accused the whole clan of 'reiving'—cattle stealing.'

Hearing her ancestral name being brought low wasn't part of the answer she'd expected. She had her own version of history, had been reared on it, and her temper rose. She didn't like his version of the story, and in no uncertain terms let him know! 'Well, it just goes to show how much you know, big Rory Stewart. Dalrymple was William's stooge. He hated everyone with a drop of Catholic blood. The Macdonalds supported your Prince Charlie during the '45. Many died for him, for God's sake. And here's another wee bit fact of history for you to puff through your pipe—during the wild days of Robert the Bruce, the two clans Campbell and MacIan Macdonald were related. And another thing, what if it was true the lassie had a fling with the Campbell; surely it was her business? But if you think killing old men, women and children—and I heard tell over forty were slaughtered in the snow that fearful night—was because of a silly affair, then you have allowed the drink to take your brain along with your gut.' She rose quickly to her feet, and with hands on hips, hissed, 'That was at the end of the seventeenth century, why should you condemn every Macdonald to this day for it?'

'Sit back down, lassie, and accept my sincere apologies. I promise to end my disgust at the name. Anyway, in Durness I heard many stories about our own people that don't do the Highlanders any favours.'

They looked at each other thinking on how senseless it was to argue and take sides in an incident long buried. When the anger subsided from her heart and the red from her cheeks, she moved closer to him, exchanging her seat of wood for a more comfortable stool. Changing the subject, she said, 'Bruar. Now there's a wonder o' a name, but why give it tae your son? I know o' the Falls o' Bruar at Blair Atholl, but I've heard nobody but my lad called that.'

Rory sat back in his seat, looked up at the high hills surrounding their small campsite and said, 'Do you know something, I never thought I'd hear myself tell anyone this, but I like you, Megan Macdonald. So I'll tell you why we, my lassie and me, chose to call our boy Bruar.'

She sat closer by the fire to give him all her attention. He would soon be her father-in-law, therefore it was only right that she knew as much of the man as she could.

'I remember like it was only yesterday,' he said, running his hands once more through his thick hair. 'Spring was bursting from a long cold winter. We were but bairns, yet felt so grown up, ready to take on the world together. We were wed that very day in a tiny church on the shore of Loch Eribol by a small priest who told us everybody belonged to God, and never to forget that. Then my lassie and I thought, if it was all right with God, we'd go on a hike round Scotland. Leaving Durness, we set upon the road, filling our teenage lungs with the fragrance of yellowed gorse and pink-white hawthorn blossoms. Not one part of that beautiful long summer did we miss a chance to thrill at nature's wondrous sights and sounds. We went swimming in the waters of the blue-green Atlantic, soaked in sunshine upon deserted beaches of golden sands without a stitch of clothes on. Oh, she was a bonny lassie, was Bruar's mother. I wish you'd known her.' Suddenly although it was a warm, pleasant day, he pulled the collar of his shirt up around his chin and hunched his shoulders. He folded his arms and lowered his face into his chest.

She watched as her storyteller flinched, and wondered if she'd opened old wounds. 'Do you want to continue, big Rory?' she asked. 'Look, if you don't want to tell me, I'll understand.'

But it was only that a sudden vision of his lassie had filled his thoughts, and for a moment he didn't want to share her with anyone. Megan gently wrapped an arm around his bowed shoulders, 'If you'd much rather not speak o' her, I'll understand.'

'No, lassie, of course I'll tell you. It's just that as I went back in my mind I could see how much I missed her. But look, sit down, and I'll tell you how we came by the laddie's name. When we found the purse was empty we went down to Blair Atholl. A landowner from Glen Tilt had postered notices on a village wall. I asked my lassie what they said. She turned on me then, and hit me hard with her fist. I couldn't understand, because I'd never seen her show one tiny spark of temper. At first I thought the notice was one saying 'no tinkers', and that's why she saw red, because we came across so many of them on our travels. Then when I read it I found that it said "Workers to cut bracken apply to factor at the castle." I asked her what had caused the outburst of anger? And that's when she broke down in tears, saying she couldn't read at all, and she was so ashamed. It made me feel more drawn to her that she relied on me from then on, but having said that, I wasn't that good a reader myself.

Well, we got the job, and with it keys to a small cottage, high up on the braeside. It was a melancholy wee place, with eyeless windows and a ruined, gaping chimney breast. Part of it was roofless, ravaged by the winds and rain from the heavens. There were traces of fastening on a wall where once hung a cupboard, and doors long since replaced by openings leading from one room to the next. We stood alone, gazing at what once had housed families, probably happy people, and wondered what they'd think of the bleak place now? We sat on a sill and wondered if it had ever held a vase with flowers. My sister Helen never put an empty vase on a sill, even in winter she'd put some plant or other in her blue vase. Every tiny low roofed cottage in Durness had them, little, rounded, glazed sea-blue they were, always filled with a few flowers.

Long grasses grew from a hole in the floor behind the front door, as if searching for some light. I told the factor we weren't too happy with the state of the place, but he just shrugged his shoulders and said, "What do you expect, a mansion? You're bloody tinkers, for God's sake, nothing more! I've scraped cleaner stuff off my boot.'"

Megan stopped him then and said, 'You're not a tinker, Rory, I know, because sometimes I speak to Rachel in our tongue, and Bruar hasn't a clue what we're saying.'

'No, but my lassie taught me some words. And anyway, what difference does it make? I'm not a tinker, but the boys are half-bred, so I suppose they're as near as can be. Anyway, do you want to hear this tale of why Bruar is so called, or not?'

She apologised, folded her arms, and asked him to continue.

'For the remainder of the summer we lived in the cottage with its partly thatched roof and worked from morning till night, clearing bracken from acres of braeside. The factor only came by to pay us, apart from the day he handed my lassie a bag of scones. His wife had made a batch for a shooting party, but she'd baked too much. We ate them heartily, even if they were a week old and as hard as stones.

Although the moorland around our makeshift home spread wide, a deep forest grew over the lower land. One Sunday we wandered off down through the vast forest, following a burn until it widened into a wild untamed river. She laughed when I said that those gigantic fir trees trapped a power of jungle heat, and for this reason, big hairy men over twenty feet tall dwelt in their midst. It certainly was a hot day, and when we were exhausted with the heat, we were so glad to see the beautiful waters of Bruar falling in sparking cascades over rocks and canyons. 'Let's jump in, my love,' said my lassie.

I thought it far too deep and dangerous, but she said that at our age there was no danger, only a challenge. So over we went, like salmon leaping to a magical spawning ground. Our skin tingled with bouncing bubbles that popped and danced all over our bodies. Oh, I can still feel the surge of water, what a feeling, I haven't the words to describe it. I felt her legs tangling around mine; her hands found my face as mine entwined her small middle.'

Megan blushed. She thought that maybe this wasn't for her ears, but her truth-teller was living again through those heart-hid moments, and not she or anyone else would stop him. He continued.

'Eventually we scrambled up on the bank, and there, while the water sparkled and danced around us in pools, we made passionate love.'

Unaccustomed to such expressions of emotion, Rory blushed too and rose to his feet, leaving Megan completely dumbstruck. She threw back her head, panting with excitement at his words, her earlier embarrassment gone. 'What wonder, what a brilliant scene! And ma lover was the result o' that heavenly day—unbelievable, simply magical.'

He smiled, glad she'd enjoyed his story and not run off red-faced. 'Yes, your lad was the outcome of me and my lassie finding the joy that only the fairies know, making love beneath the mystical water. Now, there you are, you even know the heart of me, a wee skelp of a thing. I must be getting soft, telling you my secrets.'

Unable to control the joy she felt at that moment, Megan rushed over, hugged, kissed and thanked Rory before going back to add more sticks to her own fire. At long last she had been given a glimpse into the past of this sad man, who lived only on memories of days gone by. Him sharing his innermost emotions had brought them closer now, and no matter what the future held they'd remain close, they both knew that. This man of scarred heart, his life riddled with many dubious twists and turns, hid in his depths a vision that would equal that of any great artist. His vivid descriptions she'd remember forever.

FOUR

*W*inter brought a fierce biting wind swirling round their tents, drawing the young lovers closer for warmth. A surge of wanting ran through Bruar at her closeness. He unfastened two brown buttons, opening her woollen jersey, and kissed a small inch of exposed freckled shoulder. 'Megan, I have waited so long. Are you ready? Oh God, how I hope you are, because it's time now, no more waiting. I will be as gentle as the dove.'

'You can be as dovey as you like, big lad, but me—well, I've waited all this time too you know, and I'm going tae swallow every inch of ye. So I'm for a wolf's feast!'

That night had been the culmination of a wanting and waiting that both could only dream of, and when the cold early morning frost smothered the sleeping grass around them, a love was cemented within the small canvas abode that only death could part. They knew inside that if life, with its cruel twists, separated them, then love would keep alive a flame nothing would extinguish.

Next morning the pair rose to be greeted by a freezing fog which shrouded every inch of land with its grey blanket. It rushed inside the tent as they threw back the canvas door, into their eager, youthful faces. Everybody had heard their lovemaking from the night before, and it was Rachel who asked the question, 'When are you getting married then?'

'When the frost has thawed a mite, then we can lie without blankets.' Bruar's answer had a power of barely concealed excitement. He was hardly able to keep his hands off Megan, his Megan, who was curled around him winding her eager arms through his. He lifted her into the air like a rag doll, tickling each rib, she squealed with laughter as his knees played with her thighs. Then a thought flashed into her mind, prompting a further squeal of delight. 'Never mind a thaw, let's you and I mix the fluids this Saturday!'

Many days while trekking over the heather moor they had discussed the ceremony. She wanted the tinker's mixing, just the way that her mother told her was how a Macdonald married. He didn't care what way they wed, as long as for the rest of his life she'd lie at his side. He looked around the faces half-smiling back at them. They were more concerned to light a fire, fill cold bellies with porridge and milky tea. Then he said, through a beaming smile that could melt all the frost clinging with its icy fingers upon the dyke, 'Saturday it is, then. I'll ask the good doctor to come.'

Saturday came and found the families in a far happier mood. Big Rory, O'Connor, Jimmy and Bruar were dressed in suits that they had laid by for weddings and funerals; a motley collection of clothes with frayed collars and crushed trousers.

Rachel wore a fox-furred cape, given to her mother by some old minister's wife, hoping she'd wear it and come to church, but she never did. One of its eyes had been lost in its travelling, and chunks had been ripped from the pathetic skin when two whippets had once thought it alive and fought over it. But it was all she had, so she wore it with pride.

Bruar had waited long and lustingly to a further sharing of his body with the raven-haired girl, so it wouldn't have mattered what she looked like. Nevertheless she had made an effort to impress. Her mother Annie's own wedding dress had been washed and pressed by laying it under a horse-hair mattress. That old garment had been kept safe in a wooden chest, along with family birth certificates and some old trinkets. Rachel prodded her sister, reminding her of the night of the storm when she carried it on her back all the way from Glen Coe. With gratitude and unusual attentiveness, Megan hugged her older sister and kissed her pale cheek. Rachel squeezed her shoulders in return. For all their differences, with Annie gone they were closer than they'd ever been. Rachel with the companionship of Jimmy smiled more; her tendency to ill-nature seemed to be buried by his delicate and personal attention.

Although the dress was faded and slightly torn at the hem, Megan still looked a picture: a lovely, fresh bride, in a tattered wedding frock of dull satin.

Firewood lay in massive piles between the tents. Two loaves of bread, half a pound of freshly boiled ham and several bottles of ale sat neatly on a small makeshift table made of cut logs. Bruar took a metal bucket and put it beside one belonging to Megan.

Only Doctor Mackenzie was missing, and they wouldn't start without him; he was their only guest. It was tradition to allow someone not of the culture to attend a wedding. Some believed that this person could stand witness to the joining. As government and church took little part in the ceremonies of tinker folks, such a witness served as good proof to the actual marriage. Children could then take their father's name, knowing they would inherit any meagre belongings left behind after death.

Half an hour passed. Rachel added sticks to the fire, muttering that if a spark ignited the remains of her dowdy fox fur, the doctor wouldn't like what she'd call him. Not long after, Megan and Bruar, who had clambered to a vantage point, said his horse and trap could be seen trotting along the old drove road. They were pleased and excited to see their only wedding guest, but to their surprise, he wasn't alone! When Rory saw the stranger who sat next to his friend on the trap, he stepped forward, raising his hand. 'Sorry, doctor, but we never invited another.'

'Oh, stop your nonsense, man. This is no guest, he is my present to the bride and groom.' He helped the stranger down from the trap, along with a long box and objects they'd never seen before. Then, once each contraption had been unloaded and put at the stranger's feet, the doctor said, 'Close your mouths or Jack Frost will be away with your tonsils.' He put a firm hand on the shoulders of Megan and Bruar and said, 'I went to Perth for this lad, and I hope I don't offend your customs, but he's a photographer. He's going to take your wedding pictures. Now how does that sound?'

Bruar stepped forward, awkwardly grabbed at the slender gent who had the most terrified stare on his face, shook his hand and said to his intended bride, 'Come on, lassie, have you no manners at all? Give the man a shoogle.'

Megan, arms outstretched, hugged both her dear old friend and his wedding present. The photographer was genuinely scared of this band of eager subjects. He'd never ventured any closer to tinkers than glancing warily at their fire-smoke rising from some forest, and would speed away fearing his life was in mortal danger. However, with the speed of a magician he set up a wooden tripod and fastened onto it the one-eyed box (as O'Connor called it). He popped his head in and out from under a purple blanket like a darting weasel, whispering through nervous coughs, 'Smile, please'. As quickly as it had been assembled, the three-legged stand, along with purple blanket and camera, were stacked, tied and secured again in their long box. He dropped a key as he tried with no success to fasten a padlock and chain around his box, and everybody laughed. Rory handed the man a stone jar. 'Here, lad, take a dram with us.'

The poor soul clung on to the doctor, shaking his head until it looked as if it might fall from his shivering shoulders.

Rory didn't help by curling a brute-sized arm around him and saying, 'We'll eat you later for the feast.' His growl sent the poor man white, and if Bruar hadn't supported him from behind it's a certainty he'd have fainted.

Anyway, Doctor Mackenzie promised to have him home in time to catch his train, and said they could only stay a short while.

'Please, good friend,' asked big Rory, 'stay with us to watch the mixing. After that you can go.'

'Well, why not, there's a later train, I'm sure we'll make that one. You will come to no harm among these good folks,' he assured the skinny wee man, clinging to him like a limpet on a rock.

As the small band closed in a circle round Megan and Bruar, the non-tinkers stood back. They were allowed to witness, but not take part in the circle of joining.

Doctor Mackenzie folded his arms, chewed on his clay pipe and watched as the pair wed. He remembered that not that long ago they were complete strangers, yet when he saw them together his thoughts were, 'If ever a pair was suited it is them'. He nudged the man close by his side, who by now had stopped shaking, and, although still not sure about these strange creatures who dwelt in rounded humps of stick and tarpaulin, had relaxed a little. 'You'll not see that in any church,' he said, pointing at the tin bucket Rory handed to his son, who then in turn gave it to his bride.

She, without a glance at anybody, straddled the bucket and urinated in it. Her face beamed with pride, while the photographer turned deep red with embarrassment, and didn't know where to put his eyes. Bruar urinated into his own bucket.

Then his father poured the contents of the two vessels together, so mixing their fluids. Bruar then very carefully cut a small incision with a sharp knife into Megan's ankle. She, with the same knife, made a cut in his forearm. Needless to say, this brought raised eyebrows from the good doctor, while the mild-mannered photographer nearly fainted for the second time. Bruar then rubbed his forearm over her ankle and mingled the blood. The incisions, being minute, quickly congealed and would leave the smallest scars. Then, finally, both held the bucket of their combined body fluid and poured it over the fire.

'Thank God for that,' whispered the astonished photographer into Mackenzie's ear.

'For what?'

'I thought they were going to drink it!'

With a final hiss and puff of blue smoke the ceremony was complete. No rings or promises, just a simple whisper of 'forever love' finalised their vows.

———

Soon Mackenzie was trotting off, bottle of ale in one hand, reins in the other. He had promised the couple that as soon as the picture was ready, he'd deliver it himself. What noone knew then was that one day, that wedding photo would play a powerful part in the lives of Megan and Bruar.

His companion couldn't bring himself to accept the hospitality of the nomads, and had declined food and ale. The incident with the metal buckets was sufficient to put him off food for the remainder of his day. O'Connor laughed at this, as he piled more sticks on the vigorously burning campfire. 'For sure, some folks come into this world and don't even know they've been alive. Did ye see the eyes of that skin-flinted photographer?' he asked everyone, adding, 'They were sitting on stalks wit the fear of him. I've never seen such a mouse-like creature. I should have poured a pint of the brown stuff into him, I'm sure he'd be lifting his spindles o' legs a-jigging wit the rest of us. Mind youse, I'm thinking yon lad's trousers were filled wit the other brown stuff.'

Into his trouser pocket Rory rammed his hand, drew forth a Jews harp, positioned it between his teeth and let rip. 'Come on then, you big galoot of an Irishman, let's me see the jigging of yourself.'

O'Connor needed no further prompting. With an almighty yelp he grabbed Rachel, threw her skyward and birled her like a peerie top.

62

She drew in her breath, released a fine volley of mouth music and the party began.

'If Robbie Burns just happened to be passing and him full of the drink, he'd have added tinkers alongside his witches and warlocks to his poem Tam O' Shanter,' whispered Jimmy into Bruar's ear, then added, 'Aye, and then no doubt Tam would have blamed them for cutting off his old mare's tail.'

The newlywed groom couldn't take his eyes of Megan as she lifted her wedding dress, showing perfect knees. He rose up and howled at the top of his voice, grabbed her narrow waist and began dancing around the tents.

Jimmy shook his head watching both O'Connor and Rory, who were screeching and howling like wolves, and commented, 'Nobody does weddings like the tinker.' He was aware that he and Bruar were only half-bred, but on that night and after such a ceremony, no one could have told the difference.

Hours of fun and frolics passed before an exhausted Rachel called for calm. Well needing a lie down to catch their breath, the men did as she asked.

'Sister,' she said, holding out her hand to Megan who was curled into her husband's arms, 'Flowers of the Forest.'

Megan got up, sat by her sister, pulled a shawl around both of them and, while stick ash smouldered in the circle of hot stones round the fire, they sang the beautiful haunting song of lost love, about the young men who never returned from some faraway battlefield. A single blackbird joined in from a nearby tree branch, and when the last note was sung, not one dry eye could be found among them. Even the nearby McAllisters, who had stayed silent in their tent through all the day's events, were heard sniffling.

So, as that wonderful, long-awaited day finally ended, a happy band of travellers slept in perfect peace. Love ruled in the tent of the newlyweds but only under a mound of heavy blankets. Each might have frozen to death if one inch of flesh had been exposed to the bite of winter.

As day followed d,ay each rallied to help in whatever way they could, making sure baby Macallister had enough food while keeping a watchful eye on O'Connor, who drank more with the passing of each week.

Many nights Rory and his sons scoured the frost- and moss-covered dykes calling his name, thinking that sooner or later their shouts would fall on dead ears. But he was a hardy Irishman with the luck of the leprechauns, and like a blind dog would find his way home. However, he soon discovered that trekking to the pub and broiling in fights with the ploughmen was becoming more of a hazard with the snow drifts and freezing winds, so he began to stay in his tent, brewing worse home-made concoctions than ever before.

Rory stayed off the demon liquid, and seemed to enjoy seeing to himself now his sons had wives to look after. Rachel and Jimmy too found sharing a bed their choice for the future. There was no ceremony, just a night beneath the covers and the bond was made. Jimmy expertly recovered Annie's dingy tent with deerskin and old cardboard boxes, to serve as their home from then on.

Trapped rabbits, pheasants and hare were few and far between at this time, because the rabbits dug deep down in their burrows, opting to live off their own droppings. Pheasants filled fox bellies before they came within reach of humans. Hare were the hardest to catch, staying as they did on the high mountains. Anyway, tinker people feel uneasy about eating hare. The old belief that they were shape-changers, like werewolves, put a fear in their minds. But hard foot-slogging by the men kept everyone half-fed.

The women walked once a month into town and hawked mouthfuls of bread from people hardly able to feed themselves. Doctor Mackenzie must have taken to his bed, for neither hide nor hair of him was spotted throughout the long winter months. Perhaps, they thought, the good doctor was dead. He was an old man, and Scotland saw droves of over-seventies succumb to death in those wintry days.

Farmers were a godsend to the nomads; they gave turnips, potatoes and milk without condition. Well, maybe not entirely freely, because Bruar and Jimmy had a pile of hard chores to do before the men of the land paid them in kind. Rachel hated the turnips, better known as neeps. 'They're for making soup rather than boiling,' she'd say. 'They are fit for ewes' bellies, not folks'.' She now had reason to think about eating healthily, because the first stirring of life had begun in her own belly—she and Jimmy were expecting a child.

That winter had been extremely harsh, but soon buds appeared on sleepy willows, along with bleating lambs in the fields; their fingers thawed out. 'Survival will be easy now', they all thought. Spring sang along dykes and hedgerows, in tune with the birds, which began their mating rituals.

Bruar and Megan joined the birds and the bees. 'Let's have a dozen sons,' he laughed pulling down the camp door one warm evening, 'and fill the glen with our own tribe!'

'Six boys, the same amount of girls or I'll not have any,' she teased. 'Deal!'

Their laughter within the tent, smothered by kisses, filled everyone with hope of days to come, expectation of fresh growth and an overwhelming feeling of being alive and thankful for it.

Rory called over to O'Connor, 'Will you listen to them in there going at it like rabbits! If they're not careful the tent will collapse on top of them, and we'll soon see how fast they shift.'

'Ah, fur sure we hear them, and what a beautiful sound they make. Who cares if the tent falls down, winter's over an I'm for a belly of rotgut at the public house, may God bless its solid walls. My gut's done in wit supping the green-brown dregs from my still jug. Come on, man, an' join me!'

Rory had passed a milestone in his life, a winter without the company of demons. 'I don't need the blasted stuff,' he told the Irishman sternly, speedily heading into the distance to chop wood for the fires; any chore that would take the yearning from his stomach.

Over his shoulders O'Connor slipped a shabby threadbare coat and leaped the grey stone dyke, slipping on its mildewy coating. For a minute he stopped. The yearning in Rory would surely master him, and he'd be joining him on the low road to busty, sweet-tasting women and alcohol, he was certain of that. 'You're a drinking man, me old mate, whether you like it or no, the want is there under the surface. Stay aff the stuff as long as you can, but remember this from one who knows; once you've booked inta Hell Hotel you can leave, but never check out. Remember that, Rory. And here's another thought for youse—"a tiger stays striped".'

The Irishman's words sent a shiver through Rory as his mind rushed back to his sister—her flaming eyes, pale drawn face, her parting words when he collected his sons. But the determination had never been as strong, he'd beat the craving, even if it meant his end; he'd made enough wrongs in times past; now for the rights. With two daughters-in-law to help him, things would be different. Soon he'd be big Rory, the grandfather. So many had been wronged, but more than anything else, that promise he'd made so long ago to his lassie would keep him on the right path. Sleepless nights and long guilt-filled days had hounded him until now; yes, he would stay away from the demon.

—

Summer came with a blaze of colour and warmth. Jimmy gathered armfuls of reeds for basket-making as Rachel continued to feel the stirring of growing life in her belly.

Bruar and Megan spent long days chasing the grouse and pheasants high up on the heather moors, stealing rich moments for passionate love-making and swearing on one another's lives that nothing would separate them.

Doctor Mackenzie hadn't succumbed to the ravages of the past winter as they'd imagined, and was soon tethering his horse to the same gnarled oak as before, and sharing the thick hot tea that big Rory was now supping instead of the liquid poison bubbling forth daily from O'Connor's still. 'Have you been well, Mackenzie? We thought Father Time had taken you.'

'Och no, no. There were six babies born over the winter, and we lost four old bodies to a blasted flu. I've been kept busy.'

'We only had the frost and the belly to see to. We never got any flu thing.'

'I never did see your kind take bugs, I wonder why that is?'

'Doctor, you know I'm not a true-blood tinker, and my boys are only half, but I think Mother Nature has a way of dealing with those flu things, it's her who kills the infections. You never see a fox or a rabbit with a cough or running nose.'

'That's a fact, right enough, big Rory. Now how are the girls?'

'Oh, just dandy. My boys are men now and that's for certain.'

As a warm day passed the two shared tales, laughed and gently whiled a few hours away. Before the old doctor left, he gave Rachel the once-over, saying, 'If all my mothers-to-be were as healthy as you, I'd have more time for my roses!'

—

Life was sweet and rich to the tinkers that summer, but autumn was approaching, and with the growing of Rachel's unborn infant, something else was awaiting birth!

Little did they realise that across the English Channel a race of ordinary, peaceable people was being transformed by a minority of war-mad leaders into a war-mad nation. A nation about to unleash upon the western world a horror of immeasurable magnitude; one that would reach into and tear apart the little band of tinkers hidden in the Angus Glens and nestling at the feet of the great Grampians.

FIVE

'You go into Kirriemor without me today, Megan, to dae a bit hawking. I'm feeling stirrings in my lower back, and think baby is making up its path soon for the wide world. Do you mind, sister?'

Megan picked up Rachel's basket and added its contents to hers. 'No, but I'll make it half a day, in case you need me.'

Rachel stretched her back, and when she felt only a small pain run down her legs she brushed off her sister's concern, 'First babies take ages—I'll be heaving this wee bisom out this time tomorrow.'

'Och, listen to you, like you're the expert with a heap of bairns. Mammy always said first babies could come as fast as tenth ones, so I'll be back to help you this afternoon.'

The McAllister family had left the campsite in early spring, and with the men away for a long day's harvest, Rachel would get little or no help from O'Connor snoring away the drink doldrums. She was relieved that Megan would be home early, and although she would not admit her anxiety, she watched until the skipping figure had gone before slipping in to her tent and taking up a position on the straw birth bed to get ready for the imminent arrival.

Kirriemor was quieter than usual. Megan wondered if she'd mistaken her days—it seemed more like a Sunday than a Monday. But when a brown and white mongrel dashed from the butcher's with a chunky bone in its mouth she knew she'd made no mistake. Still, it certainly was a very quiet morning.

'I think I'll go see Doctor Mackenzie, tell him Rachel's baby's coming,' she thought. After that she'd hawk her pot-scourers.

'Hello Megan, what brings you to visit me this fine morning? I hope your sister's well. Don't tell me O'Connor's got the gut ache, or is it yourself? Are you pregnant, lass?'

'Not yet, and the Irishman doesn't own a gut, he's got insides like that ticker thing there in your hallway.' She grimaced, and covered her ears as a loud gonging sound came from its depths. 'How can you be doing with such a thing?' she added. 'You wouldn't see us heaving that beast around on our backs. The sun wakes the blackbird and the moon the owl. We don't watch our life being forced around a numbered face without eyes. But I came to tell you Rachel nears her time. She's in pain, my sister, I thought you should know.'

He ignored the remark about clocks. 'Aye, seeing as it's her first time you did the right thing. Now before you take off like a linty round the doors with those pot-scourers of yours, give me the paper and the mail lying on the floor behind my own door. I'd get it myself but you're a lot more agile than me.'

Megan stooped down, picked up both items, and thought, 'Look at all these wavy lines, how can folks make head or tail of them? Bruar and I can hardly read a word between us. His Auntie brought him up, and as there wasn't a school nearby, well, it remains a doubtful point whether he ever found the need to read and write. I think big Rory can, though.'

'Well, Megan, you sell me a handful of those scourers of yours, and I'll pop the kettle on and read you a few paragraphs from *The Times*. Mind you, lass, news is usually a day old before it reaches me, but surely there'll be wee bit to interest us. We'll finish our tea, and then I'll go back with you to see to Rachel.'

Megan was more than pleased to sell her scourers to the doctor. She wasn't looking forward to trekking around braeside cottages through dung-furrowed farmyards.

Sauntering through to a warm kitchen, Doctor Mackenzie withdrew from the breast pocket of his old creased waistcoat a pair of thin-rimmed spectacles, which he positioned on the point of his nose. Megan sat down in an armchair in the parlour to wait. After what seemed like an eternity, she wondered if he was still in the house.

'Sir, do you need a hand?' she called through the half-opened kitchen door. Silence followed. She called again, not getting an answer, entered the warm kitchen of the big house and raised her voice. 'Doctor, I think perhaps I'll get myself away home to Rachel.'

69

The old man was sitting head down into his newspaper, his brow furrowed thick and tight, the spectacles slipping off his nose and dangling from his ears.

'What terrible news. This is an awful day, a real bad one for sure!'

'What's wrong? Are there bad words in that paper? Read, like you said you would.'

In the time she'd known the old man, she'd never seen him look so worried. His face was pale grey instead of its usual ruddy pink. Whatever was written in the pages of that newspaper certainly wasn't easy reading.

'Sit for a moment, Megan, here by my side. This concerns all of us, even your kind.'

As the lassie knelt by the man's chair he read from the front page: 'An announcement by His Majesty: "It is with regret that I have to inform my subjects that Britain is at war with Germany"!'

'Where's Germany, what's a subject and who's His Majesty?'

Ignoring her, the doctor hastened through into an adjoining room and came back with another newspaper, muttering to himself. 'I think it was in this issue, yes, Monday June 29th. Here it is. I knew it, I bloody knew it. I told everybody in the town and countryside this would bring a heavy price. Listen now, my girl.'

The copy of an earlier edition of *The Times* had been folded in a crumpled fashion. He pushed Megan forcefully down onto a wooden stool and read, his eyes fixed on a column of small typed words: 'The Austro-Hungarian heir-presumptive, the Archduke Francis Ferdinand, and his wife the Duchess of Hohenberg, were assassinated yesterday afternoon at Sarajevo, the capital of Bosnia and Herzegovina. The actual assassin is described as a high school student, who fired bullets at his victims with fatal effect from an automatic pistol as they were returning from a reception at the town hall.

The outrage was evidently the fruit of a carefully-laid plot. On their way to the town hall the Archduke and his consort had narrowly escaped death. An individual described as a compositor from Trevinje, a garrison town in the extreme south of Herzegovina, had thrown a bomb at their motorcar. Few details of this first outrage have been received. It is stated that the Archduke warded off the bomb with his arm, and that it exploded behind the car, injuring the occupants of the second car.'

'I remember thinking at the time that this vile act would find an end, and by God what an end, bloody war with Germany.' Tears almost spilled over as he folded the paper and laid it down. He could see that in her blissful ignorance Megan still hadn't grasped the enormous gravity of the news. He would only waste time explaining, so he quickly set aside his fear for the dark days ahead and got the horse ready for his visit with Rachel. Soon the pair were bobbing along the uneven surface of the old track. Lost, though, in thoughts of what lay in store for the young people of his country, the old doctor was almost at crawling speed. Threatening enemies waited at the door. Sitting beside him was an innocent child, a walker with nature, of a kind which had no national enemies. They suffered prejudice, yes, and persecution by certain individuals, but not the monstrosity of war! A warmth emanated from her trust in him, and for a moment he felt it. There was no evil cunning in the tinkers; to his mind they were simple survivors. How would they cope with this looming shadow of unnatural forces? What would become of their moors, burns and forests, where they cleverly blended into nature's environment?

Megan grew concerned for the old man, of whom she was dearly fond. She had never known him to miss his cup of tea. His keeping the horse at crawling speed made her lean over and offer to take the reins. Why, she asked, should he bother what happened in a far-off part of the world? 'Surely no one will come away up these glens? Let the war do its business, it won't put me up nor down. Now give me those reins, for I'm thinking my sister will be a mite worried by now.'

He let her drive his horse and trap along the bumpy road, as the events in Europe filled his head. As they left Kirriemor, it was apparent by the silence that its inhabitants had also heard the news and dreaded the consequences.

No one knows whether fate took a hand that day, but no more than ten minutes out of town, Doctor Mackenzie's old horse took a corner too fast and buckled a shoe. Drawing to a standstill the beast refused to move an inch, causing the worried pair to curse. She blamed the animal, while under his breath he blamed her driving skills. There was no option but a long walk stretching ahead of them.

Her pack, filled with scourers and bits of this and that, was no use to them, so she concealed it behind a cluster of rocks and then offered to carry his bag. 'If we don't get to Rachel's aid soon, Jimmy, who faints at the sight of blood, will have arrived back in total panic.'

Not wishing to be slowed down by the heavy leather bag of doctor's implements and medicines, he willingly handed it over.

They set off deep in thought, she for her sister, he for the countless thousands of young women carrying babies whose fathers would never return from the coming war. They would lie in a torn-up battlefield, or fall from the heavens among fragments of ripped open aircraft, or find death in the ocean, she who spares no one who sinks into her murky depths.

Meantime Rachel was having her own war! But not one with rifles and bullets. Nature demands that we come into the world with much suffering to the vessel which bears us. With her pains of labour growing in depth by the second, she cursed Jimmy and even her deceased mother for putting breath into her. Sweat oozed from every pore, and as the wretched claws of agony reached unbearable sharpness she screamed on O'Connor to help her.

'What the hell is the matter wit that bloody woman, screaming like a choked rabbit,' he thought, turning on a sweaty mattress. Rachel's small tent reverberated with her next cry, followed by a low groan, then a hiss through clenched teeth.

'That wasn't a sound o' a distressed bunny,' he thought, stretching his stinking torso and rising onto one knee.

'O'Connor, you useless bastard, get over and help me, man!' The fear in her voice brought him to a more sober level. He'd fallen asleep without removing his ragged trousers, so slipping two leather braces over his shoulders, he crawled reluctantly from the stale-smelling tent, his hairy belly protruding like a kangaroo's pouch from the open trouser front.

'My baby! Irishman, it's coming, help me! God in heaven, man, do something, please. Megan hasn't brought Mackenzie, I'm scared stiff!'

Suddenly as the sun's rays pierced through the clouds in his head, he realised the dire situation. Seeing nobody else in the campsite, he dashed into Rachel's tent, apologising with every movement of his clumsy body to the now frantic mother-to-be. When Rachel spread her legs, and screamed through clenched teeth, he fell on his knees like a stone before the unfolding drama and said, 'Holy Mother o' the God of all things, what am I to do?'

Rachel's legs were as far apart as she could physically manage. With one hand tightly gripping the tent pole behind her head, she was trying with the other to reach her tiny infant's head, which was pushing its way into the world unaided.

O'Connor quickly overcame his terror. With grimy, hairy-knuckled hands, he cupped the little mite until its mother gave one last stupendous push, and out it came, partly covered in a birth-gown of red and pink fluid. Tears fell from the Irishman's face when he held up the child to its mother. He was like a babe himself, bubbling and laughing, 'Would ye look at him, as pure as the driven snow! Little mite is as wee as a fairy. If meself had witnessed the holy infant's coming to earth,' (a subject he spoke freely about when his intoxication rendered him harmless and melancholy) 'I could not have been more humbled.' With tender care the baby was handed to Rachel, who lay back on her bed and forgot in an instant all her previous agony, as the tiny fists touched its mother's face. 'Lord, O'Connor, I feared my bairn would have come into the world without a witness. Thank God for your presence.'*

Rachel wiped her son with a flannel she'd prepared along with a basin of hot water, now lukewarm. Her unsavoury midwife dashed from the tent, coming back in an instant with a dirty pillow stuffed with pheasant and grouse feathers, and gently propped her up by sliding it under her shoulders. 'There now, my proud colleen, you rest and I'll go fetch a cup of tea, is there anything else you need?'

She smiled and shook her head, but as he made to leave she reached out and stopped him. 'O'Connor, what is your name, the one your mother gave you?'

The Irishman ran a hand through a dishevelled head of grey-black hair and turned to look at Rachel, a sad look, one she'd never seen on his usually drunken face. He looked sorrowfully at the now stirring baby and said, 'I niver knowed a mother. Some old crow dragged me up, an aunt o' sorts. Hell, I don't know if it's on any birth certificate, but me name is Nicholas O'Connor. At least, that's what she called me on a Sunday.' He was squirming in embarrassment, never having meant to say anything of his past, which up until that moment he had defended with strict privacy.

He was spared further emotional sharing by the voices of Megan and an exhausted doctor, hurriedly approaching the tent. He dashed

*Author's note: *It was a sworn law amongst travelling people that someone must see mother and baby separate their joining. In this way no one could say that the mother had stolen another's child.*

out to meet them. His abruptness startled the pair, as he rounded on them like a camp warden. 'Hello then, and where the hell have you been? Sure, we have a new little 'un. Here, you better look at this.'

As he proudly pulled back the tent door, one would think if not knowing any better that O'Connor was the father.

What a wonderful relief to see that not only was Rachel holding a very healthy boy, but that both had come through without any harm.

'All thanks to O'Connor here.' Rachel's words brought a red face to her saviour as he reappeared a few minutes later, holding three cups of tea in one hand. In the other he held a hairbrush, 'I think the father will be here in two ticks, better make yourself pretty'. To everyone's surprise he knelt down, running the brush through Rachel's hair. 'There now, that's a pretty thing for yer man's homecoming.' Each laughed at the Irishman's new attentive manner, except for Rachel who had forgotten how awful her sweat-soaked hair and drawn face must look.

No sooner had they finished their cups of tea when three famished, exhausted men came home from harvesting. All signs of fatigue and hunger soon disappeared, however, when the cry of a new baby was heard from within Jimmy's abode. 'My God, laddie,' exclaimed his father, 'there's a grand sound for the ears of a proud father. Get in there and see what you got!'

Megan pulled open the tent door and beckoned the threesome in, her finger at her lips warning them to be quiet and not frighten the wee lad.

'A boy you say? I've a wee son! Hey, Bruar, Daddy, I've a bloody son!' Jimmy leapt into the air, throwing his crumpled bonnet so high it landed between a pair of hooded crows, which screeched and hastily left their sturdy perch at the top of an ancient oak.

Rachel looked radiant. Smiling, she handed the baby to its father, who kissed his son and whispered, 'Love you.' Then he told his wife he'd never seen her so lovely, but she said the reason for that was the fussing of her midwife.

'Now that we have this responsibility,' Rachel whispered in Jimmy's ear, 'we'll think about getting away from the tent, maybe ask a farmer for a house.' She had said many times that it was the way of life of her ancestors that killed her mother, and she didn't want to go the same way.

Doctor Mackenzie joined the loud celebrations which spread through the family, but as for O'Connor, well perhaps it was all too much for him, and that's why he wandered off to his lonely tent intending to spend some time with a half-bottle he'd kept for any such occasions. Before he'd put bottle to mouth, however, Rachel's voice called out. Putting the bottle back in his pocket, he went over and peeped into her tent. 'What is it that you want of me?'

'I would like you to be here with us for a moment, my Irish friend, while I say something to my family—oh, and the good doctor too.'

'Now,' said O'Connor, 'it's not necessary for you to be thanking me. Given the circumstances, anyone wad 'ave done the same.' Clumsily he shuffled from foot to foot and turned to leave.

Rachel sensed his embarrassment and said quickly, 'Folks, I now have the greatest pleasure,' she then lifted up her baby for all to see, 'in introducing Nicholas Stewart.'

Big Rory picked the child from his mother's arms and kissed him, saying, 'That's a grand name ye have little fella, but when did it come into your head, Rachel?'

O'Connor fell onto his knees for the second time that day, and with the edge of a ragged jacket sleeve he wiped a tear from his eye along with the contents of his nose. Then he did the unthinkable. From his pocket he withdrew the water of life and handed it round to each and every one, saying; 'We'll wet the baby's head, folks.'

Later, when Rachel and her baby had fallen into a welcome sleep, the tiny band discussed the coming war round a warm fire with Doctor Mackenzie. It was with a country they'd hardly heard of, let alone knew where it was. It wasn't part of their world, so the war must be the concern of others.

'Anyhow, it doesn't matter who wins or loses a war, tinkers are treated the same everywhere.' Bruar's words seemed to take the personal sting from what was unfolding hundreds of miles away.

All night long they each excelled in the singing of their ancient ballads. O'Connor, now that he had a good reason to feel a sense of pride in himself, sang the heart from 'Erin's Isle'. Although big Rory had a heavy fist, this wasn't apparent in his beautiful baritone voice as he serenaded everyone with northern songs of the sea. He mixed traditional ballads with golden oldies he had learned about bonny babies. Megan's sweet lovesongs spoke of lost lovers going on faraway journeys, and brought tears flowing freely down the fire-glowing cheeks of the hardy men. Even the hooting owls perched above them in the old gnarled oak joined the ceilidh. A chorus of 'Auld Lang Syne' gurgled through painful throats greeted the sun's first rays, along with a squealing hungry Nicholas.

Doctor Mackenzie set off after drinking near on a whole pot of tea, promising to let them know how things were taking their course in the wider world, while the three men left to take on another long day's harvest.

O'Connor yet again spent a large chunk of the day sleeping off the night before, as Megan helped her sister with the new baby before setting off uphill. She'd her heather scourers to make. Winter money would be stretched further with another mouth, albeit a tiny one, to feed.

Afternoon was bringing a storm, she could see it forming high above her. Great white fluffy clouds had turned black and were creeping like fat fingers around the brown mountain tops. She sat down to eat a sandwich, and suddenly without any warning a massive stretch of wings swooped down several feet from her. The sandwich fell from her hand as she sat transfixed, watching the King of the Mountains soar so close she could see his fully-feathered legs and square white-tipped tail. Holding her breath, she waited on his barking or 'twee-oo' call. What happened then froze her to the spot, as in slow motion the mighty eagle glided so close its eyes met hers in a deep penetrating stare, before silently gliding upwards towards the waiting storm.

'Omen!' she screamed and ran home as fast as any deer, repeating over and over again, 'An omen!'

Rachel, who had risen from her birth bed, was washing at the burnside when she heard her sister's screams, and hastened to her aid thinking she'd been assaulted. 'Who's interfered with you, sister? Wait till Bruar finds him, he'll cut the hands from his miserable body.'

'Nobody looked my road, it was the "King"—he spoke to me! Well, not as you'd have heard him in words, but, oh my God, Rachel, he was silent above the black clouds. You know, as does every living travelling man, woman and child from the Glen of Coe, that when the golden eagle soars toward the storm in silence, then it heralds doom!'

Rachel, aware of this powerful omen, began to whimper. The sisters grasped each other's hands tightly and began to chant. O'Connor, holding baby Nicholas, had never witnessed this strange behaviour before and sat transfixed by their heathen ways. Megan spoke with quavering tones, while Rachel hummed. If he hadn't already heard that this was the way of the Glen Coe Macdonalds, then he would have taken them for witches, packed his tent and left there and then.

'What was that all about?' he asked, when the pair had stopped chanting.

Rachel with furrowed brow, frightened eyes darting to and fro from corner to corner of the campsite, told him. 'One day before a terrible snow storm came upon the Macdonalds of Glen Coe, the eagle appeared to a boy, before soaring up towards the black sky. The boy ran home, telling his parents about the great bird of the heavens which had not made a sound. That night, through a raging blizzard, their neighbours the Campbells set on them like wolves, killing all that could not flee, and there were damn few of them that could. Ever since that day, if the golden eagle is witnessed soaring in silence towards a storm, then a terror will befall the Macdonalds.' Megan nodded vigorously at each statement her sister made.

O'Connor handed over her son and said to Rachel and Megan, 'Sure, in this day an' age a superstition so old would have lost the power.' Before an answer came, he added that he was certain that the whistling heard earlier was the men coming home, and not a morsel of food cooked for them. Sure enough, almost the minute he finished speaking, the three men of the campsite turned the bend of the dusty road.

Highlanders also fear such superstitions, and all through that evening and the night that followed, an eerie silence prevailed. It was hard to imagine that the band of songsters from the previous night were the same miserable lot who now wondered what awful event was to befall them. To add to the atmosphere of foreboding, a terrible thunder storm stirred and awakened little Nicholas. With it came a deluge of rain, sagging the tent roofs, then soaking their thin canvas and animal skin homes.

Much of the rain had penetrated, leaving them damp and exhausted from lack of sleep. Just as the sun pushed through the clouds, the band of tinkers eventually fell into welcome sleep.

For several months the village of Kirriemor saw one young man after another go off to wear the King's uniform. Bruar and Jimmy spoke of nothing else, annoying the girls and reaching deep into their father's soul. He had missed a lot of their raising, and didn't want to lose them as young men just starting on the long road of marriage and fatherhood. He wanted more little babies to cheer his old age and keep the proud name of Stewart alive.

It was the sound of familiar hooves making tracks towards them that opened all the half-closed doors of the camp. Dr Mackenzie wasn't alone: the town's policeman, Sergeant Wilson, sat by his side.

Never, no matter how kind and compassionate he might appear to be, did travelling people take to a lawman. Far too many had fallen foul of a uniformed devil with the weight of the judiciary behind him. He was met by turned backs and closed tents.

'It's alright, folks,' said the doctor reassuringly, 'I've brought the good sergeant. He's come for a blether, nothing to worry about, you have my word on it.'

If any man could reassure them, then it was the good doctor. 'Come away down and join us,' said Rory, gesturing that they should sit on the old log seats by the fire. 'Here, Sergeant, this is the most comfy seat. I hope you take no offence, but we can't abide a lawman poking his nose in our campsite. We don't break any laws, and honest is our work, so state your business and be off.'

His sons stood on either side, backing up his request. Within the security and privacy of the tent, Megan huddled close to her sister. Nicholas suckled contentedly on his mother's breast, unaware his father's fate was being decided outside round a low burning fire.

'What brings the law among us?' whispered Megan.

'I haven't a clue, for we're as honest as the day's long. And O'Connor seldom goes to visit and sup with the ploughmen now, so it can't be him.'

Rachel's answer only made her more curious.

With straining ears they listened to Sergeant Wilson, who had opened a black leather satchel and was handing round its contents, telling the men how wonderful were the brave Scottish lads who had volunteered for the army.

Megan needed to hear more, so crept from under the back of the tent and slipped around so that the men were unable to see her but she could clearly view them. Rachel tried to stop her, but only managed to pull off a hairband in her attempt

Whatever it was that Sergeant Wilson held in his hands, it certainly had the men wide-eyed and eager-faced.

No matter how hard she wormed herself nearer, Megan could not get a proper look at what held their interest. Rachel hissed at her to get back inside the tent, but Megan refused. With the 'eagle omen' still fresh in her mind, she rose to her feet and hurried amongst the men. 'I'm sorry, husband,' she apologised. 'I know that us women have to stay inside when a stranger calls, but the policeman seems to be a bringer of good news, the way you lot are beaming. Here, let me see what it is that pleases you.' She pulled the paper from Wilson and laughed when she saw it was a picture of big Rory.

'Oh my, would you take a look at this—someone has painted my father-in-law's face?'

'Lassie, this isn't a painting of me, this is the King's representative, Kitchener!'

Hands firmly held on hips, she tossed back her head and shouted, 'King of where?'

Up till then the mild-mannered man of the law was an impassive visitor, only doing his duty. He'd brought the men of the campsite news of the progress of the war. He told them of a drive for volunteers, for men to enlist and protect their country, but at this fiery lassie's total lack of respect for His Majesty, his cloak of composure collapsed. 'Listen here, young Stewart, you bring a switch over this she-devil's hindquarters! If she was mine I'd whip her for sure!'

'She's a fine wife, I'm sorry but never have I heard her speak in such a manner. Megan, hush your tongue.'

'Don't you dare speak like that to me! I know why this flat-footer has come with his squirming and pussy words. Sure, he wants you all to wear some bloody stranger's uniform, to take up arms and fight in some faraway place and what for? I'll tell you—to save a land that would rather tinkers drowned in spate-rivers, or got thrown over precipices, just so long as we didn't exist! Chase him from our fire, I say. And you, Doctor, what kind of friend are you to help take away our men?' With every disapproving eye on her she turned, lifted her skirt and exposed her bare buttocks. 'See that, Wilson?' she said, slapping her bare flesh, 'you can lick it!'

'Megan, for God sake, lassie!'

Engulfed by fear and anguish, and the note of disgust in Bruar's voice, she ran from the site. Their talk for months had been of nothing else but war, and now it had come among them. She was going to lose her man and that was unthinkable.

Rachel, who'd heard snippets of the argument, came to her sister's defence, appearing from her tent with a wooden mallet tightly clenched in her hand. Jimmy grabbed it off her just in time, before it landed heavily on Sergeant Wilson's skull. Rory called for calm. 'Now, stop this at once, the good doctor has not visited us to see a fight. Wilson has come with a request, so sit you down and hear him out.' Bruar, however, more concerned for Megan, made his excuses and left.

Rachel, sobbing, went back to her son. Now, with a quieter group round the campfire, Jimmy sat on a makeshift wooden bench next to his father and asked his visitor to tell them what it was Kitchener wanted from the tinkers.

Doctor Mackenzie spoke first. He popped those familiar thin-rimmed spectacles onto the point of his nose, took the paper from the Sergeant and said: 'Now, you all know that I have no time for this bloody war, and bless me, I'd say forget Kitchener and Sergeant Wilson's fancy words, but if the enemy gets this land you will see a lot less of freedom and a lot more of evil. That's what sickens me—choice is not an option.' He shook his head as he read from the crumpled paper: 'Britain is now at war. It is every man and woman's duty as citizens of this glorious land to take up arms and fight for your country! Your country needs you!"

The good doctor sat back in his chair, rolled up the poster, and watched the reaction of the tinker men. Rachel, unable to stay out of what concerned her and her child, came from the tent, her baby wrapped in a shawl and tied around her body. It was easy to see the tears flowing freely down her face. 'Jimmy, we—me and Nicholas—have much need of you. Please, man, don't you dare say that some King hundreds of miles from this quiet glen can order you away from a loving wife and innocent wee boy, to fight for a country that spits at your feet whenever it can!'

Jimmy, totally out of character, raised his voice, 'I'm head of my family, and if I want I'll take arms for whoever I bloody like. Now go back into the tent at once!'

Crying at such an outburst from her usually gentle husband, Rachel pulled part of her baby's woollen shawl over her head and ran back to the tent.

O'Connor had been silent till then, but he'd no stomach for war and said so. 'Doctor, I'm not saying this to you, but Wilson, you can go home an tell that bloody Kitchener that he won't find anybody here to fight his battles for him!'

Sergeant Wilson, face stretched with fury at the total disrespect to his sovereign from these heathens, said, 'Come on, Mackenzie, I'm off. The taste left in my mouth from this filth is unbearable.'

Without waiting for the doctor to untie his horse he was gone, marching off down the track.

Bruar soon caught up with Megan who was hiding at their favourite meeting place, an old oak tree, twisted by the winds which blew hard through its branches in the deep winter storms.

'Bonny Megan, what is wrong with you? Surely you would not expect my brother and me to stay home like couried rats, while the whole male population is defending our rights?'

'Bruar, did I not witness the Omen? Don't you see it heralded doom? I'll lose you to a foreign enemy, who doesn't bother whether you and I are toffs or tinkers. Rachel's right, nobody cares a snot about us. To the world we're "white niggers", that's all we are. Not that niggers are bad folks; I've heard the women of Kirriemor speaking about rich faraway folk having slaves, poor souls with black faces and snow-white eyes. To this King and his Kitchener, slaves are what we are. Only we're white ones! If you gave your lives, would the so-called King mind out for us, left behind without our men? We'd die of the hunger in no time. Mark my word, that's what would happen, we'd be soon dead. And another thing, what of our plan for having children?'

The more she went on, the more it was apparent he wasn't listening. Her hysterics had no effect, and she could see that look in his face. The one she saw when he spoke of the Norsemen in olden days invading Scotland. No, he'd go, she knew that, but would he come back? Was the eagle she'd seen on the hill definitely a message of death? Too tired to run off again, she lowered her eyes to the heather around their feet and asked the inevitable, 'When?'

'Tomorrow, Jimmy and I will enlist tomorrow.'

'Then take me now, while the longing in my breast beats so strong, for it might be the last time we ever join again.'

Bruar saw in her a new weakness, she was not usually faint-hearted or limp. 'Now listen to me, how many times have you solemnly promised with hand on heart that you will rest me in Durness? I will come home, we will grow old together and you will see to my end.'

Megan nodded through her tormented thoughts, yet at that moment all she could think of was tomorrow, not many days ahead. She felt only the pain of not having him lie by her side, to rise with a hug and kiss at the lifting of each new sun.

His strong, powerful arms circled her frame. Gently the lovers each removed their clothes and as they sank into the soft heather they made intense, raw and passionate love. It moved them onto a higher plane than any lovemaking they had ever experienced before. For a long time afterward they lay together saying nothing. His head was filling with a mixture of concern and excitement; worry at leaving her and the excitement of standing on a battlefield fighting back an enemy, just as his great ancestors had done to the Norsemen!

Megan's thoughts were of one thing—a shadow-winged eagle, gliding and soaring in a misty heaven. She fell asleep exhausted, and when at last a singing nightingale awakened her, he was gone. It would have been futile for her to run home tearing at her clothes and sobbing uncontrollably, because she knew her man had to take his place within the system of war, even though it had nothing to do with their kind. He and Jimmy simply did what every other tinker laddie did in 1914—they took the path of destruction, and made, if need be, the final sacrifice.

Six

*M*egan, Rachel and her baby, big Rory and their faithful companion O'Connor, continued to fend for themselves in the now tiny circle of nomads. Two months had slipped by since the boys set off to fight. Apart from letters which had been written at their request by an army priest to each of the girls, not much news had reached them. They described France as flat, and before the shelling, a fertile land. Jimmy was in the Cameronians and Bruar the Black Watch. This meant that the brothers could no longer look out for each other, and now they were miles apart.

Rachel became increasingly worried about her man, and was convinced he'd never see his wee boy again. Many times Megan found her lost in her thoughts within her small tent, cuddling and chanting to Nicholas. Each day Megan would watch from high upon the braeside for signs of old Doctor Mackenzie bringing news of the war's progress, or better still some words of comfort, if not from Bruar, then from Jimmy, to make Rachel's burden less.

She did not have long to wait!

February froze. Blizzards were more frequent and ferocious than they'd seen before. Layers of hard-packed snow covered every visible dyke, tree and field; although the cold hardened the heather roots and slowed her pace, she still insisted on climbing the hill and watching for the familiar horse and buggy. No sooner had she reached her summit perch one day, when she heard Mackenzie coming up the old road. Unable to hold back her emotions she ran, stumbling and rolling down a good stretch of hillside.

83

She'd meant to catch him before Rachel did just in case his news was, heaven forbid, bad. But the sudden fall slowed her down long enough for the man and his horse to be met by Rachel and big Rory.

Screams of torment announced that the nightmare had come, the dreaded news which halted her dead in her snow-covered tracks. Big Rory fell against a tree as Rachel threw herself inside the tent. O'Connor, shaking his head from side to side, walked off into the forest.

She grabbed at the doctor's coat sleeve and was met with deeply pained eyes. 'He fought well, it says so here in the telegram, lassie. Oh, this blasted war! Just this very morning I had to tell two mothers their laddies were not coming home!'

'Who's gone?'

'Jimmy!'

She heard herself say in her heart, before darting off to comfort her sister, 'It's not my Bruar, not him!'

Doctor Mackenzie went into a tent, at first not sure whose, but the smell of stale, unwashed clothes told him it must be O'Connor's. The kettle simmered, a single cup lay on the ground, and into the cracked receptacle he poured tea, steaming hot, wondering how many more times he would take the news of lost sons to worried relatives. It all seemed to fall at his door since the minister of Kirriemor's church had long ago left his flock to bring comfort to the many thousands of young men on the far-off battlefield. Young Father Brennan, the priest of St Bridget's Chapel, was also overseas. The doctor hated this forced coat he wore and cursed all wars because of it.

He could hear Rachel now sobbing deeply. Once more the sound of hearts breaking filled his head. How long before the next heart would break? But life, as awful as it was, had to go on, and without a word he silently walked the horse up the narrow road, leaving the tinker folks to their grief.

For a short distance O'Connor joined him. 'Man, this must leave a bad taste in your mouth, you being a saver o' life?'

'That it does, friend, but what pains me more is that this blasted fight has hardly begun.'

When Rachel and big Rory had mourned a week, they did what is traditionally expected, buried Jimmy without his presence. All the procedure, from digging a grave to building a coffin was done. While Rory took a whole morning to break through the frozen earth,

O'Connor built a full-sized wooden box. The girls gathered Jimmy's belongings: a sharp basket-making knife, tools, a coil of snare wire, some twine for tying braces of pheasant and his fingerless gloves. Before he left he'd been whittling a toy soldier for his son, which was almost finished, but that Rachel kept.

At the foot of the forest, beside Annie's remains, they lowered Jimmy's coffin down. Along with his box of tools went clothes; what little he owned was laid neatly in the coffin and buried. Prayers and chants of olden days were offered up, hoping that wherever he was he would find rest. This was the only way travelling folk could cope with the death of a loved one who had failed to come home to them. As far as they were concerned, by this simple act they'd brought their dead back. And it was sufficient to part-mend their broken hearts. This ritual helped Rachel, but Rory only went through with it for his lassie's sake. She'd want her boy dealt with as tradition dictated. When alone, throwing a handful of soil upon the coffin, he whispered, 'No matter where you are, my son, you will find your resting. God rest you, my laddie.'

Rachel later came to say her own farewell, kissed a single sprig of mistletoe and softly tossed it on her husband's bodyless grave. 'Wherever you lie, my fallen soldier, part of me shares the cold earth with you. We only knew each other a short while, but from us came a healthy boy. I promise he will not suffer hardship. Rest until we meet again.' Gently she lowered tiny Nicholas to touch with innocent lips the earth covering his father's chosen place—the father he would never know, save in the telling of a tale.

Megan stood away from the grave. It frightened her. Thoughts that maybe her own man lay rotting in some rat-infested trench filled her with dread, her heart beat loudly in her breast until she could not bear it. Covering her tousled hair with a grey woollen shawl, she slunk away from the sight of Big Rory, O'Connor, Rachel and little Nicholas, and was soon hidden from view. Leaning her back against the old twisted oak she looked up at the heavens and cried until the salt from her tears stung the skin around her throat. 'Oh Bruar, please tell me you are still fighting. Show me a sign that a heart beats in your chest as one does in mine. Come home safe, my love. Forgive my selfish relief that Jimmy and not you died, but Rachel doesn't love with the same passion as I do. She needed Jimmy, but not the way I need you. You are my desire, my whole being, nothing matters to me but you.'

She pulled the shawl round her cold body and tightened it like a vice. 'Come home, Bruar, else I will not live without you!' She stayed there, freezing, on that cold spot, and probably would have remained there, had it not been for O'Connor who was, in his own way, trying to help his friends.

'Come you back, colleen, and see to your sister's baby, for the poor lass has collapsed in her grief. I'll take Rory down to Kirriemor to drink the passing o' his son. The fire is all right for the cooking and heat. I've seen to the kettle, so begone home with you.'

Sudden fear and anger gripped her, and a shiver ran the length of her spine. Fine she knew what it would mean. Big Rory hadn't touched a drop of liquor in ages. If he put it to his grief-stricken mouth, then he'd be unable to stop. He'd be wicked again. She had to have her say. 'Och man, you mustn't do this awful thing. Please don't take him to Kirriemor. You know as I do, he'll take the devil on himself if the demon drink runs through his veins while he is mourning. I beg you, don't take that horse to the well, for with the state of him he'll drink it dry and then kill somebody!'

O'Connor told her to see to things and not interfere in a man's grief. It was not for women to have a say in such matters, Rory had to get it out, and a bottle was the only way. She tried again to reason with him but the Irishman told her not to be so selfish. Her father-in-law had lost one son, and for all they knew, maybe Bruar was lying in a trench somewhere feeding worms as well.

Megan screamed at him before lunging at his throat, vainly trying to wrench those horrendous words from it. 'You listen to me, rat of a drunken coward, my man is safe and well. If he were hurt, never mind dead, I'd feel it in here.' She threw off her shawl, ripped buttons from her cardigan and punched the exposed flesh. 'Here beats a heart filled with devotion for Bruar Stewart. If so much as a wasp were to sting my man I'd feel it in here!'

O'Connor lifted the crumpled shawl and gave it back to her. He said nothing as he set off down to Kirriemor, big Rory at his side.

Megan's adrenaline surge left her cold and angry. She wanted to scream at her father-in-law and remind him of the Seer. A certain red-bearded, one-eyed prophet of dark futures. But little Nicholas was painfully crying for attention. Perhaps the small infant also felt the loss of his father. Nature had not formed words in his infantile head, but all the sobbing and neglect from his mother told him to make as much noise as was possible to get the cuddles and care he needed. Megan curled her arms under his small body and held him to her bosom. At her touch he stopped crying. Rachel too had ceased weeping and was holding her arms out towards her child. Megan laid him by his mother and said, 'Rachel, life has dealt you a terrible blow, but I know you will get over it. I'm worried about the older men brawling with the drink in them, though. If big Rory should get fired up, that would be worse than Jimmy's passing.'

'Why, in heaven's name, sister, should you imagine anything worse than Jimmy never coming home to see his bonnie laddie grow into manhood?'

'Because Rory has taken his pain to Kirriemor with O'Connor to drown his heart in a bottle of whisky, and God help us all if any of those ploughmen says so much as a black word to him.' Megan's brow furrowed with worry as she tried to make her sister see the seriousness of the situation.

Nicolas puckered his lips; Rachel pushed a milky breast to him and said, 'I don't think our good-father would be so stupid as to lose his senses when he has us to look after. And as for O'Connor, well, he's not as bad these days as he once was. Let's not add any more sorrow to our heavy hearts than we have already in this black time.'

The baby's eyelids closed, his belly was full; she laid him down. 'Megan, go you and put more sticks on the fire. I'll join you in a minute and we will hold hands and chant away the rest of this night. If the men feel the other side of an angry ploughman's fist, then maybe our old ancestral spirits will intervene, after all, my Jimmy's with them now.'

'Well, maybe aye and maybe no, but I feel the ancient spirits don't have much power in these evil times.'

'Oh now, sister, you mustn't go and get the weakness in you.'

'Tell me then, Rachel, when you and I sat in this very spot chanting for hours to ward off the badness, why did Jimmy end his life the way he did?'

'I have no answers to war, sister, but if our good father and his friend take a fall, then it's their own doings and nothing to do with the ancient spirit guides. Now I'm too tired to sit in vigil by the fire, instead I'll rest here with my baby. In sleep me and Jimmy will keep ourselves warm.' With those words said Rachel crawled under heavy woollen blankets. Megan kissed her head and they hugged each other until the pain of loss subsided.

Bruar would not forgive her if she let him down; so by the fire she waited out the night for Rory. As the fire burned to its last embers she heard voices, easily recognised; it was the two wanderers. Not wanting to be seen up at such an hour, she darted into her tent and gave thanks for their safe return. She listened like a mother hen to the men's sniggering and muffled laughter in the dead of the night. Then she heard a voice, one never heard in the campsite before, the voice of a woman. She sat up in bed and distinctly heard, not one, but two female voices. 'What the hell are they up to?' she thought. For a while she listened to the banter; stupid, drunk talk. Unable to contain herself, she stormed into O'Connor's tent. 'You two have a nerve, bringing back these slip morts! [loose women]'

O'Connor stared at Rory with astonishment. 'Get that bitch seen to or I'll take a whip across her arse, she takes far too much to do with us menfolk.' He stooped and apologised to the women, adding, 'Don't be taking notice of her, she's mental.'

Before Rory could prevent her, she lunged at the Irishman's throat and began to squeeze, screaming, 'What a bastard you are! You took my father-in-law into a bloody pub, and him just lost his son; not content with that, you bring him home a whore, a blasted reject from some smelly ploughman's bed!'

Rory, full of alcohol, threw her to the ground and slapped her hard across the jaw. She flinched, both in anger and embarrassment, then ran back to her now cold bed. For what was left of the night she sobbed into her feather-stuffed pillow, until sleep at last found its way into her young, and still easily hurt, mind.

Next morning she rose before everyone else. She broke a small hole in the frozen ice of the burn and washed her face and hands with carbolic soap, then set off without breakfast. Older and wiser in her hurt, she went in the hope of hawking an odd scourer or two.

Money was scarce, though, on account of the war. The lack of food was apparent in and around the hill houses of Kirriemor. Children appeared thinner, old folks sicker. Not one single penny was to be had, so with a full basket and empty belly she set off to visit the only person who would give her a welcome, Doctor Mackenzie.

'Come away in, Megan, how nice to see you. I hope there's no ill health among you during this cold spell.'

'No sir, we are doing away fine under the circumstances.'

'Something is troubling you, though. Is it the lack of news on Bruar?'

'Oh aye, he is never far from my mind, but it's more his father's carry-ons that perplex me.'

'I saw him and O'Connor stumble from the pub last night, but in times like these it's understandable. Poor man, the loss of a son is hard.'

'I know what you're saying, doctor, but big Rory has a demon in him, one that only drink releases. I don't have to tell you, surely?'

'Men have difficulty displaying their feelings, lassie, sometimes they drink to forget. You and Rachel, being from the Macdonalds, do the chanting, and if it works for you and you believe in it then fine, but remember that the Highland Stewarts are different.'

'I always feel the better of seeing and speaking with you. I'll go home now and worry no more on the men; if they want to drink and fornicate then that's their own business.'

Mackenzie laughed at her comment and said, 'I'm curious why you should use a word like that. Surely drinking alcohol doesn't involve sleeping with women?'

'Oh, I'm not stupid doctor; last night the men took two whores into their beds, and you should have heard the moans from that tent. I call that fornicating.'

He whispered to his visitor not to tell anyone in the town, for fear that the females concerned were cheating on their husbands, them being away at the fighting, or ploughmen working elsewhere. It might bring bad feeling from other women if they found out, so it was better to say nothing.

Megan assured him, 'If neighbours found they were slipping off their knickers under a tinker's canvas, they'd be tarred and feathered, doctor, never mind bad feelings.'

A loaf of bread and a quart of butter were pushed into her bag before they bade each other goodbye. As he watched this fiery lassie walk briskly up the road, the doctor thought on how wise and faithful she was; it was hard to imagine she'd not even left her teen years yet.

As she turned the last bend in the road out of Kirriemor, a woman she recognised as the housekeeper of Cortonach Castle called out to her. 'Are you one of the tinker girls? Do you want a job at the castle?'

Megan went over and said that yes, she was a tinker, and what manner of job did she have in mind?

The housekeeper told her that several workers, including two stable boys and three house staff had left to take up arms. Because of this there was a dire shortage of good working hands and they were sorely missed from the castle. 'If you know anyone, there's a small wage with board and lodgings of course. I have to go, the lady of the house has this very day received news that her beloved husband, Sir Angus, has lost his life in Belgium, a terrible thing, just awful. Of course, you tinkers wouldn't know anything about that, would you?'

Megan felt the anger tighten around her chest, her throat dried.

'Madam, my heart is sad for the mistress of the castle, but my sister's man Jimmy was killed over two weeks ago, and my own young man as we speak is also fighting with his comrades for the freedom of this fair land. So you see, missus, we're all suffering, from her lady-ship in her rich castle to us in our tents. Now if you'll excuse me, I have work to do. It turns my gut to spend a moment longer in your starch-faced company.'

The woman hadn't meant to offend. Megan turned with a swish of her shawl and hurried off. The housekeeper watched the winsome youngster disappear round a sharp bend in the road, leaving her with a faint smell of carbolic soap and a feeling of shame that one with her years should need to be told off by a young lass.

On arriving back at the tent, Megan threw down a bundle of sticks she'd gathered by the roadside on her journey home. Branches broken by the weight of snow were easy firewood, and saved her from wrestling with big ones deeper inside the forest. The ladies of the night had departed. Rachel was cooking a pot of watery soup, and the two men had left to snare anything mad enough to venture out from burrows or dens. She didn't feel it necessary to bring up the previous night's visitors who had risked their honour in O'Connor's tent, but she did tell Rachel about the housekeeper from the castle needing extra hands.

This sounded promising to Rachel. 'Why don't you and I go and see her? Anything would be better than freezing to death here in these tents. If they are so desperate for help, then I might be able to take wee Nicholas as well. Poor wee mite, if I don't eat proper food my milk will not sustain him. You said yourself the men are going to get worse with the drink. Surely anything is better than this existence?'

Megan knew all her sister said made good sense, but her place was here. Here in the campsite seeing to the fire and keeping a watchful eye on her good-father. She could not go away while he supped with the devil, though the pain in her jaw still stung from his handiwork the night before.

That night the men failed to come home, and the girls reckoned a visit to the red-lipsticked females was taking place. This time they would be in their houses, and that meant one thing, that their menfolk, whether soldiers or ploughmen, were not at home.

Next morning Megan and Rachel, with wee Nicholas snugly secured in two shawls for extra warmth, were standing outside the gigantic structure of Cortonach Castle. Mrs Simpson, the housekeeper Megan had met the previous day, opened the great creaking doors and beckoned them in. Perhaps it was the result of the talking to she'd received the day before, but the dear lady was kindness itself. For the first time in a long while meat and sweet jam found a welcome in their neglected stomachs. Rachel looked around the grand kitchen, with its rows of high shelves full of pots and pans of every size. Mrs Simpson politely asked if she might be allowed to hold the baby—such a long time since she'd had a youngster in her arms. Rachel handed Nicholas to her willingly, happy at the freedom to wander around the kitchen. Five large ovens gave out penetrating heat; she felt it reach her bones. Megan stood looking out of the window and thought how fine the gardens and grounds surrounding the place were; they brought to mind a painting she'd seen some place.

Later, as they chatted around a large pine table smelling of fresh blood congealed on three hare ready to be butchered, the door opened. Mrs Simpson almost jumped to attention. Flicking biscuit crumbs from her apron, she tugged it into line with her skirt. 'Good morning, Ma'am.'

'Hello Simpy,' said a thin, gentle-sounding lady coming down the stone steps. 'Oh, and pray tell me who it is we have here.' She was smiling at Nicholas with arms outstretched. The housekeeper handed over the boy without a word. Rachel, like Mrs Simpson, held herself straight and rigid in the presence of Lady Cortonach.

It was Megan who snatched her nephew back and said, 'This is my sister's boy, and we've come for a job.'

Angry at her abruptness, the housekeeper apologised, stuttering an explanation.

'Oh Simpy, I'm pleased you asked the tinkers, we certainly need help with so many staff gone away because of this terrible war.' She felt for a handkerchief folded neatly at the turn of a brown cardigan sleeve and dabbed her eyes, before saying, 'It would be nice to have a child in the house, it's so very dull and so empty without children.' She was almost pleading, through tear-filled eyes. Even Megan, who trusted no non-tinker apart from the doctor, felt moved.

Rachel, herself still in mourning, saw how hurt the lady was and spoke softly, assuming a genteel accent, 'Madam, me and my bairn would like nothing better than to come here. I'll work all the hours you want, and I know my sister here has a strong back; she can carry her weight in cut firewood, she can. Isn't that the case, Megan?'

Megan could hardly believe how much her sister grovelled: she felt ashamed of it and retorted, as she headed for the door, 'Listen, you come here and work your fingers into whittles if you like, but I'm keeping one eye on my scourers, the other on Rory Stewart.'

Rachel apologised profusely, took her baby and ran after her furious sister, who dashed from the house without another word. She didn't catch up until she was halfway home, leaving Lady Cortonach and Simpy bewildered.

If argument and swear words could paint their venom, then the air around the campsite was without doubt a vivid blue and red. Each sister shouted the odds like never before, with Rachel defending her use of a posh voice and listing the benefits of not rearing a child in a campground hell. With Annie and Jimmy both lost, she had no reason to continue with such a degrading lifestyle. Megan called her everything from traitor to buck mort, which is tinker tongue for a woman who deserts her culture and takes a place among settled folk. From then on, the ties that had bound the family were broken.

Next day, after Nicholas had been fed, his mother washed him till his little cheeks were like red apples, packed what belongings she could and left for a life of servitude in Cortonach Castle. Megan cried all day, refusing to cook a bite for the others, or wash her face. Her only sister had deserted her after just a brief meeting with strangers. What if her baby was put away, given to some maid to rear, what if she was whipped for not working hard enough? Why could she not be like her—proud and accepting the old ways regardless? But she was certain, after a little thought, that Rachel wouldn't like the work, and would come home. For a short while this cheered her up. After a month, however, with not so much as a whistle from Rachel, she became frantic with worry and decided to visit the castle.

At first her feet faltered on the steps leading to the large, ominous-looking building. Waiting at the door was uncomfortable, after all what would she find? Her sister, always frail and thin, might be full of whip marks, maybe even have two black eyes or perhaps broken arms. When no one answered the bell, her fear turned to anger, and running off, she soon found an open door at the rear of the house and let herself into the kitchen. On the range, pots simmered with pleasant aromas. Glancing quickly around and seeing no sign of her sister she feared the worst; that perhaps she and her baby had been roasted for the rich people to feast on.

'Hello, my dear,' it was Mrs Simpson. 'Come to help us?'

'Where are Rachel and the babe?' From a large cupboard came her answer; Rachel appeared carrying a large container of meal.

'Megan, what a lovely surprise! I thought you were too busy watching those drunkards to visit.'

'And I thought you were paggered!' (dead)

'Don't be so daft, this is the best place in the world! People are kindness itself. I only work for six hours a day, have a comfortable bed and lots to eat. Look, feel how much weight I've put on.' She grabbed Megan's hand and ran it over her ribcage, which was to the eye fuller than when last they met. Her hair shone with cleanliness and her usually pale complexion glowed warm peach. It seemed that Megan's fears were unfounded—but what of the baby, where was he?'

'Come with me, we'll find the mistress with Nicholas. Simpy, can I have leave?'

'Yes, my dear, I think I heard them in the garden.'

Megan followed behind a stranger; at least that's what she seemed like, all spotless in starched apron and pure white cotton blouse, three inches of dark tweed skirt hung immaculately. She wore grey woollen stockings, and shiny brogue leather shoes. A stiff, crisp white servant's hat topped her well-groomed hair, tightly pulled into a bun held in place by four pins.

Rachel led her into the garden towards a picturesque summer house, twined in early rosebuds of pink. Lilac trees filled the air with their fragrance.

'Madam, hello, I've brought my sister to see,' a brief pause before she finished the sentence, 'your charge, little Nicholas.'

Megan glided towards her nephew who sat on the knee of a fattish lady, his own nanny. He was dressed in blue and with a broad belt round his middle, a brass buckle in its centre. He was unrecognisable in his frilly pantaloons and blue bonnet. He gurgled and giggled at Lady Cortonach who sat opposite, and tickled him under his chubby little chin with a spoon, before dipping it into a silver dish filled with some kind of pink pudding. He loved it, and showed no visible sign of remembering his aunt, as she stiffened before this scene of utter tranquillity.

Unable to see any semblance of her kin, she turned and ran off into the rhododendron bushes lining the driveway. Rachel ran after her.

'Please try to see it my way. Tinkers are waifs of the past; we don't have a place in society. Here I can watch my baby grow healthy and strong, can enjoy good food, be content.'

'You've given the bairn to a toff! How in God's name can any mother do that! Mammy will be spinning in her grave. What kind of a mother are you?' I hate what you've become, and never want to look upon your face, not as long as breath's in me!'

Rachel clasped two hands on her sister's shoulders and answered, 'Listen to me, our mother knew how I hated the life, stuffed into a low-roofed tent, waking in the morning with spiders in my hair and earwigs under my armpits. Stinking of sweat, day in, day out, not washing until the warmer weather permitted—' Before she could continue, Megan shouted, 'You refused to wash in the cold water of the burn! Frost or not, my body smell was washed away. Creepy-crawlies only lick dirty hair, mine was clean. You never tried to live the old ways, that's your trouble. But never mind that—Nicholas is your baby, big Rory's grandson and my blessed nephew, and he sits with love in his wee eyes for the lady woman. That's unspeakable.'

'You'll judge me, I can't help that, but the poor woman is living in misery. Her man, like mine, has been killed, and the bairn has given her hope to go on. The poor soul was suicidal until his wee happy face brought joy into her life. She has promised me a new life in America. Said if she brought up my baby as her own, he'd want for nothing, and neither would I, because I'm going with her as companion and nursemaid to Nicholas. He also has a nanny. Where in our meagre existence could anything happen like going away from this miserable place, where a drunkard grandfather might teach my bairn his ways? No, Megan, I have not given up a tinker life, I've totally buried it, and God grant me the health to enjoy America with my son. I'll watch him walk a rich man's way. But let's not part with bad feelings, at least wish me God speed. Please, sister, for old time's sake.' Rachel's arms were outstretched.

They'd not always been close, but since Annie's death the pair had been inseparable. How would she cope alone? What if Bruar failed to return, leaving her to grow wizened before her time, seeing to the campsite and two lost causes? Megan walked into the welcoming arms, and as the two sisters embraced, each knew it would be for the last time.

Mrs Simpson put a comforting arm around Rachel's shoulder as they watched Megan hurry out of sight.

As she passed each familiar tree and hill, where she and Bruar had spent many a happy hour, her young head filled with thoughts. Thoughts firstly of love, then, heaven forbid, of losing that precious love, brought a surge of fear which gripped at her heart. She clung to hope like a weak dog burying his bone so prowling strays wouldn't steal it. Tears welled in her eyes as she called to her husband somewhere far across the sea. 'Without you, my man, I am useless, like a three-legged rabbit or a one-winged dove. Night brings dark shadows that haunt me with ghosts of black futures. Now that Rachel has left me, I am so alone. Watch your back, and whatever you do, keep safe. Oh, that I had the power to sleep in your thoughts, my dear, dear one.'

SEVEN

*F*rom the back of a trundling lorry he stared out at the long snaking road, winding its way through misshapen rubble, the remains of family homes that had once been filled with parents, old folks and children playing.

Every so often an abandoned dog would howl and mourn in unison with a screaming woman. Perhaps the body she'd stumbled on was her husband's. He may have been ploughing a furrowed field, hoping that soon the noise of battle would leave his land. Tomorrow, maybe, it would all be over, left at peace. Perhaps that was a vision he'd kept until that fateful blast.

Bruar closed his eyes at the sight of another battered torso; metal helmet nearby, the decapitated head intact. Crows had already eaten the eyes. 'Black-winged scavengers,' he remembered Aunt Helen used to say, 'they were designed for such a task.' She would usually add, to frighten his infant mind, 'The red seer said that a time was coming when the crows of the sky would feast upon the dead of the land.'

If ever prophesy had come to pass, then here it was before his eyes, unfolding in graphic detail. As his thoughts darkened, he pulled his wet tunic collar under his chin to cover his exposed throat. When such devil-painted artistry first spread itself before him, it brought a newly consumed plate of broth from his stomach pit. But a belly has no memory, and now he could stand a lot before it made any difference; he was conditioned to carnage.

Arras in France saw his first steps of war; his virginal battle. Marching at the rear of the 51st Highland Division, he watched how stealthily death took his prey. Seventy proud Highland pipers played into the hungry jaws of the enemy, drowning a mighty roar of artillery until only one kilted musician was left standing. Earlier their crescendo of earth-shattering sound stirred young recruits into battle; a battle that lasted three days and bravely held the town, but at what a cost!

Amidst bombs and dead bodies, Bruar felt compelled in the aftermath to retrieve the silent bagpipes, and lay them by the sides of the fallen pipers. He'd no idea what set belonged to which piper, but it only seemed right that each should not go into the other world without their beloved music. Officers called him a damn fool, but to him, a Highlander, it seemed only proper to salute the pipes.

Time stopped during the battle of Arras, but not death; he was as active as he'd ever been, piling up the corpses. Bruar shivered and thanked God he was spared.

During a march to Ypres, his battalion merged with a small division of Cameronians, and it was then he discovered the fate of his only brother. Familiar as he was now with death, the details were not important; only the fact that it took him quick was something to be thankful for. After Arras, remnants of the brave 51st were attached to other regiments; he found himself amid English lads, the King's Liverpools.

A screech of shell fire brought him back to the present, and his bumpy journey in the transport lorry. The shelling halted the convoy for a short while. When it was deemed safe again, a shout to continue came down from the top of the column, and for the next stretch of dusty miles his thoughts wandered home. He saw his young wife and imagined reaching out to touch and kiss her. How beautiful she was! He prayed that she'd never witness scenes such as these, hoped when he got back they'd spend hours in the purple heather just talking. He wanted to tell her that sometimes, when night approached, with hundreds of Very flares illuminating the battle sky, he'd call to her saying that the heavens of Europe had their own Northern Lights. The transport vehicles would also be a talking point. She'd never seen a lorry—cars, yes, but not monsters that roared and billowed smoke. He had loads to share with her when he got home—if he got home.

A loud explosion far off turned the sweet thoughts sour. He opened his eyes to the sight of another piece of burned flesh, a horse this time. An innocent beast doing chores now lay sprawled and twisted around the cart it had been pulling, torn by man-made hurricanes of unimaginable force, its grave dug by the power of the bomb. The sight of the animal cut through his thoughts and he cursed the war over again.

After what seemed an eternity the lorry came to a grinding halt. Fed up, tired and coughing incessantly, the driver shouted, 'Journey over, get off, boys.'

The bone-weary soldiers jumped down from the mud-spattered vehicle, glad to be back on solid ground, and were lined up for inspection. The driver repeated his orders in case any lad had fallen asleep, but the lorry was empty.

From within a busy group of men a sergeant stepped forward and rapped orders. 'Follow me, boys, into your trench for the night. Tuck is being served at the Ritz.'

All eyes turned to a massive pot, boiling away, filled with God alone knew what. It was covered by a khaki tarpaulin; a stink from it crowded their nostrils. They were starving, though, and soon bellies were filled and satisfied.

Entering in single file, they each found a spot in the cold damp earth. Some had capes, while others shared them. A voice called in the dark, 'That's an hour passed, Jerry will be finished his supper and wanting to play.' No sooner said, when a squeal of explosives followed by a blinding flash sent everyone downwards. There was a moment of silence, then the screams of pain. Bruar's column was so tightly packed together they couldn't get room to use their arms. Above them, two medics suddenly appeared, shouting, 'Stay where you are, the line has been breached further down.' Someone enquired, 'How many?'

'Too fucking many.' This was always the answer given.

Bruar felt a hand on his back; he turned to see a ginger-headed man who said, 'Some mother's poor wee laddies. Cannon fodder, games for the fireside generals. I'm Sandy, what do you call yourself, laddie?'

In the half darkness he whispered back, 'Bruar. You're a Highlander; which part?'

'Wick.'

'A Caithness man.'

He'd acquired a friend. Through the sleepless night, both spoke for hours, exchanging tales of mountains, sea cliffs and the Scotland of their birth.

When at last dawn crept over the eastern horizon with fingers of wispy grey fog curling around trees and barbed-wire fences, it became clear to the emerging soldiers that this enemy would not be beaten without a hefty loss of Allied life.

'Get this mess cleared, we move out at six o'clock!' snapped a weary corporal.

The 'mess' had, until the night before, been young boys, some no more than sixteen, who had never thought beforehand that another army would feast upon their flesh; marauding rodents. Fatally injured soldiers lay in pools of blood; they too were hastily rolled aside to add extra rations to the rat's larder. War was terrible, and Bruar for once agreed with Megan's parting words—it was no place for those of tinker breed.

The early sun failed to penetrate the battle fog, which was just as well; it would only add more horrors to the scene. By six o'clock they were on the move.

'Where're we going?' Bruar asked his mate, Sandy.

'I don't know, but wait on me, I've my lassies to collect.'

He was the signaller for his troop; the pigeon man. Soon both lads were making time pulling a cart of about thirty birds; these were essential in carrying messages from one part of the front to another.

For the next few months, adrift in a sea of kakhi-clad men, they stayed together, darting from one nightmare scene to another, each watching the other's back. In lighter moments they'd pretend that the Jerries were Vikings; they would scream out, 'May the bog choke the life from you, Jerry!' This brought laughter from listening comrades, and the odd 'Bloody stupid Scots' from Taylor, their Sergeant Major. These humorous moments made the madness bearable. Wherever they took bayonets in their hands, it didn't matter; there were different places but the same scenario, they had to survive, nothing else. Survival was what held the British Army together, a deep bond of comradeship.

This comradeship between soldiers is reckoned by scholars to go all the way back through history, as far back as the Romans, for example. However when a spoke enters a spinning wheel, that bond can break. It is not only enemy fire that can disturb a tight-knit unit; it can come from within the soldiers' own ranks. Captain Rokeby, a judge in civilian life, was a powerful spoke which almost ripped the life from Bruar and Sandy.

This is what happened.

After several days of hard slog, marching through the grape-growing slopes of the Loire Valley in France, their platoon of sixty was to the rear of a column of hundreds, heading from the death fields of Flanders.

Old men, women and children stopped filling baskets with grapes and waved at the dusty hordes passing through their land. Bruar slowed to watch them, as Sandy groaned at the state of his empty stomach. He curled his sore knuckles round the oiled shafts of his pigeon cart and flexed painful muscles, cursing at another bump in the road. 'This lot sit in their straw boxes, and them with plenty wing power could easy fly above us, but instead I've to push these bisoms for miles. Breaking my back, this is.'

Bruar didn't respond; a young waif-like female had caught his eye. She was running on bare feet towards the soldiers, crying, 'Bullee, bullee, you give me beef?'

She had the same colour of eyes as Megan; her hair, black and curly, bouncing around her narrow shoulders, held him spellbound.

'Stewart, get fell in.' Taylor, like a mother hen, was watching every man, counting the rifles sticking from the bulging green Bergen packs each man carried on his back. They held sleeping sacks, food if any, socks and a handful of field dressings in case of injuries. But there was only one essential item in a soldier's bag—ammunition. It weighed a ton and buckled the knees of the weakest, scrawny men among them.

'Don't get close to the natives, now lad.' Taylor took several strides to reach Bruar and repeated his orders.

Bruar fumbled with his heavy rucksack and lied that his bayonet was loose, requesting permission to fix it.

'Three minutes lad, be bloody quick,' The SM hurried off to check his men, aware they'd not eaten all day, and as an army marches on its stomach, the setting sun worried him.

Bruar stood down, and instantly the Frenchwoman was at his side, pleading, 'Please give, you have bullee, yes. I give you this.' She pulled from behind her back a small jute bag and opened it to show two dusty green bottles. 'See, fine wine for the beef, I ask please.'

'Oh, I see, you think I have food. Well, I'm sorry, lassie, but there's nothing.' He held out empty hands and gestured with shrugged shoulders. She lunged at his rucksack, thumping at it in sheer desperation. His heart ached as he watched her, crying and hitting out at the foodless bag.

She saw by his gaunt face and deep-sunk eyes that he spoke the truth. 'Take please, *mon ami*, for you, for liberty, for freedom, for France.'

He held the bag she pushed at him. A measly 'thanks,' was all he could muster.

Dejected and helpless she ran off on blackened feet. He felt ashamed, although he could take no personal blame for the war that had made her beg or turned her peaceful country into a landscape of hell. It was futile, but feebly he called after her, 'I'm real sorry, this isn't my fault.'

Two tiny children ran out from behind some vines, hands outstretched, crying 'Mamma'. She hurried them away without a glance back. Why had she chosen him? Perhaps her husband was dead, or maybe in uniform like him. Her proud family brought to the point of hiding, sneaking around like foxes. It was unlikely they'd meet again, yet an overpowering longing grew in him to see them fed; warm in a bed with a roof over their heads. Sickened and hungry he joined his mates.

Sandy whistled loudly. In seconds his silence at the signaller's side was as loud as any bomb.

'Best forget and think on your own bonny lassie back home. War takes more than soldiers,' the signaller reminded him, then added, 'We'll soon be lousing. Now cheer up, I've a surprise for you.'

Night thickly spread its darkness around and the halt was sounded. 'Sorry, boys, but the bloody supplies took a pounding this morning. The word is, no rations until tomorrow. Best chew on grapes if you find them, but don't let Rokeby know, because to leave your post is forbidden. He'd issue orders to fire at sparrows, if they flew too close.' Taylor finished with, 'At ease, men.'

'Bloody grapes, what good is that to hungry men? Marched the whole day and no food, to hell with that!' Sandy was spitting fire. Bruar patted him on the arm and said, 'Rations will be here when we wake—surely you can wait till then?'

'Listen, pal, every man has been carrying his own bodyweight on his back, but on top of this damn rucksack, I've had a cartful of pigeons. If food doesn't pass my lips soon I'll be shot for cannibalism. Keep your eye out for Rokeby, I'll show you that surprise. Firstly get a fire on, I'll sort these ladies.'

Bruar felt his hair crawl at the sight of Sandy's wide-eyed expression. It didn't take much thought to work out what was coming next. 'Man, you can't be thinking on killing them, that's the King's birds!'

'There mine tonight.' Sandy rammed a fist into the doo boxes, and in no time three throttled and silenced birds lay limp on the ground. Bruar watched in amazement as a stick was pushed inside each naked fowl, while a heap of feathers lay around Sandy's feet.

'Start a fire, the quicker we get these birds cooked the better. The King has more birds than he can count—trust me, he'll not miss these. Anyway, they had damaged wings and were no use. Hurry, man, I'm starving.'

Bruar threw his tinker skills into overdrive; he dug a hollow, a ring of pebbles at its rim. In his hands he rolled a ball of dried grass, lit it and soon tiny flames spurted and a fire was born. Around them others were doing the same. Surely they would attract little suspicion, and have the time to cook some desperately needed supper.

Over an embankment they positioned the cart; concealed from the others they warmed themselves and pit-roasted the pigeons. Rags were added to smother the delicious aromas.

Fat crackled on the roasting birds, and though Rokeby could appear at any minute, the acids building in their guts were stronger than any fear. They were starving, and the birds smelt like a heaven to die for.

'What we need to complement our meal, my half-bred tinker, is a nice wee claret!'

'I have the very thing!' Bruar fumbled with his rucksack, and retrieved two green bottles. 'The finest from the Loire Valley,' he said, popping out the corks with his teeth and spitting them in the fire.

Sandy's eyes almost left their sockets to perch on his blackened cheeks. 'Well, well, a dark horse. Where did these come from?' He gently caressed the bottle. 'Come to me, my love!'

'The lassie, remember the thin wee soul I met on the road? The poor thing was desperate for food, two little bairns to feed, my heart sank. You know we'd nothing, bur she gave me these "for France", she said.' The bottle slipped from his hand as he told his companion how much she resembled Megan.

'Listen, lad, we can't do anything about wars. Old armchair generals cause them, and they have the say on who lives or not. But never mind that, let's get on with something more important than any war, a damn good feed. God knows it might be our last! Lift your bottle and drink to Scotland!'

Roast pigeon, gulped down with ruby red wine, was on the menu that night, but it had a high price!

It wasn't either man's style to finish a whole bottle, but 'when wine's in, wit's oot', as they say in temperance circles. Ballads soon came loud and tuneful from behind the pigeon cart—so loud a certain captain had to investigate. Downing two bottles of local plonk wasn't a shooting offence, but consuming His Majesty's birds—that did indeed merit a death penalty! If Sandy had had just one ounce of sense he would not have offered Rokeby the birds' feathers for a softer pillow, but therein lay more than enough evidence to convict them.

'Shot at dawn!' screamed a red-faced, foaming-mouthed Captain. 'No trial.'

Handcuffed and still singing, the criminals were marched off, still oblivious of their impending doom.

Next morning, with a watery sun to their back and an angry Rokeby to their front, both soberly admitted the offence, but never for a second did they imagine that the Captain would have the execution carried out.

He first subjected them to a tirade about how crucial carrier pigeons were for communicating army intelligence; without these worthy birds, messages of strategic importance would be lost, and everything depended on keeping abreast of the movements of the enemy. Sandy, in their defence, assured the captain that those birds, the ones they had roasted, were injured and useless, unable to perform their duties.

This provoked another tirade of curses from Rokeby. He hit a wooden table so hard a notepad shot into the air, along with a nib pen and a pot of ink. Bruar glanced at Sandy, who had turned deathly pale, and whispered, 'Shit, we've had it, this idiot's lost his marbles.'

Twelve soldiers lined up, guns stiff at their sides. Rokeby unholstered a service revolver, straightened his peaked cap, and clicked the heels of his high boots. He seemed to enjoy the whole situation, lording himself above lesser mortals once again. But one young soldier, who'd been chosen for the firing squad, had seen his own companions die once too often. He took a brave step and laid down his rifle, refusing to take part. Rokeby threw him aside, aiming a hard kick into the soldier's back, who scrambled for cover. Rokeby was mad!

Fear gripped the platoon, and another brave lad broke ranks and went to find Taylor who was overseeing the arrival of the long-awaited supply convoy. In the nick of time the Sergeant Major came up to the command post. The order to fire was about to be given.

'Stop, ya bloody fools!'

Rokeby spat fire at Taylor, who in turn raged. Everyone listened to see what the outcome of their argument would be—none more so than two blindfolded, hand-tied Scotsmen.

'What the hell are you playing at? Taylor screamed. 'Every bloody available man is needed to fight an increasing enemy, and what are you doing? I'll tell you, will I? You're doing a fine job for them—shooting your own bloody soldiers. Has old Kaiser promised you a medal, eh, Rokeby? Rokeby stood stiffly, removed his cap and threw it at Taylor. 'They killed and ate the King's carrier pigeons.' His tone of voice lowered as he added threateningly, 'I am your superior officer. You will face a court-martial. Make no mistake, you're for the chop. The next bullet is for you!'

Taylor had taken enough from this cold-blooded man. 'I'll kick your superior arse, you little needle-faced shit, and if I so much as see a firing squad again I'll shoot you myself.'

Rokeby coolly touched his holstered handgun and sneered, 'For that outburst of insubordination, I'll have you, boy.'

Taylor had said his piece and would have walked away, but he couldn't help one last jab. 'Listen mate, when this war is over you can do what you want, but while we face a mighty enemy, it's them or us, and if the King is insulted by the loss of measly fist-sized pigeons helping to feed his own soldiers, then I'll personally apologise to him myself.'

Sergeant Major Taylor grabbed a rifle, stepped closer until they stood nose to nose, and said, 'You're a disgrace to that uniform. If I so much as hear your weedy voice barking orders at my men, I'll stick this bayonet as far up your bloody arse as it'll go, and spit roast you for the crows. Now, let's get on with the war.'

Captain Rokeby could see in the faces of his men how little regard they had for him. To save face he ordered the condemned men to be freed and walked off into his tent, cap pushed under a stiff arm.

From then on, a pair of very sober Highlanders were determined to keep eyes firmly in the back of their heads where Captain Rokeby was concerned.

Fate, that invisible stalker, has its own way of watching and waiting however. Before a week was out an enemy shell exploded, obliterating a single vehicle. This car had been ferrying the captain to a meeting with his superiors, who no doubt would have been informed of Taylor's interference with the execution and insults to his Majesty.

The bond between Sandy and Bruar grew stronger after the 'pigeon' incident and secured their friendship. As one month followed close behind another, they protected and watched out for each other like brothers.

Sergeant Major Taylor continued to lead a fine body of men, taking out the enemy when opportunities arose. Their war was a matter of brutal man-to-man combat, spying behind enemy lines, and charging blindly through fire and choking smoke following orders regardless. It was a far cry from Bruar's misty hill-roads of home.

It is only right to mention other duties which immersed them in the horrors of war. There was usually a mess to be cleared before they moved on. What one minute before had been healthy specimens of manhood had become mangled corpses to be used as ramps for the advance of an ever increasing column of lorries and black-booted feet.

There were a variety of dead. Some shot cleanly, others crushed and twisted, some blown to smithereens. Fire turned flesh to cinders and left half burnt lumps of singed bodies. Gas tormented the lucky ones who survived with breathing problems and blistered faces. Unlucky lads lay screaming as their guts protruded through bloodied fingers.

Emotion is a luxury in hell. Men who in civilian life had never so much as cut a finger had to remove dead companions from muddy shell-holes, never knowing if the next flames of death would land in their own shelter.

—

Sometime later the battle-hardened troops were lined up on shore, waiting to embark on the Royal Navy battleship *Inflexible*. The war had taken a new twist. Turkey had thrown her weight on the side of Germany. The battlefield had opened a new front—Gallipoli.

18 March 1915 saw Sandy and Bruar on deck, wondering if their luck would hold. Bruar's heart ached for Megan. He'd never been on leave, but according to Taylor it wouldn't be long before everyone was heading home, the war triumphantly over.

Sandy, who had recently abandoned pigeons in favour of Belgian gundogs which were trained to transport small cannons, asked when.

'This next one will be the big change, like nothing we've seen before. This is bloody big! I'd be shitting myself if I was the Kaiser.

The whole bloody world has turned against him and this tin-pot Turk. I bloody bet you this battle will be the last. Aussie, French, Indians, Yanks, no one could beat a force like that.'

All the soldiers tight-packed on the ship, sickened by war and desperate to see their families, lifted their arms in the air and in unison shouted, 'Hip, hip, bloody hip, hooray then, SM.'

Everyone, that is, except Bruar. He felt an air of foreboding, one he could not shake off, and the further up the Dardanelles Straits the boat steered, the more it took hold.

Sandy had been watching dolphins racing between the ships as they sailed along the narrow stretch of water separating Asia from Europe, and asked, 'What ails you, man?'

Bruar pulled a torn wallet from his tunic and handed him a photo, saying, 'I'm not going to make it. Tell her I fought well and I release her from the promise.'

Sandy slipped the picture into his wallet, muttering about how tinkers are stupid and full of superstition. As Bruar turned his face skywards, an albatross glided on powerful wings to soar high above the ship, and in that same moment a thundering thud vibrated through the hull. They'd struck a minefield. Flashes of blinding light followed, and yet another boom from below. The vessel filled with dense smoke, flames shot in every direction, screaming men darted through them like headless chickens. Sandy frantically called out Bruar's name, but at the spot where his friend had stood, a gaping hole spewed torrents of water. From then it was every man for himself.

Exposed to the heat, Sandy covered his head with his tunic and ran up the ship, searching desperately for his mate, but in such a commotion it was useless.

Lifeboats fell like stones from the deck moorings and splashed into the agitated water. Sandy caught a glimpse of SM Taylor. 'He's taken it, sarge—he was portside when the bomb hit, he's gone!'

'Look, man, you've seen enough to know the score now. Get to bloody hell off this sinking coffin, or you'll be with him.'

'Every man must live,' Sandy thought, landing in the froth. Sizzling foam and debris slammed into his face. Pushing his way through the chaos, feeling like a wee fish in a giant net, with the screams of drowning men around him, he offered hasty prayers that his life should not be tragically cut short, like Bruar's.

As he dragged himself onto a driftwood log that had caught against a rotted fishing boat, he felt sand under his feet and silently gave thanks; he'd live another day!

'No time to sit,' he thought, surveying a tidal line of carnage. So many needed help, and maybe, just maybe, his friend was among them. And to add violence to the enemy fire that lit up the sky, Mother Nature threw in her own show; a thunderstorm, so ferocious it turned injured men, who lay in grotesque shapes along the shore, into figures of mud.

The sky forked jagged blue, earth-shattering thunder joined the chorus of enemy bombardment that rained onto allied ships, sending them in every direction; it was the Devil's Guy Fawkes bonfire of destruction.

Shell-holes crammed with broken men crying for help cut to his heart and began to grate on his nerves; he curled under the upturned fishing boat, closed his eyes, covered his ears and slept.

Time elapsed, he'd no idea how long, but gradually, slowly, the enemy fire subsided as the allied battleships built up into a massive force in the narrow strait of water. The storm had rolled southwards; an eerie silence prevailed as a smir of rain fell.

Up and down the shoreline medics scurried, shouting 'He needs assistance' or 'He's finished.'

Sandy crawled from his shelter among the din and was wondering what SM Taylor might say about it all, when suddenly there was a voice nearby. 'To think bloody Greek gods lived and fought in these parts—Helen of bloody Troy swam in this damn sea. We should be bloody honoured to stand upright on this famed shore. Have I any bloody troops left, by the way?'

'Over here Sarge, I thought you'd bought it. Good to hear you in your usual fine fettle.' He scrambled onto rubbery legs and weakly saluted.

'Stand at ease, you daft bugger, I've seen sturdier legs on a jelly fish. Stewart took it didn't he?'

'I can't say. One minute he was handing me a wedding picture, the next he was gone...' The photo flashed to mind; quickly he retrieved it from his sodden tunic. The swim had obliterated Bruar's smiling face, but Megan's features were still clear. Carefully he flicked the sand off it and put it back. 'I wonder how she'll take the news. All he ever spoke about, apart from this blasted war, was his Megan.'

'We all have our families. Never mind that, the injured need help.'

Sandy touched Taylor's arm and said, 'Sarge, that's the first time I heard you say a sentence without that word.'

'What word?'

'Bloody.'

'Just saying it as I see it, man, as I bloody see it.'

The sun had dropped below a pink horizon as they pulled the last man free of the water line. Capes lay draped over the dead as the injured were stretchered off to waiting ambulances. Seagulls screeched and squawked high above them, diving at the severed limbs and broken bodies still scattered throughout the tide-line. One swooped down, Sandy threw some sand at it, then saw something moving in the water. 'Sergeant, there's a man, we missed one.' Both pulled the body free of the water, turning him on his back to look for signs of life.

'He's alive!' Taylor ripped at the soaked tunic and rubbed the exposed chest. The man groaned and they both shouted for a medic. Sandy moved closer to get a better look. Night was closing fast, but that face, that body, had a familiar look—it was Bruar, barely alive! 'Thank God, he's made it, Sarge! My mate's all right.'

'No man, he's not,' said a naval doctor, taking control. 'He's got a beating heart, but look at his face!'

Taylor recognised the muddy face, with motionless eyes staring from porcelain sockets, as belonging to Bruar, but it was not the young Highlander both men knew.

'Stretcher-bearers, shell-shock, over here, quick!' The doctor then spoke quietly to Sandy. 'The war for this lad is well and truly over.' He refused to accept what he was told, and said, 'He's built like an ox, this is nothing to him. He's tinker-bred, lives in the wilds.'

Two men, naked to the waist and covered in dried blood, rolled Bruar onto the stretcher and rushed him off to wait for an ambulance.

'Doctor, save his life, I've never known such a decent bloke,' Sandy pleaded.

'Listen, I can sew wounds and amputate limbs, but I can't treat what that soldier suffers from. It's enough to say that those corpses spread along the shore are the lucky ones. That sad bastard still breathes, but for the rest of his life won't know a thing about it. Come now man, surely you've seen all this before!'

Sandy clenched his fists, looked at his mate lying among the chaos of the scene and promised, 'As God's my witness I'll get through this and come back to find you at the end of it. If I don't, I'll search for Megan and tell her how much of a hero you were.'

From the back of a trundling lorry he watched the shoreline fade from view. Sore, stiff and lonely, he gave little thought to tomorrow, it was just another day, another battle. But for the half-bred tinker who had shared his war, the battle had finished.

EIGHT

Spring came, and with it every day saw Megan climb up on the high hills, trying vainly to blot the lack of Bruar from her mind. Doctor Mackenzie failed to bring any letters. Instead there was only the news of yet more and more battles, with the inevitable destruction left in their wake.

Her campsite companions continued to spend the nights with loose women—females, she had decided, who could only be lonely and weak.

'You won't catch me giving myself to men,' she sternly told her father-in-law one morning, slapping steaming hot porridge into a bowl held between shaking hands. 'When your son comes home, and mark my words, he will any day now, he'll find the same clean wife waiting just as he left her.'

'Lassie, I am sick and tired of you going on about me and O'Connor with the plough wives. Now shut up and fetch me a bucket so I can wash.'

'Fetch your own bucket, you filthy excuse for a man!'

Big Rory stood up and shook his head. She almost felt sorry for him, as he said, 'I never thought the day would arrive when a good-daughter spoke in those tones to her man's father.'

'Well, good-father, perhaps if you hadn't been such a fornicator and drunkard...'

He lifted a hand to strike. 'I'm fond of a skirt, aye, but I'm no drunk!'

'No drunk? Why the hell are your hands shaking so violently?

Look at them, you're spilling the porridge all over yourself like a half-dead old man.'

'Megan, please take your impudent face up the hillside and chant to the bloody eagle. I'm sure he must have some other omen to share with you.'

Megan glared daggers at him through pools of tears.

He knew how important the ancient ways were to her, so that his tone and choice of insult hit a raw nerve. He breathed a sigh of relief at hearing Mackenzie's horse trotting along the road. If the doctor saw his shaking hands, his lectures would be stern, so he quickly scraped the porridge into the fire, clasped his hands behind his back and smiled broadly.

'Come on, lassie, clean your face, get the kettle boiled, here's the doctor. Maybe there will be news from Bruar,' he said, gingerly touching her arm. She raised her eyebrows at the oatmeal sizzling in the fire and thought, 'What a waste.' Their argument was forgotten, though, and she ran to welcome the only link they had to news about the war.

'You haven't the buggy with you today, doctor, is a wheel broke?'

'Er, no, lass, it's just that my old mare hasn't been lasting the pull these days.'

Something about his tone seemed uneasy, he didn't hold out a hand with letters or anything else. He tried to avoid her stare as she searched his face for news.

Big Rory had seen that look before—the old Seer had it when he said his lassie wouldn't see a dawn! Megan was pulling at the doctor's coat. 'Still no news?'

Rory stepped forward and dropped a bombshell, 'When?'

'What do you mean, when?' Panic swelled in her breast like a giant wave crashing upon a wild beach. It swallowed her whole body and dashed it to pieces. In her head were visions of bullets ripping through her husband; of him chased by demons with no faces, plunging bayonets up and down his body, the horrors were out of control. 'What do you mean—answer me, damn you!' She bolted at her father-in-law, pulling at his limp arm. Instinctively he held her close. But she needed answers.

Breaking away she grabbed at the doctor and begged him to tell her.

'I'm sorry that it had to be me, but who else knows the heart of you? Forgive me, Megan, for this is a bad day.'

111

'No! No! I don't want this news.' She slipped to the ground, shaking.

O'Connor emerged from his tent and draped a shawl around her shoulders. He shook his head at the news bringer, who had hardly taken the time to alight from his horse before the blow of his message had struck the threesome.

Rory moved a small wooden seat next to the fire for their visitor and asked again, 'When?'

'According to this telegram—oh, I hope you don't mind, I opened it, seeing as none of you read. I hope that's fitting with you.'

'Yes, yes, now what does it say?'

Not wishing to prolong the agony further, he read: 'We regret to inform you that sometime on the 18th of March 1915 Private Bruar Stewart sustained serious injury resulting in his death.'

Rory had lost everyone: his lovely wife, Jimmy, a mild-mannered son hardly into adulthood, and now Bruar, his first-born. Filled with sorrow he wondered if the curse of the one-eyed seer had followed him like a plague-stricken victim. 'Too much pain,' he said, retrieving his jacket from a nearby fence-post. 'O'Connor, I can't take this, see to the lassie.'

The Irishman poured a cup of tea into an empty cup held by Doctor Mackenzie. He knew no amount of alcohol or company of seductive females would help his friend. A sense of complete uselessness enveloped him, as he watched his friend disappear among the shadows of trees and scattered sunbeams.

He took off his torn cap, slipped it into his pocket and said, 'What manner o' God can justify the pain that this country has inflicted upon these folks. The poorest among us, yet such sacrifice would only be expected from the highest of people, not humble tinker-folk who scrape a living among the worms.'

'I have no answer, O'Connor. But keep a watchful eye on this heart-broken lassie, there's no telling how deeply she's been wounded.'

Megan drew a hand across her tear-stained face and spoke in whispering tones. 'Don't underestimate me, good friend. You see, me and Bruar, we always said if time wasn't on our side, then he'd live in my heart and me in his. You worry about Kirriemor, I am sure there's a wife or mother who's about to get the same news as us. Away with you now. I think it's a day to be among my hills, me and Bruar always spent the best times in our hills.' She went inside her small tent and came out with a black shawl a woman had given instead of money for scourers, wrapped it around her shoulders, smiled reassuringly to O'Connor and the doctor, and then set off to mourn in her own way.

Mackenzie felt useless, and said to O'Connor, 'Watch her, there's no telling where a broken heart will lead. Now tell me, where has Rory gone, do you know?'

'As far as his legs will walk him. Then he'll rist a while an' come back.'

'But that might be some time, he's a big strong man.'

'There's no strength in those legs, doctor, only pain in his heart. He has to get it out.'

'Do me a favour—keep him away from the drink.'

His companion shrugged his shoulders, bent down to light his pipe on a fiery twig and turned his back to the fire's warmth. 'I have no control over such matters.'

Tired, saddened by war, the doctor trotted his horse off the campsite that morning; no one saw the tears trickling from his eyes. He patted his horse and said to the animal, 'Folks think I'm made of iron.' The old horse pulled onto the bit and neighed as if in agreement.

Less than a mile from his destination there was a sudden deep gurgle from the throat of his old mare. For a moment she turned to stare into the eyes of her owner, and from the depth of her belly came another gurgling sound. Suddenly her back stiffened, and his old horse of thirty years keeled over and breathed her last.

'Daft beast, you near flattened me,' he called into the early afternoon sunshine, shaking a fist at the unseen phantom of death. 'Not even my old horse escaped your fingers of doom.' He was tired, but one thing for sure, his days sitting straddled on a horse were well and truly over. From then on it would have to be one of those new noisy things; a motor vehicle. Every doctor from Perth to Aviemore had one. He'd not been one for change, though, and had often said, 'As long as the mare can walk, I'll sit on her back.'

Dealing with the disposal of the horse took his mind away from Megan and her loss.

Two months went by, and Rory still hadn't returned home to the campsite in the glen. For a time, eternally hopeful, Megan refused to believe that her soulmate was really dead, and lived day to day watching from her vantage-point for signs of him. She also spent a long time talking to herself, and this worried O'Connor.

'Are you well in the heart now?' he asked her one morning; she'd just thrown her black shawl on the fire.

'I'm as well as one could expect. Why do you ask?'

'I feels responsible for you. Since Rory has not come back, I tink maybe it has fallen to me for to look after you.'

'Oh, I reckon we'll see him before long. But don't concern yourself for me, I'm no widow woman wearing the black and keeping the head hung. He's not dead, O'Connor. I feel it, you see.' She crossed both hands to her chest. 'He'll come whistling up that road any day now, just wait and see.'

He did worry about her, though her grief wasn't showing yet, not in the normal way. He wondered if she might try something drastic as the old doctor had suggested. Responsibility wasn't his thing—he had always been a loner until he'd met these people, but as is the way, like ivy, folk grow on you. Not just that, but he was hankering after a bit of silk-stockinged leg to wrap around his body, and a bucketful of ale to help the gnawing deep in his gut.

Megan took on her role as the only woman in the campsite. She snared, caught and skinned rabbits, cut firewood, continued making pot scourers, cooked and kept a clean place.

Then Rory crept home, quiet and withdrawn, after tramping out his grief. He stared about him a lot. O'Connor could see that demons had followed his footsteps, and the only way to dispel them was, as he said, 'a good drink!' No words were wasted on where he'd been or what he'd done—his bushy beard and ripped clothing spoke volumes. In no time, both began where they'd left off before the fateful news; spending the nights drinking and sleeping with other men's wives.

Megan could not have cared what they did, she had finished with them. At night, when time stretched slowly by, she brought Bruar into her bed, making love or just talking. If life had removed him in body, in her imaginings he was still alive.

One night, with the men gone, her lonely existence suddenly frightened her. 'What if my man never comes home, what if he is dead and I am a real widow woman?' Her sorrow began to reach inward, tear at her young heart.

With the passing of time she'd failed to notice how the secluded glen had held her to its soil. That promise she had made—if her man was indeed gone—was no reason to keep her tied; why didn't she pack what little she owned and get out of the place? Rachel, she believed, had gone and was not likely to look back; her days as a tinker were buried deep in her past. Annie, Bruar and Jimmy were no more. By morning she had decided to leave forever her Angus glens.

It wasn't as simple as that, though. Big Rory, with each passing day, became more and more like the crawling fiend of a snake, freely taking what lonely soldiers yearned to come home to. He was the only reason she lingered behind. But heaven forbid if someone should inform the soldier husbands that two tinkers were sharing their sacred beds and stealing what they alone were entitled to? Perhaps she should go, before her father-in-law and his companion found themselves trapped in an act of vengeance. Already glen soldiers were trickling home; the rumours were that the war had burned out and soon would be over.

Each time that she felt more kindly towards them, the drinking bouts that had them crawling from smelly flea-ridden pits to work without breakfast through harvests and plantings and anything else which brought enough of a wage to buy more drink made her kick the grass and punch the air. So one morning followed another and her hostility to them stayed firmly in place.

One day she paid her friend Doctor Mackenzie a visit. His legs didn't take him any distance now, and that new-fangled motor car never materialised. He admitted that the ones he'd seen frightened the life out of him; they were too noisy and fast. The real reason, however, was that both his eyes were covered in cataracts, restricting most of his vision. He'd worked and lived in the area for fifty years, and was more than relieved to hand his practice over to a new doctor; someone young, eager and full of new ideas, with a wife and two lively children.

Megan almost put two and two together and got five. 'Where's my pal, is he dead?' she asked the new resident of his house.

'He's moved out of town into a smaller house, and he's not dead!' his replacement said, laughing at her forthright question.

It was a picturesque little cottage, one she often imagined living in, if she ever stopped travelling. Soon, in the confines of a cosy kitchen, the pair shared a pot of tea.

She was saddened by her faithful friend's ailing health, so rather than heap her worries on him, she asked if he missed healing folk.

'I'll always be here lassie to help the unfortunate soul who canna pay for treatment. But forget about me for a minute, and tell me about

115

those men from the campsite. I swear I've heard tales, and not the best of rumours either, about Rory and his wayward Irish comrade. Better tell them to stay away from Kirriemor.'

'Doctor, how can I stop them? They'll have to take their punishment, when it comes.'

Megan left her friend to wander back. His old home was on the near side of Kirriemor, but to get from this one meant walking the whole length of the town. Her road led past some low-roofed cottar houses. As she passed, a door flew open and a woman was bundled out. 'If I ever see your face again, I'll kill you! And see him, the filth that's ruined you, well, he's dead for sure.'

Megan quickened her pace, but as she turned the corner the woman called, 'Tell Rory to get away, or else he'll die at my man's hands. He's for it!'

She recognised the voice, and looking over her shoulder, there was no mistaking the face of the battered woman picking herself up from the pavement; it was the giggler who had shared her father-in-law's tent.

She ran home, stumbling from stone to tree until the smell of burning sticks met her nostrils. 'Good-father, there's a hell of a stink in Kirriemor over the bitch and you. I think her man won't settle until he's had his revenge!'

Thankfully Rory was sober. A pot bursting with vegetables was boiling on the fire, he'd put two bowls and some bread on the familiar tree stump.

'Calm down, lassie. I've not been near her for weeks. If her man was coming, I'm certain he'd be here by now.'

'I tell you this, he flung that woman a mile in the air, her face was like mince.'

'Stop exaggerating, Megan, and eat the soup.' He ladled some into a bowl and handed it to her. After they'd eaten, she asked where O'Connor was. He didn't know, but went on to speak about her—what were her future plans?

'Good-father, what is there for me in this place apart from sadness, worrying about you? That woman today brought it closer and more urgent. O'Connor doesn't care about anyone but himself, he'd move on and never give us a thought. Come with me to Glen Coe, my kin are good quiet folks, there might be a lassie there free to warm your bed.'

He stopped her and said, 'Megan, I'm not sure where life will lead me, but one thing I do know—it's time to leave. War breeds respect, and now men will be working to bring it back home. I know my behaviour has been, well, awful, but I thought about giving up the drink, getting a place and settling my bones, maybe a farm job, you know?'

'Yes, I do. Please mean what you say this time, because I'm worried about that ploughman. The woman had bull's eyes with the kicking, he's real pig-angry with you.'

'Don't fret, I can take care of myself. When O'Connor gets back I'll tell him we are for the off.' He smiled, eyes narrowed with smoking, face reddened by alcohol abuse, yet there was a visible change, not something she could explain, a kind of submission.

'Do you want me to pack anything for you, like this box? It seems very bulky to add to your other belongings.'

She'd seldom known Rory to be so clear and level-headed. She leant down, opened her mother's box and took out the only thing worth keeping—her and Bruar's wedding photo.

'Let me see it, lassie.' His voice filled with emotion as she carefully laid it in his hand. 'You both were a pair of beauties that day. Do you mind how the photo man shivered with fear?'

She laughed, and at that minute the vengeful ploughman didn't bother her. Next day she'd pick up her life and move on, going part-ways with Rory. The Irishman could go where he wanted, to the moon for all the good he ever did, but Bruar's father meant the world to her. He was all she had left.

Leaving Rory to sort his belongings, she decided to say farewell to her beloved hills and the memories shared with her lost Bruar. She called that she'd be back early evening. It was a lovely warm afternoon.

The last time she'd walked in such glorious sunshine was far back in the time when she and Bruar had skipped on the hills as youngsters. It seemed as if she'd lived two lifetimes. One was when happiness and joy were as common as flowers on a dyke. The other was when unhappiness and heartache were held by the icy fingers of death. She'd never fall in love again: that was left behind with Bruar's memory on the heather-fringed horizon. But who but fate knows the path ahead? For today was her farewell day, her last day in the Angus Glens. Perhaps the great winged eagle would appear to her. It could not herald doom, if it appeared when there wasn't a cloud, and there was not a sign of one in the perfect blue sky.

Leaving a patch of thick yellow broom she walked the steep hillside, filling her lungs deeply with the sweet-scented air. Grouse mothers, pretending to be injured, fell and hobbled at her feet, trying to lure her away from their young chicks, fluttering on infant wings over the purpled ground. 'Och, look at the state of you; I won't touch your babies,' she assured them. 'I'm here to say cheerio, because tomorrow, my brown-feathered friends, I'm away. Now shut up, because you're spoiling my peace.'

Lost in thought in that special place, she smiled, recognising the hill-slope on her right; it was there she first tried to seduce her Bruar. Not tears, but warm feelings welled inside her. God knows she'd shed enough tears, and what good did it do—none at all.

'From this moment, the gathered memories of my beloved Bruar shall be sweet.'

Filling cupped hands and drinking the clean, cold water from a nearby burn, she began to climb up the steep face of the hill. The mountain scenes were breathtaking, as inch by inch, rock and scree replaced grass and heather. Soon she was stretching sunburnt arms into small crevices to find handholds in the now exposed crag. One last push, and ahead lay the mountain top; a cone-shaped cairn stood alone like an ancient Pictish symbol, fashioned by primitive hands to some pagan God.

'This is heaven,' she murmured. She fell upon the ground and allowed the sun, sky and the boulders beneath her to possess every inch of her breathless frame. 'I wish you were here, my man, to share this with me.'

Suddenly a feeling that someone was there made her sit bolt upright. How could there be anyone? The whole mountainous peak spread itself before her, a vision of panoramic vastness. She lay back down again and had the same uncanny feeling. There was someone there! Something touched her face. A gentle, invisible hand ran over her body. She closed her eyes, as a soft breeze whispered, 'Don't worry any more, my precious baby.' He was there—her Bruar.

'I love you, my bonny lassie,' he called from within the warm wind.

She drifted into a dream state in the warmth of the summer day. He kissed her, she kissed him back, they touched every inch of each other's bodies, then, lost in a world of wonder and mystery, the young couple joined as if in dreams. In this world Death himself could not separate them.

How long she lay there, there is no telling, but if it hadn't been for the whirr, *tabak-tabak-tabak* sound of a mother grouse chasing away a buzzard, she may never have awakened.

Whether or not Bruar had come from the grave to make love to her she did not know, but one thing she did know was that it was a long, long, time since she had felt so refreshed. From then on, when life was sore and heavy, she'd call to him and at least in dreams they'd be together. With this thought planted firmly in her mind she set off for home.

Now and then a buzzard soared high in the sky, watching and waiting. A vile smell made her recoil in disgust, as she came upon the half-rotted carcass of a red deer, but it mattered not. 'Ah well, she thought, 'all must eat, I suppose.' Further on she stopped to take another drink from a trickle of water spurting from the earth. 'Scotland, you are a wonder,' she said, wetting a cotton handkerchief and running it over her sweated face. 'Where in the world has God painted such beauty? I think nowhere else, but where have I been, apart from here and Glen Coe? Maybe Rachel has the right idea, to go as far away as anyone willing to take you.' She smiled, thinking what a long and perfect day this was. It certainly was a hot one, so feeling tired she stretched out behind a shady outcrop of rocks, sleeping once more. She knew arguments between Rory and O'Connor would be in full swing. The Irishman, lost without his drinking buddy, would not be pleased with his new abstinence. An hour or two more and she'd trek back.

The hours fell away, and when at last she awakened a dusky night was drawing near.

'Oh my goodness, this has been a long sleep! I'd best shift my feet, better I get back in case Rory has gone into town to have a goodbye drink; heaven knows where that might end.'

The darkness of the sky joined the horizon of the heather moor. Her pace quickened; grotesque shapes appeared to hem in her path, rocks took on strange forms as the shadows grew longer and deeper. A tiny glimmer of the sun's rays danced upon tree tops for one solitary moment, before being engulfed by the night. Dew had formed on the broom; a big moor spider hung from its web as if drinking the weighty dewdrops suspended from its temporary home. In time the ground flattened out, and she sighed with relief. A lone moorfowl was a welcome sight, rising in panic from a bed of reeds at the sound of her footsteps. The broom's yellow blossom had curled into itself for the night, which had brought with it a chill wind. Her feet found familiar ground, and soon she reckoned another mile would see her home. Her phantom romancing with Bruar had given a strength she'd welcomed, for sure as night follows day she'd need to be strong to take to the long road with big Rory in tow. The flames from the campfire lit up the sky; her father-in-law was still there.

With a full moon shining a clear bright path before her, the final half mile was easily visible. Suddenly voices could be heard further up the road, and she darted instinctively behind a twisted oak. Men came nearer; they were cursing and laughing at the same time. 'Filthy bloody tinks, that's the last time they bother us,' one said. 'Yes, too true, lad,' answered another. 'Did you get the Irishman, he's a slippy bugger that one, did you slice him?'

'If he's not a goner then I'm not the best ploughman for miles. Oh aye, it went through him!' Another voice barked, 'See how the tents flamed, best fire I've seen in a long while. Aye, well rid I say. We'll not see their kind round here again. Come on, let's celebrate.'

Megan slid to the ground. She knew exactly what form of carnage awaited her. How many warnings had she given them, but they had to find out the hard way. She must have sat there for ages, stiff and terrified to go round the corner for fear of what lay and bled there. She didn't want to share such awfulness with the night.

It was a very early dawn before she dared to walk gingerly into her campsite, bottom lip trembling with each step. Her footsteps felt warmth on the singed ground; she scanned the burnt remains of what was once her small canvas home. Everything smouldered. 'They must have torched the place yesterday when I was up the hill,' she thought. Taking a stick she prodded at the remains of her material life; the family box that held keepsakes and trinkets.

Where did they put the men? she thought, because there was no sign of bodies. It was useless, she knew, to pretend that either was alive, but in a vain hope she called their names. Death had hardened her, and suddenly her head filled with wicked thoughts. 'I hope Old Nick has them planted in hell, then I will be completely free. Rory would only have stayed off the drink for a short while. No, I hope he's finished.' She wanted them gone, needed a clean slate. Feelings of desertion fought with her conscience. A desire to just run away from that horrible, smouldering ruin flooded her mind, but her heart wasn't hard. In the woodland next to the site she thought something moved.

She wanted to run away, never look back, but again she couldn't, and called in reply. A weak voice, barely audible, answered.

'I'm coming,' she called, running over to see, lying half-dead on the earth, O'Connor. A great gash slit his face wide open, and blood trickled slowly from a wound in his chest. 'Where's Rory?' she asked, helping to sit him up.

'I don't know. Those bastards tricked us. We were having a quiet drink in the pub when a boy came in an' said the campsite was on fire. The big man was worried you might have been attacked, so ran back here without me. I feel he might be here somewhere but it's been the devil of a silence all night, with not a sound but my own heart. Help me, Megan!'

'How the hell can I do that, the ploughmen have torched everything, there's not even a torn sheet to bandage you with. Anyway, what was he doing in the pub? I left him promising he'd finished with the drink, forever.'

'For sure he was. Not so much as drink o' water passed his lips. He'd come to say goodbye, but when the boy runs in he took off as I said, tinking you were in danger.'

'God curse you, Irish, I hate you for this.' But nevertheless she did her best to wash his wounds with burn water. If he was to survive, though, his only chance was Doctor Mackenzie. But where was Rory's body? She had to search for him first.

O'Connor was pleading. 'You know they've done him in, lass. Please fetch the old doctor, I'll bleed to death while you look for him.'

'Another thousand curses on you, Irishman! This is all your doing! You're the one who should be dead! Taking him to whores and pouring drink into him. I hate the very ground you walk on, and I hope you do die and I hope it takes ages, with maggots chewing you from feet to collarbone.'

Just then a great roar of an engine was heard from far down the road. In no time a motor car trundled to a halt. Their old friend Mackenzie wobbled from the passenger side. He'd brought the new doctor with him. When he saw that Megan was alright, the old man sat his shaky frame on a stone seat and said, 'One of the ploughmen's wives heard her man saying they'd killed the tinkers! I've been out of my mind with worry thinking on what state they may have left you in, lassie. But have they hurt the men?'

'Oh aye, doctor, they done a grand job. O'Connor is bleeding to death over there, and as for big Rory, well, I fear he's breathed his last. I can't see hide nor hair of him.'

'I'll see to the Irishman if you and the new doctor search for Rory. Who knows but he might have crawled off to shelter.'

The young doctor ran behind her as she called out to Rory. Her fear mounted at what state he would be in. Nor was she wrong! Lying in a crumpled heap, not far from where she had found O'Connor, was the dead body of her father-in-law. Big Rory Stewart's throat was sliced open from one ear to the other. His blood covered the ground beneath him, so he lay on a deep red carpet.

'He came to help me because he thought I was here yesterday,' she told the young doctor, who had remained silent throughout. She continued, 'This was a good man, and only the evil hand of fate brought him along a path of heartache and destruction.' She fell by his side, kissed his stony face and whispered, 'You go now and join that beautiful wife and two sons of yours.'

'We'll have to bring the law into this,' said the young man to Mackenzie.

The older man ignored him and said to O'Connor, 'Your wounds aren't life-threatening. I'll take you back to my place where I have the instruments to stitch your cheek, but you'll be badly scarred. I'm willing to let you stay with me until healed, but promise me that then you'll leave here and never come back.'

'Aye, that's a promise I'll take on me late mother's life, whoever the hell she was.'

Mackenzie turned to the young doctor, and said in answer to his request for a police investigation, 'Son, there's not a policeman in this country that will lift a finger to help a tinker. In fact I'd bet my last penny that at this moment Sergeant Wilson is supping tea with the ploughmen and congratulating them on a job well done.'

'Surely you're wrong—this is a heinous crime. Barbaric, even.'

'Son, the boys who did this have been away fighting for their country, they've killed and seen horrors you and I could never imagine in our whole lives. These men here knew what they might do and they took the risks.'

O'Connor nodded in painful agreement. He then asked if Megan could be given her time to prepare big Rory for burial. The young doctor, still reeling from the injustice he was witnessing, was further horrified to hear that the deceased was to be buried in the forest.

But this couldn't be the case. The Highland Stewarts' burial site was in the north, the far north. Megan told them that until she could afford to transport it there, her father-in-law's body had to stay above the soil. One place waited for Bruar, but now that it was certain he'd not fill it, then his father should.

'Now, lass,' said her old friend, 'there's no way a body can stay above earth in the summertime. It would need to be embalmed and boxed, not in a thin makeshift shell like you would provide. No, lassie, this is something you can't afford.' He put an arm around the young woman and assured her he would see to things. 'I'll get him sorted and pay to have you and him go up north by train, Megan.'

She raised a proud hand to say that was far too much, but he insisted, and that was final.

Her pride however could not accept such a vast handout of charity, so she point-blank refused to agree unless she could make payment in return.

He was losing a long-held patience with the whimsical lass, and told her so. 'Look, why don't you think less on your stubborn pride and more on what is fact, and that is that all you own lies in ashes at your feet? How can Rory's body be traditionally prepared in muslin? Where is the cloth?'

A wee bit taken aback by the words of the usually mild-tongued doctor, she didn't know whether to smile or frown. Yet how true, what had she got left, only ashes!

'Now, here's a proposition for you and I don't want no for an answer! You and I have known each other a long time. My heart grows cold in this chest of mine and my eyes let me down daily, and they're getting worse, that's a fact. Would you come back to Kirriemor, move in to my old house and look after me? Now I'm not telling you to give up the old ways. All I ask, is to stay in the cottage until someone offers you a better life. You never know, lassie, maybe a handsome tinker lad might pass through one day and he'll sweep you away. But until then, say you'll stay with me and be my housekeeper?'

'What can I say, my dear old friend? I must be the first tinker to be offered lodgings with one as kindly as yourself. As I look round about my feet, all I see is a life unliveable. My man, along with his brother and father, all were cursed by a seer from the far north, the

Omen came to foretell their fate, and they are stone dead because of it. My sister, who by now is living the life of a lady's maid, is probably sunning her pale skin in America, aye, her and my nephew. The forest over yonder holds the bones of my mother. You're right, I have nothing but the skin on my worthless back. Yes, I'll bury Rory at the Parbh, then I'll come back and take care of you. And I make this solemn promise, you will want for nothing! I'll clean and care like you were my own father. Come to think of it, Doctor, it's a father you've been to me these past years.'

Doctor Mackenzie put his arm around her shoulders and smiled. 'That's my girl. Now let's us get on with things.'

Back at the cottage, his colleague stitched O'Connor's face and chest-wound. Mackenzie emptied an old leather medicine bag of its contents; a few yellowed bandages and some half-filled bottles of iodine among other bits and medical bobs and gave it to Megan. 'This will take a few necessities if and when you get them, lass.'

Still feeling the doctor had been over-generous, she reluctantly shook the hand of O'Connor, kissed the wrinkled cheek of the only friend she had left in the world and set off. The good doctor had organised Rory's remains to be hearsed to Forfar train station, and from there it would go on to Thurso.

NINE

*A*s she gazed from the train heading northward, Megan looked back towards her beloved high hills. She felt she belonged there, and that in no time she'd be back with her dear old saviour, Doctor Mackenzie. She thought on Rachel and wee Nicholas, her one and only nephew, wondering if they'd ever meet again. She'd promised Annie that when she was back once more she'd tend the forest resting-place and never allow it to be flowerless.

Thinking on O'Connor's thickset Irish frame, brought a cold shiver, she pulled a shawl over her shoulders. Something about him always made her feel uneasy. Oh, nothing that one could put a finger on, just a sense of foreboding. Her old friend would give him shelter until his health was regained, but whether or not their roads would ever cross again was not for present thoughts.

Her train journey passed through the most stunning scenery she had only previously heard about from Bruar. Several times mountains of fearsome splendour threw their mighty peaks toward a powder-blue sky, leaving her awe-struck. Now she could see why her man's eyes used to open wide with wonder as he told stories of the magnificent Highlands. After a journey that was exhilarating but left her dog-tired, her train whistled to a halt in Thurso Station. Gingerly stepping from the carriage, she hoped someone had been sufficiently informed by the letter Doctor Mackenzie had sent 'To whom it may concern, The Chapel, Durness.'

Shading her brow with chilly fingers she surveyed the smoke-shrouded station. She could see no one remotely likely to ease her of her oblong burden. An officious voice cut through her growing worry. 'With respect, lassie, we have to get it off the train, we've got a schedule to keep, you know.' The stationmaster was quiet but forthright. She began to fret. Perhaps her in-laws hadn't got the message sent to the church in Durness. Before fear took a tighter grip on her, a loud voice boomed from behind the station wall. A moustached man of over six feet walked over to her. 'Are you Megan, the one with the coffin?'

It was obvious to see by the flowing black gown and white collar that the letter had indeed found a positive response. Father Flynn shook her hand so hard her neck hurt.

'There's a three-day journey ahead across wild bog land. I've taken some food for our trip, no doubt you'll be hungry. Helen isn't strong enough to come all this way, so she asked me to.' He was reading her mind, 'But I know two fine inns where we can rest.'

She was soon heading along a single-track road on a plain carriage with the coffin secured on the back, pulled by two fine heavy Clydesdales. Her sandwiches of beef and mustard tasted so good. In no time she and her constant chattering companion were sleeping soundly in the first stop: Bay Inn, a peaceful little whitewashed house with three bedrooms. The couple who ran the place were nowhere to be seen, but the priest informed Megan that it was the coffin that kept them in their rooms. The kitchen had a 'help yourself' sign, and from the table they fed on cold porridge, buttered bread and milk. The next night a similar attitude prevailed from another set of landlords. It left Megan thinking that if Father Flynn hadn't been there she'd have ended up dumping Rory in the bog, which went as far as the eye could see in every direction.

During the long journey, her fellow traveller learned the whole of her life story up to that minute and she his. He'd come to the area as a young man, and fallen in love with the wildness. He came back after graduating from theological college, rebuilt the crumbling chapel and had been there for ten years. Of the few Catholics living along the coast, Helen was the most devoted. He knew about Rory, his wife's demise, and the boys.

The changing terrain along the rough road, sea and mountains on either side, let her see another part of Scotland, one she felt close to: Bruar's birth land.

Not before time, Helen's tiny, low-roofed cottage appeared on the horizon; another hour and Megan would have left the wooden seat of the carriage for some foot work. Father Flynn laughed; she could have run faster and been there yesterday, she told him, rubbing her backside.

He lifted a hand and waved to the tall woman with grey hair coming to meet them. 'So here you are then, Rory, home once again. You won't be going anywhere this time, brother.' Megan was ignored by the woman whom she took to be Helen, as she patted the coffin and stood silently, obviously praying.

The priest offered his companion a hand, but she was already on solid ground. Helen approached, having said her piece to the coffin, and much to Megan's surprise threw welcoming arms around her. 'Lovely girl you are, Bruar chose well. This letter your friend sent us—terrible. Not just Rory, but the boys too. What manner of curse would take so many of the one line? Poor wee thing, you must be shattered.'

A hankie was already soaked with tears, and Megan could tell by her nervous shaking voice that this poor soul was grieving. The letter held all the explanations about her family's loss; there was no need to open the wound further.

The priest left them to become acquainted; he'd a funeral to arrange. It was early evening, and first thing in the morning they'd lay Rory to rest, thanks to the dedication of Megan and Doctor Mackenzie.

The two women chatted for ages, drinking tea and eating bread well into the early hours, but Megan was exhausted. The hard journey spent worrying in case anything should happen to Rory's remains had taken its toll. In a bed with soft pillows and a large patchwork quilt, she slept like a baby, not moving a muscle until a cool early morning breeze whistled through a crack in the window-frame. When she awoke, a hand holding out a warm, sweet cup of strong tea welcomed her to a new dawn.

'Did you sleep well enough? Take your time in drinking this and don't come ben the house until you feel like it. There will only be three of us at Rory's burial, us and the good Father—oh, and not forgetting two grave-diggers. I've dressed my brother's box with a black drape; the horses are fed and watered, so after a bit breakfast we'll get off. The road down to Balnakiel is short.'

'Is he not being put into the Parbh? Bruar told me that was the last place, and as he's gone, that's why I thought...'

'No lassie, we can't cross over the water with a coffin, so Father

127

has organised a wee plot down at Balnakiel graveyard. I know why you think his remains should go into the Stewart burial ground, but there's not enough men to ferry him over, so the nearest burial ground will have to do.'

Megan felt robbed, her thoughts were troubled and she wished she'd buried Rory back in the glens beside Annie in the wood. All this train journey and three days travelling through bog roads seemed in vain. However, Helen was not a strong woman, and as the priest seemed to be organising matters it was out of her hands.

After the funeral she'd say her goodbyes and trek back to Thurso. The doctor's eyesight and health were failing rapidly; he would be in need of help.

Father Flynn had dressed himself as if he were conducting a regal funeral. He'd all his purple and gold vestments hanging perfectly, his hair combed straight and a little cap perched like a scone to the back of his head. His most precious missal was clasped firmly. Megan had never witnessed a Catholic funeral and was both curious and apprehensive. To complete the entourage, two gravediggers stood on either side of the carriage, cloth caps in hand.

Nestled behind a wall of ancient stone, crossed by a meandering burn filled with marigolds, the little graveyard was filled with history. To its back, towering into mist, rose the mountains of Sutherland. Before it, Pentland Water, (near which Bruar, wide-eyed and excited, would listen to Viking tales) made its way to meet the northern ocean.

Serenely, holding a cotton hankie to her eyes, Helen held back her tears. She'd shed plenty over the years for her wayward brother. Father Flynn intoned in Latin the fitting words, as the men stood respectfully in silence, waiting with spades to cover up Rory, the wild drinking man whose love of the water of life and lack of respect for himself had proved a terrible downfall.

Looking across the land as if for a fleeting moment she saw Rory, Megan repeated to herself the words she'd heard all those years ago: 'You can book into Hell Hotel, but you can never leave.'

Megan couldn't watch as the men struggled with the coffin. It proved too heavy and after seeing them drop one end and have to jump in to straighten the thing, she decided to get away. Pulling a black cardigan that Helen had loaned her across stiff shoulders, she ran off without a word. Avoiding the path that went past the far end of the graveyard, she set off across the sand dunes which seemed endless. She didn't want to be there, all that holy stuff about repenting and forgiveness stuck in her throat; she felt stifled. But noone thought her actions disrespectful; the past war was still raw in many hearts.

On she ran until she came to a spectacular view of cliff tops, above which black and white birds hovered and dived. The sight made the hair rise on her neck. Their freedom and power over the wind made her wish she were a sea bird like a puffin, diving with folded wings among rugged rocks with such agility; then to rise with wings outstretched, hovering on air thermals.

Funeral garment now wrapped about her waist, she set off to explore that wild and wonderful place that her man had spoken of with such vivid words. In the past she had longed to see this place, hoping they could come one day. And now here she was, seeing it in all its splendour, thanks to the dead body of his father. Each step drew her eyes upward, as yet more birds held themselves steady in a powerful wind. It whipped up her hair and the frayed hem of her skirt slapped her legs. Every so often, without warning, the ground fell away, displaying a gorge of such mammoth depth it left her breathless. She walked, skipped and ran, climbing higher before falling back into long, coarse grass and staring upward until the sky's brightness brought tears. Far below, on her left, a swathe of countryside lay between one village and the other, and from her high vantage-point they appeared like tiny dots on the edge of the world. To her right, almost as far away as any eye could see, stood a high lighthouse, and she wondered if perhaps that was the 'Parbh'. She could just make out how near the cliff edge it was. Exhausted with the responsibility of recent days, she found a secluded spot to rest.

'If you stand upon that rock over there you will see the Hvarf. I mean Cape Wrath. The Vikings called it Hvarf, meaning "the turning point".'

Megan, startled by the man who'd appeared, it seemed, out of nowhere, rose to her feet.

She rubbed her eyes. 'What did you say?'

'The Cape of Wrath. The invaders, those men of Norway, had their own name.'

'My Bruar told me all about the Vikings,' she said.

'Oh, that he would, and seeing as he was from these parts, I'm sure he did a good job!'

Her strange companion faced her, and all she could focus on was a space in his head! Not the long reddish beard or the sharp jawline, but that empty hole that once housed a sea-green eye. The Seer of Balnakiel, who had flitted in and through her nightmares, stood with her on a cliff top. Who else could it be?

He sat down on grassy rocks, motioned her to do the same. As if in a trance she obeyed, clasping hands over shaking knees.

A strange silence fell across the sky; it grew dark and cloudy, and the birds flew in to rest on cliff ledges.

'Do you believe in the stones?' he asked.

'I have no time for that stuff; I am a Glen Coe tinker. And I have no time to be in the company of a pig-evil man who told big Rory his wife was dying. You could have helped him. Even if it was known to you she would die, you still should have shown compassion.' She made to stand, run away, but his bony fingers clawed her back down to the grass.

'You look to the creatures of the sky for prophecy.' His voice was slow and thoughtful.

'Why do you know this?' she asked sharply.

'I know many things, child. Now calm your heart and listen, for there is not much time and your road is long.' He took a handful of stones from a cloth bag, shaking them before throwing them on a patch of sand. When they settled, he studied them and said, 'Bruar sleeps not below the soil, but above it! You have to leave this place. Forget too, the old doctor in the glens. In the land of the King he waits. The way of a tinker lassie is the road, you're not a sheep to be kept in one place. Find him, bring the man home.'

She touched his flowing garment; it felt like spider's web. He was almost transparent. Shaking with fear, she asked if he was a ghost.

Silence followed, and for an age he ran his hands over the stones muttering in a strange tongue. Puffins joined seagulls at rest on the precarious ledges below.

'Megan,' he said, pulling her up to stand beside him on the very edge of the cliff, 'I hear voices, I must go. Listen, for this is the last time we shall meet; heed my words!

'*Run lassie, find your man, he sleeps above the earth, not below, fast go your way, like the stream, winding forth blindly, yet always aware of treacherous waterfalls cascading over sharp rock. Mind how you flow, wild child of Nature: go on until the great tide frees your tired limbs and the hidden sun shines for you once more. Embrace the warmth of him who waits in the shadows.'*

—

'Megan, are you alright?' She heard a voice calling her name, but her eyes were closed tight and would not open. When they did, it was Father Flynn putting an arm under her head and lifting it up. 'Come now, there's a good girl, drink this.'

It was whisky, and when the sharp taste slipped onto her tongue she almost choked.

She sat up to find her grassy rock seat was gone and replaced by a soft eiderdown bed. She was back in the bedroom of the small cotter house, and by her were the priest and Helen.

'Where did he go?'

'Who?' asked Helen.

'The old man with a red beard; he'd one eye!'

'You don't mean old Balnakeil?'

'Yes, yes! Him who lost his eye to big Rory! I met him away up the cliff tops and he told me things... Who took me home? Did I faint or something?'

'What did he tell you, this old man? Have you forgotten walking home alone and going to bed? You've been resting for an hour or so.'

Megan had no memory of leaving the Seer or coming back; she was frightened. 'He told me that Bruar wasn't dead, that's what he told me!'

Helen sat close, held her hand and said, 'The Balnakeil Seer could not have spoken to you lassie. Not today or yesterday or any other day. You see, he's been dead these past five years!'

The words hit her like a bolt of wild lightening; she grabbed and emptied the glass of whisky in one swallow. 'I tell you, as low as my dear mother's grave. I saw that one-eyed man. He was as real as you. Some place far away from here, my Bruar waits, and I will have to find him! Call me mad if you want, but I'm certain that the Seer came back from the other world with a message.'

Helen was angered. 'God will not allow such unholy talk. I'll tell you what's wrong with you, too young and too much sorrow. It's been overpowering and that's why you talk in riddles. Unbalanced, you are. You're going no place. I will nurse the strength back into you.'

Father Flynn, who'd been listening, stepped forward, 'Never under-estimate the effect of a broken heart, it shows itself in many ways. You thought you heard about Bruar because the laddie came from these parts. That's healthy and helps get things long buried out in the open. I bet he told you every detail about the Seer. I myself have listened to folk in these parts, and by their description, although I never met the man, I could paint a picture.'

He walked over to the little window, scanned the shoreline, turned and said to her, 'You would benefit from spending a wee bit time up here in the Highlands. Take some long cliff walks and fill your lungs with our summer winds. Help Helen cut winter peat. Find Bruar in the sea breezes and blue ocean swells. If you run away following a bad dream—and that's all it was—you'll search for nothing more than an empty wind.'

She watched him put the empty glass on the dresser, flick back his cassock, take out a packet of cigarettes and light one. Without another word on the subject, he said his goodbyes and was gone. Helen too had left the room to make some dinner.

Her head ached in pain, as all that had happened reeled inside. Had she really imagined the whole thing? Far too many negative thoughts spiralled in her head; perhaps that was the problem. She did far too much thinking.

Next day she helped Helen with some chores before heading out along the shoreline to explore, but no matter how she tried not to think about them, the Seer's words dominated every step. Miles and miles of shoreline spread themselves under foot; it was easy to cover the ground when no heather or rock hindered the way. If she was going to live in these parts it was best that she become acquainted with the terrain.

Pausing for breath she saw an old ruin among sand dunes; not far from the village of Durness and perhaps a mile or so from Helen. On investigation it seemed as if someone, many years back, had deserted it in the middle of building. It had a low wall and here she rested. Grasses dominated, but clearly visible on a concrete ledge lay a rusty trowel, hammer and scattered nails. The planks of wood that rotted beneath her feet may have been planned for a door. She wondered why this would-be home had been so suddenly abandoned.

Time passed without her realising it. It was late when she noticed that daylight was fading, and along with it a thick haar was creeping inward toward the land. 'I'd better shift myself and get back before the way is hidden in mist,' she thought, hurriedly picking up the shawl that had slipped from her grasp. As she stooped, something lying on the ground caught her eye, a part-burnt piece of paper. Usually she'd have left it where it was, but something familiar about it made her pick it up.

Fingers of wet mist, driven now by a strong breeze, pushed damp hair into her eyes; with the wind to her back she turned and looked at the article in her hand. How on earth could it be? She fell back and trembled, staring in utter amazement at the part-burnt photograph of her and Bruar's wedding. Her own face was burned off! It was the very picture that had perished with everything else in the box back in the Angus glens. How had it got here?

A whispering wind brushed her ears. She listened above the ocean's swell, which was rising in a crescendo of water music. Someone spoke—the wind carried voices.

'Surely I'm not dreaming this time!' She called out, 'Who are you?'

No response; was her imagination taking over? Did she have the photo with her all the time but had forgotten? Had it fallen from her pocket without her noticing? She turned her head to look over some rocks on the horizon, but all she saw was a faint ray from the setting sun throwing a light through the thick mist, enough to show her path. For a moment she wanted to turn into the water, to rest on the tide and let it take her away to sea, some place where the loneliness and pain, and this creeping insanity, would not penetrate. It would be a place of dreams, a place where she needed no food, just a promise of sleep forever. In the empty place she stared at the wedding photo in her hand, then was aware of something moving. She turned to see the figures of two people holding hands in the setting sun's glow; a tall man and a small woman. They walked towards the water and looked back for a moment. Megan's tears came in torrents. 'Rory,' she cried, 'you found your peace!' 'Now find yours, Megan,' the wind whispered.

In no time she was running along the sandy path, tears freely falling, releasing her from hopelessness and fear! With the burnt photo tightly grasped in her hand, her road now lay spread before her clearer than ever, with promise and hope. There was no doubt! She had to find Bruar; no matter where, when or how, she *would* find him.

Her skirt lifted with a brisk wind that followed her. She felt better than she'd done for many a long while—now there was purpose to her life. Whirling around, she called into the mist that the wind was chasing, 'You win, Balnakiel! I'm off to search in the King's town, wherever that is, for my young man, and by God I'll find him. Thank you, wherever you are, from the bottom of my heart.'

Helen could see that whatever was going on in Megan's head, she'd no control over. It was plain that her late brother's daughter-in-law had a mind of her own. Anyway, this young woman was too wild for her quiet, church-going lifestyle. It was plain that she'd other plans, which didn't include living with a staid woman, or an old man, come to that.

Helen insisted she take extra clothing for the journey and pushed a worn skirt and the black cardigan inside the doctor's leather bag.

Next day Father Flynn promised to write to Doctor Mackenzie to say she was going to find her Bruar. He wouldn't allow her to walk to Thurso, although she insisted that her feet were faster than fat Clydesdales and a rickety wagon. Helen gave her a few shillings to add to what she'd had left over from her Kirriemor friend. All in all she'd enough money for the long train journey south.

—

'Can you tell me where the "King's land" is?' she asked a ticket clerk on the station platform in Thurso.

'London, I suppose' he answered, smiling broadly, 'where the great palaces are. He stays at Balmoral sometimes to do a bit of shooting, but most of the year he lives in London.'

'London it is.'

The priest saw her on board, and just before saying goodbye, put a piece of folded paper in her pocket. 'A wee bit extra', he said. He seemed happy for her, but had a word of warning. 'Take care, and keep eyes in the back of your head.'

TEN

The train stopped many times, Inverness, Perth and Edinburgh, and by the time it reached Newcastle in the north of England it was full to bursting with passengers. Thankfully, twenty minutes break was allowed at the stops on the way for long-distance passengers to stretch their legs and have some tea in a small station café. Everything seemed to run on a smooth track. She marvelled at the changing countryside. Newcastle frightened her, though. She told a ticket collector that a city of such magnitude must have brought a million masons to build it. When he said the place was begun as a port and grew from there, she said 'the sailors were handy with a trowel, then.'

The ever-changing landscape had captivated her, and she was so wrapped in thought about her journey that she failed to see the man with the torn raincoat who'd been watching and following her. It was when coming from the station café to catch yet another connection on her journey to the south that she saw him, but failed to realise, until too late, what his interest was—the leather bag she held tightly in her hand!

'Madam, you've dropped this,' he said with a voice as polished as a duke, holding a lovely red scarf.

Never had she seen a bonny one like that before, and had it been winter she would have taken it and run. But she'd no need for a scarf in summer, so politely told the stranger he was mistaken.

'No, I saw it fall from your shoulders, and thought how much it complemented your black hair.'

It may be said that a gift horse with a big mouth should not be ignored, and this certainly was a gift, but why?

'Look, dear thing,' he pushed it into her hands, 'one doesn't tell lies.'

'Well, one certainly is mistaken,' she thought, taking it from him with a broad thank-you smile.

'Better put it away or else it will get lost again,' he said, pointing at her hold-all.

Innocently she put the bag on a slatted wooden bench and folded the scarf. Then in a flash, at the precise moment a guard shouted, 'All aboard for York,' the stranger had the case in one hand, red scarf in the other; running down the platform, he was soon gone from her astonished sight. Smoke from the trains puffed and poured over the platform, in and around the scurrying legs and bodies of passengers, concealing the thief.

'That pig-face has taken all I possess, even, heaven forbid, my ticket to London! Curse the hide off you for that,' she screamed after the thief, who had disappeared from view like a wily fox. One or two faces turned to her, but only for a second—they were unmoved by her predicament. A war had not long finished and poverty in abundance had followed in its wake. One more incident was neither here nor there. Making her way through the bodies to complain to a bald, bespectacled man at the ticket barrier, she wished that the rogue would be half way to hell by now. 'Excuse me please, missus, can I go in front of you? I have to get on that train.'

The lady in question tutted at Megan's apparent ignorance of ticket line etiquette and pushed her back into the queue. Slowly the London train's wheels began to chug, chug, chug, and to her horror it started gathering speed.

Pushing her way once again to the front of the line, she shouted, 'I can't stand here until you yap any more hair off him.' Such was her desperate situation, she took hold of the stout lady and physically thrust her aside, pushing up to the clerk and pleading in her ignorance, 'Someone has stolen my bag with my ticket for that train over there, can you give me another one?'

Several people, including the chubby lady laughed loudly and told her not to be ridiculous.

'Pull the other one,' sneered the man behind the rabbit wire barrier. She'd obviously embarrassed him by drawing attention to his lack of hair.

Megan was desperate, these people's ways were strange, she grew anxious. 'I'll pull whatever one you want, I'll pull the whole damn lot if you like, just give me a ticket.'

'That train has gone; there won't be another until tomorrow. If you want a ticket it will cost you three shillings and sixpence.'

Her heart sank, she had nothing. Pleading and begging made no difference; eventually she was asked to leave by an apologetic station porter.

'What a disaster—how can I find my man now?' she thought, before slumping down outside the train station on a similar slatted bench to the one on which she'd been so foolish enough as to put her bag earlier. Thinking on how she'd been duped by the man in the torn coat, panic at the unfamiliar surroundings and her lack of money took a grip. 'What a sleekit, fly bastard of an excuse for a man!' she cursed him for the tenth time, then thought on what he'd say on finding a grey tweed skirt and an elbow-patched funeral cardigan when looking through his ill-gotten booty. Everything became painfully clear in the full light of day. Tears welled in her eyes, though not for the loss of her bag, clothes or train ticket. Only one thing mattered to her—the wedding photo was in the case!

The more she thought about the serious situation she found herself in, the more curses were piled on the thief. 'You will never see a full belly again,' she screamed at the top of her voice. People, startled by the incoherent outburst, hurried past, probably thinking she'd lost her senses. 'What am I to do now? Here with the whole stretch of England ahead of me, and not a penny to pay my road?'

'I need to eat,' she thought as she walked away from the train station in the busy city of Newcastle, with its wide river and splendid bridges.

The aftermath of the dreadful war saw to it that there were not many pennies to be got. To date she'd managed to sustain herself in Scotland, she had never become completely destitute, so that when she came across folks begging on the street it confused her. 'Are you tinkers?' she asked two men sitting on the pavement of a broad street corner, cloth-caps at their feet.

'What's a tinker?' enquired one.

'A bloody gyppo!' answered the other, 'she thinks we're filthy pikeys.'

'You calling us gyppo, you flea-ridden bitch?' He lifted a stick and brought it hard down upon her toes. She kicked him hard on the leg before spitting at the other one's face. It was obvious Megan had been sheltered and secluded in her nomadic life. If she had been a bit more streetwise she would have rushed past such shifty-looking beggars.

Some beggars wanted money to feed a hungry family, but there were those who did it for nothing more than a bellyful of cheap alcohol. Perhaps these lads were drunkards? Suddenly they were on their feet and chasing after her. Up and down and round and on she ran, as if the devil himself was at her heels, taking right and left turns and not knowing where she was running, until no sound of them could be heard. They might have caught her, had she not had the speed of a hare and the lightness of a deer. Not even Bruar could run at her speed, and she was more than grateful for that. She kept up a fast pace until the city was a fading memory behind her.

By nightfall a long stone dyke appeared on her shadowy horizon. Behind it she found shelter, curled up and fell into an exhausted sleep. Already her search for Bruar was looking in danger of ending, and it was only three days into it.

Next morning her bones ached and her stomach rumbled. Where could she find food? More to the point, where would she get money? If another train ticket was needed to continue her journey then money had to be earned. This positive thinking took her feet a faster pace upon the narrow winding road. For the next two days she lived off berries and wild nasturtium. The scenery left her breathless, with miles of heather moor followed by drooping willow trees. She went up and over green meadows, where sheep grazed in peaceful contentment. This was the Yorkshire Dales, and like her precious Scotland, it seemed a beautiful place where songbirds sang in full-throated harmony.

Apart from a lone shepherd, she met hardly any folks at all. Three days had passed and seen her curl up on the ground behind dykes and tree stumps; how grateful she was, then, to come across a small hamlet. Snickly Rigg dipped into a green valley. Perhaps only nine or ten thatch-roofed houses made up this tranquil village.

By now she was desperately in need of a substantial meal, so she knocked gently on the first door that she came to. An elderly man, thick-set and rugged, brown pipe suspended from a small mouth, answered the door. 'What can I do for you, young woman?' he asked, looking her up and down.

'Can you spare a drop of tea, mister?'

For a while he chewed and puffed upon the pipe, before saying, 'Can you pay?'

'There's no money to my name, because a devil stole my bag back in—what's the name of that town with a train station in it, it has a river and bridges in it too?'

'Not many trains come this way, but I think you could mean New-castle. That's a long ways back, lass, did someone drive you here?'

She felt this old man would be hard-pushed to spare her water, never mind tea, with all the questioning he was doing.

'No one drove me. I can shift these legs and run thirty miles in a day. Now do you have any tea?'

He stepped back inside his house, not unlike the low thatch-roofed cottar home of Helen, and motioned her to sit on the dyke by the gate. Soon he was wobbling out on bandy legs, with tea in one hand and a welcome sandwich of cheese in the other. He sat on a wicker chair, tucked his legs under it and offered her a three-legged stool. An old shepherd dog, smelly and panting, rubbed its head against her thigh. The dog was friendly, so she gently ran a hand over its head and down its back.

'You're kind to me, sir, and I wasn't lying when I said my bag was stolen, so what can I do in payment of this?'

'Does the cow pay for her grass, and the pheasant for the wind in its wings? What kind of man would I be, if I couldn't share my food with somebody in want? God knows there's more than enough. But come to think of it, the wife's grave could do with some more of your flowers.'

She was puzzled why he should ask her for flowers.

'You're a gypsy girl, are you not?'

'I'm a Scottish tinker, never met any gypsies.'

'Can you not make the pretty flowers and give the blessing of the Egyptian?'

Before she could ask what he meant, three dark-skinned girls dressed in brightly coloured gowns, gold rings in their ears, suddenly came laughing and chatting round the corner.

'Hello, Mr Thrower, are you wanting a bunch of flowers?' one called out.

'See, here they come, the pretty gypsies with their flowers and their blessings. Lovely they are, to brighten an old man's heart. Yes, Lucy, give me six for my Jane's grave.'

Megan watched the three girls approach and felt, in an inexplicable way, drawn to them. One stepped forward and gave her a quick glance from head to toe. It reminded her of a speedy stoat, with head darting to examine every inch of a young rabbit before pouncing. The pair of steel-blue eyes gave Megan the third degree. Her inquisitor said to the others, 'She is our kind.' Turning to Megan she asked, hands on hips, 'Who be your kin?'

Megan's quick outburst of thick Scottish dialect made them laugh loudly. 'I'm from the Clan Macdonald,' she said, proudly puffing her breast out like the prize peacock in a stately garden.

They were mocking her, how dare they? Her hackles rose. They'd no right laughing at such a proud Scots name. She told them so.

'We aren't joking at your name, it was the way you said it. We've never met any Scottish gypsies before, but it's a good day this, because the more of us there is then the better, don't you think? By the way, we are the Lees. Come and put flowers on Mr Thrower's wife's grave with us. I'm Lucy, the pretty one, these be me cousins, Anna and Ruth. What's your name?'

'Megan,' she said, feeling much stronger after having eaten.

Her new friends were like a breath of fresh air. As they followed the old man down a few steps into a small enclosure of scattered gravestones she judged that they were in her age group. How she'd longed for conversation with girls of her own age. Since Rachel left she'd never even spoken to one. She watched as Lucy, without a word, laid a single rose-like flower on the grass. The others did the same. It was humbling to feel another paper flower being slipped into her hand by Lucy. Strange, they had only just met, but she felt an overwhelming sense of belonging as she laid her flower beside the others. Then the three girls held hands, closed their eyes and said in unison a blessing over the grave.

'Lie at peace in God's green earth,

Where none can hurt and none can curse.

See the light that shines for you,

Rise, gentle soul, and pass on through.'

The old man wiped away a tear and said, 'Thank you so much, what would I do without you?' He slipped some pennies into Lucy's purse, then hobbled off, clay pipe shifting in his small, toothless mouth. As he struggled to reach his door, he called to Megan, 'These girlies will see you alright, tell them what happened in the train station and they'll see you fed, nothing surer. Damn good folks, these Lee gypsies, damn fine.' He waved, adding, 'Come back soon', then was gone behind a half-shut door, the panting dog curling at his heel.

Her three companions were horrified on hearing what had happened at Newcastle, and insisted that she follow them home. Soon she was standing on the lip of a large quarry, gazing down at a most wonderful sight.

Horses, big shire ones and little ponies, grazed nearby, while brightly painted bow-fronted wagons made a great half-circle on the quarry floor. She could smell all kinds of cooking—vegetables, ham, beef, mingled with the aroma of sweet honey and boiling fruit. Never in her entire life, not even at the summer's height, did her nostrils experience such a feast of aromas from Mother Nature's bounty, mixed in the blue reek of open fires. Was this a gloaming dream?

'Come on, and meet the others.' Lucy was eager to introduce her.

'Wait up,' cautioned Ruth. 'She's a single girl, better let Mother Foy know how we came by her.' The others agreed with her. No one likes a lone woman. They went on to explain that in their circles, a lone female could be misunderstood. When she asked why, they said that gypsy men never forgave a fornicating wife. She was usually sent off without any clothes or money. 'Just like me?' asked Megan, aware now the situation was no dream.

'Yes, just like you. But come to think on it, why were you not under the protective hold of a man, does you have a husband? Did he take a stick over yer back? Or did your Daddy put the stone to you for stealing another woman's man? Don't answer me questions yet. Tell old Mother Foy the reasons for such loneness, she should meet you first, girl. If you have a shifty past she'll see it.' Ruth was the suspicious one, and needed to know why a stranger looking for protection in their midst had arrived at old Thrower's door.

'I'll tell you everything, but I'm thinking you'll find it a mite hard to believe.'

Soon the girls were standing outside a brightly-painted wagon, Mother Foy's varda they called it. Gold, yellow, green, red, in fact every colour she could imagine was to be seen, threaded into flowers and intricate designs. The artist had also painted a rainbow above the door, which split in two parts. Two polished brass oil lanterns hung at each side. Irish linen lace curtains hung like dewdrops inside the windows.

'These gypsies,' she thought, 'are fussy about their homes. I wonder what they'd think of my canvas hovel, with its black stove and sooty chimney? Our horsehair mattresses might raise an eyebrow or two also.' As she took in with her inquisitive eyes every bit of the wagon's exterior, she hardly noticed the top half of the door slowly open. An elderly woman leaned over and rested two sinewy arms on the bottom half, sucked upon a clay pipe with its stem part broken, and ran an eye over her.

'Who have we in our midst today then, girls?' she asked, adding, 'You know not to bring strangers home from the hawking, especially filthy-clothed females.'

'Begging your pardon, old humpy-back, but these clothes have kept me warm these past nights as I lay behind dirty, moss-covered dykes.'

The elderly lady laughed and said, 'No wonder the back of you is brown and green-tinged.' She then removed a brightly-coloured headscarf from her shoulders, rolled a long grey plait of hair and expertly intertwined it into the scarf. She threw a disapproving look at her new visitor's hair and scoffed, 'Avoid a mother blackbird, she'll eye your hair for next year's nesting.'

Laughter spread around Megan, tempting her to give another tirade of verbal defiance. She hadn't given any thought to her appearance that morning. Her priorities were to find a bite to eat, and some way of finding work, so that she could get on with her search for Bruar. She decided to apologise, however. 'Look, I'm sorry, missus, this tongue of mine has a life of its own, but please allow me to tell my story,' she said, and insisted that all should listen. So she explained her past to the women. Young and old, they listened in silence as she opened her heart and finished with retelling her robbery at the hands of the station thief.

Mother Foy came down from her wagon and bade Megan sit at her side on a willow seat. 'Your load is heavy, girlie, as heavy a one as would bend the back of someone twice your age. Yes, you can stay with us, for as long as you like. If I offered the money needed to end your epic journey, would you take it?'

'I will take only payment for work. I'll turn my hand to anything, but I'll not take money for nothing. I already owe my man's auntie a bob or two, and there's a debt unpaid to a certain doctor. Please give me work.'

'I'm thinking now, after hearing the woe in your life, that's the answer you'd give me. The girls here, well, they make wooden flowers, and then dye them. They use beetroot juice and get lovely red ones with it. Onions give yellow and white, oh, and when they are crushed and boiled with daffodil heads, one would be hard pressed to tell the difference twixt real and false flowers. Sometimes they go onto the moors to collect heather blooms. When these are boiled, they extract a fragrant, purpled pink dye. They also pick summer blooms and dip them into melted wax. And there are the whittling pegs, you could sell them. What turn do you know could bring in lowie [money]?'

'I gather heather and wind it into coarse balls for pot scrubbers. I can catch the pheasant, snare the rabbit and guddle the trout. I've even been known to belly-catch a sleepy salmon. I can gather the hay, lift potatoes, plant anything, harvest anything needs harvesting. Mistletoe-selling, hawking, reading palms.' She could have reeled off lots more, had the old woman not slapped her back and said, 'You'll do. But first, and don't take offence, what would you say to a nice fresh frock?'

Glancing down at her tweed skirt, plain and dowdy, and stained with travel, and well aware that the laced-up, black leather shoes on her feet would have been more suitable for a sixty-something spinster, she agreed with rose-blushed cheeks of embarrassment.

Lucy walked off, while Ruth and Anna ran to search their small clothes bags for a suitable dress. Mother Foy took her into the varda wagon, to administer a piece of worldly wisdom. 'Now, child, gypsy boys are as healthy as gorger [non-gypsy] ones when it comes to flitting eyes at slender ankles and firm breasts. And there are more than enough young men in our circle,' she smiled, then went on, 'albeit most are spoken for. But they're spunky and healthy, and might have a try on you girl. So after supper, the first thing we must do is let everybody know that you're not free for the taking. Usually our boys, who are busy on the moor at the beating, have respect and won't bother you. There is one, though...' she hesitated with her words, as she thought on him. Her shoulders rounded like an old cat apprehensive of an approaching rainstorm, her brow narrowed as the broken-stemmed clay pipe twitched between clenched teeth. 'You don't want anything to do with him; he's a bad lot and cares nothing for respect or honour, nothing like that. His heart is as black as the Earl of Hell's waistcoat; don't even look in his direction.'

Megan smiled and touched the old woman's arm, 'I fill my heart, sleeping and waking, with my man.' She went on, 'He's a big handsome brute with wavy blond hair and eyes you could swim in. No, I won't be giving myself to any other.'

The woman could see the love lighting up her young friend, so changed the subject. She spoke instead of Megan's journey south with them. 'If you do as I say, I can promise you a free passage with us through the country. We stop for the hop picking in Kent. It's there I'll show you how to get to London.'

Megan couldn't believe her luck; not only was she offered a way to be with Bruar, but these folks were good and kind. And they shared her background—yes, things were beginning to shine. 'When will we get there?' she asked, excitedly.

'Let me see, there's the horse sales at Appleby in June, there's a bit of hawking round this place and that. We might be down hop-picking way after next summer.'

'Next summer!' Megan's hopes faded by the second. 'All that time?'

They came down from the varda and sat on the seat next to its wooden steps. The old woman whistled up at a blackbird perched on a hanging branch of a laburnum tree that brushed against her wagon roof. Uncannily it whistled back, and then she said, 'It seems to me you don't know much about horse-drawn wagons, and less about the distance between the north and south of England. It's already hop-picking time, but how are we going to get there? It's a shire I have, not winged Pegasus. I'll feed and bed you, but I want help. Along with your normal chores, like filling the watering can by five in the morning, fowl has to be plucked and cleaned, rabbits skinned. Take nothing from one-eyed men, for it's bad luck, and never mention the peacock, it's real evil, that. My old Frankie, God bless his soul, is dead these last ten years, and I could do with some help. We never got blessed with young uns, so apart from the respect my knowledge brings I'm on me own. Bones creak a lot, and eyesight isn't good. You're in luck, because there's a bigger than usual pot of stew on the chittie irons over the fire, we'll eat that in an hour.'

Megan thanked the old woman; but something struck her, she was curious. If she'd no family, why the title, Mother?

'I wondered when that would sink in. I'm a baby-bringer. I know all there is about bringing babies into this big bad world. I've delivered

144

at least a hundred. Washing, feeding, healing sick uns and homing little uns whose mothers die of the birth fever, I've done it all. Except have my own. Sod's bloody law, I say!'

She looked sad, but not for long as she recalled the joy it brings to see a brand new life, so many times. 'I see them first, and that's why I'm known as Mother. Also because of that gift God has granted me of knowing what herbs heal and which poison. Yorkshire children don't suffer the scurvy because I have the cure—boil up the hawthorn flowers, that's all. Drink it down and no more scurvy. Now, here's a little advice for you. That rogue I warned you about goes by the name of Bull Buckley, "King of the Gypsies". He ain't no king, so get that out of your head, girlie. He's the best street-fighter ever lived. He can kill and has done, more than once, so keep well clear, not even a glance. He'll be back around midnight, when some publican has mustered enough courage to ask him to leave his premises. You'll hear the brute shouting with the drink. Just don't go near. That's all I'm saying on the subject. It's my varda you'll be sleeping in, so don't peer through the curtain or else you'll find a stone come through my window.'

Megan's eyes flashed fear, genuine fear, remembering how evil big Rory used to look and sound when fuelled by the demon in the bottle, O'Connor too. She assured the kind old lady there would be no involvement from her with the likes of Buckley. 'I'd rather eat glass than sit next to a man soaking himself with drink.'

When she thought back to how much trouble came by way of alcohol it made her all the more serious, and she told the old woman so. 'Honest, if you'd seen how peaceful and serene our little home of tents was in the Angus Glens before the drink took hold. I had time to notice how willow mixed with ancient oak and yew, and how the trees fought to keep ground space with yellow broom and bluebells. Wild daffodils, forget-me-nots and primroses grew along natural forest paths. Gentle, mild-mannered roe deer skipped among lily-of-the-valley, leaving the merest hoof prints on the mossy earth. Then Jimmy died and we thought Bruar had been killed too. That's when it all got serious with the drink. The older men started on that hell-filled path. They got lost, and couldn't find the way back. I never noticed Mother Nature's joys after that, only wondered what manner of state the men would be in as night came.' She did not tell Mother Foy how Rory had changed at the end, nor about the vision she'd seen in a setting sun.

'Don't blame the drink, child. It was the war that changed things.

We lost a few good men here too. Take Maggie Gaskins, over there by that palomino pony; she lost her eldest boy and her man. Georgina Boswell over by the stream, her with bright red hair, was washing her clothes in a field outsides Lincoln when her daughter saw a policeman cycling down the lane. They thought he was coming to move them on, so ran and hid. But it was news that her Freddie, one of a twin, had got killed by a sniper. The lad didn't even know what a sniper was. His brother's never been the same these whiles back. He thought at first it was a bird that killed him, you know, the snipe, so he never fails to throw stones at any he sees. No, my girl, if you need blame, then blame that blasted war.'

Ruth came over holding out a red dress, while Anna asked what size of foot she had; two light brown sandals dangled from her hand.

'I think my feet are the same size as those,' she said, 'at least I hope they are, they're right bonny.'

'If they fit,' said Anna, 'you keep them. None of us girls have such narrow feet as would fit them; see if you have.'

Like gloves her feet fitted the pretty shoes.

Old Mother Foy said, 'You pop into my varda and try on that dress, and let's see if you have a figure under those dowdy tugs. But first, why don't the girls here take you down the pool water for a dip?' Her friends were eager to wash the late summer's sweat from their bodies, so decided to join her.

The pool was a walk away from the gypsy campsite. And in no time, the happy threesome were splashing about in soapy bubbles, swirling within the deep water hole dug out by the gypsies themselves for such a purpose. Megan felt so good that twinges of guilt dimmed her joy, 'This is heaven, and I never imagined I'd smile again, but I'm having fun and I pray my Bruar will understand when I tell him.'

An hour later, out, dried and dressed, she was certainly a beauty in the red frock and tan shoes. In a strange and absurd way, she was glad she'd been robbed. Mother Foy, who complimented her on how lovely she looked, all fresh and shiny-skinned, was a blessing, and the girls were as sister-like as she could have wished. In the space of a day she'd found a new family, one that cared for her. Light and carefree thoughts lifted her feet to skip and dance arm in arm with Ruth and Anna. It was then she remembered old Mr Thrower saying something about an Egyptian blessing, so she enquired as to what he meant.

'We are descendants of slaves brought here by Romans. When

146

they left this country to defend a falling Rome they abandoned our ancestors. Left at the mercy of people sickened by tyrannical rulers, the slaves were threatened by the locals, and to avoid harm took to moving from place to place. Our ancestors' survival depended on many ploys. Telling fortunes and giving blessings was one way. Many gypsies fled north. Another wave of gypsies came to Britain in the fifteenth century. They were from India, it's believed, and they changed many of the older ways.'

Megan soaked up the stories of these dark-skinned people. She believed they were separated from her kind only by time and borders.

Back within the circle of wagons she was introduced to everyone, and while eating the tasty meat stew, chatted and exchanged travellers' stories of roads and byways. Not many English gypsies go as far up as Scotland these days, she was informed, but there were one or two who had and who had failed to return, having fallen in love with the people and landscape. That night she joined in with songsters and danced for her hosts, astonished that life felt so different. Yes, she and Bruar would find each other, the Seer had told her so, but it seemed as if her journey south would be a joyous, fun-filled road. As she watched and listened to stories and songs she thought on her man. Was he sleeping with a sickness of the mind? Would he remember her or his life as a travelling man? Were caring arms holding him in the night? So many questions swirled in her head, none she had answers to. But deep within she knew they would meet again. Nothing could prevent that, she felt it so strongly.

'What was that?' A sound from outside the varda had her sit upright in the narrow bed. She whispered again to the old woman, snoring beneath a thick eiderdown in her own bed to the rear of the wagon. 'Mother Foy, wake up, someone is at your door.'

'Too bad for them it's not daylight, cause I don't open me door until it is. Ye best get back to sleep.'

Megan pulled a faded, green velvet cover under her chin and waited. Raised as she was under canvas, her dog-like senses were flashing warning signs. She could hear heavy breathing inches from her window. A hand was being drawn along the wooden panels beneath it. Silently she slid her feet onto the floor and sat at the edge of the bed. Eyes darted, following every sound. Footsteps padded the ground. Someone was there and wanted the occupants to know it. Mother Foy's snoring was louder than ever, how could she sleep so soundly when a demon might be planning their end? Would it torch them? Perhaps break down the door, drag her out and murder her? Slit the old lady's throat? Flashes of Rory's red blood oozing away his life into the moss brought sweat beads that trickled from brow-line to ears. This new found haven was becoming unsafe by the second. But wait a minute, was there really someone there? Was it not just this springy new bed? She'd slept in a few since leaving Kirriemor. And what of the dogs lying under many of the vardas, some the size of small ponies. Surely if an intruder was hanging around in the dark a hound would howl? Of course it would! She felt silly for submitting her bare feet to a cold floor and losing over an hour of slumber. Convinced all her fears were unfounded, she at last curled up under the velvet bedcover and went back to sleep.

Next morning the dawn sunlight shone through gossamer webs spun from wagon roof to tree branches; they had been newly abandoned by fat spiders which were off to sleep away the day in some quiet cranny of the quarry wall, bellies bursting with chewed insects. People were up and busying themselves. Some collected firewood while others filled kettles and pans for the first meal of a gypsy day. Megan had risen before anyone else, setting snares around a ruined stone dyke, and came back with a fat rabbit in each hand. Mother Foy beamed proudly through the smoke of her first fill of pipe. 'Well, me little raven-haired moorhen, I've yet to meet as smart-handed a one as yourself.' She took the still warm, dead animals and held them above her head. 'See what this maid of Scotland has brought us this fine day, a change from our hedgehogs,' she said proudly, swinging the rabbits so everyone could glimpse them. Laying them on a flat stone she said, 'Now, girlie, what kind of noise had the fear of Job in you last night?'

'Oh, I had the jitters right enough, but I think my imagination got the better of me. It was hard to ignore my instincts, though.'

'And these instincts of yours, what did they say in the dead of night?'

'At first I felt a hand on the wagon. Something was outside, breathing, the heavy breath was hot, and I felt it. But had there been an intruder it surely would have awakened you. You were snoring loudly, old woman, and hardly moved, so I thought maybe my senses were overdoing things.'

'Never ignore your God-given instincts, gypsies have them too.

It goes with being hounded through the countryside just like your people in Scotland. Some authorities will punish our culture until it be no more. I'll ask if anyone heard anything in the night, while you boil up a brew.'

The old woman drew a long-fringed shawl around her body, sucked on her pipe, took a stick and hobbled off, leaving Megan's peace shaken. She'd convinced herself no one was there in the dark, it had all been her imagination, but now all her fear returned. Her eyes hardly left the old woman as she wandered slowly from wagon to wagon. Soon she returned.

'That tea looks inviting, girlie, pour me a big mug. Nobody heard a dickey-bird last night, apart from owls and bladder-weakened old men. I even asked if Bull had come back, but it seems that he had a fight down Thirsk way. He's staying there a few nights, thank the gods. No doubt we'll have his company soon, though, blast him to kingdom come.'

Lucy, Anna and Ruth scattered her fears when they invited her to come hawking round the tiny villages of the Yorkshire Dales. They had dipped dozens of briar roses in candle wax and hoped to sell some. 'Come and tell lassies they'll marry tall, dark and handsome men, watch their ugly faces light up,' said Ruth.

Anna laughed and added, 'A fortune awaits them all.'

Lucy said she could only go a short part of the way, as she had to meet someone, but would join up with them on their return journey.

Megan, excited by her invitation, hurriedly skinned the rabbits. Then, while eager hounds fought over the innards, she filled water cans, wolfed down some breakfast and was soon waving goodbye to the old woman, skipping off with the three gypsy girls for a day's hawking.

The quarry edge soon faded behind them. As she looked back, Megan felt that if she'd not been part of the gypsy circle it would be hard to believe anyone lived there at all. Only a faint smell of cooking and a spiral of light smoke marked the presence of a bustling encampment, full of families.

After a short while a fork in the road appeared. 'This is where I leave you,' said Lucy.

Megan asked where she was going.

'Not your business,' was the only answer she received.

'She's off to see her man,' said Anna.

'Ain't hers to see,' added Ruth.

'You two better keep it shut, or the eyes will be coming out of your heads, I swear! Now be gone.'

Up till then Lucy had been friendly and kind to Megan, but something about this man she was meeting changed her. She was edgy, even slightly afraid. However, as a newcomer to this secretive band, Megan thought it best not to interfere, and walked off down the path. Anna and Ruth, who'd parted from Lucy with a few choice words, soon caught up with her.

'Better not mention this to Mother Foy,' warned Ruth, and then added, 'Lucy has got entangled in a match not made in heaven. If it's discovered she'll be sent out of the camp. We don't know, having never set an eye on him, but she goes the way of Burnstall Hall, and that be the home of Mr Newton, his honour.' Ruth went on to disclose the fact that 'his honour' owned all the land for miles around, including the quarry they lived in. He allowed the gypsies freedom to roam all over. He employed the men in his fields with harvest work and also used them as beaters during the shooting season. 'He's as good a gent as the likes of us will ever come by, but he's a failing like most men—he can't resist a pretty gypsy girl. She's never said, but we think our Lucy has taken more than a fancy for him.'

Megan listened intently. After a mile or so, she asked if Mr Newton was married.

'Aye, that he is, to a damned nice woman too,' barked Anna. 'Two children they have into the bargain. That's why Lucy would be forced away. Not many give us folks such freedom and work. Every one of us stands to suffer if word of that affair ever gets out. Anyway, it's not right to be with a married man. We told you that, didn't we, Megan?'

'Yes, you did, but I'm the wife of the honourable Bruar Stewart, and nothing that breathes could prise me from my vows. I'd chase the Devil back to hell if he so much as spat near my man.'

The gypsy girls were amazed by her fierce loyalty, which prompted Ruth to comment, 'he be the luckiest of men, this Bruar of yours, that's all I can say.'

'I'm the lucky one,' was her answer, as her thoughts drew her back into the once-familiar world from which she came. 'But tell me, and I promise not a word will go back in way of gossip, why does she fornicate with a married man? I would have taken Lucy to be more of a decent lassie?'

'Why, indeed? Who can say why we walk a blind path when a

clearer, more happy one, lies ahead of us?' Ruth spoke wisely. This prompted Megan to enquire how old she was and whether she had a man? Anna was asked the same question.

Anna told her she'd a boyfriend called Tate Boswell. When the horse sales came round they had planned to meet at Appleby, where gypsies gathered annually.

Ruth wasn't so forthcoming, though, and refused to comment on her love life, instead saying they had best make tracks for Scropet.

The village of Scropet stood out like a beacon at the top of Bleak Fell. Sparsely populated, like most villages in the Dales, it offered little but the merest pennies from hardy folks who were eking a living from the soil. Half of the young who weren't casualties of war had deserted for city life, leaving a few elderly relatives pottering in small gardens, watching the world go by. It was always a treat for them to hear the gypsies come singing and calling on them. Doors opened and a welcome waited. There was not much money, but still food and drink was always offered.

'Hello to you, my dear Mrs Aske,' said Ruth, who seemed to know everyone by name. 'Want me to read the tea-leaves for you?'

Mrs Aske, who walked with a limp and had the use of only one eye, laughed out loud. 'What good would it do me knowing about tomorrow, lass, when I'm grateful I rise with the day's sun. I'm as withered as last year's briar rose.'

'My dear lady, me old gran always says, "Life can change in the flicking of a lamb's tail". For all you know, a smuggler's fortune may be lying under that flowerbed of yours. Just one more dig with the fork and up it comes. You could go on a luxury cruise. Meet some handsome fella and live another twenty years. Now what think ye of that?'

'I think you cheer me no end. Come in and have a meal with me, meagre though it be.'

The threesome stooped under the low entrance to the cottage, went inside and spent a short time with the lonely woman. Later Megan was to discover she had three sons; all lost during yet another horrific battle of the past war.

The girls did a few chores for Mrs Aske, before setting off to hawk flowers in another village further on in the moor.

Other villages offered a better return for their wares, paying them with clothes or crockery. Soon the three girls headed off across Bleak Fell to meet Lucy at the fork in the road. She was waiting with a faraway look on her young face; a bunch of misshapen red roses hung loosely between her fingers. Her clothes smelled of honeysuckle, prompting Ruth to give her a look of disgust. 'Been rolling about in the undergrowth, satisfying the gentry with your body?'

Lucy shrugged her shoulders and told Ruth to find a man of her own.

'Filth, that's all you are, my lass, sheer filth!'

'Well, better that than cowing to Bull Buckley.'

Megan felt a shiver at the mention of that man once more.

'Now, now, Lucy,' said Anna, 'you know since he battered her last she's not even going to look at him.'

'If she don't hold a torch, why was she angry that time he took back a godger woman from York, when he beat Gripper Smith at his last street fight?'

Ruth stormed off, with Anna at her heels apologising for Lucy's looseness of tongue.

Megan had no idea what they were arguing about, but thought that whoever Mr Newton was, he certainly knew how to bring a rosy bloom to Lucy's face.

'You had a good day, Lucy?' she asked, as they walked back to the camp. For a while no answer came, until the smell of cooking and the familiar spiral of smoke told her they were nearing the quarry. Suddenly Lucy drew her to a stop and said, 'Tomorrow night I'm leaving, my man is coming for me. He came last night, but couldn't find my wagon. Tonight I'll meet him at the fork in the road. Promise me you won't say a word, because when Mam finds me gone, she'll whip them that know about Mr Newton and me.'

'Then I was right, there was someone outside the wagon last night,' Megan thought.

'Of course I won't say anything, but does your man not love his wife and children enough that he has to leave them for a gypsy girl?' She felt like biting on her tongue, that she had pushed too far. After all, she was a mere guest, someone hitching a ride, so to speak. 'I'm sorry, Lucy, I didn't mean to poke my nose in. It's your business, and I'd no right.'

Lucy smiled, and whispered, 'He makes me feel like a queen. We laugh at the same things and he makes the gentlest love to me.' She opened her palm to Megan and said, 'This is not the hand of a well-bred person. I am no lady, but he has a way with him that takes the difference out of our lives. When together I am neither low-bred, nor he high—we are entwined by one thing, and that is the heaven-sent gift of love. Surely ye can see that?'

'Lucy, far be it from me to hurt you, but heaven sent him another, and what you are doing is to steal. It's not for you. My man and I, we were joined. No third party. I wish you all success, but that's all I can say. Don't worry, my lips are sealed. If your Mam finds out, I'll take a whipping. Still, it's a high price you set; everybody living in harmony here will have to move on, because you let a heart rule a head. In the glens I had to be strong, thankfully while my man fought in the war no other tempted me, but if there had been anybody, I'd not have yielded—no way!'

All the joy of a good healthy day's hawking was lost to Lucy's ill-gotten love. Anna drifted off to her wagon, Lucy to hers, and Ruth to hers, while Megan tiptoed gently over to a snoozing Mother Foy. Not wanting to waken the old lady, she added more sticks to an almost extinguished fire. Sparks shot upwards, then fell back into the boiled kettle suspended from iron chitties. Steam hissed forth and caused her friend to stir. Slowly she sat upright, and adjusted a crumpled cushion behind her back. 'Hello, girlie. Good day?' she enquired, then added, 'I have done a grand pot of my best vegetable soup; it's over by the varda wheel cooling. Get washed up and we'll eat. How was your day?' she asked once more.

'My day was just the best,' she lied, and said all four of them had wandered the moor road, stopping at each village. 'What nice folks live in these parts,' she told her host, 'they remind me of the Glen Coe people, but that was a long time ago. They gave to Mammy if they could, and sometimes gave what they couldn't afford.'

'Yes, they're a damn worthy lot, I'll agree with you. Now get your hands washed and we'll eat.'

Megan worried what problems Lucy's affair would cause if discovered; where would the circle of gypsies go? Winter was not so far round the corner, and with autumn approaching by now they should be finding a winter ground. At least that was what happened in Scotland. She asked the old woman, who told her they were already on their wintering ground, and that she prayed nothing would happen to change things, because there was no other place for many a rough mile. This made matters worse. Megan felt she was betraying everyone by keeping the knowledge of Lucy's coming elopement to herself. A

153

word once given can't be broken, though, but she still had next day to try to persuade Lucy to change her mind. If not, she would threaten to tell Mother Foy, who was held in great respect in the band. If anyone should know, then it had to be her.

A cold breeze sent most folks indoors to spend the evening. Megan sat alone by the dying embers of the fire. In time a lonely Ruth joined her. For a while both sat, staring into the red glowing ashes. Ruth spoke first. 'You wondering about me and the Bull?'

'Mother Foy warned me about him, but it's not my business what you do with your life. After all, who am I but a stranger?'

'A stranger is someone who comes among us without a voice—I wouldn't say you were like that. I don't usually talk about my love life, but two years back when I knew nothing of men I foolishly gave my womanhood to Buckley. He's a handsome brute. Made me laugh, he did. Head over heels as they say, that's what I was, hook, line and sinker, his to do with as he pleased, and by God, that he did.'

Aware that Ruth had begun to cry, she listened yet kept her eyes off her face. She knew enough about this girl to see that her sense of pride had long since suffered a blow. Should she interfere and ask why the name of Buckley was forced through clenched teeth? In whispered tones and as tactfully as she could, she asked what had happened.

While old Mother Foy snored contented in her wagon bed and the dogs sniffed round the quarry floor, Ruth shared her pain.

'Anna thinks I was angry because Bull brought a godger woman back after his fight with Gripper Smith, but what she didn't know was that the night before the fight, he held two hands round my throat and warned he'd kill me. You see, I asked him to marry me. Oh, of course, the temper was in him, but I thought like a fool that if we shared a bed, then I could stop his mad dog fighting. I was worried his head was taking too many kickings. God, if you'd seen the look on his face, you'd have thought the Devil was in his soul. He screamed at me, 'I'm the King of the Gypsies—no one has, or ever will, beat me!' There was no stopping the anger in him. I thought my end had come. I don't know to this day what stopped him from strangling me, honest, I felt the blood boil in my head. If it hadn't been for his mate Hawen Collins calling his name, I'm positive you wouldn't be speaking with me this night. And what makes it ten times worse, he broke Gripper Smith's back that night, snapped him in two. Did it bother him that he'd taken a life? Was he remorseful? Not a bit! When she came back linking arms with him and covering his bruised face with red kisses, that godger woman's presence was his message to me, saying "Back off".'

'Don't tell me you would have taken him in after trying to throttle you, then breaking another man's back?'

'No, we were finished. But I was his woman for a whole year, and that hurt.'

'I'm a stranger to you, Ruth, and I'm humbled by the confidence you put in me, but it's well rid of him you are. I say that without ever seeing Bull Buckley.'

'Oh, the pleasure isn't far off; he's due back any day now. I feel him in my bones—the pig!'

Next morning, the breeze from the night before had whipped up into a good-going gale, just ideal to dry heavy covers and blankets. Mother Foy hadn't needed to instruct Megan to fill the enamel bath with water and start scrubbing bed-covers. Years of never ignoring a strong drying wind had her well taught. Anyway, it gave her plenty of time to think about how she'd try to convince Lucy to change her mind. The rest of the womenfolk in the circle had similar ideas about harnessing the gale. By mid-morning, ropes tied from wagon-tops to trees danced and swung with bedclothes, heavy skirts, babies' woollies, old men's shirts and young men's trousers. Young women, covered in soapy suds and smelling of strong carbolic, sang and laughed their way through the wind, thanking an unseen God for his gift of clothes-drying weather.

After a light lunch of bread, cheese and apples, the four girls, satisfied with a successful washday, set off to frolic on the moor. The wind would blow a while yet. Lots of folding clothes and bed-making awaited their return, but every day has a time for relaxation and 'What better time,' thought Megan, 'to work on Lucy.'

Anna and Ruth found an area where no heather grew. As they stretched tired muscles on the warmed earth, Megan asked Lucy to walk with her, making the excuse that she wasn't tired. 'We Scots prefer to walk off our stiffness.'

Lucy knew that she'd have to talk, to explain, and so took the hint. With the others hidden from view, they sat down on some rocks further along the moor road. 'Don't try to change my mind, because last night I could think of nothing else. Even today, while scrubbing piles of dirty clothes, Mr Newton's face was uppermost in my thoughts. You must see, I'll love no other. If I don't go now, tonight, I'll never look at anyone as long as I live.' Laughing nervously, she went on, 'Take your love, for instance, this Bruar of yours, here you are with complete strangers, you take your life in your hands for sure. Not knowing if he's alive or dead, you have left familiar ground to search for him. If that's not blind faith, then I don't know what is.'

She wanted to tell her about the photograph, but the story was too long. 'I am a married woman, Lucy. I search for my husband, who I believe is a casualty of war. Somewhere in the south of this land he waits. By the word of a Highland seer's spirit, I fear he has a sort of sleeping sickness. I feel his heart beating at night when I sleep. Please try to understand, we walked our paths as children side by side, we were meant for each other. Your man is married, he and his wife share children. To top it all, he's gentry, not your kind. A match like that will haunt you both. Is it worth causing all the suffering to the quarry families, to your Mam?'

'What if Bruar is dead, eh? Say one day you find him. What if he has already passed on? Never woke up from this so-called sleeping sickness? What will you do then?' Lucy by now was showing signs of fear and anger; she rose from her stone seat and gripped Megan tightly by the shoulders as she repeated her questions.

'I shall find the money to take his remains home, and bury him beside his proud family at the Parbh Lighthouse. Then I shall spend what's left of my life tending his grave.'

The severity of Lucy's questioning settled a doubt she'd long put into the farthest corner of her mind. Never would she have continued with her quest, if her instincts had not told her that Bruar was alive and waiting. No, she'd not fill her head with such negativity, never.

Lucy sat down, apologised and went on, now in a quieter tone of voice. 'There is something I failed to tell you. We have no choice and must go away together.' For a moment she hesitated, then continued, 'Mr Newton is being blackmailed.' She shuffled her feet, closed her eyes and waited for a response.

'Somebody will tell his wife about you both. Is that what you mean?'

'Yes. It happened not long after we began meeting in secret. One night we were followed into a byre. Whoever he was, the blackmailer certainly heard enough to finish Mr Newton's reputation. I told him not to pay and tell his wife, but he said that he doesn't want me to suffer. We've spoken of nothing else for ages. Then last month he saw his solicitor to sign over the estate into his eldest son's hands. He's only seven now, but when of age all will be his. In the meantime Mrs Newton will be in charge.'

'What about the gypsies living in the quarry, surely she will want rid of them, given that one has stolen her husband? Sorry, lass, I have to be plain with you.'

'He's put in place instructions that they are to be left at peace. Everything will work out, believe me. And that evil blackmailer, whoever he is, will get not another penny more.' Lucy searched Megan's face for her response.

It was clear to see they were indeed lovers. Megan was not in favour of the union, but maybe people could fall out of love, and maybe that is what had happened to the honourable Mr Newton.

The day, the wind and the conversation were coming to a calm close. Lucy slipped an arm through hers, giving her a sisterly peck on the cheek.

'Rachel, my dear sister, probably living in luxury by now in America, never ever kissed like me that,' she thought. She felt drawn to Lucy, and sad that of all the gypsy girls she was the one soon to leave.

'Come on, Lucy. I'm thinking this last hour will have dried most of the washing, let's make tracks. Anyway do you not have plans to go somewhere with a certain person this coming night?'

'Thank you so very much, my Scottish friend, for understanding. I know you don't approve, but not many will. I thank you just the same. Once again, I trust you'll keep my secret?'

'I won't say a word. Now, will you look at Ruth and Anna, they are still sleeping soundly just where we left them.'

Anna awakened from her siesta feeling peckish. 'I have a pocketful of peppermints old Mr Thrower gave me, do you want one?' asked Ruth. She offered them in cupped hands. But before they could help themselves, she scattered the sweets over the purple heather, laughing as they cursed her for the mischievous act.

Mother Foy, sitting comfortably in her old chair, smiled as the youthful foursome scrambled down the quarry embankment, throwing peppermint sweets at each other. 'Ah,' she thought, 'how well I remember making my own nimble steps. Oh, that I were their age again.' She'd managed to gather in half the washing load which was folded on the varda steps. 'I couldn't reach the high sheets,' she said, pointing at a rope Megan had suspended from two trees, then added,

'You can get that lot down, and it's a mystery how you managed to tie the rope so high.'

'I've what you call a good stretch o' arm.' She clambered the steep wall and removed, from a narrow ledge, a line of net curtains.

'You seem in fine fettle. Had a good day, girlie?'

'Yes, I suppose I have at that.' She felt a lot better having talked to Lucy.

From a bend on the road leading into the quarry a small boy appeared. He was shouting and panting. All eyes turned to see what the commotion was. 'Bull's coming, and he's doing a fight, right here, here in the quarry. Big bare-knuckler, twenty-rounder with Moses Durin. They'll be here anytime now. Move aside! Move aside!'

Megan, surprised and confused, turned to the old woman, who bade her to get a quick bite and then to go to safe quarters with the womenfolk. Already some were hastily throwing cardigans on, shawling babies and herding youngsters up the narrow path leading from the quarry. Anna called over, 'Come on, Megan, best you don't see this bloodbath. Back to the moor until it be over.'

Megan had heard so much about Bull Buckley that a form of morbid curiosity was half-telling her to stay and see if all the build-up was true. 'I think I'll stay here and look on,' she answered.

'You'll do no such thing, my lady. Now, here's a bit bread and ham, take yourself off. That's an order. I'll fetch me old pals and we'll play cards in the varda, while the mad maulers batter what little sense they have into the dry earth.' Mother Foy flashed her a serious look, and without argument Megan nodded.

She'd never heard her host speak so forcefully, and thought it better to smother her cat inquisitiveness and go with the others. Still, a wee peek might be possible if she hid up on the quarry lip. She followed as far as the vantage point, then found a big rock. From here she'd witness what was sending people scurrying like mice in a dark cowshed from a torch held by the farmer.

Way down below, men were scattering their campfires and dousing flames, loudly exchanging opinions on which fighter they thought would win. 'Bull will mush him,' said one, while another swore Moses had the height to beat Buckley.

She could just make out Mother Foy's wagon, and already the old woman had it shuttered and locked. 'No doubt she'll have several old folks crowded inside playing cards, having seen it all before,' she thought.

Butterflies fluttered under her ribs. Adrenaline forced her eyes wide, ears strained to hear the fighting talk down below. Then a giant of a man walked briskly into the quarry. Circles of excited men chanted 'Moses—Moses—Moses!' Fists punched the evening air. He stopped, darting eyes from wagons to trees, as if checking his fighting ground. He grabbed a boy, a small elf-like youngster, and ordered him to make certain there were none of Bull's men hiding to knife him when he got the better of his opponent. Like a rat the tiny lad shot in and out of every available corner, calling out repeatedly, 'Nothing in here, Mo.'

Then, little by little, the baying of the crowd for blood fell silent. All eyes turned toward the man who would fight Moses—Bull Buckley himself.

'So this is the beast, then,' she thought, 'let's see if he's as bad a bear as I'm told.'

He wasn't as tall as she'd imagined, but by God he was broad all right, like a small bullock. 'He's well named there,' she thought. He'd thick, wavy, red hair that fell over one eye. His shirtsleeves rolled above the elbows exposed hamshanks for forearms.

She couldn't make out either man's facial expression, being so far up, but she was glad in a way she couldn't.

Ruth, who had wondered why she wasn't with them on the moor, came back to find her. She huddled down. 'God, look what the night's dragged in,' she snarled, eyeing up Buckley. 'He'll rip Moses to shreds. I'm glad we brought in the washing, it'll stop it getting blood-splattered. Durin will feel a pained man by this night's end.'

'Do you mind if I stay here, Ruth? Being from a mild-natured tribe we never did that—the bare knuckling, that is. I'm curious to see how they perform.'

'You stay, fill your mind. I promise you, though, that by the end of it your bread and ham will be yellow vomit on the grass.' Ruth crawled away, leaving Megan to watch. She didn't scare that easy, though. After finding big Rory with his throat cut and O'Connor's face split open, it would take a lot to sicken her. 'It's only a fight,' she told herself, 'There's nothing scary about two brainless mongrels bleeding each other, just something to tell my Bruar about when we meet.' As she hid in relative safety behind her natural hiding place of slate rock, down below more and more spectators poured into the circle. Torches were lit and held high, so no one would miss a punch or a spit. Voices screamed odds on Moses, while as many did the same for Bull. Four men came running up the road. Daylight was fading fast, but she could just make out that each held a chunky pole; a bit like a small caber. For a minute she wondered what they were for, watching as each of the men dug holes an equal distance apart, then dropped their wooden posts in. A young lad ran around with a rope, and in no time the pair of fighters stood facing each other like gladiators in a square booth.

Moses had a large cigar clamped between his teeth. Every so often he'd remove it, spit at Bull's feet, toss back his head, laugh, and shout at the sky, causing every man there to fall silent as the grave. 'Look what thinks can beat me—a shit-stump pikey, and me the best street-fighter ever drew breath, born with raging knuckles.' He seemed to bite the air like a coiled snake, lowered his eyelids, and then popped his eyeballs to roll them around in his head. Each movement was to his followers a message of aggression. Another jerk of his jaw almost shoved his eyes out of their sockets, and his head, which was shaped like a rugby ball, turned a deep purple. 'Moses,' he roared, 'I'm the only one.' Then, as if an invisible demon had leapt out and begun playing fiddle music from hell, he performed a form of war dance, clicking red leather heeled boots and swirling his coat tails back and forth like a dancer.

This was looking more like fun, but the fading light was creating shadows and obscurity. From her hidden spot she couldn't make out who was who. The hand-held torches were dimming. 'I'll have to get down there,' she thought, 'I have to see who wins.'

Folding her petticoat and flowing dress over one arm she scrambled down the rough quarry wall. Halfway down she found a sturdy tree stump and twined her free arm around it. Resting her chin onto knees she waited with eager excitement. From this new vantage-point she saw every sinewy muscle of the caveman-like pair.

Bull, who'd been silent throughout Moses' ranting and dancing, turned to his mate Hawen and stretched out an open hand. A hush spread within the crowd. Hawen pulled something from a bag and put it on the waiting hand; it was a curled-up hedgehog. As Bull grabbed it and pushed a fist into its belly, a great gasp of 'Oooohhhh!' came from the mesmerised crowd. The prickly little animal stretched its curled spine. Then, without warning, he sank his teeth into its nose. It squealed and he crunched into its head. He spat out an eye and cracked its skull between two rows of flashing white teeth. Looking around every single person—and by now there were dozens—he slowly sucked out the poor beast's brains and swallowed them, then handed what remained back to Hawen.

Ruth had warned her. The yellow vomit came forth like a fountain, spattering the moss-covered tree stump. She felt faint, her grip weakened, and had it not been for Lucy who'd joined her she'd have fallen to the quarry floor, probably breaking a limb. 'Stupid thing, why did you not go with the others? A fight with these pigs is never a sight for squeamish bellies.'

'I haven't got a sickly gut. I can take a lot, but not seeing an innocent animal being mauled for fun I can't. It makes me ashamed of being related to gypsy origins if this is what's done.'

'This is not our ways, but there are evil types in every group. Those people down there are the dregs of society. You never see them until something like this brings them from beneath stones. Beggars, drunkards, thieves, murderers, they seem to crawl from the sewers. Surely you have them in Scotland?'

'I think we do, but I never saw any, apart from a certain Irishman. I heard Mammy call them "blue bucks".'

'Never mind watching anymore, this will get worse. Come with me, I know of a narrow path just over here.' She pointed to a shadowy corner concealed behind other tree stumps.

'No, Lucy, you'd better get off and meet your Mr Newton, I'll find the ledge path myself. I was born among mountains and rock faces. A small quarry wall is nothing to me, honest. No, I'm going to watch this fight, even if only this one time. I want to tell my Bruar all the gory bits when we next meet.'

'Then I'll keep you company, because we don't meet until midnight.'

The pair snuggled closely, sharing a shawl, while down below the crowd was being roused to fever pitch by the brutal antics of both Bull and Moses.

'The more they perform, the faster and heavier go the bets. Along with the rats, some men in that crowd are cattle-thieves, horse-dealers, true life outlaws. A lot of big money is being pushed back and forth,' Lucy informed her.

'Who would you back, Lucy, if you had the lowie, that is?'

'Bull Buckley has the devil on his side and has never been beat. Moses is here like many more to take him out.'

'Yes, but you haven't said—who would you put money on?'

161

'I pray both kill each other, then this quiet part of England will revert back to the peaceful place it once was. Ever since that beast has taken the road with us we've had nothing but a bad name. He brings the lawless with him, and nobody likes a hair on his head. I tell you, if I were a man he wouldn't be standing there. He'd be six feet under.'

'You really hate him that much? I heard it was Ruth he ill-treated.'

'Ruth's my full cousin, and if you'd seen her two eyes when he'd finished with her then you'd hate him too. Her Daddy and mine were killed by a runaway horse. They had spent days breaking a big red stallion. It was a rogue animal, had a brain sickness and couldn't be trusted. Her mother never got over his death, so took a mixture of deadly nightshade and black throat mushrooms, witch poison, and died in total agony with her innards coming up her throat, dark green coloured. That's what witch poison does to you, though.' She began shaking, Megan held her close. 'What's wrong?' she asked.

'My mother lives for me, that's why she'll go mental when she knows what I'm doing. But you promised not to say.'

Megan promised, but wasn't paying much attention, for down below things were turning uglier as the two fighters were by now eye to eye, hissing and spitting. 'He's like that mad horse.' Megan's heart was beating fast.

'What horse? Who?'

'The one who killed your and Ruth's fathers; him, Bull Buckley.' Without realising it, her voice had carried to the crowd below.

Bull looked up and for a moment she froze in terror as their eyes met. Never had a man's eyes held such evil. She turned away, closing out the stare. Then, as if hypnotised, she found her face being drawn back, back to stare into those pools of sheer wickedness.

A right hook from Moses' clenched fist broke the spell. The ground shook along with Bull's jaw. Pieces of hedgehog brains spewed into the crowd. The fight had begun in earnest.

Bull lunged forward, then putting one foot back threw a punch that caught Moses square on. His head dropped to the left, Bull straightened it with a hard right elbow; teeth and blood spurted from his half-open mouth. He fell. Bull picked him up with two punches below the ribs. Moses teetered for a moment, then over he went. Clouds of still warm fire ash spiralled in the air. Punters began choking on it, while others rubbed their eyes. It made the crowd's fury worse. The boxing ring got flattened, and soon Moses, not getting to his feet, began to feel theirs.

'No!' roared Bull, 'he's mine.' Like rag dolls he threw aside the fired-up spectators until a form of calm was regained. The crowd spaced themselves and waited for Bull Buckley's special ending. 'Wait, boys, now he be a dead man,' someone dared whisper. Buckley grabbed the offender by the neck. Hissing like a viper, he asked through clenched teeth, 'Who be a dead man, then?'

The one who had dared to open his mouth was left with no choice as Bull's grip tightened on the grimy muffler around his neck. 'Bloody big Moses Durin, that's who,' he said, gasping for air, then scurried away on all fours between fire ash and trouser-legs, like a terrified rat, when Bull loosened his vice-like grip.

Moses began to stir and slowly rose on hands and knees, when Bull let out a scream, drew back his right leg and with inhuman ferocity let his opponent take its full force to his stomach. Bull growled, ripping his shirt off at the same time. Megan was gripping at Lucy's arm, wondering what manner of end was coming Moses' way. It surely was coming. Bull Buckley was holding every card. Lucy began to shake. She rose to her feet from her precarious seat and screamed. All eyes looked upwards. 'You wicked bastard, Buckley. Don't you go and kill him, bringing the muskries [police] here, because you'll shoot with the crows, leaving your mess on our backs.'

Megan yanked her down and whispered, 'Why should you worry, are you not this night deserting everyone?'

'I'm thinking on you all—me Mam, Mother Foy, the children, Ruth, Anna, the old ones. Moses ain't a gypsy; he's a godger. If Bull kills him the wagons will be broke to smithereens by those searching for that hound from hell. Oh, it don't matter if us gypsies kill each other, but lay a wrong hand on a godger, then every law officer in the shire will be on us.'

Bull Buckley couldn't hear them speak, but he had heard Lucy shout. He sneered while he lifted the limp head of an almost comatose Moses and called up, 'Look, little Lucy, see how a fool meets his maker.' He drew in a deep breath, laid the head down in a gentle fashion, like a cat teasing a mouse, and bestriding his prey he fixed a steely gaze on the man lying below him in the dirty ash. If a leaf had fallen it would have been heard, such was the silence of the crowd. For the last time of his wild existence, Moses Durin opened dazed eyes.

'You've breathed the same air as me for too long.' Like a sledge-hammer splitting rock, Bull's metal capped boot thudded in, and the skull made a gruesome popping sound. But that didn't satisfy Bull, he had to finish the job. 'Get me a hatchet Hawen,' he called out. Hawen seemed to live for every command from his friend and soon stood at his side, holding out a big butcher's hatchet. 'There ye go, bully boy,' he said, like a teacher's pet offering an apple

'Don't do it,' someone screamed from the crowd. 'Leave 'im for the muskries to find, Bull,' another voice called out. 'Come on now, Bull, that's a good lad; King of the Gypsies forever, eh Bull?'

'Shut your coward mouths and watch how I does me work.'

Rays from the rising moon caught the blade for an instant as it sliced into the exposed neck. Like a stone the head wobbled and rolled to rest awkwardly at Bull's feet. He lifted it up, blood dripping from the gaping neck. 'Look, the lot of ye, this is what makes me King. I does what I likes, to whoever I want!'

Megan buried her head into Lucy's chest. 'Please tell me that's a trick, and Durin will get up and both take a bow.'

'What ye saw was what ye got, but try to blot it out. The only good thing is, Bull will not hang around, there'll be a big price on him after this. But Mother Foy might decide it best to move away from here anyway. I'll have to go myself, it must be nearing midnight.'

'Lucy, take care of yourself. I don't want to stay here now, so in the morning I'll take my chances alone on the road.' She watched as Lucy disappeared up the quarryside. Down below the crowd had gone, including Bull and Hawen, leaving Moses' body and his head for the resident gypsies to dispose of. She felt disgusted and sick. One by one she watched the other women return, then silently followed them down.

Old Mother Foy opened her wagon door. Her guests walked past Moses' remains, shaking their heads as if they had seen it all before. Ruth and Anna called up to her, 'Megan, give us a hand to bury big Moses before word reaches the law.'

'No,' she screamed. 'I want no part in that. I'm away tomorrow, hell to the lot of you.'

Her words trailed off as she ran away and onto the moor. Tears welled in her young eyes. 'I want my Bruar,' she called inwardly, 'I want my man.'

She seemed to wander the moorland for ages, the earlier horrors bursting into her innermost thoughts. That awful demon that derived such pleasure from sucking hedgehog's brains and severing heads was stalking the depth of her troubled mind. If she fell blindly into heather clumps once, she fell a dozen times. How could such a peaceful day have so bitter an ending, she told herself, hardly believing the sick events she had witnessed. Then, while lying in the undergrowth she heard raised voices, men shouting, and a woman too. How close they were she had no idea, and with only the odd glimpse of moonlight peeping through an ever-thickening cloudy sky, it was difficult to see anything. Still, she had to get nearer. With her knowledge of moor terrain, she knew how to slither through thick heather. Soon a narrow sheep track could be felt beneath her feet, and she edged closer to the raised voices. 'Lucy—that's Lucy,' she thought.

The wind rose and whistled around her; suddenly the track lost itself, pushing a spur of rock in her way. She huddled behind it. The voices grew louder, but so did the night wind. Apart from Lucy, she couldn't make out who the others were. Mr Newton would no doubt be there, but who were the others, and why the arguing? Someone was full of rage, that was certain.

'You pay up, or else I tell the madam everything, do you hear me?'

'Tell her, if that's all you're good for. I've parted with enough money and won't pay you a single penny more. Now get out of our way, you filthy dog.'

'That must be Lucy's man friend,' she thought. Clear moonlight scattered yellow light across the sky. Now she saw four figures: Lucy and three others.

'Get him,' shouted one.

'Don't hurt her. Lucy run home, save yourself, don't worry about me.'

Megan held her breath, heart beating like a drum. There was something terrible taking place, but earlier events had taken their toll and she curled back behind her rock, too afraid to look. Noises indicated a fight, she could hear thudding, shouting, and then silence.

'Did you kill 'im?' some one asked, panting.

'Sure as stone I did. What about her?'

'Consider it done, easy as snaring a rabbit it'll be.'

'Good, now strip him, there's bound to be a few shillings. When ye kill the girl, take the cases and meet me up at Stropet. We'll head to York from there. I've to meet up with some men and get me winnings from the fight.'

Megan covered her mouth with both hands, felt her face set hard like stone: it was Buckley. The other man obviously was his sidekick, Hawen Collins.

The moon seemed sickened by the night's events and shrouded itself with cloud. How long she sat with her head in cold hands, in pitch dark, was anybody's guess. Only when she'd mustered enough courage, and with eyes become accustomed to the dark, did she rise to view the scene of murder. Her worst fears were confirmed. The corpse of a man lay face down among the heather. Blood had already congealed on small rocks by its side. Rory's stiff form flashed into her mind. Far off in the distance she thought she heard a scream, but perhaps not. Maybe an owl had misjudged its prey and taken a large rabbit. Slowly she walked away, glancing backward. The plot was all too obvious. Bull Buckley was the blackmailer. How could she tell on him, though? He'd kill her, suck out her eyes and feast on her brains. She had to get away, and hoped poor, broken-hearted Lucy had done the same.

Back at Mother Foy's a hush had fallen. There was no sign of Moses or his head; they'd sufficiently cleaned up. A fire was blazing where hours earlier a baying mob stood circling a horror unequalled in her eyes. She sat on an empty seat and warmed herself. Should she tell the old woman about Mr Newton? No, she'd let Lucy do that when she came home, if she came home. She put more sticks on the fire and waited on the coming dawn. What would it bring?

—

'Everybody get up, quick now, come on, let's be having ye.'

She'd fallen asleep at the fire. In a daze she watched black uniformed men banging on doors and shouting. They were kicking dogs, knocking over water cans, throwing seats and benches all across the quarry floor. 'Get out of your flea-pits, bloody gyppo killers.'

Quickly she stood up and composed herself. Either Moses' murder had reached the ears of the police or Mr Newton's body had been discovered.

Mother Foy threw open her half-door, fear etched on her old face. It had turned her lantern jaws white and drawn. 'What's wrong, girlie?' she asked, seeing her standing fully-clothed by the fire.

'The muskries must think someone's been murdered, they are acting right mean and angry.'

The old woman stepped slowly down the wagon steps, shaking her head, 'Bull Buckley, blast him to kingdom come, he never fails to get us the bad name. I knew the minute big Moses Durin walked upon our peaceful ground that the devil would be at his heels, and he'd come in the guise of that goblin from hell, bloody Buckley!'

Megan stretched out a helping hand to steady Mother Foy, avoiding eye contact as best she could, the previous night's terrors tearing inside her brain.

'Girlie,' she said, 'I get the feeling something mighty bad has come upon us.'

Her words made Megan tremble. She whispered, 'I never seen a man's head come rolling off his body before, I ran up onto the moor last night to escape this place. This very fire we heat ourselves at was probably built on a pool of blood. Now I'm going to fill the kettle, I think a cup of tea will be all we'll get this day.' She righted a water can that had been kicked over and went off to fill it at the stream. However, before she could go, a thin-faced copper grabbed her arm and told her to stay put. She sat the can down and walked over by Mother Foy, who was being spoken to by another policeman. The elderly lady was shaking, eyes glazed and staring.

'What's the matter? Surely a dozen or so muskries are a common sight to you?'

'They've found a body on the moor. It be our dear Mr Newton. He's been murdered! Whoever brought this on our heads will bring our destruction. Oh God, that nice Mr Newton, and him happily married with two good children. Who could have done such a thing? Four generations of his family line have given us freedom to roam on their land. This be a bad day, oh a bad day.'

Megan wrapped her arms around the visibly frightened old lady, lest she fall from shock. Soon the police made their way round to them. She prayed the awful scene from the previous night's grisly happening wouldn't show up in her face. It would be hard, though; she wasn't one to lie.

A thick-set middle-aged man dressed in plain clothes walked over. She'd watched him poking under canvases, lifting baskets, going in and out of vardas. He said very little, but by the slit-eyed look on his rugged face she could tell he was a thinker. He was taking everything in, and it would be hard to pull wool over those eyes.

'Well then, I suppose you both saw nothing, heard nothing, and like the rest slept peaceful in your beds.'

'I heard the wind get up in the night, a pair o' owls took to fighting. Blasted tree branch scraping agin the varda roof put paid to a good night's slumber, but other than that we heard nothing.' Mother Foy had composed herself to appear almost normal.

Megan nodded in agreement, then tried once more to reach the water can, but was again hindered by the thin-faced policeman. 'Can I fetch some water for the old woman's breakfast, arse with moustache?' she asked.

'Impudent bitch,' retorted the man, then, 'That's no English accent. If I'm not mistaken you're a Scot. Why are you here with this lot?'

'Leave the girl alone, she's the daughter of a cousin. He married a Scot. I'm looking after her for a while, Mr Martin, sir.'

Why did her old friend need to lie? After all, she'd no knowledge of last night. But it dawned on her that here was a wise old woman who'd been around a long time. Maybe she sensed something.

The detective accepted her reasons for Megan's presence, then warned everyone they'd be back the next day, so his parting words were 'Nobody move on'.

A fearful silence settled on the campsite, it was stifling. The gypsies held their breath, watching as one by one the policemen piled into two charabanc-type motors, that looked like square tin cans on wheels.

Detective Martin had a car, which spurted and spat into life, taking him and the thin-faced constable off down the road. They had not travelled fifty yards when a young man almost threw himself in front of the vehicle. He was in a terrible state, panting and sweating as if he brought news so awful it would shock trees from their roots.

'A young lass! There's the body of a girl on the far east side of Bleak Fell.'

Megan's heart froze. 'Lucy! He's murdered Lucy!' she cried out. Visions of last night's mist-shrouded events flashed vividly on her mind's eye. She dropped onto her knees, remembering the scream she'd blamed on an owl. The one she thought had taken a heavy rabbit. It hadn't been a rabbit, but poor, sad Lucy, and her killer had two legs, not wings.

'What's that?' shouted Martin, hearing what she said from the open window of his car.

Megan ignored him and ran towards the gypsies. 'That beast Buckley, the one you cowards gave ground to fight and kill another man, I saw the fiend kill Mr Newton, and order Hawen to get Lucy. You let him come and never lifted a finger to stop him. Bloody cowards you are!'

Every one of the gypsies turned their backs to her, older children joined their dogs beneath the wagons, while little ones clung to their mothers' skirts.

Detective Martin caught up with Megan and held her tightly by both arms. Here was a witness, a gypsy willing to expose another gypsy, unheard of. He wasn't letting her go. 'Constable,' he summoned the thin-faced one, 'take this young lady into custody.'

Mother Foy hobbled up and called to the eager detective, 'A word in your ear if you please.'

Beady-eyed Martin, impatient to get Megan away from the gypsies, said, 'What is it, old woman? Can't you see I've a crime needing solved?'

'Now, everyone in these parts knows you to be an expert policeman, a real clever fella, a solver o' crimes. Would you agree with me?'

He pushed out his chest, swallowing her compliment as she continued.

'I've seen you come and go onto sites ever since you had the brain of a babe and the face to go with it. I've watched you find wisdom dealing with us gypsies. Now tell us, have you ever come across a single gypsy who'd say anything agin another?'

'Can't say as I have, but there's always a first.' He'd found the first one, as far as he was concerned, and needed to find out what she had to say further. The old woman raised her voice so that all could hear, including the police.

'She's not fit in the head, my poor little niece; she'll only fill your good selves with nonsense. She thinks Bull Buckley was the killer. Bull came here last night for a bare-knuckle fight, no one denies it. He fought well he did, won a few rounds, but I picked him up from the gutter and washed his wounds. That man, well, let's say he was out for the count; the end of the fight saw both of his eyes closed with bruises. If he killed anybody, then it must have been with eyes shut."

Megan could hardly believe that her friend was defending a killer. She broke away and ran over to Lucy's distraught mother, who was donning her coat to go and identify her daughter's body.

'She was going away with Mr Newton. Buckley was blackmailing him. He killed him and Hawen killed Lucy. I'm willing to be whipped for saying it, but if it puts that devil from hell behind bars, then I'll gladly tell all I know, because Lucy told me herself.'

Lucy's mother pushed her aside abruptly. 'Shut your mouth. My girl didn't fall by his or any other's hand, and she took her own life. I begged her not to fret over a boy she'd met during the war. We heard recently that he was dead. She warned me she couldn't live without him, foolish girl, and now she's dead because of it.'

The policemen stood around, watching and waiting.

Megan's head was spinning with all kinds of dark thoughts, 'How could a mother distraught about her daughter's murder tell such lies,' she thought. Her mind was in turmoil; drastic measures were called for. 'Take me into jail. I did it,' she screamed. 'Come on, get the bloody handcuffs on me.'

Mother Foy lifted her stick and brought it hard down across her back 'She's a gowpie, don't take any notice. She sees demons everywhere.'

She fixed her gaze deep into Martin's eyes, and summoned him close to her so that only he could hear. 'Now, she may be telling truth or she might not, but what would folks say if they were to discover that Mr Newton, the finest gentleman around these parts, had been dipping into gypsy flesh? What would that do to his family's standing among the nobility? And what about his dear wife and innocent children—what of their reputations?' She lowered her eyes to the ground and waited for his response.

Mother Foy's words made crystal clear sense to him. He knew that his hands were tightly bound by the need to protect the aristocracy of the land. He summoned his troops.

'Come on boys, let's go. She's just a stupid gypsy gowpie, with nothing between her ears.'

Megan, powerless to persuade a living soul of the truth of her story, watched until all that was left of the law officers was a cloud of thin wheel dust.

'What the hell got into you just now?' asked Mother Foy. 'We know who killed Newton and Lucy, but we gypsies never, ever, bring the law into our affairs.'

'How the hell are you going to punish Buckley? He'll chew you all into little balls and spit you out. Bloody cowards, that's what you are. And what's a gowpie anyroad?'

170

'There are ways to sort Buckley, gypsy ways. Now, maybe we haven't got a fixer here in the quarry, but word's out now and soon others will tighten a noose for his neck. You take a look at the face on Lucy's mother and tell me she's not planning revenge. If the law get to him first she'll rot with anger for not having avenged her girl. No, his days are numbered. And a gowpie is simple.'

'Simple what?'

'Touched.'

Ruth and Anna, who had stayed silent through out the commotion approached her and said, 'We are going onto the moor to fetch Lucy's body, will you help us?'

'Of course, but surely the police will be watching over Lucy's remains, seeing as a murder has taken place?'

'They don't care about my Lucy, only the Honourable Mr Newton,' the dead girl's mother called across, thanking her for caring about her dear daughter. She then added that other women from the camp were going to fetch her girl's remains, and she was welcome to come.

Thoughts about all that had happened, and what was going to take place now, teemed in Megan's aching head. "They might be strange people, but they are certainly not cowards," she thought. It had been to protect the gypsy code of secrecy that Lucy's mother had remained so composed while the police were present.

Megan planned to leave the encampment that very hour, and for sure that was what she wanted to do, but somehow the pain that Buckley and his evil ways was spreading over her hosts was also penetrating her heart, so how could she go now? 'Tomorrow, then,' she thought, 'I'll take to the road in the morning, get right away. Find Bruar without gypsy help.'

As the women walked up and over the quarry edge, no one spoke. They just followed the youngster who knew where a young girl, with so much to live for, lay cold and motionless on the rough purple heather. A breeze swirled around them, who numbered a dozen or so. The wind prompted one to say solemnly, 'She be round the corner, she be.'

Megan asked Ruth what that meant.

'Winter,' came the reply.

A small form could be seen ahead on the ground. It was Lucy, covered by a dirty blanket. 'Oh God in heaven,' screamed Lucy's mother,

'Look at my innocent baby, my beautiful babba, lying in the heather like a lurcher's discarded prey.' She broke free from Ruth and Anna who were supporting her, falling and stumbling until she stood trembling over her daughter's lifeless body. 'My little, sweet flower. Why did you give yourself to the master of the moors? Plenty good gypsy boys, but oh no, you had to pick him. Now look where it got you.'

She threw herself on top of the dead girl, sobbing uncontrollably. Then gently she lifted the lifeless body by the shoulders and cried with such depth of sorrow as only a mother can feel. It was pitiful. Megan remembered her own mother, Annie. Thinking of her lying in the woods of Kirriemor brought tears. She sat down gently and began to mumble. The gypsy women were silenced by astonishment; they'd never heard this before. Ruth sat down on a rock. Anna joined her. Then one by one the rest sat in the coarse heather and listened as Megan chanted the call of death. When, after several minutes, she lowered her head, the others asked her what it was she was chanting. 'It is a simple call to Mother Nature. I asked that Lucy be at one with the earth, the wind, rain and sun; to be free to join her ancestors.' She turned to Lucy's mother with outstretched hands and said, 'Now that she has climbed the highest mountain, she can dance the dance of freedom.'

'Freedom from what?' whispered Ruth.

'From her limbs,' came the simple reply.

Anna, who had brought Lucy's shroud, called out, 'see what took the life from her!' She was pointing at a cravat around the neck; a green and red scarf. 'We all know who that belongs to.'

Everyone nodded except Megan, who asked if it was Buckley.

'That piece of silk belonged to Hawen Collins. He killed my girl, and for that his fate is well and truly sealed.'

Soon the women with their burden of grief were back at the quarry campsite. Once they had all returned, Mother Foy called for Thamas. All eyes turned toward a wagon at the far end of the quarry, as the door slowly creaked open. A big man, wearing only an undervest and trousers, stepped down. He sat on the bottom step and retrieved boots from beneath the wagon, slipped them on and walked over to the women. 'Thamas,' said Mother Foy in her sternest voice, 'Hawen Collins did strangle Lucy. Find and kill him stone dead. You know if the muskries find him before us, then he'll escape his punishment.' She went inside her wagon and came out brandishing a small, shiny dagger. 'Stick it to the heart, one to the left side, then one to the right.

Before he breathes his last, whisper young Lucy's name to him three times. Now find Hawen Collins and kushti bok [good luck].'

Thamas went to Lucy's mother, laid a gentle hand on her shoulder and said, 'Tis the grave that waits for him, not a muskrie cell in a warm, "eat-yer-fill" prison. Take it for truth, he's a dead man.' Then, after a shave and donning a coat, he walked silently off down the road. His eyes were fixed ahead.

Megan watched in silence, as did everyone until Thamas turned the bend of the quarry road and was gone. She wondered what the words of the old woman meant, and asked her.

'Hawen took a gypsy life, therefore only another true blood can take his. We believe that when first born, our heart turns in our bodies to meet the rising sun first to the left, then towards the right; to the setting sun. To whisper the victim's name means that God hears it and will not allow the murderer entrance into heaven. So between the sun's lights he is bound to wander the earth, never finding peace.'

Megan walked away, and found solace by the peaceful water of the pool. She thought seriously on all that had taken place over a few short days. She'd not changed her mind about leaving, but wondered how the old woman would respond. 'Probably pleased to see the back of me, after that episode with the muskries, I don't doubt.' How long she sat there in her quiet spot she'd no idea, but soon the sound of a stranger's voice made her go and find out who had come among them. As she went into the site she saw a tall, chestnut horse tethered to a fence post. A handsome, slender woman was talking to Lucy's mother. Megan sat down beside Mother Foy, and Ruth and Anna joined them. 'It's Mrs Newton. She wanted to pay her respects, and she needs to speak with you, Megan,' the old woman told her, then whispered, 'I knew those rumours would bring her here. She knows you were the last to see Lucy.'

'But why me? I can't help her. I never set eyes on her man. Surely you all knew him?'

'Yes, that we did. But who told the muskries about Lucy being murdered? You did, and I bet they went up to Burnstall Hall and mentioned to her what the gowpie said.'

Megan turned and said to her host, who was sucking away on her familiar broken-stemmed pipe, 'Mother Foy, I am forever in your debt, but in the morning I will leave. My man is somewhere and I can't wait until next year to find him.'

'You are frightened by the murders and the bare knuckling; to be truthful, girlie, I am too. But while you were away down by the pool we had a talk.' She gathered Ruth and Anna into a circle. 'I am taking to the road meself. There's further down the way a nice bit of land known to gypsies as "the gorse field". Now there comes a time when a gypsy head has to stand down. My time has come. The girls here will tell you I've been getting a mite pained in this 'ere chest.'

'That you have Mother, that you have,' said Ruth. Anna added, 'She wants you to look after her, Megan.'

'I was getting round to that,' the old woman scolded the two girls and said, 'I'm going to speak to Megan.' They both nodded.

Megan stayed quiet, then asked, 'Is the group breaking up? Because Lucy told me that Mr Newton was arranging things with his lawyer. The quarry will be free to live in, so there is no need to concern yourselves over that.'

Ruth spoke next, 'His widow has already told us we can stay, so that's not the problem; it's Bull Buckley! He's caused so much worry that we are all splitting up to avoid him bringing his fights and whatever else to darken our doors. We leave tomorrow after resting Lucy. Now, you better go and speak with the widow, see what she wants.'

Megan, who once again found her tie with the gypsies twisting and turning, threw a glance at her old friend. She'd been a source of kindness and wisdom. What harm could be done by spending a quiet winter seeing to her needs?

'Alright, I'll look after you for the winter. We'll set off tomorrow. Now I'd better see what the lady wants.'

She saw Mrs Newton chatting quietly with Lucy's mother, and so not wishing to interfere in the shared mourning of the two women who'd recently lost so much, she walked down toward the chestnut mare and stroked her nose. 'You're a beauty, aren't you?' she whispered.

When as a child her father took her up on the hills to bring down the deer, she loved leading and riding the garrons, sturdy, thick-set little hill ponies. Although seldom with horses since, she always felt close to them, the few times she was. Doctor Mackenzie's horse was old and short-tempered, yet never like that with Megan; she could do what she liked with that animal. Gazing into the black and brown eyes of this regal beast brought floods of emotions, and for the second time that day her heart ached for Scotland. 'Will I ever be there again?' she thought.

'Hello, are you the gowpie your friends have told me not to listen to?' It was the grieving lady.

'I'm no gowpie, but they want me to keep quiet about a certain man, so don't waste your time, because I'm doing just that.'

'You seem to have a way with my horse,' the lady said, changing the subject and watching her animal nudge Megan's face.

'She's beautiful, you must give her plenty attention, with the shine of her coat. Fed well too, by the feel of these flanks.' She stroked the horse and it nudged her even more.

'All credit goes to Sam, my stable hand; he's a delightful boy and a natural with horses. Walk with me a little and tell me about the part of Scotland you come from. My husband and I...' Mention of him brought tears. She pulled a silk handkerchief from a black-sleeved velvet jacket with cuffs of leather, 'we spent many happy times hunting deer in the north.'

Here was a person who had been to her Scotland. She had seen and breathed the air of her moors. She was keen to walk in this woman's company. 'Yes, I'll walk with you. Where in the north did you hunt?' They began to stroll along, leading the horse by its bridle.

The old woman, watching her with the lady, raised a hand in concern and called to her not to go away from the site.

'I'm alright, don't worry.' Megan hoped that all the gypsies, who were silently watching her every move, would hear and know that, as far as Buckley was concerned, she'd make no mention of him.

Ruth joined her and drew her back from the lady. 'Tonight,' she told her seriously, 'no one goes to sleep. It's our custom that everybody stays up the night before a funeral. I'll wait up by the quarry lip till you and the good lady have finished walking.'

Megan could see how worried Ruth and all the gypsies had become in case she mentioned Buckley.

'Mrs Newton and I are talking about my Scotland, that's all. I'll see you later.'

Soon the expanse of moorland stretched out before them, and late autumnal breezes spread amongst heather and rock. What was recently to her a place of wild beauty was now a desolate region of murder and whistling, haunting winds. She was glad she'd put on her coat.

It was plain to see her companion was a mistress of horses. 'Move on, pretty girl,' she ordered the mare, taking off the halter. 'I like to give her freedom now and again,' she said, patting the horse's flanks.

Megan was astonished at how dutiful the tall horse was, as it circled and galloped, then fell in and walked behind her mistress.

The pair chatted and discussed Scotland. 'Although we hunted on friends' estates, Glen Coe was my favourite place. I loved its seclusion, its mighty gliding eagles, the rugged beauty of the place left me breathless.'

Megan could hardly contain her excitement. Not only was her companion a visitor to Scotland, but of all places she knew her very own birthplace—her ancestral home!

'You'd not hunt the monarch of the glen there. It was forbidden. No one hunted in the Glen of Coe, maybe in the Rannoch or the Etive, but never the Coe.'

'No, to be honest, we found the area far too dangerous with all those jagged peaks and sheer giants of mountains. It was hardly a safe place to stalk, but a wonderful place to dream. Look, those are the lights of Burnstall Hall, we're nearing home.'

Megan had seen plenty of stately homes, another one more or less meant little to her. Her heart was chasing the red deer back home. She was laid on her back staring up at the soaring eagle as it stretched its wings toward a powder-blue sky.

The woman broke into her thoughts. 'Please come in and have some tea before you go back.'

'Thank you, madam, but the gypsies will be thinking I'm telling tales, so best I get away.'

'I insist, it will only take a moment.'

'Darkness is not a time to be upon the moor, any moor. I must say again, no thanks.'

'Then Sam will walk you back, he has no fear of the moor.' At that she called for the young stable boy who came instantly. He was quickly introduced, and said that of course he would take Megan back.

Without a word she followed the lady inside, to be met by a rather stern housekeeper, who was obviously somewhat taken aback by a gypsy being allowed inside a stately house.

'If looks could kill,' was Megan's first thought, noticing the housekeeper's apparent disgust at being ordered to fetch some tea.

'Surely Madam doesn't expect the good china cups for this person, who, and if Madam doesn't mind me saying, should be in the kitchen?'

'Mrs Simms bring us a tray with—yes, china cups, cream and sugar.

176

Now, if you don't mind, I wish to discuss some matters of importance with this young woman.'

Still the hard-faced servant, with her grey hair stretched across her head and tied tightly in a small bun, just had to have her say. 'Madam, we in this house are in deep mourning. It is understandable you wish to find out who took the master's life, but not by giving hospitality to a filthy gypsy.'

Her employer stood up, stiffened her spine and ordered Mrs Simms to cease her offensive remarks.

Mrs Simms clicked two black brogue heels together and marched off.

'Pay no attention to her, dear, we are all in a state of shock.'

'Mrs Newton, I am well aware you need to know who took your husband's life but it's more than I am worth to tell about that terrible night.'

'Look dear, I know of the affair, and also that he was being black-mailed about it. But if the killer's identity is known to you, then please tell me. I swear no one will be any the wiser as to who disclosed the information. Please tell me, for our children's sake.'

Before she could repeat her refusal, a small girl walked slowly into the room, followed by a pale-faced young boy. The girl hurried over to the lady and threw herself into her arms, sobbing. 'Mummy, I want my Daddy,' tears streaming down her elf-like face.

'Daddy isn't here anymore, Lavinia,' said the boy trying not to do anything other than what was expected of a gentleman, albeit a seven-year-old one.

'Where is he? Mummy all the servants are wearing black, why? Didn't they do that when Grandma died? Daddy's not dead, is he Mummy?'

'There, there, my sweet child, so many questions. Mummy is very tired. In a moment I shall speak to you about Daddy. Now David, why don't you take Lavinia upstairs and wait till Mummy comes.'

'Poor wee bairns,' thought Megan, and to think bloody Buckley is prancing about somewhere in freedom. Probably sitting supping in a public house and boasting like a puffed cock.' She watched them go up-stairs, heads hung, weighted with aching sadness, poor little innocent mites. It was then she thought, 'Well, I may be a gypsy of sorts, but I'm first and foremost a Coe Scot. She remembered her own mother telling the story of the 'Massacre'. 'If someone had forewarned the

177

Macdonalds all those years ago that their neighbours, the Campbells, were on their way to slaughter them, then perhaps it never would have happened. Who's to say Buckley won't come to Burnstall Hall and terrorise this defenceless family?' These thoughts twisted and turned inside her head. 'Will I? Can I? Should I?' Surely he should be caught, imprisoned, punished? Yes, it was only proper. So as she sipped tea with her host, she told her all she had heard and witnessed the night her husband was murdered, finally adding, 'tell the police that Bull's in York, wherever that is.'

When she had finished her story, she asked the woman to promise not to inform detective Martin until two days had passed. That would give the gypsies time to conduct Lucy's funeral and leave the quarry.

The woman was strangely quiet as she rose to touch a silver photo frame with a small family photograph hidden among a dozen or more upon a grand piano. Her gaze stayed softly on her late husband's smiling face.

'It pains me deeply to say this, Megan, but it's not who killed Mr Newton that is important, it's the fact he was involved with the gypsies; sadly it is that we have to keep secret, even from the police. The future of his good name depends on it, and that of the children, of course. I promise that what you have told me will remain with me, and thank you so very much. I shall put my demons to rest, now that I know the truth, awful though it is.' She laid her pale hand on Megan's arm, adding, 'I do realise the sacrifice you have made in telling me, but I had to know the murderer's name.'

Before leaving, Megan gazed round the massive, marble hall. The walls were hung with portraits of men in uniform, soldiers. While hawking her scourers in Kirriemor she had seen similar pictures. They reminded her of what Bruar would have looked like. 'My husband was a soldier, was yours?'

'Yes, a proud captain in the Queen's Cavalry. That's a portrait of him over there.' She pointed to a large painting suspended above the curved turn of a broad winding staircase. Megan took a closer look. Indeed, he was a very handsome fellow. Tall, tanned skin, thin moustache above a firm lip, ocean-blue eyes, perfectly groomed brown hair. She could see how Lucy had fallen so heavily for him.

'My lad, he too is a looker. Not nicely ironed like him. Wild and strong, that's my Bruar.'

Mrs Newton touched her arm again and asked where he was.

She told her everything.

'The dream disclosed to you that he sleeps above and not below the ground?'

'Yes, missus.'

'And you think "King's Land" is in London?'

'Yes.'

'It may be something or nothing, but I happen to know that in Sussex there's a home for shell-shocked soldiers, called "Kingsland House".'

Megan's eyes nearly popped from their sockets. 'He may well be there, then!'

'Don't get your hopes up, my dear. He might be in any one of the homes, and believe me there are plenty, but if I have given you some clearer hope, then this night we have helped each other, don't you think?'

'Oh missus, little do you know how much of a misty veil your words have lifted from my eyes. Thank you so very, very much.'

Her road ahead looked so much clearer, her heart was freed of a heavy load. However, standing on the doorstep saying farewell, she just had to ask the lady what she had really thought about Mr Newton going off with Lucy.

'My dear girl, my husband, wonderful man though he was, did, like a lot of men have a weakness, and for him that was pretty young girls—mainly gypsy girls. I think it was their air of wild freedom; their windswept beauty drew him like a moth to a flame. Lucy wasn't his first, and if it hadn't been for that awful man, she certainly wouldn't have been the last.'

'But they were going off together.'

'Just as he had done before with the others. My dear, I knew his failings but loved him in spite of them. I think he paid the blackmailer, because the last time he ran off he promised me faithfully that it would never happen again.' It pained her to continue talking of him, that was becoming obvious. 'I'll ask Mrs Simms to call on Sam, he'll walk you back to the camp. Goodbye, and thank you so much.'

Before she slammed shut the massive oak door behind her, Megan stared into the beady eyes of Mrs Simms and whispered, 'I feel you don't care for me.'

Keeping an inch of open space between them she answered, 'I hate you. If not for your kind, my master would be alive and well and sharing supper with those broken-hearted children.'

As the door was bolted and noisily locked, Megan, although totally innocent, felt pangs of guilt at having been part of Lucy's secret, contributing to a heartbroken family's pain. But her new-found knowledge sent a wave of energy surging through her body. Looking for Bruar would be a lot easier now, and that was her only reason for existence.

Sam smiled and offered an arm, which she refused, saying there was none more capable than she on the moor. 'I have the eyes of a cat and can see for miles in pitch darkness.' Having just uttered those words, they both laughed as she stumbled and fell over a water barrel at the far end of the stables. 'Well, even a cat has its moments,' she said as he helped her up from the cobbled courtyard.

Sam had none of the other servant's disgust at gypsies, and said he knew and liked most of her quarry friends. He faced a problem, though, because Mrs Newton had informed her staff that she planned to sell Burnstall Hall and move away from the Dales.

'Surely whoever buys the place will need staff to run it,' Megan asked.

'Might do, but who can say? Sometimes property in these parts changes hands and new owners bring their own workers. Some even get shot of horses, don't use stables, and leave them empty. I have a big problem, lass, 'cause me Mam, ye see, she's real sick. Takes all me wages to pay for her medicine. What'll I do?'

'Get another job—say with a blacksmith or horse breeder. Surely someone will employ you. Mrs Newton told me you're a dab hand with her mares.'

'Aye, she's good to me. Hell, listen to me rambling on. I hear the quarry will see the burning of the gypsy girl tomorrow.'

'Burn! No, she's to be buried. After her funeral the gypsies are breaking up, after all that's happened.'

'Well, unless my knowledge of local gyppos is wrong, a funeral means the body and all it owns is to be burned.'

Megan felt her flesh crawl at the very idea of Lucy burning, and was certain Sam was pulling her leg. She spoke no more on the subject, opting instead to listen to the night creatures calling all across Bleak Fell as she walked back with the stable boy. In a short while, fire smoke drifted into their nostrils, telling them the quarry was near.

Ruth, who'd been watching for her return, came running up to meet them. 'Hello Sam, how be your mother these days?'

'Oh, you know, some days are worse than others. I'll get off home now, Megan. It was nice meeting you.'

She wished there was something she could give him for his kindness. Having a sick mother to care for was a heavy burden. She searched deep in her coat pocket, hoping a penny or two might have lodged in the stitching. There was a piece of paper and as she felt it a memory flashed into her mind. It seemed so long ago, but she recalled that when Father Flynn had given her a tiny piece of paper she'd put it deep in her pocket. When she unfolded it, she was astonished to find a ten shilling note. She smiled and gave it to Sam.

'I can't accept this, it is a whole week's wage, that is.'

'Well, it's yours. Now, cheerio.'

'First time a gyppo ever gave me money,' he called to her.

'I'm not a gyppo, Sam, I'm a clan tinker!'

She thought to herself, as she sauntered down the quarry path arm and arm with Ruth, 'Now, if I'd known I had that money, then I'd have got a ticket further south, and would never have been involved in the downfall of these gypsies.'

Not believing what Sam told her about burning, she asked Ruth, 'What manner of funeral will send Lucy to her rest tomorrow?'

'We burn our dead,' was the horrendous answer.

Ruth noticed how she'd turned quite pale. 'Don't fret, it's not as bad as it sounds. Listen, I've helped Mother Foy to bed, she ain't got the energy to sit up the night, but she insisted you go to her when you got back. I think she's afraid if any mention of Buckley took place, we all are.'

Megan noticed anxious-looking faces; they'd waited for her to see what had happened, what would she do? If Mrs Newton kept her word, and after all she was a lady, then she wouldn't reveal the truth of the murder, and all the gypsies would be gone the next day, none the wiser. She had no choice but to lie.

A great sigh of relief spread through out the campsite when they heard her say she'd not spoken Buckley's name. One by one they touched her shoulder, thanking her and saying, 'You done good, girlie.' Buckley would dig his own grave one day. With all the men he fought, sooner rather than later he'd take on one who'd whip him good.

She knew, however, it would take a lot of disguising the truth to convince her wise old friend, who thankfully was asleep by the time she tiptoed into the wagon. Wrapping herself in a heavy wool blanket, she

181

went outside to sit alone at the fire, and glanced around at the others who also sat in solemn silence. It was a long, cold night, and by dawn it was clear by the whiteness that lay around that the first winter's frost had covered the ground and the wooden wagon tops.

Lucy's mother began sad and mournful singing as she finished preparing the pyre.

'Here, girlie, pay respect.' Megan took the black scarf from Mother Foy, who didn't ask about Mrs Newton's questions, and covered her head.

The strongest of the men pulled Lucy's wagon out of the circle. All her bits and pieces, including scarves, headwear and shoes, were intertwined with colourful dresses and undergarments. Then each article was arranged methodically across the small barrel-shaped wagon. Everyone gathered round. Lucy's mother stooped and retrieved a burning stick from the blazing campfire. Firstly she lowered it, whispered her final farewell, and pushed the stick under the wagon, where firewood had been piled. Anna and Ruth both pushed clenched fists up toward the calm, early winter sky and said, 'may he who stole your young life soon perish. And let his ghost wander this earth, never to find peace.' It took several minutes but soon the whole wagon was engulfed in flames that leapt and burned into the small home. All heads stayed bowed, and holding hands they said goodbye in their own gypsy way.

Megan remembered how Father Flynn, when burying Rory, said in melancholy tones, 'And into God's hands...' but she couldn't remember the rest, so mumbled under her breath incoherently.

Ruth was right, the burning wasn't such a horrible sight, in fact it seemed peaceful and proper. Earth to earth, ashes to ashes.

Lucy's distraught mother, now homeless, was taken in by a cousin. They were the first to leave. Then, one by one, the womenfolk said farewell to Mother Foy. They warned Megan to take extra care of the old woman whom they held in high esteem, as the men harnessed up the big shire horses to their wagons.

Watching them go, she wondered if she'd they'd meet again, especially her two special friends, Ruth and Anna. They hugged and kissed, then soon they too had gone. Before parting, Anna whispered, 'Once a friend, always one. When me and my Tate Boswell meet at

Appleby, I'll be wanting to introduce you, so make sure you find a way of getting there come next June.'

Eleven

*U*nder the watchful eye of her old friend and following strict instructions, their wagon, the last to leave, was harnessed and yoked for the open road. Mother Foy's was, without doubt, one of the sturdiest horse-drawn wagons ever to fill an English country lane. Built by both herself and her late husband, it was every bit a labour of love. However, unable now as she once was to hold the leather reins between her arthritic fingers, she asked Megan to take them. But she hadn't a clue how to drive. Oh yes, horses she loved, and they responded likewise, but this was a different matter. At first the poor horse was drawn up, then trotted on and so forth, until the old woman managed to exert a form of verbal control (of which a large part was expletives) and was able to teach Megan the basic skill of straight line driving.

'God, whoever you are, keep our way on a line without bends or hills, and we might just make it,' prayed the new driver.

Three long weeks later, after much swearing and sweating, the area where they were to winter settle appeared on the horizon. In a field edged by a forest on one side and an open plain on the other, they snuggled the wagon into a sheltered spot.

'My man and me came here many times to winter stop. Folks calls it 'the gorse field'. It's near enough to village and town for hawking and dukkering [fortune telling]. There's a farm a mile up the way, nice people run the place who deal in a pound or two of good horse flesh. I know them who own it.'

'Not horses for the slaughter?' Megan curled her lip in disgust.

'No, racers they be. I've heard there's been many a top runner come from them. If you take yourself there I'm a certain you'd enjoy it, with you liking a horse. Maybe tomorrow when chores are finished, we'll visit the couple who own the place. In past days I always found a pleasant welcome. Now I have just enough power in these twisted fingers to unharness me dear old grai [horse]. Hold the shaft handles until I've finished.'

Megan learned such a lot from Mother Foy about gypsy ways, and it didn't take long before she was almost mastering Beth, her shire horse.

The flat land allowed the horse a freedom seldom seen in Scotland, and when they had stopped for the day Megan would often climb onto its back and ride the large animal as fast as it could go. Shire horses are not usually to be seen galloping with a rider straddled bareback, so when horse and rider took to the open plains it was not a graceful sight: it could be quite comical watching the pair. Beth with her clumsy, skirted hooves shifted clumps of grass in their wake, Megan bounced like a rubber ball on her broad back, hanging on to the thick ginger mane. But someone who was fanciful might have seen it as a pretty painting come to life. While she rode, Mother Foy slept a lot, so Beth the fifteen-year-old shire mare was the only real friend Megan had.

Because of the recent events in the quarry they decided to keep a low profile. The need to know if Lucy's avenger had sent Hawen Collins to meet a fate worse than death, or, more to the point, whether the police had decided to pursue and imprison Buckley, was soon eating into the old woman, and she had to know. Sooner or later such news trickles to gypsy ears, though, and one way or the other she'd find out.

She may have had her own doubts regarding Megan's talk with Mrs Newton, but she thought best not to question the girl when they were back at Bleak Fell quarry. At night, though, when the pair sat warming themselves in the wagon by the stove, a movement from outside would silence any conversation, sending them to close any small openings in the curtains. However, if Buckley did come seeking to silence Megan, what could defenceless women do—one far too old, the other not a match for that beast?

—

Time passed and the fear diminished. Megan familiarised herself with the small villages scattered here and there. She hawked long hours, which were fewer now that winter had shortened daylight, and she brought home mere handfuls of pennies. Her old companion taught her tea-leaf reading, palms and fortune-telling. She wasn't a natural at it, though, and soon doors were staying closed at her knock. The villagers had heard that a woman had been told by Megan that she'd meet and marry a handsome dark-haired stranger. Imagine her shock when the lady in question informed her she had mothered six kids to a shepherd with thick red hair. So it was decided that she would not go a-dukkering any more. She also felt unwilling to go gathering and bunching heather; it didn't seem appropriate after all the bad memories of Lucy, her lover and Rory all being found dead in the stuff.

Add to this that old Mother Foy had taken a few falls from the wagon steps, and Megan felt that it would be better to stay with her.

Winter brought sporadic snowstorms and biting winds. Her concern for the old woman became a constant worry, and Beth's lack of adequate shelter bothered them both.

The old dear had a quirky sense of humour, and one morning after a battering of snow she stroked her backside and said, 'What a horror of a night it was—did you hear the howling gale? The sleet, needle-pointed, tore into me arse by that blast of a gale. I went out for a pee in the frozen gorse and when I lifted my skirt the wind bit and stung like gunshot. Buttocks were solid for hours.' Megan laughed, it wasn't what Mother Foy was expecting, but she soon saw the funny side.

Later, when they went outside, Megan ran over and rubbed Beth's body. She shook her head, saying, 'That bloody wind is merciless, the poor horse will be got dead. I think we should break our silence and ask the good folks at the stud farm to give Beth a shelter till spring.'

The older woman had seen and lived through it all before, and so had the horse, but this nature-loving Scot would always put animals before her own comfort. Her protest continued.

'Girlie, that horse has the hide of an elephant. See how her mane thickens to keep frost from her neck. Her tail curls under, keeps the openings warm, stops her kidneys cooling, and those skirts covering her ankles are like fur boots, they are. No, she's all right.'

But Megan, now with the bit between her teeth, was persistent. 'Just the other day you told me you'd not seen a winter severe as this before. It's as bad as the ones we have. Please let me visit the horse breeders.'

Up till that point the old woman had decided to stay away from the stud farm. Buckley too, knew these people, in fact most gypsies did.

At the annual horse sales in Appleby they were there in the midst of the gypsies, dealing, buying and selling. The old woman thought for a moment, and replied, 'If Buckley had been caught, surely the stud farmers would know of it, so I suppose it might be a way to get the cloud of worry off our shoulders.' Another thought occurred to her: Megan might at any time leave her to search for Bruar.

'Beth might do well having a bit of shelter. We'll ask if she can be stabled with them for the winter. They won't do it for nix though, so give me my tin box from 'neath the bed.' Under the bed in a metal box the old lady hid her savings. From the box she took several pound notes which she put in a leather purse.

The snow had ceased to lay its cover of white across the fields and dead bracken. Megan had cleared it away around Beth, sufficient to allow her to sleep, walk and graze on a bundle of crunchy hay brought with them for winter feed. Feeling the sting of long, cold nights, Beth had eaten more than her usual ration, so perhaps the horse farm was the best place for her survival.

Christmas Eve arrived cold and damp, a thick freezing fog covering every inch of the land. Without a glint of sunshine or a murmur of wind, the day's start felt as though a leaden hand was turning time. Megan helped dress the old woman before haltering Beth. 'Look at the icicle dripping from your nose, big soft beast,' she whispered in the horse's ear, rubbing a coarse blanket up and down its spine. 'There now, that should stir up some warm blood. Before breakfast, let's ride a mile or two.' Half an hour later the pair were back eating a hearty breakfast of fried bread, eggs and black tea.

'I'm anxious to meet your friends. Do you think they'll take to me?'

'Who could fail to like such a girlie as yourself? These folks, being an Irish family, will love the celt in you. Now hurry and rinse these dishes, before the grease hardens.'

As they walked towards their destination through a thick mist, Megan worried about whether her old friend would manage the journey. 'What a miserable day, is your shawl warm enough?' Her concern grew with each slow, dragging step of the old woman. She would have liked to take her companion's arm to steady her, but she was walking Beth. The elderly lady was, however, of a hardy breed and told her so. 'I'm fine. Now, watch that we take the right turn on this road. If we go left we'll put another mile onto our journey. In this pea soup I'm certain my joints will fix stiff if I go another step over the distance.' Minutes had passed when she stopped, squinted her eyes into slits and said, 'Yes, there's the building, thanks be to God for keeping me eyes sharp. I don't show gratitude for me bent back and stiff legs, but I thank him for the eyes.'

In the thick fog Megan could just about make out outbuildings with low roofs; these were stables. Beth, on smelling other horses, quickened her pace. The old woman laughed and said, 'Now, girl, don't get too frisky, you'll be there soon. We'll put her in the barn meantime. We don't want to seen too pushy by taking up a pew in the stalls, better I get permission.'

Megan walked into a cobbled yard and led her equine friend into the giant barn at the farthest end. After scattering loose hay in a trough and hobbling the horse, she was soon standing alongside her companion, outside a grand ranch-style door.

'Well, well, well, would you look at who has decided to brighten our doorstep,' said a young man, holding a newspaper in one hand, brown-stemmed pipe in the other. 'Come away in, dear friend, out of this confounded fog. Now tell me, who is this young filly?'

'Stephen, what a sight you are to gladden the eyes of an old gypsy woman. This is Megan, and before you start prodding at her mind, let me say she is a Scot and her business is her own. Now, what have you done with Bridget?' At these words a young woman appeared.

'He's not got the energy to do anything with me, Mother Foy. Oh, it does my heart the power of good when I see that wrinkled face of yours. We noticed the bowed wagon down by the gorse, is it yours?'

Megan was ignored momentarily as the friends greeted each other on the doorstep.

'What couthy folk,' she thought. They certainly had a fondness for her old companion, and she wondered why. Her answer came running breathlessly down the stairs in the form of a little girl. Her face, on seeing who was visiting, beamed as she threw herself into the old woman's arms, 'Mamma Foy, my lovely old Mamma! Why have you taken such ages to come? Did Daddy tell you what Uncle Michael has given me for Christmas? Can I tell her Daddy?'

Her father waved his hand in a gesture of approval.

'Oh Mamma, she is just divine, wait until you see her, are you staying for long? Uncle Michael will fetch her over in the spring because she's too young to leave her mother.'

'What a load of questions; me little princess, let me look at you.' The wide-eyed child blushed and turned on tiptoes, pirouette-fashion. Her golden ringlets skimmed the air, then fell one by one upon tiny shoulders and cascaded down her back.

'A living doll if me old eyes don't deceive me, how you have grown. I think you must be about seven or eight. But what is this gift that has my sweetie so excited?'

'Oh silly Mamma, I'm nine now. It's nothing other than a brand new Irish foal, whose mother is none other than Fiddler's Fancy. You remember her, don't you? She won the National twice.'

'Well, she must be a pretty picture if she's her foal; I won a small fortune on Fiddler, I did.'

Megan couldn't help but wonder, with a little awe, at the attention, nay respect, this family paid to her old friend. They were not without wealth, that was apparent, but why the red-carpet treatment to a mere gypsy?

The child smiled. 'I'm Nuala, what are you called and why do you come with my precious Mamma Foy?'

Before she could answer, the old woman called Nuala over and said, 'This young lady is my friend, and has kindly offered to take care of me until the winter be over. Like you she has a pretty name, Megan.'

Nuala threw her small arms round the new visitor and said excitedly, 'I think you are the loveliest person in the entire big grand world.'

'Why?' she asked curiously.

'For taking care of my Mamma Foy, that's why.' Then as fast as she had come she dashed back upstairs, to gather armfuls of dolls and teddy bears to lay at Megan's feet, small hands arranging the toys in a little circle, giving each a name and asking Megan to play with her.

Her mother seemed to delight in the child, in fact both parents did. However their visitor intervened. 'Nuala, my little sweetie, why don't you sit here beside me and we will tell her how you came into the world?'

The child needed no prompting, and jumped up into the soft armchair to gaze into Mother Foy's grey eyes.

Silence settled around the family as outside the start of a gentle wind could be heard. Rain began to spatter against the windows. Bridget drew shut the curtains, then joined her husband, who sat on the floor beside a roaring log fire, waiting for their friend to share, once more, the story of Nuala's birth.

'It was around this time me and me old man Frankie, God bless his rest, took ourselves to settle out the winter months down at the gorse field. We had just arrived and were tying Beth to a tree, in fact to the same tree we had her tied to up to this very day. Well, Stephen here comes galloping like the devil was on his tail. Oh, what a state this poor young man was in, hair all windswept and needing a wash and shave if I remember rightly. Me old man helped him in to the wagon. 'What ails you?' he asks him like.

"My wife is fretting and I'm certain she is dying. Oh God, gypsy, do you know anyone who can help her, please!' He was near on breathless, poor soul, he was. I heard all the commotion and asked what was wrong with his wife. "She has gone pale with labour. Been two days pushing and screaming, but now she has gone silent. I think the baby is dead, and if we don't find help, then I'll lose her too."

I could see by his fearful-looking brow that there wasn't a minute to lose. Onto his horse we went, and did not draw a breath until we got up here to the house. When I did see Bridget with that awful greyish colour, I tell you for true I had me doubts if the girl was alive or dead. Frightening it was. But when I stared down at her lifeless frame, her eyes opened and she whispered, "Save my little lamb."

Now I tells Stephen to take a good grip of 'imself and follow my instructions to a tee. "Get me a glass of cold water, and when I lift your wife's head, I want you to drip it down her spine." I could see the look on his face and knew he was not trusting me. "Do it!" I shouts in 'is ear. Then, when he was fetching water, I spoke little words to the swollen belly. "Please don't think this child dead," I reassured Bridget. "All these past nine months, tell me what words did you whisper to your unborn?" I put my ear close, for the mother-to-be had hardly the strength to speak, let alone deliver her child. She whispered one word: "angel". I put my mouth to the womb and said over and over, "Mummy's little angel." Stephen came back, water dripping from a shaking hand. I lifted Bridget's head and he did as I told him—poured the cold water gently down her spine. At its touch she flinched. This was to keep her awake, she wasn't far from unconsciousness, and if that happened, both mother and child would have died. The cold water forced her eyes to open and she screamed: "my angel is moving—I can feel the tiniest movement." I warned that she should lie very still, because I knew through delivering many awkward births that this little madam was exhausted, she needed to be encouraged. In other words,

190

she was going nowhere otherwise. It took Bridget and me some time, but eventually tiny Nuala here came into the world. Bridget couldn't rise from her bed for a week.'

'And I was a very happy and contented father who did all the caring for our little angel,' beamed Stephen, relishing the importance of fatherhood.

'I was the best baby in the world, wasn't I, Mummy?' added Nuala, whose big blue eyes stared wide with wonder at the story of her birth.

Mother Foy cuddled the child snuggling into her side in the silk brocade-covered armchair, and whispered, 'And I became your God-mother.'

Megan listened with pride. Here were people with enough money to buy the best medicine. Yet when no doctor of experience was available, nature brought a woman into their midst to safely deliver a desperately wanted child. She held no honour or distinction, just the knowledge of how precious life was. She lived in a simple barrel-shaped home, and transported all she owned from place to place. The night they so needed her, she just happened to be down at the end of the gorse field with her husband, tending to their horse and boiling a kettle.

Quietness settled around as they sipped on tea. Outside the breeze was gathering force now, and Nuala was yawning for bed. 'But,' she protested, 'I won't go unless you both promise to stay for Christmas.'

Before either could answer the large door blew open and in strode an angry young man. 'Blasted English weather pelting down out there, hardly a Christmas scene. And what bloody idiot put a sleepy old shire in the barn? I fell over the mare in the dark. Who the hell could be so stupid?'

Mother Foy, seeing the funny side, laughed, but his tone brought Megan to her feet, 'I put Beth into the barn, because Mother Foy said I should. She didn't like us helping ourselves to a stall in the stables without permission.'

The young man closed the door at his back, then striding past her, knelt down by Mother Foy and planted a big kiss on her cheek. 'I should have recognised Beth. How are you?'

'I'm getting old. But Megan did as I asked.'

He brushed a hand across his damp hair. 'Sorry, young lady.'

Megan blushed red; she could feel her face glowing. He called her a lady; no one had ever done that before.

'Michael, me dear friend, Nuala tells me you have the foal of Fiddler.'

'Indeed I have, Mother, and what a beauty she is, the image of her mother.'

'Do you still have the horse?'

'Yes, I do. I could not see me part with the love of my life.'

'Can I see her?'

'I wish you could, because she still has a fine sway, but I keep her at home in Ireland. Sorry.'

'Well, you take good care of that beauty, because she runs like the wild Arab steed, she does. Listen to us going on about horses and me not introduced you proper to Megan.' Much too comfortable to rise from her warm chair, she gestured at the pair to make their acquaintance, while she bade Nuala goodnight with the assurance that they would most certainly stay for Christmas.

Michael Riley was as handsome a man as Megan had seen in a long while. Unable to say exactly what it was, she knew there was something about the man. Her body felt on edge, slight confusion entered her brain, why?

That evening passed with conversations of little or no consequence, yet all the while she felt drawn to him. Perhaps it was his wild, devil-may-care attitude. She was at a loss for words to explain it, she just knew he had a power. It made her feel vulnerable, but what of him? If she'd caught his glance once, she'd done so a dozen times.

'I can't help but feel a fondness for them who have grand Scottish blood flowing through their veins,' he said, after hearing her broad accent.

She smiled and heard herself say, stupidly, 'In what part of the Emerald Isle did you see first light? Is the gypsy in you?'

'In honest answer to your second question, is not the wandering gypsy in us all? To your first, I saw the light of day in my parents' tiny cottage on the shores of Galway Bay, but I was brought up in Wexford, and there it was where my father began a lifelong love—buying and selling horses. Needless to say, my old Dad passed his horse sense to me. My dear father is no longer with us, having died of pneumonia. My blessed mother found her bed cold and empty without him, and was gone herself no more than a year later. My only living relative is my dear sister Bridget, over there putting the finishing touches to the Christmas tree. There now, pretty colleen, you know the very heart of me, and I don't share that with just anybody.'

Mother Foy heard the last part of the conversation, and thought it best to rescue Megan before she shared more than she needed to with the handsome Michael.

'I wonder if we can leave me old Beth with you for the winter. The gorse field gives little shelter, and with her being on the old side...' From a concealed pocket in her skirt she brought a little pouch to pay her animal's feed, but Stephen, who put an arm around Bridget, assured his old friend that they would care for her horse as long as she wanted, and added, 'No payment for feeding'.

'Now, why did I know that you would say that? Bless you all, and thanks.' She pulled her shawl across her shoulders and drew it tight. 'I wonder if I might enquire of you something else before the girlie and I take to our beds. Bull Buckley—you haven't seen him sniffing about these parts, have you?'

Much to their great relief, no one had seen or heard of him for many a month. They had heard, though, that his life-long sidekick, that weed of a man Hawen Collins, had met a bad end.

'What happened to him?' Mother Foy pretended not to know anything about it.

Stephen took a log from a basket at the side of the fireplace and placed it in the big iron grate, 'Bridget, you met a gypsy girl didn't you? Remember the one who told you about that fight?'

'I do remember something, now what was it?'

The old woman glanced over her shoulder at Megan and winked.

Bridget continued, with the undivided attention of her visitors. 'It was in a pub on the outskirts of York, the Dog and Gun. Seems a bunch of locals were having a laugh at a mate's birthday party when Hawen, being drunk, tried to gatecrash. He was for the chop, when one bulky guy threatened to fight him. The stupid fool took the challenge, probably thinking that because he was known to be the great Buckley's friend, the big chap would back down.

'What happened?' asked Megan, lowering her voice to disguise an obvious panic.

''Well, there's a mystery as to what really happened, but this big chap took him out in the back-alley. The next thing, someone passing saw Hawen's body all hacked.'

193

'Did you find out how he died?' Mother Foy asked quietly.

'Stephen met a policeman he knows. You tell them, dear.'

'His neck was broken, but he'd a knife wound at either side of his heart. My friend said the big man, him who did it, wasn't a guest at the birthday party, nor had he ever been in that pub before. Locals at the Dog and Gun thought he was a passing gypsy having a quiet drink. No one was sad to see Hawen's end, though, and that goes across the board. Just a pity his mate Buckley didn't get it too.'

'He won't be so easy caught, he has the sign of the Devil, that black-hearted one,' Mother Foy said in a low voice. She leaned forward in her chair and spat in the fire. 'That's what I think of him! Now, I feel we have taken far too much of your hospitality for granted, it's time for bed.'

Megan helped her onto shaky feet, and guided the tired old lady off to a very comfortable bedroom Bridget had prepared earlier. Michael said goodnight with a long lingering look at Megan. A tingle ran the whole length of her spine. He made her feel strange, but he made her think less of Bruar and that was wrong. She wished Christmas Day was over, and they were home in the wagon. She said so to her companion.

'Now, child, try not to think too much on the young master. Mind you, if I was your age I'd be hard-pressed not to give him the eye.'

Megan blushed; her old friend seldom spoke of romance. She continued, 'I don't doubt for a minute you're not tempted, none of us are exempt from temptation, but it's the consequences that you have to watch out for. It's been a long time since a man held you, and the longing will be there, you're human after all. But might I add you are not like others. You have a living husband somewhere, waiting. It might be the case he knows little of what is going on, but the time will come when his eyes will see again. I have a feeling you are joined to this Bruar of yours. A force far stronger than any mere mortal controls things, and if I'm not mistaken this force guides you. Remember this!'

How could she forget? Here she was on her quest to find him, indeed a long road lay ahead. A longer one lay behind, but while she could breathe and walk she would not give in.

'I feel a lot better now. Is this not the night the Son of God came; the great star shining in the east?' Megan was peering from the bedroom window at a beautiful starry sky.

'So they say, girlie, so they say.'

'Then I shall do something I very seldom do.'

'What be that then, my young friend?'

'I shall pray.'

'What will you pray for?'

'For the safe union, one day soon, of me and my Bruar.'

'What a perfect place to dream,' she thought, sinking into a soft warm mattress covered in spotless linen sheets. It sported a shiny brass bedstead with bows of yellow silk tied here and there. 'I can't remember ever seeing pillows of this size, nor sleeping with an old gypsy.' She nudged her bed companion, laughing, 'They are as big as my tent bed was, these pillows.'

'You make me laugh, you do, girlie; but best get some sleep now. And as for myself, well, after that news that Buckley is out there somewhere, I'll sleep with one eye open.'

'Surely he wouldn't be so stupid as to risk coming here?'

'That beast crawls the earth without a brain, his skull's filled with bad brawn. He's like a mad bull. He'd come here alright.'

'But why should he?'

'Listen, girlie, you might think me short of a shilling, but I knows how much is in a pound. You told Mrs Newton what you saw the night her man got murdered. Don't tell me you didn't, because I can see a lie like I see a rainbow. If Bull Buckley so much as sees a muskrie, he'll know who fingered him. He's got scores to settle.'

'Then perhaps you had best stay with these kind folks, and I'll take off to find my man. Surely he won't bother you if he knows it was me who did the dirty on him?'

'Stay the winter. This is a big lonely country, full of rivers, country roads and dales. To travel you need to know the place where you're going, and money. Now let's be honest, you have neither. Come spring, I'll give you a shilling or two and help, but not just now.'

'But if Buckley comes he'll know you've helped me, and heaven forbid, hurt you. I couldn't stand that on my conscience.'

'If Buckley wants to come, he comes whether we be together or not. Now, get some sleep, will you, girl.'

If they wanted a long lie in bed, then Nuala put paid to it. Ages before the cock crowed, her eager little legs were running up and downstairs, and along to the bedroom at the far end of the ranch-style house where her visitors slept. Megan listened both to her constant knocking on the door and her oohs and aahs on opening another gift from Santa. Although she hardly knew the child, it would have been nice to have something to give. But then, here was a girl who had a world of material wealth. What could a mere tinker give such a one?

She was certainly the better for the early morning call. Bull had flitted in and out of her dark dreams, his red hair hung over one eye, and a helpless hedgehog held between his gruesome jaws. But thankfully, a bright morning pushed him to the back of her thoughts.

She gently lifted the covers from her side of the bed, not wishing to awaken old Mother Foy; but there was no need, her companion was already up and about. With a feeling of embarrassment and guilt at resting longer than the old woman, she washed in a basin of water left for that purpose, dressed and quickly brushed her hair, and rushed along to the large sitting room. Nuala had taken herself upstairs, probably to share her Christmas joy with her parents. Apart from a smelly hound curled in a dog basket by the stone fireplace, the room was empty, just as it had been the night before. 'I wonder where my old friend has got to,' she spoke out loud.

'Megan, I'm here.'

She glanced around the room, it was empty. She asked, 'Where?'

'In this blasted chair.' A limp hand fell from a blanket covering a wickerwork chair by the far wall next to long flowing curtains; it was the old woman.

'I didn't see you under the cover. What's the reason for deserting a warm bed at this ungodly hour?' She knelt down by her side.

The old lady was pale and sickly looking; she was holding her side, obviously in pain. She made a weak attempt to sit forward, but the pain forced her back.

'What in the name is the matter?'

'I felt cold in the night, then I felt hot, my head got to thumping and this sharp pain like a hot poker in my chest. It'll be little or nothing, probably just the walk yesterday. Nuala too, she was all over me like a nettle-rash, dear sweet child. Yesterday was too much for me and this is the result. If we can persuade Stephen or Michael to hitch a buggy, take us back to my varda, I'll be the better in a couple of days.' Through the grimace of pain she forced a smile, then laid her head back against a brocade cushion perched behind her.

'Do you want a doctor?' The old lady was far from well, and her colour worried Megan.

196

'Phew, a doctor, that'll be right. No, just give our hosts a call, then put the kettle on for everybody, it's the least we can do.'

'Nuala will be sad that we don't share Christmas dinner with them.'

'It can't be helped. Old age is what it says, and things old don't work well.'

A concerned Bridget, who'd heard their voices, came downstairs. 'What's the reason for my guests in this cold sitting room, without so much as a hot morning cup of tea?'

Megan thought she should be aware of her friend's condition. 'It's Mother Foy, Bridget, she's not at all well and wants to go home.'

Bridget rushed over, leaned forward to examine the old woman's face and said. ''Tis the saddest news now, how did you end up being sickly on this, the day our Blessed Virgin gave birth to the Lord. Little Nuala will be heart-sorry for sure.'

Just then Stephen came downstairs carrying Nuala, who was already dressed in riding gear; part of her Christmas present from Uncle Michael.

'What's wrong, Mother Foy?' asked Stephen, gently dropping Nuala on a chair.

'Nothing a good rest in me own bed won't cure.'

'She wants to go back to her wagon. Could either you or Michael rig up a buggy?' asked Megan.

Michael said, 'Ah, you poor old thing, why don't you stay here. Spend the day in bed, we can bring you a fine spread of turkey and stuffing on a tray.'

Little Nuala came rushing into the room, and when she heard what was going on, cried, 'I have a present for you, Mamma, please stay.' A parcel, loosely wrapped, was retrieved from beneath the Christmas tree and put gently onto the old woman's lap. It was a green, paisley-patterned shawl.

Bridget, who'd been making tea, set a warm welcoming cup on the small table beside Mother Foy's chair and said, 'It was our mother's Sunday best. We want you to have it.'

Mother Foy unwrapped the present and draped the shawl over her knees. 'A fine present. Thank you, Nuala, I shall treasure it.' She looked at the couple, then at Michael and said, 'You know me well enough that if I say I'm sore, then I am very sore. There's nothing more I'd rather do this day than to have Christmas with you. Me pain is strong, though, and I wouldn't eat or drink. I'd hate not to enjoy a grand feast after all the time and effort you'd put into it, Bridget. No, all I want to do is sleep in me own wagon-bed, but if Megan wishes to stay, then it's me blessing I'll give her.'

'No, I'll look after you.'

Michael seemed rather annoyed and she couldn't understand why. He walked outside, muttering that he'd get the buggy ready and take them back to the gorse field.

'Nuala, sweet child, will you do Mamma a favour and keep an eye on Beth?'

'Of course, but you must stay nearby to see my beautiful foal when uncle brings her over on the ferry.'

'I'll come first time I feel better. But if she be like her mother, I remember her beauty very well.

Help me to my feet, Megan, we'll be off,' she said, holding a hand out for assistance.

Little Nuala and Bridget gave the old woman a hug, making her promise to hurry and get well. Stephen promised to keep an eye on them. His parting words, though, brought a chill to both as he said, 'If I hear any news of Buckley, I'll be sure to let you know.'

Mother Foy closed her fingers tightly over Megan's arm; these were words neither wished to take back with them to the lonely spot down by the gorse field.

'You do that. Now a million blessings on all for this Christmas Day.'

Hugs and kisses over with, Michael drove up with a small two-man buggy. 'Sorry, but we'll have to squeeze together,' he told them.

'I'll sit to the outside, me stomach feels a bit under the weather,' said the old woman, adding, 'talking 'bout weather, I've got cold ear-lobes, and that's a sign of more snow.'

As they huddled close for warmth, Megan, while keeping an arm round her companion's shoulder, couldn't help but feel the way Michael's muscles rippled as he controlled the reins. It was only a mile to the wagon, yet she wished it were longer. It had been such a long time since she had felt the breath of a young man against her face and the movement of strong legs rubbing hers. Feelings she'd not experienced since she and Bruar made love on the braeside returned with a fire to them. Even although a fierce wind blew a torrent of bitter cold at her body she was warm. Beneath her breasts, little beads of sweat formed, making her feel more and more uncomfortable. Confusion took hold: how could her face sport a bright red nose, yet such a heat burn beneath her collar? The same feelings that had been generated by Bruar's closeness filled her mind; she was attracted to this stranger.

'Never,' she told herself, 'I will not do this, I can't think this way.' The wind lifted her skirt; she curled it down under her shaking knees. Deliberately she stiffened her legs, hoping he'd get a message of hostility. His gaze forced her to look into his eyes; she turned away, but only for a second. She was lost under a spell.

Suddenly the old woman called for him to slow down, and as he did so she vomited over the side of the buggy's leather seat.

She had been so wrapped up in her newly discovered emotions, Megan had forgotten her friend was suffering. Guilt and anger spread through her, she felt so ashamed. Rachel's words, away back at the campsite in the Angus Glens filled her head—'You hussy, have you been working the pants off yourself?' Perhaps her sister was right. Was she was a hussy? 'No, I'm the proud wife of Bruar Stewart, and I will not betray him unless he has gone. If he's alive I'd never forgive myself, nor be able to look him in the eye again! Oh no, surely I am not letting words like "unless" and "if" creep into my head,' she scolded herself. 'My love *is* waiting for me, and that's that.'

Soon the young man was pulling gently on the reins as the horse came to a halt on the gorse field edge. 'Thank you,' she said, as she helped them down.

He offered to help by carrying the old lady into the wagon, but Megan protested. 'I can manage fine, we don't need help.' Then she added, 'Best get back to your celebrations, you don't want to miss your dinner.'

At first he didn't turn his face in her direction; instead he jumped back into the buggy and turned it around. 'I feel easier in my mind that you are with the old woman, but there's a favour I want to ask of you.' His smouldering brown eyes now held her gaze. 'Let me wait until you put Mother Foy to bed.'

'She'll freeze to death without the fire lit. No, I'm sorry but I've no time to waste chatting—Jack Frost is already closing around our feet.' She was trying harder than ever to avoid his eyes.

'Then let me light the fire.' Without a word from either, he was up the steps of the wagon and in a flash had the stove emptied and filled with a heart of kindling. He seemed to know where the matches were kept, and soon had a grand flame pushing thick smoke up the long chimney that projected from the roof.

Mother Foy slid under her bed covers, while Megan made her a cup of tea. Before half of it had been taken she was sound asleep. Outside Michael tended the horse and waited.

Quietly she opened the wagon door and asked, 'Do you want a drop tea?'

Now that her old friend was asleep, something of the closeness with him made her feel vulnerable. In an instant he put his strong hands around her wrist to steady it while the cup wobbled in her shaking hand. He gently took the tea. She watched as it slid over his throat, rippling down his fine broad neck. Shivers danced up and down her spine. She pushed her hands in her pockets and asked, 'Well, here I am, what is it you ask of me?'

'I almost forgot there for a moment,' he said. From his jacket he took out a small black velvet box and gave it to her. She'd never seen or handled one like it before, and for a minute didn't know what to do, except stare at it nestling in her cold hands. The feel of the material was warm and pleasurable.

'Open it, then, sure it's not going to bite!'

She felt awkward and stupid and thrust it back into his hand, then turned and opened the door; but he held her arm tightly and said, 'Nobody should go through this day without a gift from someone, here.' He lifted the small, compact lid displaying a shiny necklace.

Although no light from the sun or any other source fell upon it, the shine was magnificent. 'I cannot under the cloudy sky accept such a bonny thing, now put it back into the box and away with you.' Smiling, he simply ignored her protests and slipped it on her slender neck. 'Christmas gifts must never be refused, sure now, that's the height of ignorance. Anyhow, what's a little bit of gold between friends?'

At his words her chest thumped like a hammer—gold! She'd never ever seen the precious metal, let alone been given it. His gift would indeed be kept close to her beating heart, but it was the last part of his comment that felt good—the word friend. Yes, if he was to be a friend, then she could keep it that way. Yet all the time, her wildest innermost thoughts were of intimacy. It would be so much easier if they were friends. She took his hand, shook it clumsily and said, 'I'd be honoured to be your mate, and thanks a million for this beautiful necklace.'

The brown, leather-upholstered buggy with its handsome driver held her gaze until it disappeared up the road. She smiled and ran a finger over the lovely gift hanging around her neck, before going in and spending a long Christmas Day with her other friend, who was still sleeping soundly beneath the quilt. Night came, and with it a blizzard unlike any she'd encountered in her life before, even wilder than that night she had searched for help in the Angus Glens. She listened as Mother Foy snored in unison with a nagging wind blowing smoke down the chimney. She felt lonely, her eyes filled with tears. 'Christmas Day, and look at me hunched over a reekie hearth. No family, saving this old gypsy and a bowdie wagon.' In the gorse field the blizzard was laying walls of banked snow, choking trees and pathways. Mother Nature was giving midwinter his place.

She closed her tired eyes and went back home in her thoughts. Home to stand over Annie's grave. She visualised the secret spot; now also covered in a blanket of snow. Beneath that covering, sleeping snowdrops and wild crocuses would soon be pushing up through the ground and she so wished that her dear mother could reappear with them, if only for a minute. She remembered the last time she saw her before sickness stole on her, sitting at the campfire stirring tattie soup. 'I miss you, Mammy, and Rachel,' she whispered to her memory. 'Can you see us, Mammy, from wherever you are? Or do you stay sleeping, forever? And what of Rachel, do you walk about America like a toff? Wee Nicholas will be getting big. I wonder what kind of Christmas you are both enjoying.' Lost in a reverie of self-pity she rested her head on her narrow single bed. The wagon was rocking violently; she worried it might topple but knew enough of the wagons to understand they were of hardy structure. The wind must have changed direction, because the smoke ceased to blow down the chimney; instead it was sucked up and away leaving a red, glowing hearth. The rocking, coupled with the cosy hearth, soon found her eyelids heavy, and at long last she fell asleep. 'What will come with the new day?' she thought, as she drifted off.

TWELVE

'**O**pen up those blasted curtains and let some of that bright winter sunshine fill the place.' The old woman, having slept all night and half the day before, had awakened with a crabbit head and was shivering cold. 'Hurry up and get the fire lit. What possessed you to let it out? No gypsy worth her salt would see cold ash in a hearth. Tells me there's less of the gypsy in you than you think. And where did you put my baccy?'

Megan rose to her feet, fists firmly on her hips. 'Listen here, you moaning-faced old crab, I'm preparing the fire, and when I've rubbed some of this black ash off my hands I'll make some tea. Pull open the curtains and fill your own pipe.'

Both looked at each other and burst out laughing.

'I'm glad you're feeling better. For a while in the night you'd stop snoring and I thought the bucket was getting kicked.'

The old woman, not having heard that saying, looked puzzled; but when Megan explained it, she laughed louder. This time, however, a strange crackle could be heard deep in her chest, prompting Megan to say, 'I think you might have a chesty problem. Do you want me to fetch a doctor?'

'Me with a doctor? What does a doctor know that I don't?'

'He spends his whole life studying ill folk. My doctor back in Kirriemor can heal every ailment, so I expect others can too.'

'I know the herbs, the roots, the mushrooms. I also know me body is done. Now give us a fill of me pipe.'

'But what if there's something in your chest?'

'The baccy will keep it company!'

She could see that arguing with Mother Foy was pointless, so relented and brought the box of tobacco, pipe and matches from the small cupboard above the bed. The old lady was still feeling unwell, so decided to stay put in bed. Megan helped her outside to toilet behind a holly bush. This brought more laughter, as the old woman sat too close and felt the holly prick her bare bottom.

Back inside, she washed in a small enamel basin while Megan dusted the two ornamental china dogs on a narrow shelf at the back window, then remade the bed.

An hour or so later a warm fire heated the heart of the place. They'd breakfasted on eggs and bacon, a gift from Bridget. Stewed tea grew black on the stove as the pair chatted over things. Bull Buckley filled their conversation, him and a certain Irishman called Michael Riley.

'He's got the hot eye on you; I felt it on the way back yesterday. Are you going to tell him about the poor soldier who waits for you somewhere?'

'He will be a friend and that's all. See this pretty golden necklace? Well, it was a Christmas gift. Do you like it? And no, I don't see what business it is of anybody where my man is.'

'Look, girlie, I'm an old woman, coming near the end, I am. If life has taught me anything, then it's always start with coming clean. If he knows all about you, then no one will get hurt. Do you see what I'm saying? Now give us another fill of me pipe, and a fill of me teacup which has gone as black as that bloody baccy.'

Megan handed over the tobacco, thoughts running through her head. Should she tell Michael about Bruar, or keep her man a secret? Once again, like fingers of grey mist, doubt and confusion filled her mind.

However, the day wound down to a quiet close without a visit from anyone from the farm. Mother Foy was both disappointed and relieved. Relieved that she'd found a peaceful day, and disappointed no one paid a visit. 'Contrary thoughts of an old fool,' she thought.

Megan was glad that Michael stayed away, at least until her head was cleared, or was it her heart? She didn't know, but one thing she did feel, was that her legs needed stretched. 'A long, brisk walk and I'll come back to prepare a light meal,' she promised her old friend, adding, 'you get another sleep, it can only do you good.'

Leaving Mother Foy with a fresh brew and her baccy tin, she set off along the gorse field road. Only knowing one way, she found herself heading in the direction of the farm. There was only an hour left of daylight, so why not pop in and see Beth.

Just where she'd left her the old horse munched away on a bundle of hay in the giant barn. Seeing a familiar face the big shire raised, then lowered her head in a nodding motion, and looked around as if at someone entering behind her. 'You looking for the old woman, Beth? Yes, of course you are. Well, she's in bed, and between you and me, that's where she'll be, until the crackle from her lungs goes.'

'Are you always in the habit of talking to horses?' Startled, she turned to see, leaning on a wooden barn post, handsome Michael.

'Aye, dogs and birds and worms and snakes—in fact, if it crawls, wriggles, flies and canters, then I'll have a conversation with it. Hello, did you have a nice day yesterday?'

He did not answer, nor laugh at her remarks, just stared with those smouldering eyes. Those forbidden thoughts she had tried so desperately to eradicate came slinking like a thousand hungry foxes seeking their prey. He was the prey. Both their bodies met in a tight embrace like two adders coiling around each other. It had been so long: her skin tingled, every sex-starved inch of it. In seconds they were ripping at each other's clothes until they stood before each other's bare flesh, she naked apart from a thin torn petticoat, his torso like a stone statue at the gate of a stately home. For moments she ignored him, teasing him. He kissed her hands, her arms, and her neck. Very slowly, in rhythm with his advances, she relaxed herself, and he kissed her half-opened lips. They lay down on the soft hay, caressing each other's warm, youthful bodies. His tongue opened her soft lips; he thrust it gently inside her mouth. She tasted it. Muscles flexed and danced from his powerful neck to toes that were finding the contours of her slender legs. Then when she thought this passion, like the forbidden apple, would burst out through her beating heart, she slowly opened those slender throbbing legs and freely gave what had been promised to another man.

Afterwards she lay in his arms. A long time passed with nothing but the sound of Beth munching and breathing. He spoke first. 'Ah, for sure you're a real beauty, Megan. I cannot let you drift out of my life like a wind-blown seed. Please stay with me, my pretty colleen, please say you will.' Again, unable to control his body, he was exploring her entirety. She was like mercury through his fingers. He was ravenous yet gentle, and she responded with willingness that frightened yet excited her. She was lost again in the arms of raw passion. Later, as she lay in his strong embrace, she said, 'Today I came here convinced it was to see Beth, but my heart knew it was to find you. Yes, I so want to stay, to lie like we did this day... but...' Before another word fell from her quivering lips, Bruar flashed into her mind, pointing a stern finger at her naked form. She closed her eyes and covered her face with her hands. 'It is impossible.'

'Then why did you give of yourself so freely? It felt so right. Tell me.'

For a minute silence fell upon them. She shuffled her bare feet in the chaff-covered ground. Beth gave a snort, then a whine, as if telling her not to stay another minute, but to run and never come back, fool that she was. Still, what kind of person would use another and not be truthful. It wasn't her way. Cupping his face in her small but firm hands she said, 'I am a married woman.'

A look of utter disgust spread across his face. He lifted his scattered clothes and hastily dressed. His strong Catholic religion and upbringing forbade the cohabiting with another man's wife. Adultery was a dreaded sin. It was looked upon with horror by society. Quickly he finished dressing, and without a word left her alone with the horse.

Her inner self was merciless. 'You deserve to be whipped,' it told her, 'making sheep's eyes like a true hussy at the innocent man.' On it went, 'And what of Bruar, how could you do that to him?'

Tears streamed down her face as she begged his forgiveness, shouting it aloud as if he were there, a witness to this abomination. His lassie taking another man like a bit of free food, picking him up like a pheasant left behind after a day's hunting, shot and discarded.

Such was the power of her guilt she took no notice of the biting wind now driving yet another snow storm into a new night. Soon she was sobbing into Mother Foy's arms. 'I knew it would come, it just had to. My sister was right, I'm a hussy. Oh, how I wish I was stone dead!'

'So you been playing with fire then, eating at the forbidden fruit. Well, I did forewarn you, but never mind. We all fall in our lives, it's not like you lied, killed or blasphemed, is it?'

'Yes it is! I have lied to myself. Murdered my marriage, my blessed union, and broke a promise to my man.'

'That's not blasphemy!'

'It is if he's your God, and Bruar is my God, you know.'

205

For all her words of comfort, Mother Foy could see none were easing Megan's guilt. 'Maybe another dawn will take the sting out of things,' she assured her. 'Now, have you eaten any supper?'

'Yes, I've just eaten a man!'

'Now listen here, girlie, I'm in no mood for your silly nonsense. This man of yours, a ghost sends you off on a mission to find him, even though the army have informed you he's dead. He might be waiting for you as we speak, and then he might not. If things are meant then they will be. You don't have to flog yourself every time you fall.'

'He is alive—why else should this pain in my heart be so bad?'

'Because you refuse to let go. I knew a gypsy girl, so inconsolable was she that only death brought relief, she jumped from a cliff. It isn't hard to understand your hanging onto threads. Let him go. Find Michael, tell him about your missing man, see what he thinks. But like I said, if a path is set you'll walk on it. Aye, you might get lost every now and then, but you always find it again.'

Megan buried her head into a welcome pillow. Floods of tears later, she sat up. 'Do you believe my man is dead, and it's stupid imaginings that I cleave to?'

'I will not say one way or tither, but so what if you steal a passionate moment? Remember, 'tis a long cruel war to our backs. Do you think other good women haven't pinched a tiny bite of the cherry? Don't be so hard on yourself, that's all I'm saying. Now, when tomorrow comes and you have finished your chores, take a walk up to the farm and speak with him. Tell him the truth and see how he takes it.'

'Mother Foy, do you know something?'

'What is that, girlie?'

'My Bruar breathes! I *will* find him, and it's thanks to my wayward ways that I'll have a lot of confessing to do. As for you, do you know that I love you like a mother?'

'Well, slip your hand into the back of that cupboard 'bove your head and fetch me whisky, I'll not take no to you sharing some.'

This was all that was needed, a little tender care, a word of worldly wisdom and a few nips of the cratur. Things seemed crystal clear now. She'd no stomach for strong drink, but after downing those three nips the world had a rosy hue to it. In the morning she'd go off to the stud farm and tell Michael everything, but the night was young and the amber liquor plentiful.

Next morning, as she tried with great difficulty to lift her head from the feather pillow, a thought struck her—why did she have a leaden head and ache like a billy drum?'

'You'll be better when food and warm tea fill you.'

'I feel sick even at the mention of food, and my skull is bursting at the seams as if it's full of rocks. If it's all the same with you, I'll stay here in this warm bed and nurse a cracker of a sore head.' Like a tired badger she curled up, head to knees beneath the bed covers.

There would be no peace for her, though, and as the thump of Mother Foy's stick came across her back she screamed, 'Leave me alone, stupid old woman, can't you see I'm ill? And it was all your doing.'

'It's many a horse I've walked to water, but none I've forced to drink, so don't blame me for the wild state of you. Now get up and see to things.'

'Where is the mercy in your heart? I'm dying here.'

'So I'll just slide out of bed and bump me arse with full bladder down the snow-covered steps. Then, if I'm not frozen to death I might manage to relieve meself, is that what you're telling me to do? Anyhow, have you changed your mind about telling Michael? Talk of the devil, here he comes, I see him from my back window.'

Like a flash Megan was pulling on her skirt and fumbling with buttons, the stones that filled her head ignored. She yanked open a drawer, searching frantically for the hairbrush and thinking, 'I'll die for real if he sees the state of me.'

It must have taken her ten seconds to get dressed, put a quick brush through her curls, and open the wagon door.

However, there was no one to be seen. She peeked behind and up the side of the wagon, yet if the old woman had seen him, then he certainly wasn't there now.

'Wait a minute...' the sudden thought that she'd been tricked entered her aching head. She mused, 'Ha, ha, I can see how that wizent old dame is known as wise—she tricked me. Still, I must say I feel acres better now that I'm up.'

In a while she'd lit a fire and filled the kettle with warm water, and after Mother Foy had taken a wash, she helped her outside to toilet, this time avoiding low-hanging branches from the holly trees.

With breakfast over and the wagon tidied, she decided she would visit Michael and explain her situation. Leaving the old woman comfortable and a kettle on the boil for tea, she set off. Snow had settled, and an icy breeze blew tentacles of mist. 'This place reminds me of

Glen Coe,' she thought, as the dewy mist found its way down her collar and over her shoulders. She drew them in towards her breastbone. Her fingertips nipped, 'I could do with a pair of woolly gloves. It's a small mercy but thanks be for pockets, although this coat is useless,' she thought. as her cold fingers peeped through holes. 'I will have to start hawking soon, and see if some benevolent soul will part with a cast-off coat.'

Here and there small fir trees full of rustling under branches lined the road, a low breeze bringing them to life. From side to side she darted her gaze. Usually walking lonely roads was nothing to her, even the dark seldom ruffled her, but there was an strange feeling of menace that gnawed into her courage. As the way bent through gorse bushes someone moved swiftly across her path. 'Who's there?' she called into the thickening fog. Far off the wind howled like a werewolf lamenting its accursed form. Her steps froze as the body appeared again from the heart of the mist, hovered for a moment, then slipped backwards into the swirl. 'Is that you Michael? Stephen, is it you?' Silence followed. Fear grabbed inside her and squeezed her heart. She remembered O'Connor's tales of sinister beings who practised magic in the boglands of his Irish home.

There was a storm of silence. Her heart beat like thunder. She stood her ground and waited, then no more than ten feet from her stood a figure, cloaked, face hidden under a black hood. It was a phantom; slowly it lifted its hand, pointed and said, 'Hell comes soon!'

Its croaky voice chilled her to the bone, the hair on her scalp rose. Gathering what scrap of courage remained to her, she called again, 'Who are you, and why do you follow me, what is it you want?' Nothing, not even a heartbeat, was heard from the beast. Unlike the beat of jungle drums pumping from her own heart. The thing's outline was just visible, its outstretched hand, finger pointing.

At that moment her resolve broke and something in her screamed, 'Go!' In blind panic she was a child again, running down the hill to escape the evil Green Man. She abandoned the familiar road for snowy grass, which instantly hindered her pace. A rotted fence post didn't appear until she had fallen over it. Buttons were wrenched from her coat by the fall, the hemline was held by the barbed wire and chunks ripped from the garment. As she attempted to pull herself free, a broken splinter tore into her hand, she screamed in pain. Strength was sapped from her as the terror of the mist made her already vivid imagination hear voices not of this world. But she was a tinker and should have known that the voices were the sounds of a gurgling stream. And as if she'd not endured enough, a rabbit snared by the fence was writhing in its last throes of life; it stiffened and died. Her foot caught under the rodent. As she lay face down, her ears felt the ground vibrate. She knew that sound! There was no mistaking the noise of horses' rattling hooves galloping nearer.

Fear of what might be shifting behind her back lifted her up. 'Stop!' she screamed, and threw herself directly into the path of the oncoming horses.

'Megan, we nearly killed you, what in the name of heaven are you doing running about in this freezing weather?' Her rescuers were Stephen and Bridget.

'Some idiot dressed like a banshee frightened the life from me! I ran off the track, got lost. He'll die for doing this to me, the stupid, senseless fool!'

Seeing the raw wound in her hand and the blood-soaked coat sleeve, Bridget jumped off her horse and examined the injury. 'Our house is round the corner, that splinter is deep, it would do no good if frost got into the wound. I'll soon have it cleaned and dressed. Now, who would be out on a day like this, trying to put the terrors on you? A thousand curses on his black soul, whoever he is!'

Stephen promised to get the fiend. 'He'll get my riding whip across his back when I find him, for frightening a solitary colleen.' The Irishman spun around his horse and quickly trotted into the desolate, grey mist.

'I'm worried about leaving Mother Foy any longer. If it's all the same to you, I'll clean my hand back at the wagon. Would you take me, Bridget?'

'You're going nowhere until I've given that hand a good clean with iodine, we'll be round at the farm in no time. Anyway, we've left Nuala playing on her own with her toys. We don't want to leave her longer than planned.'

'Isn't Michael with her?'

'Well now, here's a strange thing, this morning me brother, fine boyo that he is, up sticks and left.'

The icy air stung into the wound, but it was Bridget's news that drained the colour from her face. 'I must have chased him away,' she thought, with a rush of panic. 'Where's he gone to?' She tried to disguise her obvious disappointment by adding, 'I hope Stephen chases that cloaked demon away.'

Before Bridget could answer her husband cantered back, saying he'd seen nothing.

She didn't ask a second time about Michael's departure, in case her interest caused Bridget to imagine she'd something to do with him leaving. Yet how she longed to know where he'd hidden himself. 'Poor Michael,' she thought, 'it's my fault.'

Nuala copied her mother by bandaging a dolly's hand, and asked Megan how Mamma Foy was keeping.

'She's coming on, but very slowly,' was her answer to the inquisitive child.

Bridget had donned a white apron and was looking every inch the caring nurse. Pointing to a small three-legged stool she said, 'Sit down here and put your hand on this table.' The table was covered in yellow gauze. 'I'm going to try and remove as much of this jagged splinter as I can, and it might hurt' She produced a large set of pincers, and after wiping the injury with orange-staining iodine, proceeded to remove a bloodied piece of rotten wood. 'Would you take a look at the size of that,' she proclaimed, holding the pincers and the offensive splinter so Nuala could examine it.

'I didn't feel a thing, you have a touch of gentleness about you.'

Stephen curled a hand round his wife's narrow middle and said, 'that's because she is a trained nurse. She gave it up to take on me and our Nuala.'

The child grinned, agreeing with her father.

'My mummy is the best nurse in the entire world. When Uncle Michael was sick, she stayed up all through seven nights until he was better of a bad fever.'

At the mention of his name, Megan's memory picked up the threads of what had passed between them. Should she ask where he'd gone, and why? Her unspoken questions were answered by the little girl. 'Mummy, when will Uncle Michael be back from Wexford with my pony?'

'He didn't say, pet.'

'Sorry, Megan, in all the commotion I didn't answer your question—my brother has gone home to Ireland. He seemed depressed and worried about something. He'd promised to spend New Year with us, still that's him all over, can't make up his mind about anything.' Bridget then noticed for the first time the necklace around Megan's neck. Her tone changed, and she shot forward, eyeing the trinket. Angrily she asked how a necklace that hung over Michael's dressing table should be draped around her neck, 'Did you steal it?'

Nuala stopped her. 'Mummy, Uncle Michael asked me to put the necklace into one of my little trinket boxes as a Christmas present for Megan. He said what a sin she should not get a present. Remember we gave Granny's shawl to Mamma Foy? Yes, you do. Well, poor Megan didn't get a thing. That's why he gave her the necklace. Shame on you, Mummy, for thinking it was stolen.'

'I'm so sorry, I didn't realise, forgive me.' A blind man could see she was genuinely distraught.

'Forget it, I'm a tinker and it's not the first time I was blamed for stealing. First day I went to school the teacher said it was me who pinched her purse from her handbag. I was only six years old and wouldn't have known what a purse was, but I can't read nor write to this day because I was too afraid to go back. So don't fret, but thank you once more for your charity and tending my wound. I'll have to rush off now; Mother Foy's been too long on her own.'

Bridget ran off to the kitchen, returning with a large wicker basket bulging with eatables. Her clumsy attempt at covering her obvious sense of guilt caused her to drop things, prompting Megan to say, 'Why don't you visit with the old woman, give her those yourself. I'm certain in a day or two she'll be ready for visitors.'

Bridget for the second time felt her face blush with embarrassment, 'Nuala would love to. You can tell her what Santa brought.'

'Yes, Mummy, I can't wait to be inside the story wagon again.'

Stephen spoke. 'Every time Mother Foy had Nuala to herself she'd sit her on a wee stool near the wagon stove, and tell stories of princesses, toady men, shape-changers and the likes, she just loved the tales.'

'I knew another Irishman who when drunk would shout on the toady men and the little green goblins to get out of his tent. But he wasn't surrounded by bairns, it was just the amber liquid sliding down his throat.'

Stephen and Bridget laughed.

Just as she was about to leave, the necklace came back to mind. 'This isn't yours, is it, Bridget? What I mean is, he didn't give it me knowing it wasn't his to give?'

'Dear me, no, a man owed him money for a horse. He could only

211

scrape half of what it was worth, so paid him the rest with some jewels. I'm glad to see a part of them round a female neck rather than in a box in his bedroom. It's just that I saw that one and thought he was planning to give it to someone—I didn't think of you. He spends his life with horses, it's good to see him spend time with a pretty colleen, for sure.'

Dare she ask when he might be back? The question was already formed in her mind, but she thought it best to show little interest, and bade them goodbye.

—

Soon the buggy with brown leather seats was hitched, and she was being trotted back to the wagon in the gorse field. The creepy cloaked one had drifted into the innermost regions of her mind. 'It must have been a dafty—some simpleton from a nearby village out to make a nuisance of himself,' she thought. It was certainly nothing to bother about.

The wind rose and lifted the fog. Sleepy sunshine covered the wagon with a yellow glow. Her old friend had slept on and off, and happily had encountered no one.

Stephen popped in to say his hellos and how-are-yous to the old woman before departing. Promises to bring Bridget and Nuala drifted on the wind as he hurried away. Mother Foy answered Megan's query as to why the Irish folks, with their obvious affection for her, didn't visit as much as she predicted they would. 'The part of Ireland where they come from is steeped, not just in superstition, but in the best manners you are ever likely to encounter,' she said. 'They'll not come unless I invite them.'

'But I have invited them, twice.'

'But this is my home, they wait on my invitation, not yours, it's their way. You have ways of doing things in Scotland, don't you?'

'Aye, but we can hardly send out invitations for a-coming to the tent. We don't all live in fine varda wagons. If folks chance by they either get a welcome cuppy or a hard stick. All depends on why they stop.'

Her comments made the old lady laugh. 'It's a tonic you are! Now, how did you manage to hurt that hand? Bridget has done a fine job of rolling it in muslin strips, but if you want it cleaned right, get them off. Tell me now, did you find time to speak with Michael?'

'No, he's gone off to Ireland, and I know it was because of me. Will he come back?' She asked un-ravelling the bandages from her hand.

'He has the foal to fetch over, else little Nuala's parents won't get a minute's peace. You haven't told me how you got such an injury.' The expert hands of the old woman were busy rubbing a concoction of dried nettles and a vile-smelling paste into the wound that Bridget had cleaned so well with iodine.

'I fell against a rotten fence post in the thick mist. What the hell is that, it stinks like dung?'

'I dunno what dung is; this is Beth's shite!'

Megan drew away her hand, but it was already covered in the muck. 'Let the air dry the thing, keep those bandages on and the wound will stay wet and rot. My stuff will put a hard scab on it. It'll heal from the bottom up. Now don't argue with me!'

She didn't. It was dark outside; the cloaked figure that had caused her accident began to concern her.

'You seem afar off, is something bothering you?'

'Nothing at all, except...' she stopped for a moment, wondering if she should tell her about the thing in the cloak.

'Except what, girlie?'

Just then a low eerie rumble of wind followed by heavy sleet spitting hard against the windows brought back the earlier encounter. 'What if he decides to come a-creeping round us?' Megan thought with a shiver. The spooky vision she had seen earlier in the mist ushered in new fears. 'Strange, that one day a merry dance of passion is followed by another of hidden terror. Better lock up early, just in case, but before I set the wagon for the night, I'll take my old mate outside to pee.' Mother Foy would not have this, however.

'No, not even a cat would squat in that weather. Bring in the bucket, the one I fed Beth with; we'll both use it in the night. Anyway, me warm bed would freeze if left empty for a time. Now what did you start to say earlier?'

'I'll tell you when I've fetched the pail.'

As she opened the door, the pitch darkness filled with wind and sleet engulfed her like a dance of ghosts around gravestones. 'God bless me, if this is not the dreichest weather,' she said, groping for the wagon steps. The bucket was hung on a broken branch of an old tree trunk. Pulling her coat over her head and shoulders, she rushed into the gale and retrieved it. Gripping the pail tightly, she turned and forced her steps back up the wagon stairs. At the top, movement amid the nearby bushes stiffened her. Forgetting the old woman and still shaken by her earlier experience, she screamed out, 'I swear, bastard, no way will I run from you again.'

Who was this person? Feelings of vulnerability and a sense of worthlessness battled within her head. If she'd mistakenly imagined someone was watching and trying to put the fear of death in her earlier, then all doubt now vanished as the figure of the cloaked phantom stepped out of the shadows, pointed a finger once more and said, 'Hell comes, Megan!'

Fingers closed tightly around the metal handle of the bucket, as the weird words crept inside her ears and chilled her brain. The creature threw something. It landed at her feet, then rolled heavily down the steps. If fear could be measured her earlier encounter was tiny in comparison with what she felt at the vision of the dead hedgehog dropping onto the bottom step! The animal had been dug out of hibernation, to prove that Bull Buckley was here!

She threw the bucket, a rook squawked somewhere, then she flew into the wagon, locked the door and piled baskets, cooking pots and anything not bolted down against it.

Old Mother Foy was sitting up and one look at Megan told her trouble was afoot. 'I fell asleep for a moment, did I hear a scream?' Megan's whiter-than-snow face and staring eyes were enough to tell her how serious the situation was. 'Girlie, last time I saw such terror was on the face of a rabbit before I throttled it. Quick now, and tell me what's wrong.'

With eyes darting from one dark corner to another, mouth curled down at the corners, lips trembling, she just managed to squeeze out the words, 'We've a visitor.'

'This has to do with what ailed ye before, isn't it?'

Megan sat close and draped a blanket over the old woman. 'It's him!'

The elderly lady laid her hand on Megan's. 'For several days I've smelt the murderer, he has an unholy presence, has the Bull. But calm down, 'cause he lives on fear, he does.'

No sooner were the words spoken, when out of the black night a bloodcurdling scream was followed by mad laughter, which sent both women into a corner of the wagon to huddle like rats. 'Did this swine do that?' Mother Foy was pointing at Megan's hand.

'Like a witch of the mist he appeared, I should have realised when he called out "Hell", but my mind was full of Michael. When Stephen assured me that it could be some dafty I didn't bother. Will this mad-man do away with us?'

'I wouldn't put anything past him, but I have a feeling he's playing cat and mouse. If that really was him in the mist, he'd have throt-tled you, if that was his plan. Now, quiet your tongue and keep your strength, for it could be a long night.'

'He'll not linger long in such cutting air—in no time his balls will be stone hard.'

Mother Foy stifled a laugh and said, 'Them things were kicked flat years ago by a horse.'

Both smiled at the idea as they huddled close under a large quilt, waiting on a far-off dawn. Each agonising minute slowly ticked down, as they strained their ears, listening. Just like mice in a hole, they knew that he, cat-like, was out there in the dark, but they didn't know if and when he'd strike. Exhausted and thirsty after a long night, the terror-struck couple, one young, the other old and sick, gave grateful thanks for a glint of daylight at last. Cats sleep most of the day, but would the one from hell?

They looked at each other as sounds drifted to them in answer. A knife being dragged across the wagon side turned them to jelly, fol-lowed by, 'I'm off now, but keep your eyes in the back of your heads. Oh Megan, I'll take the high road and you take the low, ha, ha, ha!'

Ribbons of light coming through the curtains shone fully on her face. 'This beast insults my land,' she stood up and shouted to her companion. 'That's a song of my countrymen, I'll kill the pig.' Her mood turned instantly from cowed terror to anger. That flea-carry-ing low-life had used a song written for her countrymen. Who did he think he was?

'I'll rip the bastard's tongue from his throat,' she hissed, tearing away boxes and baskets from the door.

Mother Foy shouted a warning, 'That's what he wants, girlie.'

Too late, her Scottish fire was now kindled. She wrenched open the door, iron poker in hand, and bounded down the steps, screaming. Two hoodie crows shrieked skywards without breakfast. 'Listen, you horny fiend, don't ever use words unfit for your shit-pitiful mouth. That song was for Scottish soldiers who never came home to their loved ones, decent people. Come and do your worst, you pus-filled maggot. See if I care. Never again! Do you hear me, never again will I shiver in fear of you or the whole breed of you.' Taking two steps at a time she was back inside, smiling reassuringly at her friend and brandishing the poker. 'He's gone, and I reckon won't come back near us, or I'll cave in his skull with this.'

'Oh girlie, you stupid thing. He's not human, the Bull.'

'I couldn't give a toss, that's the last time I spend a night in fear of anybody. Now let's get out and relieve ourselves.'

'Put me coat on, girl, and mind the prickly holly.'

It had been a horrible night, Buckley had seen to that, and showing flames of anger would not deter him. The old woman was aware of this, and when Megan cooled down, she knew it too.

Breakfast was a solemn affair, as the wooden mantel clock standing over the stove on a narrow shelf ticked louder than it had ever done.

'Listen, Megan,' said Mother Foy in her sternest voice, 'without argument or protest go to the farmhouse and invite my friends. Ask them to come for the day. Tell them I'm well and want to see them. If he's lurking nearby, maybe the sound of others will send a message that we're not as alone as he thinks.'

'Better I tell them of what he's done.'

'No, I wouldn't put it past the beast to terrify the child. He's got no soul. It's our problem. We'll wear it out. But I'll tell you one thing, my pain is back today, and its worse than ever.'

'The pain you suffered on Christmas Day?'

'Yes, blast it.'

Mid-morning saw her running the mile to the stud-farm, but not before she had checked and rechecked every nook and cranny before securing the wagon door, locking it from the outside. Clear skies and no wind made it a fine pleasant journey, yet every step found her darting frightened eyes in and out of the bushes that from time to time lined the way. Her new-found courage, like a spurt of steam from a boiling kettle, had gone, vaporised. If he did return, how could she defend them both? This thought, coupled with her concern for the old woman's deteriorating health, slowed her pace. In time, though, the farm outhouses appeared and she felt safe. One short visit to Beth in her barn, and then she was knocking on the doorstep, jumping nervously.

Nuala bounced around. 'Can we go visit Mamma Foy?' She was all over Megan, pulling her excitedly into the house. Bridget opened the door further, smiling a welcome. 'Come in. What a pleasant surprise.'

'Mother Foy invites you to her wagon for the day,' she said, her tone formal but anxious.

Stephen, who'd been grooming his horse, sauntered in through the back door. Bridget and Nuala told him they were going out to see the old woman.

'Well, I'd best change my breeches, these are filthy.'

'No need, come as you are, we don't mind, come now quickly.'

Bridget, taken aback by Megan's insistent manner, asked, 'Are you all right? You have the eyes in your head of a hunted fox. Sit for a moment and give us time to gather our boots and coats. And as I never visit without a basket, I'll be filling one. Stephen, find out what's the matter with her while I pack some food.'

The house was a hive of activity, Bridget singing from the kitchen, Nuala rummaging in cupboards for her outdoor wear.

Stephen also noticed how anxious Megan was and said, 'You've not been followed again by that shadow figure?' When no answer came, he tried another approach, 'How's the hand?'

Megan wasn't listening; the bright blue sky was once more filling with that dreaded mist. Buckley may have already crept back and be hidden in the gorse; lying in wait until night came. He'd see the Irish folks come and he'd hear them go, leaving her and Mother Foy at his mercy. 'Let him try,' she told herself. 'Just let the beast try. I'll give him the bloody poker!' Her fist came hard down upon a cushion.

Stephen turned her to face him, 'There *is* something the matter?'

'Och, not at all, I was away in another world. What do want?'

'Well, I'd not fancy being the person in that world. Look—' He pointed to the crushed cushion lying on the floor, before slipping on his coat and going outside to harness the buggy. But Bridget told him not to bother, she was in a mood to walk.

Megan was horrified by this decision and said, 'Mother Foy wants you to spend all day with her.'

A good brisk walk to disperse the aftermath of Christmas indulgence was sorely needed, so Bridget insisted. Stephen ran on ahead, making little snowballs, which he gently threw at his excited daughter. She squealed and laughed, and did the same.

Megan was rushing through the snow ahead of the others, when Bridget caught up and threaded an arm through hers. 'Want to share it with me?'

Should she tell her that Bull Buckley, wild man and beast, was

217

stalking and terrifying them, or like all gypsies, should she say nothing outside their own circle?

'Mother Foy...' she began softly, 'That horrible pain she suffered at your place has returned. I'm worried for her health. She thinks her knowledge is better at healing than a proper doctor, and so she refuses to get help.'

Thinking it was the old woman's welfare that caused her anxiety, Bridget reassured her, 'Well, I for one felt the power of her healing hands. Don't underestimate her wisdom—there's many folk walking and talking today been sorted out by her.'

She ran off to return another snowball to Stephen, who'd playfully thrown one, only to be pelted by little Nuala.

For a moment their laughter and shared joy made her think of home, when she and Rachel would chase their men in the newly fallen snow.

Bridget, with her green velvet coat trimmed with fur, her soft red hair bursting from a thick-brimmed woollen hat, was so alive. Stephen smothered her in a light covering of powdered snow, then stole a kiss.

'Why can't I have a share of that?' Megan asked inwardly. 'Instead I am far away from home, taking care of some stranger unrelated to me. Curses on the thief from Newcastle!' This thought was dismissed from her mind as the wagon, vulnerable like its owner, came into view snuggled in the far end of the gorse field.

They arrived at the wagon with its welcome spiral of blue smoke rising into the mist. Nuala sighed deeply. 'Daddy has pelted me sore,' she told her mother, annoyed because her efforts to hit him had failed.

'Next year, when the snow returns, you'll be taller and won't miss. Now remember your manners, and be gentle with Mother because she's not very well.'

Stephen dusted most of the powdered snow from his daughter's coat, and soon they were walking up the steps into the wagon.

Mother Foy was spruced up and sitting at her fire, warmed by a rug draped over her lap. She greeted her guests like royalty. 'Hello, hello, and a special big cuddly hello to the world's most beautiful girl.'

She lowered her eyelids in a sign to Megan that their unwanted guest had failed to appear.

'Sit here by me, Nuala, and after Megan fills us a warm cup of tea, I'll tell a few tales, you'd like that.'

So, as the old woman told mystic stories from days of old, her visitors munched on biscuits and drank tea. Having the wagon full of bodies created a sense of security, but when Stephen reminded his family they'd not got the horse to get them home quickly, Megan and Mother Foy felt the uncanny fear of the previous night crawl back over them.

'I shall pelt you to bits, Daddy, and then I'll feed you to the monsters from the green valley in Mother's tale.'

Megan had not intended to ignore her friend's stories, but her fear of Buckley kept the back of her mind filled with terror. Soon the Irish folks would be gone, and once more they'd be at his mercy. While Nuala and her father had slipped outside to play once more among the soft snow, Megan asked if they might come up for New Year.

With Stephen and his hound at the farm to chase off intruders, both would be a lot safer. Bridget however put a stop to that possibility. 'We're off for the holidays, but don't worry about Beth. She'll be in the capable hands of a young lad that Stephen hired yesterday to see to the horses while we are gone.'

Megan's heart began pounding when Bridget continued, 'We have received a letter from Michael, he wants us to join him in the old home. Oh, and one more thing, I nearly forgot,' she lifted her basket and emptied its contents onto Megan's bed. There were sweeties, eggs, cold beef, Christmas cake and lots more. 'Goodies to see you over, in case the weather deteriorates again.'

She thanked her host, but it was late and they had to make tracks for home, 'Nuala, Stephen, come in here from the snow and say your goodbyes.'

Megan and Mother Foy sat close, listening intently until little Nuala's laughter and her parents' chatter faded away in the distance. Once more they were at the mercy of a cold midwinter's night and those who inhabited it, what or whoever they may be.

Like soldiers preparing for war, they weaponed up: forks, knives and any sharp object that came to hand went beneath the old woman's pillow. Megan positioned the poker and carving knife by the door.

'Were you frightened while I was away?' she asked

'To tell the truth, I busied myself and did a little rummaging in my old clothes for buttons. I found green ones for that coat of yours, girlie, but me fingers couldn't hold a needle. I dare say you're a dab hand with it, though.' She was trying to get Megan's mind off Buckley.

'You must be kidding, Mother, I'm useless at sewing. But Rachel, well, she could sew clouds together, could that sister of mine.'

'Where is she? Did I hear you once say to Ruth she went to America?'

'Oh, it's a long story—but yes, with her wee laddie, Nicholas.'

Her companion smiled in a sad way. 'Do you know that two centuries or so past, hundreds of gypsies were rounded up and sent off to America as slaves? Dreadful times they were, bad days indeed.'

'Rachel was promised a far wealthier existence than a slave's. I would imagine it wasn't without sacrifice, though.'

'And do you wish to tell me what it was that cost her so dear?'

'She handed over something precious to a woman who had lost her husband when he was killed in the war. She's a nice woman, owns a mighty big chunk of land with a castle sitting at its head.'

'She sounds like aristocracy.'

'Her full title is Lady Cortonach.'

'What is it your sister sacrificed?'

'For a better life than our ancestors provided, my sister gave her only child to the stranger, and for that I think she was wrong.'

Mother Foy wasn't judging, or listening for that matter: her old head lay upon the pillow and snores filled the silent night.

This time the pee bucket sat in its corner, and as the clock on the narrow mantelpiece tick-ticked, Megan found her eyelids weighing heavy.

But, thank heaven, whatever plans Buckley had for that night, they didn't include the wagoners in the gorse field.

—

New Years Eve came, and much to their relief he continued his absence from their remote campsite. Yet this did not stifle the awful memory of his presence, or the nagging fear that if a sound awakened them in the night, it would be him. While it was dark, Megan would stay forever vigilant. During the daylight hours, her thoughts turned to Beth. Without doubt Stephen had left her in good hands, but she needed to see for herself, anyway. Bull Buckley wasn't a day person, she'd convinced herself of this. His type haunted shadows, moonlight and misty dawns.

Mother Foy's chest was sounding that crackle again. This worried both of them, but she too wished to know how Beth was doing, so agreed that Megan should pay her a visit. 'I will be back in no time,' she promised, 'try to sleep.'

With bedcovers wrapped under her chin, she said weakly, 'When you return, I'll show you how to prepare a cough medicine for me.'

'All right, but keep your eye on the clock. I'll be walking up those steps before the hour hand circles twice.'

The weather showed no sign of mist, rain, sleet or snow, and the sky was clear blue. She could see for miles. High upon the horizon several sheep mingled with cows and munched on scattered hay. Spirals of smoke curled towards a frosty sun from faraway cottages. The silhouettes of naked trees and fence posts dominated the scene, and beyond was a church spire. Yes, it was a day to fill one's mind with positive thoughts. 'Us Scots look toward the coming of a brand new year,' she mused. 'Tonight I'll share a dram with my old mate and toast my Bruar, and hopefully she'll regain some strength so that I can make plans to move on.'

Bull Buckley faded into a dark memory as she came upon the out-houses of the ranch. Beth was tied up outside in the cobbled courtyard. She called to her. The horse lifted her head and neighed back. The young man who'd been left in charge of the Irish stables came out to see who had arrived. At the same time both shielded their eyes from the sun's glare to see each other. 'Is that you Sam?' She called to the young man walking nearer. 'Is that Megan?'

Of all people it had to be the lad from Burnstall Hall. He must have been in need of employment after all.

'What of your mother?'

'I was most grateful for the ten shilling, though it done little good. To tell the truth, she was already dying, but didn't tell me.'

'That's a mother for you, always protecting her chicks. When did she pass away?'

'Only last week I buried her. It felt lonely in our house—well, it wasn't ours, it belonged to the landlord, so I had no choice but to leave. I knew of this place, and with me being all my life with horses, it was good luck the Irish took me on. Mrs Newton's gone away, poor woman. Do you know they haven't caught the killer yet?'

She knew all right, but because she'd put his life in danger by telling the police, he was after her. Once more she found that staying silent about Bull Buckley to safeguard Mother Foy was the best option. Also, his ugly face being absent meant perhaps that he'd been forced away by another rival predator. Changing the subject, she asked how Beth was faring.

'Come and see for yourself. I think she's a beautiful shire. If I had a horse like that, I'd get me a plough and do work for farmers and woodsmen.'

'Well, she belongs to Mother Foy for pulling her wagon. Talking of my old friend, I'd best hurry back to her.'

'You've only just come, don't rush off. I'm alone here with the animals, and could do with a bit of company. Have some tea.'

Beth seemed in fine fettle, and it was obvious with the nudging going on she'd a fancy for Sam. A quick cup of tea and chat, then best get back to the wagon.

As they parted she wished him a Happy New Year when it came, followed by a promise to visit tomorrow. 'Mother Foy is sickly, so it might not be possible to leave her. You come to us, there's good whisky for the thirsty.'

He laughed and said, 'You won't catch me refusing a dram, I'll be there by ten.'

'Bring Beth down with you, my dear friend could do with a look at her horse to perk her up.'

As she hurried back, to her disappointment a stabbing wind was already whipping up storm clouds on the horizon. 'Bloody weather, not clear one whole day. Ever since we arrived, if it hasn't been thick mist it's been sleet, rain or snow.' The thought had no sooner left her mind when sleet, harried by a rising gale, forced her head down. The wind was merciless, she wasn't wearing a hat or scarf, her exposed fingers soon froze and her buttonless coat blew all over the place. 'I'll have to find shelter, else this will be the death of me, but where?' The only place was the old stone dyke and an occasional holly bush. She opted to crouch down behind the wall and curl her head under her arm like a robin under its wing. She lost track of how long she stayed there. What was certain, though, was a great deterioration in the weather. Suddenly her wet hair prickled on her freezing neck. Following hard on the torrents of sleet came a storm of thunder. A zigzag of lightning earthed into a far-off tree, and as it crashed into the ground she shivered. Cowed and at the mercy of the elements, she wanted to run. But if it was holding her back, then it was hindering Buckley too; if he was around he wouldn't want to be out in these conditions.

After another peal of thunder she rose and dashed blindly back down the rest of the way. Dripping wet and frozen through, she stepped briskly into the wagon.

Nothing in her young life had ever prepared her for what lay on the bed! It was Mother Foy, bereft of any sign of life, eyes wide open and staring at the ceiling.

The dear, kind old gypsy who had given her an unquestioning hand of friendship was dead. 'Oh please, not you, my only friend in the world, Mother, poor old thing, to die alone!' She cradled the still warm body, rocking it back and forth, sobbing uncontrollably as outside the storm wreaked havoc through all the countryside.

The presence of death didn't frighten her: she'd seen it before, but never faced it entirely alone. 'What a horrible end to the year,' she thought selfishly, then scolded herself for not thinking on her friend facing death alone. If she'd not sheltered from the sleet or wasted time with Sam she'd have been back when she'd promised.

She remembered her last words of reassurance, 'I'll be back before the hand goes twice round'. Glancing at the mantel clock, she saw not two but four hours had gone by.

Megan's mind was in utter turmoil, what could she do? Sudden emotions, mixed with guilt and sadness, engulfed her. Buckley wasn't an issue now. Here was a much-loved and devoted old woman. Her funeral had to be prepared, and her traditional incineration. This was far too great a responsibility for such as she, a simple tinker lassie; but where were the other gypsies? Who would take matters in hand? It was all too much.

The stove had but a few red-grey ashes, throwing out little or no heat, but it mattered not.

Old cant words that her mother used at her granny's funeral came to mind. It was as if they had been tattooed deep inside her head. All she had to her name to give was the respect those ancient chants offered. Covering the corpse she put a small cushion beneath her knees and chanted:

'*Tre banni, tre banni,* [Three prayers, three prayers]
Femma tori marra, [Woman to earth]
Femma tori glimmer, [Woman to fire]
Femma tori panni.' [Woman to water]

On and on she repeated the chants, and hoped that her friend's soul would go wherever her heart and truth lay. All that she could give her friend was what the Earth offered all people—the elements of earth, fire and water. Nothing else mattered, and this then was her parting gift to Mother Foy.

When at last she ceased chanting, the faraway clock tower rang for all to know that a New Year had begun. There was no way gypsies could be found to deal with the elderly woman's death; anyway, Megan's knowledge of the countryside amounted to the mile between the ranch and the gorse field. She decided to burn the wagon herself.

'Perhaps when Sam comes,' she thought, 'he'll help.'

A long night lay ahead, as all across the land a nation would be drinking, dancing and celebrating. A solemn duty rested on her young shoulders, a preparation of the final event, and the last ceremony of Mother Foy's life.

Having no one to talk to or help with the preparation, she started conversing with the corpse. 'You have plenty bonnie petticoats and blouses, ideal for cutting into strips to bind you with.' This helped her loneliness. During wakes she'd listened to many of her own tinker folk having conversations with the dead.

By first light she stood back and congratulated herself for a job well done, and wished someone would come and take a look at her fine handiwork, such a perfect job. Before bandaging her body, Mother Foy's earrings had been slipped into almost paper-thin lobes. Gold rings were placed onto every sinewy finger. 'You'd a great love of jewels, I bet each tells a story,' she said. Once more it seemed appropriate to explain to the corpse what her work entailed. 'I put two pennies on your eyes and shined and laced to perfection these narrow shoes of yours. I wish you could see yourself, old friend, you're a right bobby-dazzler.' It took her a long time to plait the long grey hair, then to arrange it over her head with pretty ribbons. But it was worth it; she was lovely. Death removes wrinkles to such an extent that the skin of a corpse takes on a semblance of near white porcelain. 'Do you know, my old friend,' she said again, 'I wish you could see yourself, you'd be right pleased.' With these, her last words to the woman who'd taken her in and given her hope, she very delicately bandaged every inch until not a single hair was visible.

One thing which troubled her was the thought that no burning should take place, not on New Year's Day, it would only attract attention when there were so many people on holiday. So she decided she'd conduct the ceremony the next day.

There was no way she could continue to use the wagon as a home, not even for a day, as the dead have to be left in total peace. But this wasn't a problem for a tinker who'd survived summer and winter in the open, so she set about building a small tent behind the wagon and lighting a good fire.

She had to get a fire lit—after all, for a tinker, is this not the first thing to be done? After clearing the area of snow, the mattress off her wagon bed was folded over a bent tree and secured with stones taken from the dyke, with silent promises that they'd be put back. She cut and piled branches to form a barrier at her rear, then used some more to build walls on either side of her mattress roof. From the wagon she gathered as many bedcovers as she could and packed them inside her tiny abode. Hunger pangs were by now gnawing deep in her stomach. She added extra firewood to her rapidly dying fire. Soon she'd a kettle boiled. Bridget had left lots of good things to eat, and in no time she was fed and watered.

The long busy night took its toll, and if Sam hadn't come as promised, she'd have slept a lot longer than the noon hour. He was confused to see her huddled inside a tent, instead of in the shelter of the wagon. 'What are you doing outside the wagon in the middle of winter?'

Pleased to hear another person's voice she welcomed him in. 'Sit down here and warm yourself by the fire. Now, if you don't mind, I'll ask that out of respect you lower the tone of your voice.' Then she told him what had happened. He was genuinely sad and said there would be a lot of tear-shedding by gypsies when this news reached them. He knew where several families were wintering, and if she wanted he'd go and inform them. For a moment she thought it would indeed be proper, but something nagged at the back of her mind—Buckley! If others heard, he most definitely would. 'I might as well send a news bulletin,' she thought, and then wondered if Sam should be confided in.

'Sam, I can't tell anyone about this. I have good reason, and I'm sorry I can't give you the promised dram, I'll need it to fire the wagon.'

'Are you telling me that a funeral of one as revered as Mother Foy is to be carried out by, and I mean no offence, a Scottish tinker of no relation?'

'I have good reasons. She knows why too.' She ran a hand across the wagon. 'You must know, Sam, I can't bring attention to myself, and if I say Bull Buckley, will you understand?'

He turned quite pale, shook his body as if a giant spider was crawling up his back, and spat into the red ashes. 'When are you going to burn her?' he asked, looking into the embers.

'Tomorrow, will you come and help?'

'The Irish are back in two days, and I'd promised to clean the stalls, polish the brasses and oil the leathers.'

She lowered her eyelids at his rejection.

But when he saw this, he said, 'Hell, I'll work through the night and finish my chores. Yes, I'll come. Wait for me, don't start until nine in the morning.' She brightened up no end.

If ever a night dragged on with no sign of morning it was that one. Snuggling inside her small tent and looking at the clear night's starry sky, she was transported back to a campsite at home, her head filled with stories of ghouls and doom-slayers. An owl hooted, she held her breath, it hooted again. Thinking of those old faces telling tales of werewolves and witches only added fuel to her already heightened imagination. A wind rose, and on its tail came devilish groans; she could almost reach out and touch the cloven foot of a she-demon. 'What a night to be alone.' She shivered inside, but not with cold, for she was warm enough in her home-made tent. No, it was the fear that maybe Buckley might be joining the foxes and the rats watching her from the shadows. The hairs rose on her neck, while nearby a stream where she and old Mother Foy drew their drinking water gurgled with otherworldly chit-chat. Her chest heaved as she panted with fear. Her promise to keep vigil was scattered on the chill wind; she opted instead to bury herself under the heap of blankets and covers lining her shelter. And there, until early light, she remained.

'Thank you, whoever you are, who looks after vulnerable folks in unsafe places, including me. Give me enough strength to carry out this day's farewell to my old friend.' Her predicament seemed to call for such prayers but to whom was she praying? Somehow, under the cover of the endless sky it mattered not if her ancestors or an unseen God listened, something mightier than humanity was what she needed at that time to support her through each fathomless minute.

With a fire lit, kettle boiled, breakfast eaten, she began the funeral. It was not so easy when the bushes and tree branches hung thick with snow and morning dew. Still, there were plenty of bits and pieces to light a fire from Mother Foy's bottomless hoard. Old books, boxes of rags and piles of torn curtains soaked in whisky were scattered under and around the wagon. Making certain that no eyes, prying or otherwise, were in the vicinity, she waited for Sam. If he had fulfilled his promise to work through the night, then surely he'd soon appear, but when nine o' clock passed and ten followed with no sign, she decided to go ahead without him.

So, with a lighted rag dipped in paraffin and lamp oil, she lit the undercarriage of the bowed wagon, the pride and passion of an ageless gypsy woman who had been held in the highest respect of anyone she knew.

The resin in the wood flashed instantly to life, flames fighting for control of the fir's breath. She stood well back, such was the intensity and speed of burning. Suddenly a thought flashed into her mind. 'The tin box was full of money—if I am to leave this place, I'll need that money for train fare and food.' She might just have time to get it from the wagon.

She remembered how her friend always put all her money in a pouch then into the box. Already a heat was spreading through the wagon, she felt it as the door opened easily at her touch. Inside the mummified remains waited for incineration, strangely still. The impatient voices of the wood groaned and spat beneath her as the fire got going.

She dragged the heavy metal container from beneath the bed with apologies. 'Forgive me, I need this a lot more than you, and where you go there's no call for money.'

Flames found a route up through the floorboards, one singed her ankle. She hesitated whether to remove the pouch and leave the box, but a growing fire has no patience. With as much strength as both arms could muster, she pushed the box out of the wagon and followed its path down the steps. Once at a safe distance, she opened it. There was an assortment of bits and bobs, including four green buttons for her coat. Seeing them brought tears, their salt stung her fire-reddened cheeks. 'Dear old friend,' she thought sadly, 'you were ill, yet thought of my buttonless coat.'

Disappointment on not finding the pouch distracted her from grief. She was certain the old woman put the money Stephen refused to take for Beth's keep in the pouch; she had seen lots more bundles before the box was closed and pushed under the bed. She never went into it the box again, so where was the money?

'Are you looking for this?'

Fear spread through her shaking body like the flames in the wagon. Her fingers tingled, and sick visions of mutilated hedgehogs grew in her mind. As flames of red, yellow and gold, now twisting in unison, completely engulfed the gypsy wagon, she turned to see, in all his evil glory, Buckley, the demon stalker, directly behind her! He who snapped heads from bodies and sucked brains from defenceless animals.

There was no wagon to run into and lock the door now. No man or woman to help. She was totally at his mercy. Blood drained from her heaart: she could feel it sap all her strength, from head-tip to toe end, every last drop. She collapsed weakly onto all fours like a terror-struck mouse, stared up into the soulless black eyes of the wild cat, and waited.

'I watched you all the while, and may I say, it was a darned good burning ye done. Foy would have been well pleased with ye, I for certain would have been if it were me ye burned. Not to mention the earrings and hair pleats and that bandaging.' His words sent a further surge of fear into her body, thinking that he'd actually been out in the darkness watching every move. Was it coincidence or had he read her thoughts?

'I've been as close as this to you for ages, Megan, my pretty thing. That night on the moor, I knew it were you hiding in the heather, I smelt ye. And what good did it do telling Mrs Newton? King I am, and no prison cell or deep jail can keep me for long. So you see it did no good at all. But me, well, I think you'll provide me with a bit of fun.' He lifted her up like a rag doll and bit into her neck saying, 'You taste real nice, you won't mind if I help myself to some more.'

One hand gripped her thigh, the other pushed back her head until she was at his demonic mercy. Her clothes were ripped from her body as if they were made of gossamer. Another bite, this time to her exposed breast, drew blood. Her futile attempts to push him off amounted to nothing; he was far too powerful.

'Real tasty, I'm surprised no one has taken a chunk of this before.' His tobacco-yellowed teeth found another part of her shivering flesh. With a clenched fist he hit her stomach. She fell flat. Still forcing back her head he straddled her body, and like a ravenous caveman, untamed, he tore her undergarments from her trembling hips. His red hair hung over one eye and gave his appearance further menace. She was at the mercy of a maniac. One who did not believe in such a thing as mercy.

'I'll take this high road,' he said, cupping her breasts with filthy, clammy hands as slavers dripped from his mouth and trickled, hot and steamy, onto her now naked body.

For a second his grip slackened, she got half free and screamed, 'Not over this border! Bastard, bastard breed, I'll rather be dead than let you enter me!'

One knee came up and caught him under the chin, while the other found its mark.

'You bitch, she-devil!' His face for a moment turned pale as the pain between his legs shot deep, but it was nothing he'd not felt a hundred times before; much to her horror it heightened his pleasure. 'Kick me again,' he laughed insanely, and drooled.

'If you insist,' she wriggled free and stood away from him, but in her eagerness to escape failed to notice that in her way was a bulky oak branch that had succumbed to the ravages of the storm. She went sprawling over it.

His eyes widened at her vulnerability; again he was like the cat standing over its small prey before the final pounce. She was trapped and she knew it!

'If you plan to rape me, kill me first. I'd not want to live after you'd been inside me.'

'What cat kills its prey quick? I'm not going to rape you once; I'm planning to make a meal of you. I might even keep you breathing and do it tomorrow as well.'

He threw back his head, rested two sinewy hands upon thin hips, and for what seemed like eternity said nothing. Her body was shivering with cold, she bit her bottom lip; it bled profusely. Yet this creature would not see her tears.

'Am I not a power unto myself? I control every living gypsy in England. For instance, see that burning wagon of poor Mother Foy's; it's turning into a pile of ashes, see how the wind scatters them. For all we know them ashes might be hers.' He leered at her nakedness, and with sadistic pleasure slowly, one by one, opened the buttons of his trousers, eyes narrowing into slits. When finished he dropped his body onto hers. She waited, her breaths coming in short pants, but she would never beg; not to a weasel like him. He was toying with her, and now that she was gripped by the arms, had to have his fun.

'Did you notice the bruising on the old woman's neck while plaiting her hair, or did you accept she passed away peaceful, like?'

Was she hearing things? Surely no human, no matter how low, could kill a dying woman who hadn't a day of natural life in her. His nodding head was already answering her question. Her temper, that the circumstances had buried, began stripping away the fear. He could rape her to kingdom come, chew every inch of flesh, but no way would she go without a fight. England and the gorse field with its dead and its demon were gone. She was home, beneath her heels once again the wind-teased heather, and a sea of stars sparkling in the heavens above the mountain tops of Glen Coe called to her from an open moor. 'Megan,' their voices joined those of the ancestors calling through the holly trees, 'get his eyes.'

His face contorted, he leered at her exposed, bitten breasts and revelled in his merciless control. Second by agonising second he held back, letting her arms go, drinking in the sordid infatuation of his power, but in his savage enjoyment he failed to see her curl fingers around the bulky branch that had been her earlier downfall. Now tightly held in her freezing hand, it came thumping into the side of his head. Dazed and confused he staggered onto all fours. With dominance now transferred into her hands, she wasted no time in swinging the heavy wooden weapon so hard into his ribs he buckled under its force.

'I'll not let the likes of you interfere with me, son of darkness, fiend that kills an elderly body waiting on a quiet death! You're no king! You're a shit-pit dweller, a lowlife, unfit to breathe the same air as Mother Foy or any decent gypsy.'

But he was no ordinary human, she knew that well enough, and soon his bent back was straightening, his eyes widening, staring fire, smirking; the victim once more was at the mercy of the cat.

Her momentary courage deserted her. Her fingers, unable to hold onto the weighty branch, loosened their grip.

Slowly he shook his red hair clear of snow and dead twigs and hissed through clenched teeth, 'Hell's here!'

Inside her head, voices screamed to her to run and run until exhaustion would deny him the sick perverted pleasure he'd planned, but an invisible magnet held her to the spot. She stood her ground and waited.

Suddenly, beneath their feet, loud thumping was felt, her tent and kettle moved upon the ground, the bushes sleeping under blankets of snow parted as if a fury of wind was tearing them apart. Something was thundering towards the campsite. A shout from a familiar voice along with loud thudding hooves filled her ears—it was Sam riding Beth. Pulling on her reins, he steered her to charge in Buckley's direction. 'Go on, girl, run him down,' ordered the feisty stable lad. Buckley was sent flying three feet in the air and came down in jaggy holly bushes. Megan raged for vengeance as she ran towards him. Claws unsheathed, she rammed stiff fingers into his face, ripping and gouging at his eyes. Blood spurted around his face. 'I have you now, Buckley, your eyes. I'll blind you and see how far you'll travel without sight!'

Sam had other ideas; swiftly turning Beth he leaned down and scooped her up. 'Hang on, Megan, leave him to the police to catch.' She clung tightly to him with her naked frame as Buckley rose from among the holly bushes, bleeding and raging and swearing vengeance.

Back within the welcome safety of the farmhouse Sam didn't spare a minute before wrapping Megan in coats and garments. She shook with cold, so he gathered her into his strong arms, desperately trying to bring some warmth and colour to her grey-white skin. But she'd been too long exposed to the freezing temperature without clothes. Her head lolled and eyes rolled, she was turning blue, there wasn't a moment to lose. Inside his bedroom, the same one she had shared on Christmas Eve with Mother Foy, he put her into bed. She wasn't responding, so he then took off his clothes and spent hours warming her frozen body. Once or twice he thought she'd died when no breath could be heard, but she'd sunk into a deep sleep and he didn't give up. 'I thought you were a goner,' he said with obvious delight, on hearing her wake with deep sighs.

In her weakened state Buckley still stood over her with a leering face of the wild cat. Her screams on feeling Sam's naked body next to hers pierced the air. It took all his energy to explain things. 'I didn't know what to do—you were turning blue.'

'You promised to come early, why were you not there when I needed you? He was ready to violate me over and over, then suck my brains out.' She sat up and began to hit out. He put his arms round her warmed body and set her back down.

'I couldn't get away,' he apologised, 'and before you ask, did I fall asleep last night, the answer is no. I had a huge lot of jobs to do, tons of leathers, tack and brasses to polish. Now I'll have to get some warm milk into you, Megan.'

She wasn't having that! Staring wide-eyed at the bedroom window, fully expecting the pig Buckley to burst in and start the nightmare over again, she begged Sam, 'Don't leave me—he's watching somewhere out there. Please, Sam, stay here in the room. Get a gun or knife, but don't go about without a weapon.' When she told him about Mother Foy and how the poor lady met her end, he put a protective arm firmly round her shoulder and said, 'His days are numbered. The Irish will be home today and the police are going to be told, I'll make damn sure of that.'

'They'll not catch him. He's afraid of nobody, he can escape from every ball and chain. Nothing, I tell you, will hold that beast.'

'Listen to me, when the police trap him, it's the jail for him and no one gets out of there. Now keep cosy while I fetch hot milk. I've got your skin warmed up, time now for your insides.' Slipping another log onto the bedroom fire, he took her hand and said, reassuringly, 'For a while there you'd given me a fright, with your pale face and lifeless body; thank God you're all right. But there's a few nasty bruises on your body. I'll fill a tub. I'm sure a relaxing soak will ease the pain.'

She held a crumpled pillow to her body and said, 'I'll never relax until I see his lifeless remains. But thank the heavens you had the good sense to use Beth against him today, or else you and I might both be smouldering on Mother Foy's funeral pyre.'

'He would have to fight me first. I'm not just a stable lad, you know.'

Thinking back to the quarry and remembering the rolling head of Moses Durin, she said, 'Bless you, Sam, but Buckley has no soul. I'm pretty sure he's made of devil-skin with a lump of coal for a heart. Now, if you ever have the nightmare task of facing him, make sure there's nothing wrong with your legs, because you'll need them to run.'

After a bath and some warm food, the confusion of the past events began to clear in her mind. She felt much better; perhaps not stronger, for strength had deserted her, but silently relieved that maybe one day she'd live to fight again.

Later that afternoon, when the Irish came home, they were horrified to hear that their dear old friend had been murdered at the hands of Bull Buckley. Sam's detailed account of Megan's near-death experience left them aghast and speechless.

Poor little Nuala had been so eager to show off Fiddler's foal, but on hearing that her favourite person was dead, she became inconsolable, and blamed the angels for not looking after the old woman. Bridget, to protect her child, simply said that Mother Foy had slept away peacefully, and being so young, Nuala accepted this.

In view of the fact that there was a murderer on the loose, she refused to allow Megan to leave. 'Stephen has gone to fetch the police, so you have to tell them everything,' she sternly insisted.

'If I'd kept my mouth shut about a certain wayward landowner and done as the gypsies said, then I would be fine, and Mother Foy would have passed away as nature planned. Because of my blabbering tongue, choice is denied me, I have to tell them all I know. I feel in my bones it will take more than the law to finish Bull Buckley, though.'

'He's had a free hand far too long that one; they'll get him, and before those bruises have healed on your body, we'll hear news of him dangling from a rope.'

Megan had suffered a devastating experience; she might have died at his hands. She longed to lie in her man's arms, protected and cared for. At that moment she ached for him. Was he waiting for her in a high-walled asylum? Did he look to the North Star at night, wondering if she'd ever come for him? If he was alive, that is. It seemed there was not a single person in the world apart from Sam and these good people who cared if she lived or died. Yet she had come through a terrifying ordeal, and she wondered once more if some unseen force was looking after her. And if there was, then it was surely done for a purpose. A clearer picture emerged; her mission had to be to find and bring her husband home.

Finding her surroundings comfortable and secure, she divulged to Bridget, as she'd done to her deceased friend, the quest she had undertaken, and why her journey had taken her to their door.

'You dear, poor thing, what a burden sits on those bruised shoulders! Stay in bed now, I'll be back in a minute.' She hurried off, muttering and shaking her head, and presently she was back, smiling. 'I have brought a friend, will you allow a visitor?'

'Bridget,' she told her, 'is this not your bedroom and me just a tinker guest? Of course, now who is it that hides behind your back?'

She stepped aside, and standing there like a shy child was Michael.

'Megan, why in heaven's name did you not tell us about Buckley? We would never have left you and Mother Foy at his mercy if we'd known.' He sat on her bed with no hint of the shame that their brief encounter in the barn had once put on his conscience. All that concerned him was that she had survived a terrible ordeal. He continued, 'I'm going home to Ireland next week again, and you're coming with me.'

If life was to throw her once more against its rocks, could she survive another shock? 'Hasn't Bridget told you about Bruar, and why I have to find and take him home?'

'Yes, but what good are you to anyone in this state?'

She cried, the strain of the day's awful events, of seeing him again and now waiting for the police proved overwhelming. Burying her head under the pillow, she demanded to be left alone. Bridget walked quietly out of the bedroom and summoned her brother to follow, but he couldn't; he needed to speak to Megan. Her pain seemed to penetrate his heart. He felt her agony; gently he touched her limp hand, held it firmly, and then whispered, 'Come for a few weeks' holiday as my friend, it's the least I can do. Oh Megan, what wonderful dreams I've had since last we met. When the bloom returns to that bonny face of yours I'll pay your fare home. Come to Ireland with me, no strings.'

He was talking with two tongues, yet at that moment as his body touched hers, she didn't care. 'Hold me someone, anyone,' she thought, 'Whoever leads me to Bruar, lift the veil from my heart and help me find the right answer.' Instantly her wedding photo flashed before her and drove away the hazy pictures in her tired mind; she knew what to say.

He was a proper gentleman, but there was no way she'd go anywhere without Bruar. Bull Buckley had it in for her, time was a luxury now, and one she couldn't afford.

'Megan, in a couple of months the ground around my home will be blooming with the tiniest snowdrops. Buds will be sprouting from the ends of willow branches; birds singing to their mates in readiness for new life. Come home to my green isle to live without fear or worry. There will be no Buckley or hidden Bruar to weigh down your pretty head with worry. It will do you a power of good.'

He felt her push him back, both with hands and eyes. Thinking she needed more time, he left her to consider his offer, said he'd a week more before going home to Ireland.

The sleeping powder Bridget later gave her was a blessing; it emptied all worry and fear from her as she drifted into a deep slumber. It may have been after midnight when a slight tap on her door was followed by Bridget's head peering inside the dimly lit bedroom, asking if she were awake. 'The police have arrived to question you, and both Michael and I said we thought you too weak, but it's up to you. Can you face them? If not, I'll tell them to come back tomorrow.'

'Give me a minute to wash my face and get dressed,' she said before remembering she'd not got a stitch of clothing.

'We're the same size, so I've taken the liberty of hanging a few things in the wardrobe.'

'You read my mind, Bridget.'

Ready to face the police, she hugged and thanked her host just as Michael entered the room.

'Well, thank God you're smiling. I've been worried Buckley's scars have gone deeper than we could see.'

His eyes were bright, his concern genuine. It touched and warmed her, she felt safe. She was dressed in a fine tweed skirt, cosy brown twin-set and nice dark leather shoes. A quick flick of the comb through her black curls and she was prepared to meet the police. Immediately on seeing the uniformed men with a mean-eyed detective, her old tinker fears flooded back. To give eye contact was beyond her, never mind speak with them. 'Hello,' said the plain-clothes detective rising from a hard-backed chair to greet her, then exclaimed, 'Oh, it's the gowpie!'

Of all the policemen in Yorkshire it just had to be Inspector Martin.

Her strength returned and that same old flash of anger at all law officers with it. 'I'm no idiot and fine you know it, now where do you want me to start?'

'Look, Megan, let me speak as a friend and not, as your lot think, an enemy.'

He told her to sit, and even went as far as to take her arm and help her gently to a chair. When settled she looked at the others. Bridget sat in a large settee; Stephen sat close to her and over by the window Michael stood beside Sam. By the door were two policemen. Any other time she would have felt like a trapped fox, surrounded by six bloodthirsty hounds, but not now. These were nice people, concerned for her well-being. She'd been seriously assaulted, a defenceless old woman killed. They all shared her sense of injustice, wanting the same thing—the imprisonment, and eventual hanging, of Bull Buckley.

'Seriously, Megan, it is imperative we find this beast. Never a week goes by when his name isn't linked to some crime of major proportions. He's thrown folks, not just weak people but healthy ones as well, into a world of fear. Mothers tell their children if they don't go to sleep, the "Bogey Bull Man" will get them. He is terror with a capital T. Please, lass, if you can help us catch this brute you'll be doing a great service.'

Bridget laid a gentle hand on her shoulders in support, and asked if she wanted a drink before giving her harrowing account of events.

She nodded. 'Make it a big one! Blame it on Mother Foy, because she was the one who said a whisky opens gates and closes eyes.' She certainly had gates to open. When the whisky was downed, she opened the floodgates and told the company all the sordid details. She began, 'I was so proud of my handiwork on Mother Foy's body, even down to the bonny braided plaits but if I'd looked closer at her neck I would have seen the black and blue marks that beast left on her tired old frame. He even stole her money pouch. All the while we stayed in the gorse he was listening to our conversations, coming and going whenever he pleased. Yet not once did I sense his presence, not a single sound. Back in the quarry I lay terrified listening as he murdered Mr Newton.' She wanted to tell the inspector about Moses Durin as well, but that might have involved the gypsies, so she said nothing. One thing that was of vital importance was his ability to disguise himself. Inspector Martin agreed that this was the reason he'd evaded capture—the police had no definite picture of Bull Buckley.

Knowing how Megan had suffered, it was young Sam who interrupted them. 'Inspector, hasn't she given enough? Can't you see how tiring this is for her?'

'That's all right, Sam, I don't mind. If it puts him away, I'll sit here all night.'

'Well now', said Michael butting in, 'it is four o'clock in the morning, and that is, as far as I'm concerned, all night. So if you are quite finished, Inspector, we all need our beds.'

'I'll come back later,' the lawman told Megan. 'Better we continue this here, rather than you come to a police station.'

She smiled and nodded in agreement, then said, much to everyone's surprise, 'I gave him a right slap in the face with a piece of heavy firewood. I'd arrest everybody with half their face bruised.'

'Did you hear that, lads?' the inspector called to the policemen who were dizzy with lack of sleep, 'Let's find this fiend.' Holding out his hand to shake hers, he added, 'And it will be all thanks to you, my dear gowpie.'

There were still enough hours of darkness left for the welcome blessings of sleep, and Megan did sleep right through until six the following evening. Thankfully Martin didn't come back that day. 'He is probably far too busy checking every public house in Northern England for a bruised face,' Stephen said, while they shared dinner.

There was not much in the way of conversation, and the household took an early night. Next morning the police would probably be back, so the house was made ready for them. However, after breakfast and still no sign of the law, Bridget and Stephen went for a ride.

'Come and see Fiddler's foal,' Michael asked, but Megan couldn't rest in her mind until she had news that Bull Buckley was captured, and at first she refused to step outside even in daylight. Yet Nuala went on and on about the lovely foal, so with great reluctance she gave in, and went to admire the young horse. It certainly was a beautiful little animal, and had the look of a future champion about it. It was chestnut-coloured with a flash of pure white running from the tip if its black nose and from eye to eye.

Its young owner pulled at her sleeve asking for her opinion on the horse, since most of the time Megan's eyes were elsewhere, watching the horizon.

'She's a born royal,' she told the child after being tugged at and questioned, 'a lovely wee horse, but to me there's only one great horse and that's Beth. Can I see her, Michael? Will you walk me to the barn?'

Leaving Nuala playing with her foal they were soon in the barn, where memories came flooding back to them; she blushed, her eyes on the loose hay scattered underfoot. He turned her to face him, hands firmly on her shoulders, and said, 'I don't know about you, but I have neither been sleeping nor thinking clearly since that day. You made me feel alive, special. No woman will ever reach me as you did. For that one heavenly, stolen afternoon I give thanks to you, my darling.' He drew her to him and kissed her quivering lips. She didn't flinch or run off, frightened and confused, as she thought she might. Instead, much to her surprise she kissed him back.

Buckley had done as good a job of knocking the stuffing from her, she felt so weak. She needed someone to pick up her pieces and remake her shattered spirit.

'Listen to me, Michael, I too found great comfort and pleasure in your arms, but one day was all it was, and now it's a bittersweet memory.

It's in the past and best left there. In the south of this country in a place called Sussex there's a home for shell-shocked soldiers, Kingsland House. I have no money to get there, nor can I read or write, but I will not take another decision regarding my life until I know for certain if my husband is alive, buried or if his brain is dead. It is a promise I made, and as a Macdonald from Glen Coe I am duty bound to keep my word. Now, if you mean what you say, then take me to him and let that be an end to things.'

'Leave his memory, for that's all he is, and come back to Ireland with me, stay with me. I can give you the world on a plate if you want.'

'Michael, you're not listening. If he is buried in some soldiers' graveyard, I will close our door and go anywhere with you. If his mind is gone, I will take him home and together Bruar and me will live out our lives. When I have that knowledge, then and only then will I be free to decide.'

'I feel in my heart your man is dead, and my heart also tells me that I will spend my days with you!'

She smiled at his passion, and felt in a strange way that his love went far beyond any she might feel for him, even if Bruar was indeed gone.

He lifted her into the air and swung her round like a flag on a pole. She begged him not to, her wounds were smarting, so he gently apologised, putting her feet on the ground just as Sam came in and began packing his leathers into a bag.

'Are you leaving?' she asked.

'Yes, it was only while Mr Stephen was in Ireland he needed extra hands to work the stables. Now he's home I'm not needed.'

'Where will you go?' asked Michael

'I'll find somewhere, sir.'

'So you have nowhere to live, is that what you're saying?' Michael enquired.

'Like I said, sir, I'll find somewhere.'

Michael thought for a moment and said he knew of a small derelict farm in the Lake District. 'I'm friendly with the owner of the land, and I bet he'd be pleased to put a man in it, a hard-working man like you, Sam.'

Megan added, 'A hard-working hero like you, Sam!' She kissed him and thanked him again for saving her life.

'Look folks, don't think me ungrateful like, but what good is a farm to me? I have no livestock.'

Megan slipped an arm through his. 'Yes you do,' she smiled. 'You have a fine Shire horse.' She pointed to Beth, who was oblivious to everything apart from her bundle of hay.

'Are you giving her to me, honest, really?'

'Mother Foy loved that horse, and I know she'd be right pleased if one such as yourself looked after her.'

'That's that settled then,' said Michael. 'I'll write my friend a letter and say we've found him a tenant farmer, with a bloody good plough horse.'

⟶

'Oh look,' she said, as they walked back to the house with Nuala, 'there's Inspector Martin's black car.' His familiar vehicle with its mud-splattered bottom was parked at the front of the farmhouse. Seeing it again brought the thought of Buckley home to roost uncannily in her mind. 'If that man hasn't caught Buckley I'll never sleep soundly again,' she told Michael.

'Don't fret, colleen. He'd have to face me to get to you, and my brother-in-law has a cabinet stuffed with firearms to help me put him in the cold earth.'

His bold words made little difference to her. She'd seen a man twice his size part with his head at the hands of hell's messenger. 'Don't be so sure, Michael,' she warned him, 'he's not known as the King of the Gypsies for nothing.'

'Don't underestimate the Irish fighting cock in me neither, my bonny Scottish lassie.'

She giggled at his antics as he danced a jig on the cobbled courtyard.

Inspector Martin saw them approach and sucked upon a fine ma-hogany pipe. 'Hello, Megan, and how are you doing this fine day?'

His tone was quite upbeat for a man like him. She told him her state of health was improving, thanks to such hospitable hosts. Bridget and Stephen came back from their ride just as the police arrived. 'Is there any news of the fiend?' she asked, her voice filled with fear.

Before he answered, little Nuala came running in, breathlessly saying, 'I think the name will be Foyranday!'

'What name?' asked her mother, calling the child over.

'The foal's name, Mummy—"Foy", after Mamma, and "ran" as in

239

running like the wind, and "day", the special day she came to bring me into the world. There now, what do you all think of that?' She beamed with pride, awaiting everybody's response.

Both parents were delighted and hugged their child. Michael told her she would be a great leader some day with such a sharp mind, and Megan cried as sweet memories of her old friend and the days they shared brought a sudden surge of emotion. Bridget handed her a handkerchief before addressing Martin, asking what they were all eager to know—had Bull Buckley been apprehended?

There was a 'cat's got the cream' look on his face and his answer almost took the feet from Megan. 'Very early yesterday morning, a young boy delivering newspapers to a hotel in York saw a man hiding behind a row of barrels to the rear of the building. He thought little of it, it being a favoured place for down-and-outs to sleep. The man asked the lad if he had a smoke. When he said no, the man tried to grab him, but he broke free. The boy ran off round to the front of the hotel, shouting that someone with a blackened face had tried to grab him. Now, at that precise minute there was a constable doing his round who heard this commotion. He goes into the hotel and gets several strong lads, then out and finds this here blackened-face chap crouching behind the beer barrels. Word reached me that someone resembling Buckley was being held. We need you to identify him.'

'Why me? There's gypsies the whole skelp o' this land that could do the job—get them.'

'I know the gypsies could testify and I've asked them, but they say because he hasn't killed a gypsy they have no argument with him.'

'He killed Mother Foy, for God's sake, strangled her until all her breath was gone.'

Martin approached her and said calmly, 'You refused to take that information to the gypsies when you took it on yourself to burn the old woman. Did you not think the evidence would also be burned? How do you expect anyone to believe you?' Martin's words resounded in her brain. The honest fact was, he was right. Sam did try to tell her, even offered to bring the gypsies himself, but she hadn't thought about consequences. Her only way of freeing herself from Buckley was the way she took. She tried to explain that in Scotland her tribal upbringing had taught her always to think for herself. 'We moved from place to place, with sometimes babies being born at the side of the road and old folks buried in a passing forest. We were always thinking, living and acting on our feet. I know no other way. All I did was help my friend because, in troubled times, she helped me. I knew the gypsies burned everything, so that was what I did. And the fact Buckley was terrorising us made me act swiftly. I never would have known if he hadn't admitted to killing Mother Foy. Perhaps if I explain to the gypsies they might believe me and identify Buckley for you.'

Martin, with eyes almost on a level with hers, said, 'We know if they thought he killed such a powerful lady as Mother Foy they would indeed seek gypsy justice, and in all honesty I wish you had told them. It would have spared the public purse from paying his trial and the length of rope needed to hang the fiend. He murdered a certain gentleman—not mentioning names—and for that he'll dangle long and hard, that's why I want him. But for what he did to you and that nice old woman he should be drawn and quartered inch by inch. Now, if what I've heard about you Scots being tough is true, then get your coat on and put Buckley away. That is, if it's him locked up in York.'

Michael, who was worried by Megan's fear of facing Buckley, said, 'Don't fret, I'll come with you'.

She nodded, though the truth was she hadn't the stomach to look into that beast's face again. But Martin was right—his rampaging through people's lives had to end, and as she was the only person to hear him on the night Mr Newton was so horribly killed, then it was solely down to her. Michael slipped on her coat and squeezed her shoulder in reassurance.

York was a great city, and apart from Newcastle she'd never before been in such a place with high spired churches and regal buildings. Something else she'd not seen was the inside of a moving motor car. It seemed so strange travelling faster than a horse along the road. Quite a change came over Inspector Martin behind its steering wheel: his shoulders hunched, eyes darting, and he cursed as the vehicle screeched on every bend in the road. Regardless of his cursing and jerky driving, she'd gladly have endured it all day, rather than face Buckley, but soon their journey ended.

The black uniforms of the constables coming and going at the police station made her cringe. Perhaps it was a lifetime of being aware that these men had the power to take tinkers, imprison them and throw away the key. Many horror stories she'd heard from relatives made her shiver. Michael felt it and circled her waist in assurance.

'This way, please.' A friendly sergeant with handlebar moustache ushered them into a side room down a long corridor. 'You can stay with the young lady, sir,' he told Michael. In time he brought them both a welcome cup of tea, wobbling on large saucers with a water biscuit soaking up the spillage. Martin came in and sat down. 'Megan, in the corridor we have a man who might be Buckley. He's all shackled up, so don't worry about your safety. All that's needed is a simple nod of the head if you are sure it's him, do nothing if it's not. Is that clear?'

'Yes, now please get it over with before I soak my knickers.'

Michael chuckled, gave her a big hug and said, 'Do you want the toilet first?'

'No, that was only a figure of speech. Please, Inspector, let's get this over with.'

The door separating her from the haunting nightmare creaked very noisily open. The word 'oil' came into her mind, 'the door hinges need oil'. Then she saw a chunk of wood had been kicked from the bottom of the door. 'Anger did that, maybe a heavy ploughman's boot, probably drunk.' She wished the door had other features to look at, rather than having to raise her eyes and settle them on what now stood staring at her.

His very presence sent trembles through her, sweat ran from beneath her hairline to gather under her breasts.

'Is this him?' Martin asked impatiently, but the answer did not come from her, it came with the words of a poignant ballad. With ice-cold malice, for every man in that place to hear, he spat out the words—'You-take-the-high-road-I'll-take-the-low-road.'

Hell opened, she heard witches, werewolves, banshees screaming, every kind of devil screeched at her. Her joints were frozen in fear, 'Is there no end to this red-eyed dog?' she cried into Michael's strong body. What did she do to deserve a living nightmare such as this?

'Deserting me again, Megan? Just when we were enjoying ourselves! Ah well, another time—yes?' He stood inches from her, motionless as a tombstone.

In the space of seconds she'd found enough composure to take a good look at the man who tormented her; his ruddy brown face, yellowing teeth and newly shaven head displaying jug ears. 'Yes, it's him—the murderer of Mother Foy.'

Trapped by chains and large guards he snarled. The veins in his neck, red and swollen, were near bursting. 'Hell will come for you,

Megan,' he hissed, as the guards dragged him off, shouting 'We're not finished with one another!'

'That's a positive identification, then,' said Inspector Martin.

'Hang him slow!' she said, with a mixture of anger and fear.

Later, back in the warm farm house, with promises from Martin that she'd never see the Bull again, she felt stronger and happier. After dinner, Michael told his family what he and Megan had planned to do. 'She will not come with me. Until she has definite proof of her husband, we don't know one way or the other,' he said. 'I will help her find him after I return from Ireland. I've several horse deals to sort, so can she stay here with you?'

They thought Megan was a nice and pleasant girl, they'd become quite fond of her; yes, she could stay with them. Bridget loved her brother, who clearly held a great deal of affection for the Scottish lass. It did concern her that if Bruar was alive and well, his hopes to further a relationship with Megan would be dashed. Later, when the men went to bed, she spoke with the tinker girl who had stolen her dear brother's heart.

'To be sure our Michael seems taken with you. Be honest with me now, do you feel the same?'

'In total frankness, I do not know. Hell, Bridget, my feet have hardly touched the soil while all manner of mishaps have befallen me. I can't think straight at all. But one thing I do know, your brother sees worth in me. I will find Bruar, and I'll tell you this, if he's got a tiny spark of working brain, then I will take him home and live my life with him. Michael is aware of this, yet he is prepared to take a chance and wait on this outcome.'

'Tell me something else, and it's entirely up to yourself if you answer me. Have you slept with Michael yet?'

She waited for an answer, but Megan wasn't ready to tell of tasting the serpent's apple in the barn, not yet.

'Part of me is hoping you find your man... dead. But it's only because I hope my brother finds your love. I can't imagine a nicer, more sensible girl than you. I know that's an awful thing to say, but surely you can see the reasoning behind it?'

She smiled, but a stranger who had never met, let alone looked into the eyes of her Bruar, could never understand how painful those words were. She didn't want him to be dead, but the opposite; she wanted her handsome, windswept laddie to walk again on northern soil. Yet she knew that was only a fleeting dream. Reality might prove a far more demanding master in the days that lay ahead.

While filling the kettle and cutting bread for toast the next morning, she glanced from the kitchen window at the handsome Michael already risen with the cockerel. Shirtsleeves rolled up over elbows, he strode about the yard scattering corn to a regiment of hungry hens. His thick mop of brown hair was already combed to perfection. She'd not noticed before, but a thin line of hair was growing above his top lip. He wore green tweed breeches held by two leather braces buttoned at either side, rubber boots already covered in horse-dung and straw. Lifting the boiling kettle off the hot stove, she slipped out to join him. 'What are you planning to do with the hairy lip you've on yourself, laddie?' she teased.

'I'm going to grow a handlebar moustache like that police sergeant back in the station in York; sure I am.'

'Well, I hope you haven't plans to go kissing me, only clean-shaven men will have the privilege.'

'Is that the way of it?' He laughed and lifted her clean off the ground and rubbed his unshaven mouth into her face.

'You big brute, I'll get you back for that.' He let her go before turning on his heels. Breathlessly she chased him through the yard then back into the barn where he caught her in a firm embrace and began kissing her neck. Gently he rolled her onto the hay, but this time however she did not respond to passion's temptations; quickly she rose and dusted the hay from her clothes. 'I can't, Michael, not this time, not until I know of Bruar. He will always be there, try to be patient. If you want me, then I can only be yours when totally sure.' There was no need for an answer; the disappointment on his face said it all.

Within a week, Michael began to pack for his trip home to Ireland. She watched him carefully roll socks and gloves in balls, before slipping them into the side-pockets of a brown leather suitcase. Feeling slightly awkward and at a loose end, she asked, 'Do you need a hand?'

'If my mother was here she'd tell you I always pack things myself. Never mind that, me lovely colleen. Can I ask you to promise me that you will you stay indoors unless my sister or brother-in-law goes out with you?'

'But what have I to worry about, with Buckley locked up in jail and in chains?'

'Sure, it's not him that bothers me, it's some other fella stealing you.'

'Don't be so silly! Two men are quite enough, you know.'

They laughed and talked until, his packing finished, he stood on the back step. He'd bought a car, one with wipers to flick off rain and a loud horn. 'I never was in favour of these blasted tin horses,' he said, 'I'd much rather have my bicycle or a good thick-rumped horse to get to the nearest train station. But it's a long way to Liverpool to catch the ferry to the old country, so this boyo with its four wheels can do the job faster. Modern toys, eh, Megan?'

Just as he was about to say his farewell, another car was heard braking on the driveway; it was Inspector Martin.

'Wonder what he wants?' Her heart murmured low and questions teemed wildly in her mind. Both waited as the policeman dropped his hunched shoulders and stepped from the ominous black vehicle. 'Nice day, folks,' he said. 'Can we go into the house?' He was leading the way; without a word they followed.

'I won't beat about the bush,' he said seriously, 'but last night, while being transported to the main courthouse for trial, that slimy eel escaped. Bull Buckley has managed to evade capture since. I'm sorry to tell you, but he's slipped right through our fingers.'

Michael wrapped his strong arms around her to no avail. She felt only the beating of her terrified heart. Martin offered protection in a safe house, yet she failed to hear him. Bridget and Stephen's horses clattered loudly on the cobbled yard, and still not the slightest sound did she hear. Her vulnerability put a cloak around her, she was help-less. Seeing the police car, Bridget quickly came in to see what was wrong, while Stephen stabled the horses. 'What manner of man is he, and shame on a useless police force,' Stephen said, on hearing the awful news.

Bridget strode to a drinks cabinet, poured a stiff whisky and asked, 'Anyone else want one?' Emptying the glass she added, 'To think of that terrible man running around out there makes my flesh crawl.'

Megan took a glass and did the same. 'Mine doesn't feel too great neither,' she shouted; then apologised for raising her voice.

Michael forced her to sit down, and she instantly withdrew into herself. Even circled as she was by friends, their presence failed to drive the demon from her side. Vivid images of terror loomed above her, of Buckley whistling the 'high road,' biting hedgehogs and promising to take her to hell. Buckley, in all his evil dominance, was right back in her body and soul. She began to scream hysterically, and only when Bridget slapped her hard across her face did she come out of it.

With dogged insistence Inspector Martin assured her they'd get their man, but he was wasting his breath as far as she was concerned. He was uncatchable. That inhuman product of evil would never hang from a rope-end until she'd been dealt with by him.

'I'm so sorry Michael', she told him in sombre tones, 'this is too much for me. I think if I lose myself on the open road it will offer me more safety than these four walls. Anyway, I wouldn't put it past him to come here and terrorise these kind folks.'

Her bedroom offered sanctuary and privacy to fill a suitcase with the clothes Bridget gave her, and she was soon standing on the doorstep.

Michael's jaw had a stiff, determined look to it as he took the case from her hand and said she was going nowhere. 'I'm not afraid of him, I told you that, But this trip is important, else I'd set off and catch him myself; or wait here and shoot his hide full of holes. He's a coward, and can only hurt weaker people with fear. Stephen has his guns.'

Stephen was worried though, and not for Megan; his responsibility was to his wife and child. 'I agree with her,' he told Michael, 'and I feel it would be better if she left. I'll take her to a station.' He brought a wallet from his jacket pocket, took out some money and pushed it into her hand.

The men began arguing, but Inspector Martin intervened and said, 'Buckley will be caught; now his identity is known. Fugitives don't get far.'

His words meant nothing.

Michael directed Megan outside, where he put the suitcase into his car. 'I'm taking you to Ireland, and that's that. And before I hear "What about our arrangement to find Bruar", I'm a man of my word. We will definitely search for him, but just not in the near future while Buckley's around. We'll come back to see him hang.'

The police officer seconded his words. 'Oh, you can count on that. No stone will be left unturned until he dangles from the rope.'

Michael went on, 'Buckley will never know you're in Ireland, and will have no idea where to search.' To his sister and Stephen, he said it was highly unlikely a hunted man would come where there may easily be police waiting. 'No, I feel he'll lie low for a time. Now come on, Megan, let's go—over the water to dear old Erin's Isle.'

What should she do? If she took her chances on the road she'd be forced to come across circles of gypsies, where in time he'd discover her. If she ventured alone somehow their paths were bound to cross. There was no choice.

THIRTEEN

*T*he port of Holyhead near Liverpool was a sprawling mass of humanity, struggling and jostling for space. Ship-hands, using every minute to get their ships moored or ready for sailing, were oblivious to other harbour business. Only the gangways along which they unloaded and loaded precious cargo mattered to the dozens of burly sailors whose job it was to see the goods on and off the huge carrier ships.

This was a new sight to eyes that had seen only hills, moors and mountains high. She clung tightly to Michael until they were safely onboard the giant ferry which carried all kinds of folks to the south of Ireland. The simple words 'haste ye back' came from the ancients in her head, and tears rolled over shiny cheeks while she watched the mainland fade into a thin horizontal line of mist, then disappear. Michael wiped the tears from her face along with salty sea spray, squeezed her arm in reassurance and whispered softly, 'He can't reach you now.'

Who did he mean, she wondered, wild Buckley or her Bruar?

People thronged the decks, some passing with a smile or nod, others with stern looks, although few seemed sad. This uplifted her heavy heart.

The sea, like her mood, was serene and quiet, and soon, with their journey over, they were disembarking at the capital port of Dublin. This city, where she imagined men stood on street corners sharing tales of great politicians, and the country where there were tiny magical people called leprechauns, fascinated her. Dublin was full to bursting with all kinds of people, talking, it seemed to her, in several different tongues.

Michael told her she was privileged to hear the Irish Gaelic, which much to his dismay might soon be heard less as more folks spoke the English, especially the young. She said that in Scotland the northern folks were being forced to go the same way. She'd even heard some say that in schools a child not speaking English should go home and not come back until they'd scoured the Gaelic from their mouths. 'My father-in-law told me that,' she added.

'Here's our Paddy now,' Michael said, as a noisy car drew alongside them, horn honking loudly. 'This is Megan,' he told the plump character with small twinkling eyes and rounded rosy cheeks nesting in a greyish beard. A bonnet sat on the side of his head, with thick grey curls sticking out beneath like a spiky broom. She held out her hand, which he accepted with a flourish, then planted a kiss on it.

''And this, dear, is my friend and right-hand man, Patrick O'Neil.'

'Tis a fine evening, and may I say it's a pleasure to meet you at long last. Sure his nibs here spoke of little else last time he was home.' A blush spread across her face and she lowered her eyelids.

'Well, bless my soul if this colleen isn't a mite slip of a thing, hardly a picking on you. I dare say you'll be putting a bit of beef on yourself when Mrs Sullivan feeds you up.'

'Leave her be, Paddy. Tell me now, how are me girls doing?'

'Sure, the mares couldn't be better with all the love me two hands have been giving them. They're better treated than frilly females, I'd say.'

With each passing mile Dublin was fading into yet another memory. She smiled, thinking of the Gaelic tongue, and remembering how Bruar would only utter it if annoyed at big Rory and O'Connor.

For the whole length of the journey, apart from the odd times that a jolt brought the car's engine to halt and each man took turns to yank it into life with a starting handle, all they spoke of was horses. This was fine because it gave her time to think; not about Bruar, but about the presence of Buckley somewhere over the stretch of sea, which seemed to her not that far away.

Darkness had settled around, and only silhouettes of the countryside were visible. Michael tried, with clumsy words, to paint a picture of how lovely the place was, but with the disappearance of the light, all she saw were lengthening shadows.

It must have been two in the morning when they jolted to a sudden halt. Mrs Sullivan, the housekeeper, had stayed up to greet the master of the house with a giant yawn. 'Hello dear,' she said, after hearing the brief explanation given for Megan accompanying him. 'I'll put you in the room on the first landing where the guests usually sleep unless...' Michael answered her questioning look by saying, 'Yes, I'm sure she'll be comfortable.'

They were exhausted, so after sharing milky cocoa with the others, Michael showed her to her room. Smiling, she asked him whether or not she should mention her marital status. 'Do I mention Bruar, or would you rather I didn't? It's just that I don't know how to present myself. Can I talk freely or is it best to say nothing?'

'I have simply told them you are a girl I met at Appleby Fair and that's that. No husband, no search. Don't mention him, because in these parts it would look wrong if I had another man's wife under my roof. It's a religious taboo here, and one that's seen less fortunate women tarred and feathered.'

Saying goodnight, she slipped quietly into her comfortable bedroom, slightly opened the window and listened to a solitary owl calling from some treetop into the night. She was troubled; it felt like a betrayal not to mention her man. She stayed up well into the night, pacing the bedroom floor, before deciding what to do. It wasn't the fear of being tarred and feathered, but she knew she had to keep the peace, be accepted.

When sleep overpowered her, nothing and no one entered her subconscious mind, and because of this she felt as refreshed by her sleep as she'd done in a long while. Morning brought bright sunshine, flooding rays of its welcome light into the bedroom.

Through the open curtains she saw what Michael had tried to describe; miles and stretching miles of beautiful fields. Although it was still winter, in her mind's eye she pictured a summer scene of luscious green, with wild clover and tiny daisies.

Over a satin-backed chair hung a red silk robe which Mrs Sullivan had hurriedly prepared for her the previous night; she slipped it on hastily, tying the soft belt around her waist. Running fingers through her tousled hair, she almost floated downstairs, feeling every inch a lady of the manor. Michael was already up and about seeing to his precious horses. As she set her feet on the paisley-patterned carpet of red and green in the hallway, he came in and filled his gaze with the vision of loveliness standing before him. At once she was in his arms being kissed and embraced. Pushing him gently away she reminded him of their agreement.

'If you had my eyes and saw this beautiful filly standing in front of you—well, need I say more?'

'If I were a filly, I'm certain Mrs Sullivan would have something to say about my hooves on her carpets.'

'Carpets can easily be replaced, but the look of you all fresh and blooming cannot. And that red robe goes with your black hair like a crimson sky on a shimmering ocean at the setting of the sun.'

'My, oh my, what a charmer you are this fine day, Michael of the Irish.' She wondered what title this fine gentleman held and asked, 'What is your other name? Though to me, forever the tinker, names matter little.'

'Why is that?' he asked.

'Because we seldom stayed long enough in any place to care what people were called.'

'Riley is my name. Now, will we annoy Mrs Sullivan by demanding a cup of her special tea?'

Morning tea, he insisted, was part of Mrs Sullivan's breakfast chores (and hell mend anyone who got in the way of her duties) so while they waited for the housekeeper to prepare breakfast, Megan dressed and went for a walk around his stables. These were several more in number than his sister had, and because of this more men were needed. Already Paddy was up and about and eager to introduce her to Johnno and Terry, both stable hands who'd worked many years with Michael and his father before him.

'Ah, she's the picture of a princess she is,' said Terry, smiling with approval. 'Tell me now, colleen, why have you come here wit this piece of useless flesh when I'm free?' He laughed, pointing at Michael.

Johnno joined in the laughter, displaying a toothless grin. Shoving his mate aside he said, 'Niver mind him, Megan, and I'm the one wit the looks.'

Paddy, haltering a fine stallion, laughed at his two mates' fanciful shenanigans and said, 'Would you listen to the two of you? One would think you'd never set eyes on a woman before, and the both of you with fine wives.'

'Less of the fine there now, Paddy me lad, me old bird is as broad as that barn door there and as bald as the church roof.'

'Terry, the nixt time I sees your good lady, for sure I'm telling her what you said.'

'I'll flog the life from ye, Johnno, if ye do. And who are you to speak, wit that skeleton wit flesh wrapped around its bones that you have for a wife.'

Both men playfully tapped each other with horsewhips.

'I'll have to be speaking with these men of mine,' joked Michael, 'for they are as mad as hatters.'

She enjoyed the light-heartedness. She didn't usually stir grown men to such frolics, so she flicked back her head and smiled broadly, almost flirting. Then, realising what she was doing, she blushed red.

Michael held her hand, already signalling to all that his visitor was spoken for. It made her feel important. Strangely, she felt a sense of belonging there in such a lovely place; but was she fooling herself yet again?

Later that day, after a breakfast served to perfection, Michael took her on a tour of his kingdom. 'This is Ballyshan, my home,' he told her proudly, indicating the land for as far as she could see. 'To the front of the house and stables is where we graze and exercise the horses. To the rear of my property there is a vast area of moorland.' He went on, 'It would be best if you kept yourself within the miles of flat land to the front of the house and don't go near the moor, because it has bogs so deep I've lost horses in them. Sank, they did, into the ooze of hell, never to be seen again.'

She reminded him that next to her birthplace of Glen Coe in Scotland lay Rannoch Moor, the location of the country's deepest bogs. They made slimy graves for whoever didn't know the area for certain. Pools of wet, black peat covered the earth further than the eye could see. Once, many hundreds of years past, it is believed a whole battalion of Roman soldiers, out scouting suitable routes to the Highlands, were swallowed up by the wet lands of Rannoch. 'Fear not for my safety, Michael, I know boggy moors like the back of my hand. The secret is never to walk in straight lines, and always test black peat with a stick,' she assured him.

'I don't doubt your knowledge of bog terrain, my lovely, but nevertheless I'd feel a lot better if you took walks on solid ground. There's lots of lovely quiet ways here, though I'm afraid there's no village for miles. In fact all we have in the way of neighbours is a few solitary tinker families who come and go on the edge of the moor.' His words sang out to her.

'Where are the tinkers exactly, Michael?'

'I might have known you'd want a visiting with your own kind.'

'Can you blame me?'

'No, of course, I wouldn't dream of it. If you ask Mrs Sullivan, although she doesn't say, I know that sometimes she takes food to a small family living way out by Runny Brook. It's an area of woodland on no man's land between moor and forest.'

'Do you think she'd take me next time she goes?'

'Ask her and see. It wouldn't do any harm, and I'm sure she'd be glad of the company.'

'I'd be happy to take you,' said the housekeeper, folding her arms over a snow-white apron, 'but bless me soul, if the family isn't away to Glendalough. Kathleen, the young wife who comes with her man and children, winters there beside her parents. I dare say though, like the curlew, the folks will be bundling into their summer haven soon. Her man is called Robin, a fine name for a lad who wears a red waist-coat given him by a lord whose life he saved at a shoot near Wicklow. Nearly shot the head off himself with his own gun, had Robin not grabbed the blessed thing off him; folks say the lord was on the edge of committing the mortal sin of suicide. By the Holy Virgin, I can hardly bring meself to utter the awful words.'

Megan was just getting interested, when the old body refused to continue, sat down on a high-backed chair and began running rosary beads through her podgy fingers and muttering prayer after prayer. Yet her eyes seemed to say, 'If you press further I'll tell you.'

So sitting close she said, 'Go on, Mrs Sullivan, tell me why the gentry was killing himself?'

'Oh, something to do with a lot of debts he owed, and don't ask me another thing about that, cause me lips are closed. The tinker couple have been blessed wit three lovely little boys, and it's them I takes the food for, beautiful sweet childer they are.' Then she raised herself from the chair and said, 'The lord was so grateful to Robin for saving his life, as his worries turned out not to be as bad as he thought. He gave him the red waistcoat, and that's why I said the name Robin suits him fine, because since receiving the gentleman's clothing it's never been off his back. They'll be passing any day and you'll see for yourself. He always takes the lead, pushing his red breast to the front. As the purple crocus raises its bright head from the brown soil, that's when they'll head up to Runny Brook, and that's not a flicking of a lamb's tail away.'

Although Paddy stayed in the farm at Ballyshan, Terry and Johnno lived several miles away in the nearest village, going home at weekends and holidays to their families. And going by their stories, each had about a dozen kids.

Megan settled down to live a normal life in and around the homestead, but unknown to Michael had become quite an expert in the causeways through the boggy moors.

Michael had been taking trips and not coming home for days at a time. In the beginning he was always there, to-ing and fro-ing between the house and stables, yet after a month he began to be absent more often. When she asked, all he would say was, 'I have deals to do, horses to sell and people to meet.' Although she didn't say anything, loneliness had taken its place in her heart.

It wasn't her place to be interfering, but perhaps it was that loneliness that had her press Mrs Sullivan to accept her offer of an extra pair of hands around the house. Much to her disappointment she politely refused, saying, 'If you're to be a lady one day, and its no use saying the master hasn't got plans for you, my dear, then those hands should stay soft.'

One morning, while Michael was away, the old housekeeper hurried into her bedroom. 'I have a sighting of the Fureys coming to the house. They'll be passing any minute, and you'll miss them if you don't rise from that bed.'

'Who are the Fureys, Mrs Sullivan?' she enquired sleepily.

'Why girl, do you niver listen to a word I tells you. Kathleen, Robin and the three little 'uns, that's who.'

She dressed, and standing at the door minutes later saw a sight that lifted her heart boundlessly in her chest. Robin came first just as the housekeeper said: red-breasted Robin with a mountainous pack on his back. Kathleen, heavily pregnant, followed behind with three lively wee boys marching at her heel like little soldiers.

'Hello, Mrs Sullivan,' called Robin, sporting a red face to match his waistcoat. 'I sees our Holy Mother's been sending the angels to make you look ten years younger than last time I had the pleasure of your fine company.'

Megan smiled at his banter. How many times had she herself used those soft words, buttering folks up so they would show acts of kindness; she waited eagerly on the housekeeper's response.

'Ah, that'll do with the smooth tongue. Tell me now, how have the children been? Take them round the back door, I've a parcel.'

'Bless me soul, if they aren't just after saying they hoped Mrs Sullivan, God's very own angel, wid have a bite to fill their little bellies.'

'Yes,' thought Megan, 'he certainly knows how to charm the old woman, a handy skill when feeding hungry bairns.'

At the rear of the house, wooden boxes were set out for the tinkers with food and drink. She'd also been preparing provisions for them, putting the odd titbit in a basket. This she would give to Kathleen, who'd take it with her to their campsite on the forest edge. When a week had passed, the old woman would go back and refill the basket. This was the usual way of things until the small band set off to winter elsewhere once again. Kathleen, because of her shy quiet nature, left all talk to her husband, giving only a gentle nod to her dear old friend who was eager to introduce Megan.

'This is a Scottish girl who spent her early days on the road like you.'

'And what's up wit the roads o' Scotia that you've left them?' asked Robin, showing a slight annoyance.

'Nothing but circumstance,' was the only answer that came to mind.

For a while he ate and said nothing. Then, when he had finished, he removed a green cotton muffler from his neck, wiped his mouth, folded the neckerchief and put it back on.

'Begging your pardon, Mrs Sullivan, but time is agin us this day. It will be dark if tracks aren't made now. Will we see you and what's-her-name here, later?'

'Sorry, Robin, I failed to say, this is Megan. Yes, she wants very much to visit you and maybe help Kathleen. I see another baby is in there.'

These words seemed to trouble them, so they gathered their boys who were happy playing in the stables and were soon gone to camp up on their usual site.

'What did you say to upset them so much, Mrs Sullivan?'

'Me an' me big mouth. I forgot that Kathleen has already lost four babies. All girls, and all born dead they were, bless their tiny little souls.' She reached into her apron and kissed several beads, whispered a prayer and popped them back into the pocket. She continued, 'Two years past I helped bury the last one. Oh, what a mite it was, no bigger than my fist, didn't have a chance. Strange thing when a womb rejects girls. All I can say is, God needs angels when he takes the newborn, them being void of all sins.'

Megan told herself that Mrs Sullivan was far too holy, and perhaps if she thought more along the lines that Kathleen might not carry girls for reasons going on inside her body rather than Heaven's declining population of angels, she'd not need to pull that rosary from her pocket every two minutes. She thought this, but never would she dare insult such a lovely old woman by stating the obvious.

That night, when Michael came home, she couldn't wait to share the day's visitors with him. His mood, however, was dark and as if he was angry. He reminded her that the Fureys had been coming to the area for so long now he hardly noticed. 'It's women who fuss over tinkers,' he said, to her utter amazement, 'Mrs Sullivan has a thing about Kathleen and her boys.'

'Why should she be so concerned? And by the way, just in case it's slipped your notice, *I'm* a tinker.'

He ran his fingers through his hair and apologised for his lack of compassion, 'Mrs Sullivan had two sons, oh fine young lads they were, but in 1916 she lost them. You see, her man died when the boys were little, and she brought them up here with my mother's help. They were like brothers to me, but...' his words trailed off as he dropped his head on the arm of his chair.

'Tell me, Michael, I need to know—was it in France or Germany they died?'

'Hell no! It was in bloody Dublin during the Uprising. Those blasted British ambushed a dozen young men, and killed every one. Look, here I am, rambling on about something you know nothing of. Anyhow, it's finished now and in the past. But it split the country in two, it did, and as far as we're concerned the politics have hardly begun.'

She removed two coats from the rack behind the kitchen door and said, 'It's a nice moonlight night, Michael, why don't we walk awhile and you can tell me all about this fight in Ireland. In Scotland, on our small campsite, there was an Irishman who told us of unrest in his homeland. He came from the south and said he might go back and take up arms, and now that I hear you, I feel this struggle was what he meant.'

He was lost in thought and hardly heard a word she said, as arm entwined in arm, they walked and talked. Then she asked him if he had any involvement in matters concerning his country's politics?

It might have been the gentle breeze blowing about her ankles that made her move closer to him as he went on and on about the problems in his land. She couldn't say why, but once more she was back in the hay barn in Yorkshire, finding his lips and kissing him with as eager a passion as the coming spring. Pressing her body into his and running her knee up and down his inner thigh, she felt out of control like a wind searching for an autumn tree laden with dying leaves. Nothing seemed important, only the hunger rising in her body as she ached for love, she needed him. This time, however, it wasn't she who was pushing him away, the opposite was the case. 'Stop it—have you heard a single word I've said?'

'No, and to be honest I don't give a diddle damn about struggles, politics or any war, whether a homegrown one or a world one. Get this into your stupid skull; a tinker is a tinker and always a tinker. Who wins wars makes no difference to us, because we get treated the same by everyone. Och, you make me sick, can you not accept life and be done with it? Anyway, things seem to fare well for you, I can't see hungry folks with begging bowls in hand here.' She turned and ran off in the direction of the house, only to be pulled abruptly back on her heels by a red-faced and furious Michael. 'You listen to me, my lady, father and mother worked every God-given day to build this place and I'll do the same, but it doesn't get round the fact that there are those who aren't so fortunate. Look, I love you because I've never met anybody who makes me feel so happy, tinker or not, but if you stay here as my wife, then the Republican cause will definitely be your business, as it is mine.'

She'd never seen this side of the fine Michael and shouted, 'Stuff you and your war up a hen's arse!'

He grabbed her arms and hissed, 'How am I supposed to take a mouth like that into county circles?'

She broke free and screamed, 'You can stuff your county circles up the hen as well!'

Without another word she ran to her room, leaving him fuming, and was soon lying face down on her bed sobbing into the pillow.

Their first row, and what a whopper it was. Sleep was a luxury that came after hours of tossing and turning, and her only relief was in calling a certain smiling face into her mind—that of Bruar, her husband.

Breakfast was as quiet a time as she'd ever known. Michael had gone while the moon was still in the sky and Mrs Sullivan was washing bed sheets. Apart from the natural shuffling sounds of horses in their stables, outside was just as still, telling her that the stablemen were also gone. She needed to do something with herself; Bull Buckley or not, she'd be taking the journey home if things didn't change.

'After me chores I'll be taking the road to Runny Brook to visit the Fureys; do you want to come?'

No need for the housekeeper to ask twice; soon the pair were sauntering along a long narrow lane on the way to visit the tinker family. 'Well, would you look at that,' said Mrs Sullivan, pointing to the grass verge, 'The earth is giving birth to a purple crocus. On our way home that will be in bloom,' she added.

Robin sat outside the tent, tending the open fire while the children played around him.

'Lovely little boys. The eldest reminds me of someone.' The house-keeper wiped tears from her eyes as she greeted the tinker children who rushed around.

''Tis a happy man I am to see you come and sit by me fire,' said Robin, who had the charms of a prince stepped from the pages of a fairy tale book.

Mrs Sullivan took a bag of freshly baked biscuits and shared them amongst the little boys, all jostling for the biggest ones. 'Good day to you, Robin. Lord, I'm feeling the legs sore, it's easy seen I've done little walking since last you were here. Tell me now, how is Kathleen?'

'If you take a squint into the tent, sure she's started her labour and won't want to be a-talking. I wonder if you'd do me a favour and keep yer eye on me boys until I get back?' he asked, slipping some snare wire into a bag slung over his shoulder. 'You see, I need to catch some rabbit for to feed the family.'

Megan thought his snares were far too thick; not at all like hers. When she snared dinner she used thin wire, and she never left the snares unchecked more than three hours. 'How often do you check them?' she asked, unable to hold back. The natural ways returning to her mind, she could almost smell the rabbit, both raw and cooked.

258

'It's just that no good comes of long-snared rabbits, they lose a lot of flavour. But my ways are not yours.'

'I see that the way is in you. Well, that's good, so it is. Now, if you'll excuse me, I'm off.' He didn't share his ways with her and left her question unanswered, which is just what she expected, because a tinker never shares his ways with anybody. Before setting off, he warned the boys to behave and turned to Mrs Sullivan, repeating his request. She assured him his children would be in safe hands, but that he shouldn't be too long. Then she tiptoed over to the tent mouth and very gently peeped inside. She didn't like the colour of the pregnant woman, and asked if she needed assistance.

Vigorously she shook her head.

'I see things are in hand, then. But how long do you think it will be?'

Kathleen went blood-red as another push of labour forced her face into a contorted grin of pain. She screamed out an answer, 'I think it's another one of those curses, because my agony is terrible.'

Megan didn't understand, and said quietly, 'Poor woman, what's wrong with her?'

Mrs Sullivan moved away from the tent, not wishing Kathleen to hear and said, 'She feels this is another one that will die, a girl. Look I'll take the little ones down to Ballyshan just in case Michael comes home and wonders where I am; the men might be hungry, having left early without a breakfast. Why don't you stay and help Kathleen? She's never needed it before, but I always feel another pair of hands won't go wrong.'

Reluctantly Megan agreed. She watched her friend hurry away with three little boys in tow, then sat by the fire and waited. Several times Kathleen screamed and cursed, before at last she let out one frenzied screech, then everything went deathly silent.

Although Mrs Sullivan told her not to bother the pregnant woman, she just had to see how mother and baby were. She peered inside, and what met her eyes was the most awful sight. Kathleen was cleaning herself in a basin of water she'd prepared for when her labour took hold, but there was no sign of a fresh new life. Instinctively Megan searched the tent bed for the baby, expecting to see its bonny wee face snuggled inside a cosy woollen shawl, but only a blood-soaked sheet lay crumpled at the foot of the thin mattress. Her eyes searched every wrinkled inch of the bed, but there was no infant. 'What did you have?' she asked, with increasing concern as there was no sign of the newborn.

Kathleen turned with obvious discomfort and said; 'Another one, it's lying over there.'

Megan scanned the tent floor until her eyes fell upon two tiny blue fingers protruding from a dirty rag at the base of the canvas. Trembling she bit onto her fist at the small size and helpless posture of the dead baby and cried out, 'How did you lose it?'

'Oh shut up. Now throw it over by the burn and the dogs can eat it when Robin comes back.'

'Eat a human being, a little innocent baby, how can you even think on it? I'm no Christian but I thought you folks were believers in God?'

'Think on it, is it? God is it? Listen, you. My womb carries these useless things. They move inside o' me for nine month, and when I put them into the world, they die. And don't mention God to me, its all his fault.' Kathleen fell silent as exhaustion engulfed her. She fell upon her mattress and turned her back on the dead child.

Megan felt as useless as she'd ever done in her life, yet the female instincts of her heart weighed heavy. Trying not to disturb the wretched mother, she gathered the still frame of the baby and took a long strip of flannel from a pile of rags. Sitting the mite on her knees, she began rolling its body carefully into a proper shroud as delicately as she could. When the little arms and legs were straightened and tightly wound in the cloth, she spoke gently to the mother. 'Kathleen, will you allow me to bury your baby? You see, like you we live in tents and also our women folk lose as many babies as are saved. Let me send this tiny girl into the earth so that Mother Nature can accept her flesh. Such sacred bones should be left in her tender care.' She waited patiently for a response.

Kathleen in time opened her eyes and whispered, 'You're as bad as that Mrs Sullivan. Do you know she walked for miles with the last one and buried it? So if you want you can do the same, I don't give a damn.'

The finishing touches were taking place just as Robin came back, two small terriers at his heel eagerly sniffing at the trickle of blood that had congealed around the noses of three big buck rabbits tied expertly to a piece of wood; thick snares or thin, he certainly brought home the dinner.

Seeing Megan kneeling beside a small mound of earth in a peaceful spot at the dyke's edge, it didn't take much for him to realise his wife had once more produced what she'd predicted. The sadness that spread across his face was the opposite of that of his wife. He knelt down, cap screwed in his bloodied hands and said, 'Strange, is it not? We hardly know you, yet here you are burying our poor wee mite of a child. It was a girl, then?'

She nodded and said, 'I'm a Macdonald from Glen Coe, and this is our chant of death. Kathleen has given me permission. If you can allow me the same, I'll give your baby up to the earth.'

'On you go,' he said, wiping a tear with his crumpled bonnet.

Tre banni, tre banni: (Three prayers, three prayers)
Chavi tori mara, (Child to earth)
Chavi tori glimmer, (Child to fire)
Chavi tori pani. (Child to water)

Three times she whispered the earth prayer, and as she did so, not a sound was heard either from the vast bog or the mighty forest, apart from a tiny Jenny wren whistling happily from a small hole in an oak tree. When finished she went back inside the tent. Kathleen was sound asleep. Leaving her in peace, she and Robin went back to Ballyshan, he to collect his boys, she to reflect on the day's events. The tiny purple flower she'd noticed earlier while going to the campsite had been joined by several others, and the dark brown earth now sported a small carpet of purple, pink and white.

'Poor Kathleen, not again.' Mrs Sullivan, who was visibly saddened by the grave news, slipped small woolly cardigans she'd knitted during winter months onto the three boys before giving Robin another food parcel. 'This will keep the wolf from the door, and let you see to the children while Kathleen regains her strength.'

Sitting the youngest on his broad shoulders he set off with little said. The other two ran on ahead. Megan watched from the kitchen window until all that was left of them was the curly top of the child on Robin's shoulders.

'Look at them,' she told herself, 'just another day in the life of a tinker family. Who but this elderly lady and myself know what agony and pain they've suffered this day?' To an outsider walking up by Runny Brook, all he'd see was a small encampment with three dirty-faced little boys, a red waistcoated father and a sad-eyed mother. He'd not be aware that, sleeping beneath a small mound of earth nearby, was the result of a night of lovemaking followed by months of uncertainty and wishful dreams that the child just might be another boy.

Her bedroom offered sanctuary. Her heart grew heavy at what she'd been forced to do. Still, if she hadn't done it, what was the alternative? Two sharp-toothed terriers ripping legs and liver from a human being who'd not yet sinned? Her day's burden, hard as it was, was one she was grateful to have undertaken.

Neither Michael nor the men came back, and by early evening she and Mrs Sullivan had stabled the horses and locked the buildings securely. Before retiring, Megan asked where Fiddler's Fancy was stabled. Her companion showed her quickly to another part of the stables, a place fit for a queen, never mind a horse. A plush room with a carpet of hay, walls half-lined with sheep skins, just enough food and water to keep her healthy and shining. Megan could well understand why everyone said what a beauty she was. 'She's an Arab, doesn't like the cold. Michael treats her like a princess.'

Mrs Sullivan's constant yawning signified she sorely yearned for bed. The day's events had opened wounds. Linking an arm through Megan's, she said softly, 'let's have a nice cup of milky cocoa before going to bed. Now, do you want to speak of today's sadness, or will we settle for the hot chocolate?'

Megan did have questions, but they would be better kept for another day. And maybe this kind lady would share the memory of her lost sons.

Cocoa cupped between hands, they both retired to bed. It was hard finding sleep, as those blue fingers and that tiny bundle kept flashing in her mind.

It was about four in the morning, the darkest hour, when her new-found sleep was disturbed by the sound of a car engine coupled with whispering voices. The men had come home.

Morning found a happy-faced Michael wakening her with a broad smile. 'Come on, lazy bones, I have news for you.'

She was grateful for the presence of his manliness, and his smile beamed warmth into her body. 'Whatever it is, that smile on your face tells me it's mighty good,' she said, running a hand through his wavy hair.

He took from his pocket a letter. 'Now, darling girl of mine, I want you to listen. I never told you because I didn't want to raise your hopes, but before I left England I sent a letter to the war office.'

'You did, and what about?'

'I contacted the body concerned with displaced soldiers, injured ones that is, and asked for a list of hospitals in the south. They sent me a list. I wrote to them again, and this is the reply. I would have had this news sooner, but if I'd written from an Irish address I hardly think they'd have answered. No, I used Bridget's home address, and this is why a reply has taken so long in coming.'

'What is it, Michael?' she asked sternly, then added, 'That piece of paper has an official look about it. Does it hold news of Bruar?'

He sat on her bed, laid a hand on her shoulder and opened the brown envelope.

' "Dear Sir,

Regarding your enquiry as to the whereabouts of Private Bruar Stewart who served with His Majesty's forces during the recent war: it is with regret that I have to inform you that Private Stewart, having sustained severe shell-shock while in action, was hospitalised in France before being transferred to Kingsland House in Sussex. He never regained any form of normal mental state. It is my sad duty to tell you that he was found dead at the foot of fire-stairs adjacent to the building. It is believed he fell while walking in his sleep. This is a common symptom with shell-shocked soldiers."

There, at long last we can put Bruar to rest. Now, say you'll marry me!'

She hit him hard on the jaw. If he had any regard for her feelings, he never would have spoken of Bruar's demise in such a selfish fashion. Visions flashed into being behind her wet eyes. Questions filled her shocked mind. 'My man gone! Why did the Seer tell me he was not dead? Why have I felt such pain at the distance between us, why did I think my life could be fulfilled with finding him, regardless of his state?'

Questions without answers fell like a deadly shower around her ears. With not a single glance at Michael she dressed. He stood awkwardly against the dressing table, waiting for a clear answer. He was puzzled by her apparent shock. 'Isn't this what you wanted?'

'It's what you bloody wanted, not me.' There, she'd said it, and she meant it.

'But the other day, it took all my strength to fight you off. You're not telling me that was the feelings of a sad lonely wife, because if so, it was a funny way of showing it.'

His blunt words clarified everything. Now that the truth was revealed, she realised all she'd been doing in Ballyshan was living a lie. 'I know what you're saying, Michael, but the uncertainty of whether he existed seemed to leave me in limbo. All this time my imagination sent me off on roads of wild dreams of being your wife, living here like a lady, but the truth is, I'm a true-blood tinker. We don't marry outside our own. My Bruar is dead, and half of me with him. Do you want half a woman?'

'I'll take a fraction if you'll say the word. God almighty, Megan, surely you know the heart of me? Who cares for you as I do? I love the wild tinker in you!' He folded the letter, putting it back into his pocket, but through heartbroken sobs she asked for it. 'Why, if you can't read or write?'

'It's all I have of my Bruar. Please let me keep it Michael, it's the only thing left to say that he's finally gone from me.'

He told her defiantly it wouldn't do her any good because of her illiteracy. She said that didn't matter. Grudgingly handing it over, he left her to think things out. After all, he thought, it had been wrong of him not to show respect, or a flicker of melancholy at Bruar's death. Yet it hurt him to know that a memory from her past would share their bed; if she decided to stay, that is.

She pushed her arms into a warm coat and was soon heading up onto the boggy ground. Here her pain could be given free rein, she could grieve naturally. Ghosts of her past relatives painted scenes of her forbidden love, they whispered in her ear, shame on you for not finding Bruar yourself. Needle-tongued spectres told her that with Michael there could never be a future, nor a present for that matter, because something was missing in their relationship. Whatever it was, she'd no idea, but maybe the truth was that Bruar was never meant to be shared, dead or alive.

Michael didn't follow her, which was just as well, because she'd found routes through the bogland that no one had ever walked on before. The seclusion was welcome. The green and mystical Ireland was like Scotland, and yet at that precise moment she craved to be home. At least in such wild terrain her savaged heart might find solace in its similarities to her homeland. Try as she might, though, Bruar's spirit would not rest, and somehow a future with Michael seemed impossible. Her mind was made up; come the weekend she'd ask to be taken to Dublin.

How pained and lost he seemed after his agonising wait, as his face searched hers for an answer. When she saw this, it wasn't in her nature to hurt him. 'I'll wait for the right moment,' she promised herself.

She yearned to leave but her comfortable surroundings and the beautiful heather-filled moorland offered her a place of peace, to dream of times past and those never to come again. Anyway, who did she have in Scotland who cared about her? With Rachel and Nicholas in America, and Bruar gone, there was nobody apart from old Doctor Mackenzie, who was probably dead for all she knew. Buckley would be very much alive, however, with his catlike ways, and would certainly be prowling around. He was another good reason to stay.

Summer was almost upon them, and still she delayed her answer to the ever-patient, doting Michael, who did not press her, much as he wanted to. Then, one morning after breakfast, he summoned everyone into the kitchen where he dropped a bombshell!

'I wonder what he's doing now,' she thought, listening to him giving his orders. Mrs Sullivan was just as much in the dark. One by one they gingerly stepped into the warm kitchen, to see a bottle of champagne and several tall-stemmed glasses.

'My,' said Paddy, scratching his head and removing a faded cloth cap, 'I wonder what the celebration is.'

'Might be that new stallion he's been on about. I reckon he's bought the beauty,' said Johnno, lowering his voice as Michael strode into the room, smiling from ear to ear.

'Well, me hearty fellas, I have a fine bit of news for you all!' Striding over to Megan, he took her hand and kissed it. Hoping she was wrong, she waited for his next romantic gesture. This wasn't how she'd imagined it to be. He took a small box from his pocket, opened it, and then on one knee he asked her in front of everyone to be his wife!

Why did she feel like a fish hanging from a hook, suffering its slow, agonising failure to breathe? Unable to take in this awkward situation she was stunned into silence. He stood up, uncorked the bottle and began to pour each of his friends a glass.

There were yippees and choruses of 'He's a jolly good fellow', along with 'Bloody time ye got yourself a wife.'

Terry, who'd said little, was eyeing Megan. 'Well, colleen, put the poor man out of his misery with an answer.'

The words didn't come. They were there deep in her dry throat, but not one came. What did come though was action. Her hand reached out to grab a cardigan, and a severely frightened black-haired tinker rushed from the room and did not stop running until she'd found her secret rock seat in the middle of the bogland. Here she drew breath and tried to clear her clouded mind. How could he do that in front of his friends and workers, and Mrs Sullivan? But on the other hand, what was so wrong with a romp in the hay and then accepting his ring? Her thoughts had until then been focussed on grieving the loss of her man, and now the sudden reality of becoming a rich man's wife was terrifying. Was it what she wanted? Why did she have to be such a loner? 'If only Rachel or my mother was here to share this episode with, they'd soon tell me what to do, but as things stand I'm so mixed up.' All morning and into the afternoon she thought about nothing else but taking on the role of Michael's wife. Could she fulfil his expectations? Would she open her mouth and shame him at such times as his county friends came calling? Up till then she'd seen none of them. Everything seemed to fade off into the distance as a rumble of thunder rent the air. She'd been so wrapped up in her thoughts, the blackened sky above her head had gone unnoticed. 'I'd best get back and face the music,' she thought. 'They'll all be waiting on an answer.'

Thankfully, Ballyshan was in sight as another loud clap of thunder shook the earth beneath her feet. The short time between the flashes of forked lightning and roars of thunder forecast a wild, storm-filled night ahead. On approaching the driveway she saw someone at the front door talking to Michael. Was it the last peal of thunder following on the heels of a severe flash that had momentarily blinded her? She couldn't say, but something inside said, 'hide!' Hidden from sight behind a wall running up the side of the house she waited until the visitor had gone. She watched him as he walked past. A mighty flash of lightning stopped him in his tracks. He pulled a torn collar under his chin and stared skywards, and as he did so she saw the unmistakable, lean, sallow face of the Devil—Bull Buckley was back!

Every sinew tightened like a vice. Tearing free from her hiding place when he'd gone, she bolted through the back door, screaming hysterically.

Mrs Sullivan got such a fright she ran into the front room for Michael. Her screams brought the men hurrying from the stables.

'Is it the storm, lass?' asked Mrs Sullivan, 'it's the time of year for them, so tis.'

'God love us, woman, yiv put the fear o' death into the beasts, and them sparked up with the storm already,' cried Paddy. Terry and Johnno also were vocal in their displeasure at her ridiculous screams. But none of them knew the cause except Michael. He'd seen that jutting jaw and those protruding eyes before. 'Come on now, boys, give her a bit of peace. Megan doesn't scare easy, something is wrong. Tell me now, what terrible thing has put the fear of death into my love?' He put an arm around her as she snuggled into his body, clinging for dear life.

'You're right, Michael, I have seen Death!' She got up and ran to the door. 'Standing on the other side of this door no more than five minutes ago was Buckley! He's found me. I tell you I'm as dead as stone now.'

'This was the reason I took Megan away from England,' he told everyone, then added, 'Megan has been stalked by a street-fighter, and he seems hell-bent on terrorising her.'

Bull Buckley, the man who laughed in the face of the mighty law enforcers, had followed her across the Irish Sea. Perhaps the Seer of Balnakiel had destined her to be a victim of this hellish demon, and not, as she had once firmly believed, to find Bruar and live happily ever after. Was this the reason for her search—to allow her to be chased by a cursed beast? Was it the curse of Rory now laid on her shoulders? This man could not be snared because he wasn't human!

'What did he want here?' Terry asked. She waited for Michael's answer.

'Looking for a job, he said. I told him I didn't need anybody, but he insisted on coming back tomorrow anyway.'

'He will, but not for a job—he'll be coming for me!'

'Then he's in for a big surprise,' said Paddy rising to his feet. The others nodded in agreement. Johnno seemed disturbed by the stalker, and said he'd a power of stealth if he managed to find Megan here. 'Better get some help, Michael?' he said uneasily.

'Aye, best we do. Come on, Megan, it's time I let you meet some friends.' Michael held her close, and she felt his strength.

In a soldier-like fashion, Johnno and Terry brought the big saloon car from its garage. How often had she heard its whirring engine gliding out to take the men on some secret mission or other, and now she too was part of that company.

Behind her on the bog-ground a stray dog howled, 'The auld Pooka is heralding some man's doom.' Terry stretched his neck, sniffed the wet air and added, 'He'll linger around the place until the Banshee shakes the victim's shroud.'

Megan's background told her what was out there: it was a demon dog come looking for a newly dead soul. Her flesh crawled with images of deep-seated superstitions.

Rain fell from the heavens in thick sheets. It was all the wipers could do to keep the windscreen clear. Terry, Paddy and Johnno sat silently in the back.

After about an hour the vehicle crunched to a halt. Michael laid a reassuring hand on her shoulder as he took a black and green handkerchief from his pocket and tied it round her eyes. 'This is for your protection; I'll take it off when we're inside.'

Beneath the blindfold she could just make out a fringe of dandelions bunched intermittently along the bottom of a whitewashed wall. It reminded her of Helen's low-roofed white cottage in Durness. Rain puddles were scattered everywhere; she squelched through one, soaking her shoes. A creaking door opened and she was led inside.

'Hello, Nick, we have a problem,' said Michael, sitting Megan down on a creaking chair. He went on, 'This is the colleen I told you about. She has a problem needs fixing. We think you can fix it.'

Nick shuffled to his feet, and she heard him lighting a cigarette. He cleared his throat, then to everyone's surprise insisted the blindfold be removed.

'Are ye sure now, sir? Begging your pardon, but she's not one o' us.' Terry was adamant.

Johnno joined him. 'Aye, Terry, she's not given Michael an answer, and for all we knows she might be a spy. Na, I'd keep her eyes shut, that's my opinion.'

Nick quietened them both, 'Boys, boys, let's ask her.'

She'd heard that voice before! That same low growl when he cleared his throat... but surely it couldn't be?

He leaned closer to her, and she could feel his breath on her face. Her heart thumped so hard against her ribs she felt that any minute it would leave her body and roll onto the floor. His fingers felt clumsy, yet with a gentleness to them as he unfastened the blindfold. As it fell from her eyes, there in the dim light of a candle, standing smiling with an unsightly gash running down his face, was Nicholas

O'Connor! The useless Irishman she couldn't wait to see the back of in the Angus Glen.

'It's a small world now, is it not?' He held out a hand, changed his mind and hugged her instead. She was speechless, as were the others. Putting his strong arm around her shoulder, he lowered her into a more comfortable chair. 'I knew when Michael described you to me wit that black curly hair an' devil o' a temper, and said you were a Scottish tinker, it had to be the same lassie who shared me campsite back in those bitter cold glens. But tell me, why wid ye be in England?'

Michael was prancing up and down. 'What manner of madness is this? Why did you not say you thought my Megan and yours were the same? I'm speechless.'

'Coincidence is a strange thing to be sure,' O'Connor said, patting Michael on the back. Megan was no stranger to life's twists and turns, but when he asked again why she had left the north she simply said it was how things turned out. She wanted to tell him about Bruar, but rather than upset Michael she just said, 'Folks were telling me about hotel work, and while there I got tangled with some gypsies.'

'And was this when you and this poisoned person crossed paths?'

'Aye it was, and for certain he'll kill me.'

'Oh, well now, we'll see about that.'

'He has nine lives, and has so far lost none.'

He put his hands on hers, smiled and said, 'I sit here this night a proud man who has organised many exploits for the good of this old country of mine. Not a drop of liquor has passed me lips in a long while. I'm respected now. If it hadn't been for your saving my life that day after them ploughmen left me for dead, like Rory, I would be nothing. I owe a lot to you Megan, and as God's me witness, if a man wants to harm you, then he'll have to come through me.' She winced as a revolver was laid on the table. The Irishman added, 'Me and this old friend.'

'I'm puzzled by the changes in you, O'Connor.' She had to find out why his path had led him here. 'Remember when Sergeant Wilson came among us that time with a picture of Kitchener, and I thought it was Rory?'

'Aye, and you were goin' to stick him for telling the boys that war was for the good o' the country. Sure now that face on you was a sight.'

'Yes, but I heard you say that war wasn't your thing. Yet here you are hiding from your enemies, blindfolding visitors and so on.'

'War with Germany was one thing. We fight for our independence, and that's different.'

'Its not, if all you do is shoot each other!' She wondered what Doctor Mackenzie would think of him now. After seeing his bloodsoaked body the last time, his weatherbeaten and destitute face, and saddest of all, those begging eyes.

'When me wounds healed I went back to the auld campsite. Oh bless us, it wis all burned and empty; a lot like meself. I sat down near where your mother sleeps, under the willows, listened for the birds singing, but it was eerie an' silent. Not hearing you and the cracking o' Rory's voice, just echoes in me head. I sat awhile in me loneliness with only wind for company. The night came an' I wanted to light a fire; you know, for the last time. But have you ever heard of a campfire in a graveyard? That's what it was like, Megan; a place for peaceful ghosts. Sitting on me log, I suddenly sees a path in me head. All lit up it was; on and on it wound until I could see in the distance—the auld country. So me feet got moving, and when I came back to see all the troubles, I decided to turn around me life. One man tells another, an' before I know it here I am—a fighter for the cause.'

'So you've ended up poisoning yourself with bullets, instead of gut-rot drink.'

He laughed loudly, and agreed that both have the power over man. 'Oh, me little wild Megan, sure there is no understandin' in that head o' yours. Now, let's make plans to catch Bull Buckley and rid you of him once and for all.'

She smiled. It was hard to believe how many bends circumstance had pushed her around. She was beginning to feel like a cork caught in the coastal tides of two estuaries. Looking into the scarred and rugged face of her late father-in-law's boozing buddy, who would have ever imagined he'd find his feet and respect from his fellow Irishmen? A picture formed in her mind of him in his smelly clothes, the beer belly, hairy and fat, hanging over loose-fitting, greasy trousers; unshaven, vomiting over dykes. 'Funny old world,' she thought, but was too much the lady to remind him.

A wobbly-legged farmhouse table served as the focal point both for them to chat over journeys past and, more importantly, how to dispose of Buckley. The serious intensity of the night discussion brought moths to join them and flutter close to the candle flame. Singed wings fluttered through the smoke-filled room adding to the atmosphere. Daylight was pushing between clouds left after the storm had passed through; the earth became bright as they decided on the plan of action.

When Buckley came back they would be waiting. She gazed at the men, each of whom showed a determination the like of which she'd never seen before. It gave her a feeling of inner strength. Maybe this time, finally, Buckley's end was in sight. Somewhere far off a bell in a church tower tolled a slow recurring note. She felt cold sitting close to Michael, yet her skin sweated. After all, Bull was no ordinary man, but her companions were.

O'Connor joined them on their return journey to Ballyshan. They arrived before seven am. Buckley wasn't expected until noon, enough time for them to catch some sleep. It came easy to the men, but not to her. Each time her heavy eyelids closed, his leering face loomed above her with a croaking voice singing 'I'll take the high road you take the low'. Mother Foy's old wrinkled neck was being throttled like a farmer strangling a chicken. Shire Beth rode to the rescue, hot breath snorting from nostrils, with Sam on her back knocking the beast-man face down on the muddy ground. Memory followed awful memory, until at last Mrs Sullivan called to her through an opening bedroom door, 'Breakfast is ready'.

After a quick bite the men set their plan in action. Terry would wait behind the far end of the stables; Paddy and Johnno by the back door. Proud O'Connor, armed with his trusty pistol, would hide by the wall. Michael would open the door, as Mrs Sullivan, who'd been informed of the trap, was to try to do her dusting as normal. Megan was instructed to stay in her bedroom. She went without protest, armed with a good sharp meat knife.

Eleven o' clock struck loudly from the grandfather clock that stood like a guard beside a cast-iron umbrella stand. If the old housekeeper dusted it once she did so a dozen times. 'Go and chop up some kindling, Mrs Sullivan,' ordered Michael. 'God, woman, I'm sore in the head watching the speed of that duster.'

'I'll not be doing anything of the kind. Chopping wood, an old body like me? Where's the respect in you?' He immediately apologised, and told her to find something else to do apart from blasted dusting. 'Go see how Megan is.'

Megan smiled at the old woman. 'He's chased you in here, has he?'

'Oh, the cheek of him. I was coming anyway, thought you might need a bit of company.'

'Is there any sign of Buckley?'

'Don't worry, they'll get him and whip the flesh inch by inch from his hide.'

'He's not got any hide,' she told her, 'only green slimy scales.'

The well-dusted grandfather clock struck the hour he had named for coming; Megan grabbed hold of Mrs Sullivan's hands and clung until her knuckles turned bleach white. 'Don't fret, my dear, those boys have fought battles up and down the land. They know what's to be done.'

'They have no knowledge of Buckley.'

The silence seemed to stretch from wall to wall of the room, and if a pin had fallen on the paisley-patterned carpet it would have been heard. Outside the men, with hawks' eyes and owls' ears, listened for every movement, as shadows from a cloud-strewn sky played hide-and-seek with their vigilance. Everyone waited on the thud of the doorknocker. But nothing came; another hour and still no Buckley. The raw stress was placing Megan once more under enormous strain. Mrs Sullivan couldn't stand the waiting, saying, 'I'm away to get you a drink of water in case the faint comes on you, all colour's gone from those cheeks of yours.'

After the old lady left Megan ran over and locked the door. 'You're out there, Bull Buckley. I feel the evil, I know it!' With all her strength she pushed a large oak wardrobe over against the door, then piled up chairs and carpets and even her bed until a mountainous barricade imprisoned her in the bedroom. How long she sat shivering in fear she'd no knowledge. No sound from outside, no shouts, no gunfire, nothing, yet she was certain he was there, leering from a hole.

Michael and Mrs Sullivan began banging loudly on the door. 'Megan, for goodness sake, let us in,' he called.

'I will not, now go away. If Buckley comes, he'll kill every mother's son of you, but not me! Oh no, he'll not get me. I'd rather starve to death than go by his hand. Do you hear me? Get away.'

'My darling girl, he's not coming. It's three in the afternoon. Come and have some tea with Nick O'Connor before he goes home.'

'No, I will not!' She was about to scream at them, when a shout from outside drew Michael away, leaving Mrs Sullivan to talk to her.

'Some scoundrel ran along the dyke, Michael, he's heading for the back of the house,' shouted Terry, then added, 'Nick, he's ran up the back o' ye, try to head him into the open, we have the devil for certain.'

O'Connor, buttoning up his trouser-front, cursed, 'Blast him to kingdom come, he must have sneaked past while I was havin' a piss. Come on, boys, he won't get far.'

The men left their vantage points; two went to the far side of the house, while three ran round to the rear. They met halfway, but there was no sight or sound of anyone. Megan, with her ear to the door, called out to the housekeeper, 'Have they got him yet?' There was no answer. She shouted louder, 'What's going on, Mrs Sullivan?'

Mrs Sullivan must have gone outside to see what all the commotion was, because there was no sound. What a blessed relief after a time to hear the shuffling footsteps of the old woman who had come back from wherever she'd been.

'Mrs Sullivan, can you tell me if they've got Buckley?' Megan called through the door.

A sense of déja-vu overwhelmed her. Every fibre in her being knew who stood on the other side of that door, as a low hissing sound from the keyhole turned her ice-cold. 'I'll take the high road and you take the low... Hell's back!'

She slumped against the bedroom wall and slid to the floor. The meat knife fell from her limp hand, the strength drained from her body as she stared into nothing. He'd killed them all, and once more wanted her! There was scuffling outside her door and loud noises, but she failed to hear them. Suddenly the door almost came off its hinges. She grabbed the meat knife and almost rammed it into Michael, who along with O'Connor stormed through the barricade. 'We have him, Megan, we have him!' Eager faces swarmed around her. 'Mrs Sullivan was in the kitchen, when she saw a shadow by the clock. She looked along the hall and saw him kneeling on the floor outside your room then tip-toed out for us. Come on, girl, the boys have him tied to a chair.'

In a flash she was running along and into the cobbled yard, knife fiercely clenched in her hand. Terry was putting the finishing touches to the prisoner, tying his hands with strong rope. Paddy and Johnno smiled at the restrained criminal as he tried to wriggle free from his bounds. Johnno kicked the chair from under him, saying, 'Where does ye want the bullet, ye wicked fart of a man?' Buckley was to be executed, army-style.

At the first sight of him she stood petrified, words and thoughts lost in a maze. She could only stare down at him, shaking. 'But I'm not a mouse,' she told herself, 'a little helpless mouse.' In a strange attitude he lay on the cold ground, tied tightly with his legs up in the air. His eyes narrowed and centred on her gaze.

From the purple hills of Glen Coe she felt the power of her ancestors. 'Megan,' they said, 'remember who you are, take back the pride that many died to leave as your legacy; keep it with passion.' The voices faded, leaving a single whisperer who repeated, 'Remember the bogs of dread that beat the Vikings.'

The cruel fear of this monster had imprisoned her, sent her to another land with her tail between her legs. If he were there, Bruar would have failed to recognise her after what she'd been reduced to. Buckley had her shaking in her shoes like a cowed dog. Nick O'Connor interrupted her train of thought. 'Best you were away inside, you don't want to see this.' His words signified Buckley's coming end, yet as she gazed deep into his eyes he was still challenging her to take the low road.

He tossed his head back in that so familiar way, causing a shock of red hair to fall over one eye. He sneered and grinned at her. It was as if no one else was present, only she and him. Suddenly everything became as clear as the sky when a cloud gives back the sun. This was her fight. Not O'Connor's, nor Michael's with his stable hands, this was between a Glen Coe Macdonald and street-fighter and killer Buckley. If he died, then it had to be by her hand. Paddy and Terry righted the chair. Buckley shook sand and gravel from his hair, then in answer to Johnno's earlier question he said, 'Put it right between my eyes.'

What Megan did next was utterly insane. Sudden powers of energy rushed through her body. She dived behind Buckley and in one swift slash of the knife had cut him free from his bonds. 'Get up onto the moor, Buckley, we'll finish this there.'

'Ha,' he called, running past the men and away, 'the low road it is, then.'

The men watched helpless, as he took off like a red deer and was soon gone onto the moor to wait for the next move.

'You've gone stone horn mad, girl,' O'Connor told her. 'What stupid idiot takes on a monster like that?'

'I have no choice, that beast has sent a fear through me. I have been living a nightmare. Can't you see? If I don't face my fear it will never leave me. Dead or alive, he'll always plague my waking thoughts. Now, give me that gun, I'm not so daft as to match my puny strength against his.'

Michael immediately forbade her to go after Buckley, saying he and the men would go instead.

'I know the moor bogs,' she replied. 'While you pottered with your horses and ran that blasted war of yours, I spent days marking causeways through them. That will be my advantage over Buckley.'

Then, before they could stop her, with a new-found power and speed she ran after her demon.

As the mist swallowed her up, Michael said to his men, 'I love that mad tinker. God help me for it, but I have to follow her. You lads are free to make up your own minds about the risk.'

'Aye, I love her too, an' for different reasons, so I'm coming. Any road, she's too good to fall at the hands of a fiend that kills old wimmin,' said O'Connor.

Mrs Sullivan watched as they chased after Megan, and were swallowed up by the thick mist covering the land.

Treading softly through the bog on strips of firmer ground, where nothing but the creatures that live in that godforsaken place know the way, she soon found what she was looking for—the heavy, unmistakable footprints of her prey. The men behind her were calling out to each other in the mist; one minute they were within touching distance, the next, far off. If they found him first she was certain they'd shoot him. She kept her eyes on the oozy earth, following the deep-sunken prints until they disappeared. Underfoot, the heather wove a thick carpet and there was no clear track forward, so she waited. There in the damp mist she found her rock seat, almost hidden by bracken and rye grass, and sat stealthily down. It wouldn't take long; she knew he'd back-track. A moment later, she also knew her prey was inches away as hot breath touched her neck.

'Show yourself, Bull. You're not frightened of a little tinker mouse are you?'

'You be a good girl and throw away the gun, and make me feel a mite luckier.'

Before she could answer, fingers wound around her arm and whirled her to face him. Once again the devil stared into the depth of her soul, red hair covering one eye, grinning.

This time, though, the veil of terror that so long shrouded her had lifted.

'Not as easy to kill as Moses Durin or a helpless hedgehog,' she told him, 'am I?'

'Or old Mamma Foy,' he laughed. 'Honest, though, I have to thank you. I've never had such fun since you shopped me to the muskries. All those killings, and here I am seeing a bit of old Ireland. It's a power of joy you are to me but,' he threw a quick glance at the gun held tightly in her hand, 'that puts anger in my head, and you know what I do when I'm angry.'

'Surely a wee gun isn't turning Bully scared?' She goaded him and waited for his familiar response.

Tossing back his head he snarled like a dog and growled into the shroud of mist, 'Give me that gun!'

'Oh, does Mr Pussy want this?' She dangled it inches from his leering eyes, then threw it behind him.

It thudded onto tufts of rye-grass and lay awkwardly, with the barrel facing upwards.

'There's the weapon, take it from the marsh if you dare!'

'It's not to harm you, my pretty little mouse; that weapon will rid me of those idiots who think I'm easy meat.' He turned and stepped towards the gun. His feet landed on soft ground that instantly began to suck him down. 'What the hell is this!' he called as he began to sink up to his knees into the marshland. 'Megan, I will not be beaten—throw me a hand or stick! I won't hurt you, surely that is clear. I'm really in love with you! Help me out and together we'll rule this place.' The bog sucked and inch by inch he went down. His chest heaved as he sank to his waist. 'Listen, how would you like me to take my fists onto the Irish scene? We'd be rich; I'm King, never been beat.'

Down he went, slithering under, now up to his chest. Soon only his head remained above the bog.

She could hear the others calling, hear the crackle of dead twigs under foot. They were closing in. Carefully she knelt at the edge of the bog that had brought his doom. His pleading eyes filled with fear. 'Fetch the men, I'd rather they shot me than die like this.'

'Sorry, Bull, but that's not my way.' Mocking, she repeated his own words—'Hell's here! Well, seeing as you have such a liking for the place, welcome, you're in it. Before you leave me, take a look around—do you see them waiting in the fog, those ghosts from the past, people you murdered? Oh yes, my fiendish friend. No one escapes vengeance.'

She smiled as the ooze sucked mercilessly. His struggling only hastened his grisly end, and as he made one last desperate attempt to gasp for air, she ran her fingers through his red, curly hair and sang, 'I'll go the high road, while you go the low...'

Deep and black, the bog left only the smallest bubble of his last breath. She stood up and breathed clear air. The mist was wet but it tasted good. 'Revenge should taste sweet,' she said, turning on her heels and skipping along the secret causeways threading through the hellish puddles of liquid peat.

O'Connor was first to meet her and asked if she had his gun. She winked, smiled and said, 'Sorry, but it sank with Buckley.'

'Oh, 'twas a fine pistol was that, but I'll get another.'

Michael joined them, caught her in his arms and asked anxiously, 'Are you alright? Tell me where he is, and I'll rip out the evil bastard's throat.'

She glanced over her shoulder and said, 'The thing about cats is they have no idea of the power of water, even muddy water. My granny used to say, if a wild cat frightens you then find a bog. They'll never follow you onto a moor where peat puddles lie. Yes, he's gone, and will bother no one again, ever!'

As they made a happy journey back to Ballyshan little was said. No doubt each thought of Buckley's last moments, and about how this slip of a young woman had shaken off her fears. She had replaced them with a solid, positive vision, and faced down a fear so awful it would eventually have strangled her. Megan had dealt with a killer whom others could not. She hadn't felt so good in ages, she was new, alive and needed to share her joy. So she linked an arm with Michael and asked, 'What would be a good time for a wedding in these parts?'

He stopped dead in his muddy tracks and lifted her into the air. A strong breeze parted the mist, revealing a deep blue sky. A sleepy sun scattered its rays across the moor behind them, and everyone shouted 'Yahoo!'

She was determined now to put all thought of her past as far away as possible. Ballyshan and all its splendour would be her domain. She would be mistress of its lands and keeper of its bogs!

Mrs Sullivan met them at the door, her rosary beads tied in knots with praying. 'Oh, thank the Holy Virgin you're all safe and sound. Me heart's been going sixty to the dozen, so it has. Is that bad man dead or chased away?'

All eyes turned to Megan; after all it was her story to tell. But instead of saying what happened between her and Buckley she waved it away with a gesture. He'd been buried. How could she describe her feelings of release, watching the top of his head disappearing into the mire? She didn't need to put it into words.

The weekend arrived with O'Connor getting ready for home, his secret hidey-hole somewhere an hour's drive away. Paddy would work the morning and take himself off to Dublin in the afternoon, leaving Terry and Johnno to head home with a juicy tale to tell, no doubt.

Michael and Megan were lovers now and not ashamed to show it to the world. 'You shall want nothing,' he told her. 'All my attention will be you first, horses second. Lord, I'm a happy man for sure.'

She smiled, kissed him gently and said, 'Time is beginning to heal a lot of scars in my mind, dearest lad, but time has its own pace. Be patient with me, a lot has happened that I'm still not over.'

'Whatever you want, my love, as long as it takes.'

'Oh Michael, I'm such a fortunate lassie. What female wouldn't give an eye-tooth for what I have?'

'I'm the lucky one,' he told her, heading off to saddle his favourite horse, adding that she'd soon have her own to ride. She settled for a chat with Mrs Sullivan, who was busy sorting through the muddy clothes left for her to wash.

'Me hands will be shrivelled into black prunes by the time I've worked through this lot of muck. Sure they'd be better set on fire.'

'I'll help you, and don't bother telling me I'll ruin my hands. Good God, woman, what are hands for?' She lifted her own filthy cardigan and shook it. Something fell from the pocket. 'What's this?' she thought, then remembered the letter. Ever since Michael had given it to her, she'd kept it on her person.

The old woman scooped it from the floor and said, 'Is this yours?'

'Yes, it's a letter from...' she wanted to tell her about Bruar, share his memory. After all, her boys had died as a result of war, she'd understand.

278

'My husband, and before you say anything, he's dead.' It was obvious by the woman's shocked look that her strong religious convictions were uppermost in her mind.

Megan pointed and said, 'In that letter is the proof he's dead. Go on, read it if you don't believe me.'

Mrs Sullivan sat on a small stool and opened the letter. Bits of heather and moss fell from its folds. She shook it and smoothed it flat with the palm of her hand and began to read, out loud at first, then she stopped abruptly.

'Go on, read it. Michael's already told me what's it says, so it's alright.'

Mrs Sullivan finished reading the letter silently, then said, 'Megan, can you read?'

'No, of course I can't, that's why he read it for me.'

'And did Michael organise this?'

'Yes, but why the look of disgust? Surely your religion has nothing against a widow remarrying?'

'Oh, I'm not thinking about that. This letter says nothing about anyone being dead. I'm puzzled, not disgusted.' Touching Megan's arm, she shook her head and re-read the letter out loud. 'Private Stewart, having been pronounced mentally incapacitated, has been transferred from Kingsland House to Horton Home, London, where he shall spend the remainder of his life. Wives of Army officers fund this establishment.'

Each word opened floodgates: her heart was once more upon the braes of the Angus glens; there he towered in all his Highland splendour; there he stood on the mountaintops with windblown hair, holding his big strong hand to her, there once more was the face of her beloved Bruar whom she'd buried in the darkest recesses of her mind. Tears rolled freely down her face and ran onto the white lace collar of her blouse. The letter was indeed from the Army authorities, but Michael had blatantly lied.

Mrs Sullivan set about her chores, while Megan went into her room and packed. Paddy hadn't left yet for Dublin, but when he did, she'd go with him.

Michael was brushing a slender chestnut mare, whistling happily, when she entered the stable with the opened letter in her hand. 'Don't say a word, my love, because I know why you did this. I feel very honoured to have been for a short while your intended wife. I'll never forget or stop loving you. But this letter, and your lies, prove that my path still leads elsewhere.'

Michael knew no amount of grovelling excuses would change her feeling for him; if he'd dared to hope for her respect, it was now gone. Like a child found stealing, he buried his head in his hands and cried like a baby. He, a fine upstanding son of one of the finest families in Ireland, had been reduced to lying to such an extent that he'd even said someone was dead while knowing full well that person was as alive as himself. He made no attempt at begging forgiveness. She was lost to him. He knew it.

She said her farewells to Mrs Sullivan, but not so much as a sideward glance did she afford Michael as she left him standing, stiff and dejected, and galloped off with Paddy.

The entire journey to Dublin's fair city gave her time to think. Paddy sat in silence, and only when they reached the city did he say, 'Michael asked me to give you this. He said it will help put right his wrong, but only in a small way. He'll never marry any woman instead of you, and maybe it's just as well. Now he'll get back to breeding the finest racers. What will you do?'

The ferry had docked, the passengers hurried on board. There were lots more eager faces than when they came. Megan was fond of Paddy, and as they kissed their farewells she whispered an answer to his enquiry. 'I have a man waiting for me somewhere, Paddy.' The choppy water slapped noisily against the ferry's hull, and she remembered one man who might be the better of a wee bit of good news. 'Will you tell Nicholas O'Connor that Bruar never died?'

'To be sure I will, and I'm not a judge of anybody. I fancy where the heart is, then best be there as live an empty life. Me prayers will be that you find him, whoever the lucky fella is.'

A strong wind whipped up sprays of salt sea as Dublin merged back into the land of many shades of green. She had found a new life there, albeit short-lived, she had loved and almost died there and would be forever grateful to Ireland. It taught her how to live a different life and love a different way. She'd buried someone's tiny child, apart from young Nicholas the only newborn infant she'd ever held. She'd met O'Connor again from the old days, who was treading a lighter path than that of previous times. She had laughed with the humorous stable boys who had hidden another side; they were soldiers of an army ready to kill when ordered to for the sake of their cause. An artist could have searched the whole of his life and never found another wrinkled face and childlike smile like that of Mrs Sullivan, dear lady of the rosaries. And what could be said about evil Bull Buckley? He who flipped life's coin once too often, and lost. Finally, Michael. What lengths he had gone to, to secure her heart, yet let it slip away because of lies. If he'd stuck to their original plan and found Bruar, then maybe they could have shared a future.

The cold, silver-dark waves whipped freezing winds around her, that blew up her skirt and breathed life into its hemline. She laughed loudly as the posy pink hat lifted from her head and became another item to add to Davie Jones' locker.

One heaving roll of the sea sent passengers to the warmer lower decks. Megan found a quiet corner to sit out the rest of her journey across the Irish Sea and to think of no one but her husband. Aching for him, she promised, 'My love, you're no ghost, nor a brain-lost soldier, because in my entire being I feel you breathing. It is love that will carry me to you.' Reaching into her handbag for a handkerchief she felt the envelope: Michael's apology. Fumbling to open it, she felt a surge of shame mixed with relief: it contained the sum of one hundred pounds, more money than she'd ever seen, let alone handled, in her life. She'd planned to find work, for how else would Bruar be found without funds? Yet with this welcome gift he was within her grasp.

FOURTEEN

*S*everal trains and horse-taxis later, an exhausted Megan found herself sleeping on a comfortable bed in one of London's better hotels. She had the means to afford such luxury now and after breakfast began her final search in earnest. 'Well, my laddie,' she whispered to herself, stepping out onto the capital's busy pavements that were filled with a constant tide of humanity, 'where are you?'

Street names meant nothing to her, and she cursed her handicap of being unable to read. But Mrs Sullivan had printed out in large letters for her, HORTON HOME; if she saw those words, then for certain he'd be there, or at the worst there would be information about him. All day she searched, until the capital turned grey-red with fog and people dwindled home, leaving the night-prowlers and down-and-outs the freedom to rummage through bins for morsels of food to see them through another night. It wasn't so much the fog or the undesirables that ended her search but her legs; they ached so much that she abandoned her efforts to lie in tears on the comfortable but cold hotel bed.

Two tortured weeks later she was as no nearer to finding him than she was at first. Policemen and taxi-drivers, beggars, old ladies, young boys and a constant stream of faces all said the same thing, 'Never heard of the place.'

Horton Home was proving harder and harder to find.

It was a Sunday when she found a quiet spot by the River Thames and sat down to think. London, with all its thousands of faces, was as lonely as a graveyard. She'd stopped many people who gave her an evil look then rushed away. She found herself shouting out, 'Have I the mange or something?' It was the worst place she'd ever walked and breathed in. 'How can sane people live here?' she asked herself, then thought if it held her man then surely he must be sick or worse. This idea only sent her into a depression, and to add to that, her funds were running low.

Somehow, going to London for Bruar was nothing like she imagined. Every day she pushed her weary feet through more new districts. 'This city is as big as the sun,' she thought. 'How will I ever find him?'

After a while, as she gazed thoughtfully into the rippling water of the river, she turned as someone called to her. 'Hello!' A man sitting with a fishing rod dangling over the water had been watching her. 'I hope you don't mind me talking, but I couldn't help notice how unhappy you look.'

Megan didn't wish to speak to strangers unless they wore a uniform, yet it was a fairly busy riverbank. Little children fed ducks, while couples sauntered along under parasols. Surely if this stranger meant any harm to her, he'd picked the wrong place to do so.

'Some place in this mass of mortar and stone is my long lost man, and I can't find him,' she told him.

'My wife will swap places with you,' he laughed, and instantly she lowered her guard. They chatted and shared stories for ages. It seemed this middle-aged man knew London like the back of his hand, but like others he'd never heard of the place which she searched for daily.

'Horton Home, you say, are you sure it's called that?'

'Yes, look—I've got it written down.' She gladly put the piece of paper that Mrs Sullivan had given her into the stranger's hand. He read it, then said, 'I think whoever copied this read it wrongly. There is a place I know of that is run jointly by the Army and the Church. Now, if my memory serves me right, I'm sure it's called Morton Home. The H and the M have got mixed up. It's in Kingston-upon-Thames, not that far from where we sit.'

Her mouth fell open, prompting him to say something about flies, but she didn't hear him. Flashing like bright stars in her mind were the last words of the Seer from Durness to her: 'Find him in the town of the King.'

'Whoever you are, my friend, there is no amount of money can pay for what you tell me this day. I feel it in my heart and soul, my man's there.'

'Now, don't you go getting your hopes up, there's a lot of places filled with broken soldiers. Many have now been closed down and this might be one of them. If I were you, I'd be prepared for this.'

She threw her arms round this man who held all her hopes and said, 'It might close tomorrow, but not today. He waits there for me. See, feel my heart.'

Before he could stop her, she'd put his hand against her breast. 'Yes,' was all he could mutter, withdrawing his hand in case a passer-by thought he was molesting her, and added, 'Best of luck, and Godspeed.'

The horse-drawn taxi stopped outside the tall grey building. She stepped down and made her way towards two iron gates. All kinds of emotions swept through her as she surveyed the ominous building with its shutters closed and barred.

'One could imagine Bull Buckley locked in a place like that, not poor broken laddies who gave everything for their so-called country,' she thought. Nerves trembled down her arm and tingled at the fingertips. Holding her bag nervously to her chest, she went through the gate and knocked on a double-sided door. Ages went by, or at least it seemed that way, then eventually the door was opened. A middle-aged gentleman asked what she wanted.

Her voice low, yet barely containing her eagerness to get inside, she said, 'Where's my man?' Not waiting for an answer, she pushed past the closing door and the man. Inside she found a seat in a large waiting-room and sat nervously down. Sniffing the air like a bloodhound for her husband, she blurted out, 'Come on then, take me to my Bruar!'

The man at the door seemed a decent sort and sat next to her with a notepad in his hand. He held a pen dripping with fresh ink and asked what her maiden name was.

'It's my man's name I've given you. Now, do you have a soldier here by the name of Bruar Stewart—he's from Scotland? If so, get him so I can take him home. London stinks like a sow's arse.'

Her dry throat hurt, three times she repeated her question, swearing and cursing in her anxiety. There was whispering and shaking of heads from others who were in the waiting area. If they only knew how much pain and time her quest had taken then they might have been more understanding. The man still persisted asking her questions until she could take no more. She left him abruptly and ran up the main staircase. Through an archway she saw a long corridor lined with narrow doors. In each was a small opening through which she peered. There was a man in each room. Her eyes widened as each sad, gaunt face looked at her, then lowered its head to stare at a cold stone floor. Banging on every door, she called his name over and over. 'Bruar, it's me—Megan! We must go home, Bruar, where the hell are you?'

All she heard was an echo of her own voice and footsteps behind. With her heartbeat quickening she began running again, came to a winding staircase and started climbing. 'Wait there, young woman, you've gone too far, no one is allowed up there!' The man who had questioned her, who by now had been joined by another, got past and physically halted her.

Convinced they were hiding him from her, she screamed out, 'Bruar Stewart, you get down here now! It's me, Megan.'

Both men, gently yet firmly, led her back to the waiting-room, where, overcome with emotion, she fell into a chair and sobbed.

After a time the man who had been questioning her again sat next to her and asked if she felt more composed. He assured her it wasn't uncommon for young wives seeking news of their husbands to react as she did. He told her that they wanted to help but needed information, and could she fill in a form?

'What's a form?' she asked, drying her eyes.

'Before allowing visits it's very important we establish who comes here. All that is required is name, address, and relationship with inmate, and so forth.' He laid the form in front of her on a small desk where an inkpot sat neatly beside a nib pen and piece of blotting paper.

Ignoring the writing materials, she said, 'Look, mister, I can't read nor write, so don't waste time. Just show me my man, or at least tell me if he's here.'

This man was obviously a stickler for the regulations and said, 'This information is not in my power to divulge. You must understand that some of our inmates are extremely violent, and only close relatives are given permission to visit. If you cannot provide the necessary details, I am within my rights to escort you off the premises.'

'I have no proof of who I am! All I want to know is, have you got my man?'

A sledgehammer would not have broken this man's resolve; she had no identity therefore had to be put out of the building. It took three sturdy male nurses, all wearing white coats, to remove Megan as she continued to scream and shout for Bruar.

Out on the street, feelings of the deepest despondency spread over her like a shroud. 'Some kind of demon is fighting me all the way, but I won't let you win,' she screamed up into the noise of London. No one seemed remotely interested as she kicked carriage wheels and spat at dogs. Street after lonely street presented a heaving mass of bodies heading everywhere yet nowhere. London reminded her of a weather-beaten oak tree. From a distance it looked like any other tree, but as one got nearer its bark showed all the creatures living off it. Maggots, flies, mould, moss, worms, the list was endless, and the nearer you got the more could be seen, eating into its bark, a never-ending army of devourers. Until one day the old oak could feed them no more and began to crumble and die. London, the old oak tree, would live on forever in her mind as the guard who kept her away from Bruar.

Exhausted she continued to walk along the bank of the Thames. She did not want to go back to her hotel, and thought another walk might clear her head. If a fisherman on the riverbank could lead her to the door of Morton Home, then someone else might help her find a way into it. 'I mustn't give in,' she forced the thought to the fore, 'not when I've come so far.'

Down by the water were countless ducks and geese, and she wondered how they stayed alive. Standing by the water's edge she saw a man with a bag of stale bread surrounded by birds feeding excitedly who answered her question. He looked shabby, as if every penny in his pocket was counted, and she thought it odd he could afford to feed wild birds. Suddenly he began shouting at several teenagers who had started to throw stones at the birds. In time the boys tired of their play and ran off. She watched the man pick up an injured bird. He stroked its feathers, speaking words of a gentle nature. Megan moved closer to hear what he was saying, but before she could do so, the bird had recovered and was flying high above her. Watching it she hardly noticed the man approach. He went to her side and said, 'Excuse me.'

But with only a few pounds left in her pocket, she remembered the Newcastle thief running away with all she owned and the tramps who chased her. 'Sorry,' she told him abruptly, 'but I've nothing to spare.' Wrapping her coat tightly round her, she turned to hurry away.

'No, wait a minute, I'm not going to harm you, please.' There was a slight pause as he fumbled inside his jacket. He took something from a wallet and held it up. 'Yes, I knew it was you.' His words frightened and puzzled her. But this was a big city and lots of tricks were played in the cities. Convinced this was another ploy to rid her of what little money she had, she ran off as fast as she could, but he wasn't giving up and gave chase. It took a long time to shake him off. With heart near to bursting and breath almost leaving her body, at last, with great relief, she saw her hotel. When on its steps, she dared to look back to see if he was following her, but she'd lost him. Panting up the steps, she told herself that in the morning Morton Home would see her back again. Until they told her where Bruar was, she swore every single day she'd do a Bull Buckley on them.

This determination gave her renewed strength which quickened her step to the hotel door. Just as she put a foot inside, a voice called out, 'Megan!'

Turning slowly, she saw the shabby man who'd chased her. He held up a photograph for her to see. 'Oh my God, you have our wedding photo!' She had found Sandy, Bruar's wartime friend!

Inside her hotel room, he told the story of how, after the war, he found Bruar in a hospital and kept in touch with him while he convalesced in Sussex, and also visited him here in the place named Morton Home. He was near there because he had been to see Bruar that day.

'Do you have any idea what it means to meet someone like you?' she asked him. 'My man has been a long time in finding, but now, to see you and talk about him! Oh, Sandy, I could kiss the face off you.'

'Steady on, lassie. I promised, you see.' He went on, 'Before he was hit he begged me to find you; gave me the photo so that I'd recognise you. I had meant to come north and seek you out, but getting a few pennies to live on was as far as I got. I'm heart-sorry, lass.'

'Och, never mind that. I've been searching for him myself, and only this day did I find Morton Home. But can you tell me why, when I went to the home, they refused to even tell me if he was there?'

'They have to be extra careful since a lad went mad, escaped and murdered a postman. Since then it's locked rooms and round-the-clock guards. Don't worry, though, tomorrow I'll take you there myself.'

'Sandy,' her eyes were pitiful as she asked, 'Is he sick? What I mean is, does he have memories?' She searched his face; it was easy to read.

But inwardly her picture was not to be smudged. 'Don't say a word, because when he sees me things will come back, you'll see, and he will know me.'

The night fog had come down and all the night people were to be heard out on the street below when Sandy finished his story.

'And he lay there on that beach among the dead? My poor laddie, what must have gone through his mind foreseeing his end? He must have witnessed it, otherwise he'd never have parted with our wedding photo. She went into her bag and took the burnt half of her photo showing his face and laid it over the one brought by Sandy. How uncanny that they fitted together like pieces of a jigsaw. 'We are meant to be, Sandy, nothing will stop us.'

Her visitor was tired and had to go home; this was a dingy shelter for homeless people, but now that he'd found her and kept his promise it wouldn't be quite such a bad place.

After he left, it took all her willpower not to climb to the hotel roof and sing from its chimney tops. Soon, at long last, they'd be together.

—

The man who had forcibly removed her from the Asylum the day before was a nurse who knew Sandy. With her new male companion she felt stronger facing him.

'She can neither read nor write,' he told the man who, on seeing Megan, at first totally refused entry. 'That's why she got so flustered yesterday.'

'My sincere apologies to you, dear, but surely Sandy has told you about the serious situations that can arise within these walls?'

Megan nodded, desperately trying not to scream. The closed doors, mumbling voices and high ceilings made her ache. She wanted them to know that as soon as she and Bruar returned to Scotland the freedom of moor and glen would be his domain. The tiny piece of affection she felt for this grim place was that it held her man in safety, but now at last she would take him home. 'Can I see my husband?' she asked quietly.

'As soon as Doctor Cunningham has finished his rounds he'll speak with you,' said the nurse. 'Meanwhile I'll fetch you both a cup of tea.' He walked off, leaving Sandy and Megan to wait. 'Lassie,' Sandy laid a hand on hers and continued, 'far be it from me to pour cold water on this day's meeting, but I think the doctor will try to put you off.'

'If he does then I'll slit his throat. Surely he'll let me see my man?'

'He'll tell you that within these walls your man will be safe, whereas outside he may react differently.'

'Sandy, no doctor breathing will separate us. I promise you this, if I can't take Bruar home then I'll set fire to this place, if that's what it takes to free him. Do you have any idea what a place like this does to tinkers? My flesh is crawling as we speak, man.'

In due time a small man sporting a tartan bow tie, metal-rimmed glasses and wearing a white coat far too big for him came in and sat by her side, took her hand and shook it warmly. 'My dear girl, I'm so glad you've found him at last. Now what do you think of his condition? Fine, isn't he? Oh yes, we look after our lads in here. They want for nothing, not a thing. Wholesome food and a warm bed, that can't be bad, now?'

Sandy stopped Dr Cunningham because he could see Megan's eyes narrowing. 'She'll thump him in a minute,' he thought. 'Excuse me interrupting, doctor, but Mrs Stewart hasn't seen her husband yet.'

'Have you not? I was under the impression you came yesterday.'

Sandy again interrupted, 'She was unable to sign the documents.'

Just at that moment the nurse came in with two teas. Rather than speak to the doctor, Megan drank hers down, an easy task because the tea was half-cold. She thought, 'If that's included in the good food, then Bruar will kick the walls down if he's a spark in him.'

It was obvious she was impatient, so the doctor rose to his feet and said, 'Well, best go to see your man, then.'

She stared at Sandy, then back to the doctor. Was this is it, then? After all this time they were to come face to face! Her hand reached out for Sandy's; quickly he grasped it, linking her arm through his. She seemed unsteady.

The walls of the narrow corridor streamed past. She stared up at the winding metal staircase, feeling her head swoon. Grasping Sandy even tighter, she counted the clanking of their steps on the metal stairs.

Her heart sank like a river stone when Sandy pointed to the door. She looked into his eyes pleadingly, yet not knowing why. Perhaps she wanted him to wave a magic wand and bring Bruar smiling into her arms. As the doctor turned the brass door-handle she stopped him.

'It would take a week to tell you all I've suffered to reach this moment. Can you give us privacy?'

'Of course,' the doctor assured her, 'but just a little word of warning, if I may. War can leave scars of dark and ugly scenes where once beauty and happiness reigned.'

'I have recently witnessed dark and ugly scenes, doctor, but behind this door is all the beauty and happiness I need.'

She waited until her companions' footsteps were reduced to a whisper on the stairs before turning the shiny brass handle. It was difficult; she didn't imagine it would be, yet why was her arm feeling stiff? For all her love and devotion, would Bruar's reaction be hostile? The experts made him sound like a lunatic. One final push of the door and it would be too late to turn away.

Quickly she stepped inside. The door was a welcome support for her back. She closed her eyes, then opened them. Sitting like a school child on a wooden chair, his hands on his knees, staring through the iron bars of the narrow window was her lost husband. At long last, here was her Bruar in all his wonderful glory. Mind sleeping or not, here he was—safe.

Apart from a haircut he'd not changed at all. She approached and turned him to her. Cupping his big chin with shaking hands she kissed him full and passionately. 'Would you look at you, my bonny proud laddie, what are things coming to when Bruar Stewart sports a bowl haircut! Love, my love, I thank all that's divine for bringing us together. Nothing will part us, do you hear me, nothing. Soon we'll be chasing the grouse among the wild beauty of our glens, beneath Scotland's blue-grey skies.'

He sat motionless, staring at the floor as though a chilly morning frost covered him. For an age she held him, kissed and stroked his hair. 'My boy, oh my dear silent love, soon this will be a bad memory and you'll smile again, tell tales of those Vikings. Wait and see, I'm going now to get that doctor. He can please himself, but you and me, we are getting off home.'

His dead face and listless body would have sent many in tears from the room, but they made her more determined. 'Sandy told me what state you were in on that bloody beach. I know you can't recognise me, but one day soon you will. We'll walk upon the cliff tops at Durness with the wind blowing through this blonde hair of yours. These eyes will see again. I feel it, I promise it will happen.'

His hand fell limp from her grasp as his empty eyes continued staring into nothingness. Yet how warm his body felt as she pressed herself into his. How sweet was the aroma of his flesh; this was their heaven.

Sandy and the doctor were thoughtful enough to give her plenty of time, but she so wished it would stand still. Time, however, will not be halted, and soon the door was opening into her world, intruding on their privacy.

'Mrs Stewart, as you can see this is only a shell of the man you once knew. When young wives come here and see their husbands' condition it seems to paint a clearer picture of where their future lies. I feel now that you too will be of this mind.'

'Oh do you now? Well, I have news for you, Doctor, sir, but my man walks and hears and sees. He eats and no doubt can piss. As far as I'm concerned that'll do for starters. Can his belongings be brought together? I'm taking him home.'

Sandy closed his hands over hers and shook his head. The doctor said that under no circumstances could Bruar leave the premises, he was unable to function in the wider world.

She pulled her hands free and wrapped them round Bruar's neck. 'Look, I will not leave my man here, not after all this time, all the searching, you ask the impossible.'

Sandy closed the door. He was all too aware that Doctor Cunningham had positioned two male nurses outside and was about to call them in. He'd spent enough time with Bruar to know the mind of this couple; he'd try and make the doctor see sense. 'Would it make a difference if I told you that he was a tinker, and, in the eyes of society, worthless? I feel the board would take a dim view of this model asylum housing vermin.'

Megan could see what Sandy was trying to do, so gave him a hand. 'Aye doctor, wait until he starts shitting in that nice disinfected corner. And tearing the feathers out of those fine pillows on that bed and stuffing them through the window bars. Imagine what passers-by will say. My God, man, this place might get shut down if it's discovered such a filthy person is taking a room, paid for no doubt by the King's good purse, or is it those kind officers' wives?'

'Listen, both of you, this man has been under my care for some time, and has never shown anything other than impeccable behaviour.'

'Just wait, though, he'll change, us dirty tinkers always do. Like old dogs we don't bother licking ourselves; the smell will be awful.' Megan was clutching at every excuse to allow her man to be freed.

'But maybe I could get him transferred to Scotland, would you accept that?' Doctor Cunningham was beginning to see sense.

Megan shook her head. 'Give him back his freedom, sir,' she begged. 'Let us go home to the hillside, and I promise nothing will be heard or seen of us again.'

The doctor sat on Bruar's bed and thought long and hard before saying, 'Well, I certainly could do with the room. The Army Wives Committee is always looking for spaces, there are plenty more unfortunates needing a bed.'

Megan felt her knees weaken; she sat close to Bruar clasping her hands together and gave thanks. Sandy retrieved a small suitcase from under the bed and began packing what few possessions Bruar had. They were going home. It had taken so much time, yet at long last Scotland was only a few hours away.

———

At the station on the platform Bruar stood between his wife and Sandy, each linking an arm. 'I have been so swept up with things I forgot to ask, but where you are from?' said Megan.

'I'm a Highlander, that's why that big softy and me had so much in common.'

'Why are you not going home then, Sandy?' She was wiping Bruar's nose, every bit the carer, and although she'd been told he would never be any different, she'd enough of her lad to love.

'I expect it's because of two things. One being I promised always to take care of Bruar, and secondly, as I said, lack of funds.'

'Sandy,' she said excitedly, 'There's enough money for the three of us to go home. Come with us and be there when he opens his eyes, for mark my words he will speak again. If you knew about the Seer and how circumstances have swept me here, then I know you'd have faith.'

'He always said you were a dream of a wife but not a dreamer. The doctor made sense when he told you this man of yours was severely brain-damaged. Better get used to it. I've been with him a long time now, and there's not been so much as a blink of an eyelash.'

'You don't know which parts to touch or words to whisper. I'll take over now, and if this is all I get then so be it. He's mine, and if we can't join in life then we'll do it in dreams. Please understand, Sandy, there's no way I'd let him rot like mould on cheese in that barred prison. He can live with the wind in his hair and the heather beneath his feet. Now come on, here's the train. Be there when I open his eyes.'

Sandy shuffled his feet and pushed his hands deep inside his pockets. For a moment he looked around and then shook his head.

She could see all he needed was a wee push. 'I can't take this big lump on and off trains, come on, man, give me a hand.'

It worked! With a grin spreading from ear to ear Sandy helped her escort Bruar on the final journey home.

'Never,' she promised herself, 'will we be parted again, not as long as we both live!'

—

Sandy left them at Inverness, after solemnly promising he'd visit them when he'd said hello to relatives in the north. In Thurso, with the last of her money, she bought a small buggy and an old horse, sturdy enough to trot the moor road to Durness.

Finding Helen's tiny cottage locked up, she went to call on Father Flynn.

'Well now, would you believe in miracles?' he said, seeing her clinging to Bruar.

'He'll come back to me. It might take ages, but I can see even now a sparkle in his eye. If you'd seen how blank and dead he was, sitting in a hard chair staring out at iron bars and smoke-filled skies in that bleak asylum! I kid you not, it was a pitiful sight. Here though, where he was brought up, this place will stir life into him. Now, where's Helen?'

'So many boys come back from the war like that, I knew of two lads in Sutherland, grand clever heads on their shoulders too. But now they can't even tie a shoelace. Lassie, be prepared for little improvement. Helen, bless her, is no longer with us. She took a severe stroke. There was no pain, I can say, because she spent a week under my roof until the end. Come away in and have something to eat, can he manage to do that?'

'Yes, he can function normally. But tell me if Helen left word of her house? I need a home for Bruar.'

'I'm so sorry, dear, but she never thought a relative was alive, and so she left her small home to the church. Young men entering the priesthood visit periodically and live in it; it's a kind of sanctuary, if you like.'

In that instant the feelings of homelessness and her new responsibility weighed heavy on her. Durness was a bleak, cold place and without a roof, no place to heal a broken mind.

'Father, I'm desperate. Do you think as there's no one living in the old place at the moment that we can stay, just until I can find some other suitable place?'

'I'll fetch the key, but meanwhile have some food.' He ushered them in to sit, and marvelled at how Megan sat Bruar on a seat, placed cutlery in his hands and watched over him as he ate. He thought about how remarkable it was that a young woman should shoulder such a burden, but in the same thought put it down to God, as he did every miraculous event.

Every day Megan spent hours talking Bruar through past experiences. 'Think on big Rory, and how he and O'Connor would stumble home drunk. And try to remember old Doctor Mackenzie with his crabbit horse. Do you remember Rachel, and Jimmy your brother? Their little boy Nicholas? Oh my love, try to think back.' She pointed to his head, and over and over again repeated those tales of family and memories past. Day after day she'd come back, sink into a chair and cry with exasperation. Bruar was unresponsive. Whatever damage had been done, she was now totally convinced that if she wanted her man then she had to start to create a new one; the same person, but a new mind. In other words, his life's learning had to begin at that moment. So, as if with a newborn infant, she began from scratch. To her it presented yet another challenge, but for her all life was a challenge.

Progress crept like a tortoise, and for every step forward, ten went back. Each and every waking minute was spent working meticulously on what was inside her husband's head, but the work stopped at night. This was her time. Cuddling close into his back, she'd close her eyes and pray to whoever controlled dreams. Gently, as sleep swept over them, they'd be transported back to a secluded, peaceful, sun-kissed Highland hillside where the vibrant, healthy and passionate Bruar would take her in his strong arms and claim her inch by inch. Morning, with its reality, would rush into the tiny bedroom along with dancing sunrays. She'd turn him towards her and say, 'Thank you, my love.' And as usual the response was the same, a blank look.

'Still,' she'd say getting him dressed, 'thanks be for dreams.'

Nothing much changed apart from an odd glance or half-smile. 'If there was one single thread that I might cling to, my love,' she whispered, walking him along familiar footpaths he would have played upon as a child. 'I'd hang on and not let go. But it's so deep inside, that river of horror that finds no sea, and only you can swim in it.'

It was a warm day, a brief spell of windless blue sky, when she decided to take him to Balnakiel graveyard and tell him of her visit from the Seer. She'd speak at length, hoping one word might release a spark. Everything was a long shot, but worth trying.

She sat him down near the simple stone with the words Rory Stewart on it and told him of her experience. He stared at the place of his childhood days with no sign of recognition. She left him sitting there as she wandered onto the white sandy beach.

For a moment her charge was forgotten as her own memories flooded back. Bruar would be safe sitting in the graveyard; the high cliffs with the views to the northern ocean called her.

The Indian summer may have been responsible for her giddy mood that morning, or perhaps it was her night of dreams, but she headed off, light-footed, to climb the cliff tops. 'This is a magic season of the year,' she told herself, reaching an alder tree growing bent beside a willow. The first frost had arrived the night before, and she saw how the flow of sap had been halted. She ran her hand over the barks of both trees, and already crimson and gold leaves lined the path. She wondered how bad the winters would be so far north, and wished at that moment Bruar was gushing about the weather in his land and the Vikings and boggy ground. She wanted many times to tell him of Bull Buckley and his fate. 'Mother Earth, will I ever get him back? If only you could show me a sign.'

The day was easy as she stood overlooking the ocean. Puffins dived and soared skywards; she whispered to them, 'I have brought him home.' Throwing back her head she closed her eyes and called out, 'Big Rory, Balnakiel, I did it!' She sat down amid the late summer offering of warm air and full-grown grass. A sudden movement in the sparse undergrowth caught her attention; it was a tiny vole rushing back and forth, nibbling bits of foliage. 'You wee thing,' she said into herself, 'I bet that's a layer of fat you're busy storing round those tiny flanks to see you through the winter ahead. Well, keep out of the owl's sight when night comes.'

Suddenly it dawned on her that Bruar was still down at the

295

graveyard. Running like a mother seeking a lost child, she rushed breathlessly in through the gates, but he'd gone from the grave seat; he'd wandered off. Panic-stricken, she dashed everywhere, but there was no sign of him. The only place he could be, as far as she could determine, was on the far-off cliffs. There was no safe footing there—she remembered Helen telling her that when the boys were small that cliff path was forbidden. 'Bruar,' she called, 'wait for me.' Finding the path treacherous and breaking away underfoot, she scrambled onwards. Reaching the top her heart stopped as she saw him teetering precariously on the edge.

'Oh no, get back from there,' she gently whispered, edging nearer. 'Bruar, look at Megan, turn and see me. Come to me.' His dead, blank stare gave her the answer she least wanted to get. 'I have no choice but to inch my way over and drag him back,' she thought nervously.

Then, at the moment her hand touched his jersey, a voice shouted out, 'What the hell are you doing up there with him in that condition?' It was Father Flynn, but it would have been better if he'd stayed away, because his sudden appearance startled Bruar so much he jumped backward, knocking her over.

She tried to leap forward, but the crumbling rocks beneath her feet gave way, and over the edge she went. 'I'm finished,' she thought, as her fingers clung desperately to a cluster of ancient water-battered tree roots. Above her, Father Flynn lay flat on his stomach and called down to her. 'I haven't got the reach, can you hang on until I fetch help?'

'No time! I'm gone—just take care of my man,' she called, as her fingers began to slip. She thought of thudding onto the rocks below and tightened her eyelids shut.

Then, as the last finger lost its hold, she relaxed her body and gave in to gravity. Instantly two strong arms grabbed hers and pulled her up like a rag doll. Her eyes opened to find her husband; no one else. He had saved her from certain death. The blank eyes still staring from their sockets showed no emotion, and those lifesaving arms once again hung limp and dead.

She knew what had happened, she was breathing and living proof of it. The old priest had also witnessed the miracle. Yet how could it be explained, what would their words be? That a young man without a thought in his empty mind had reached down and pulled his wife to safety?

'It's a blessing from God above,' came the explanation from the man of the cloth. 'There are those that swear angels are sent with each priest. Oh, and for sure I felt so privileged to have taken in this sight. I tell you, Megan, an angel entered into Bruar and saved the very life of ye!'

'Yes, Father, you could well be right.'

Her arm hugged Bruar tighter as the threesome took the road home.

'That was a frightening experience hanging from that tree root, Father, I really thought my end had come. Tell me, why were you there?'

'To say I received a letter addressed to you. I have it in the presbytery. Come with me and I'll read it for you.'

'For me, Father? But who would know where I am?'

Passing the church and heading toward the presbytery, another wonderful happening blessed her day. Bruar, to her astonishment, pointed to her head and said with a slow mumble, 'One grey.'

'One grey what, my love? What is it you're trying to say?'

'Tell us, son,' asked the priest jerking him round to face him. But there was no explanation, nothing, just the same limp arms and glassy eyes.

'He's trying, though, Father. I tell you it's a good sign. Somewhere under that mop of blond hair are threads of memories, all searching for each other.'

Soon with warm tea in hands they were sitting within the sparsely furnished interior of the Durness presbytery as Father Flynn proceeded to read. Megan could not help but feel excited, and yet with all the roads, places and people she'd encountered, it also entered her head that the contents of the letter the old man was about to read might not be pleasing. There were in fact two letters inside a large envelope. The first letter, larger than the other, was buff-coloured and had a look of officialdom about it. It was from a firm of Perth solicitors.

Father Flynn began: 'Being solicitors in charge of the affairs of Doctor Roger Mackenzie, we have been instructed to inform you, Mrs Megan Stewart, that our client, being of sound mind, has bequeathed his entire estate to you. Following his recent death, it our duty to hand over keys of said property to yourself.' The priest went on, but not one word made sense, apart from those that said Doctor Mackenzie, a dear friend of her family, had died.

'You seem to own a bit of property, lass. What are you going to do?'

Her eyes welled up, at the memory of that sweet old man with the crabbit mare. His usual call, intended to be for a few minutes, would undoubtedly last all morning or afternoon; it would depend on his mood or just the flow of tinkers' crack. The ease his visits brought to Annie, her mother, in those last agonising days of life. His parting left a hole unfilled, and in that moment she saw and yearned for the Angus Glens.

'I think I'll take my man back to Kirriemor, Father,' she told him. 'Dr Mackenzie's house isn't big, but it holds memories, good ones. Tell me what the second letter says?'

'I forgot about it,' he said, opening the small, whitish envelope.

'Dear Megan,

It has been a long time since Rachel, her son Nicholas and I set sail for America.

We settled in the great city of New York. We spent a wonderful time there and loved our Manhattan apartment. Nicholas is almost ready for school. He is a handsome child and resembles his father, his mother informed me.

The reason I am forced to write, is sadly to inform you that recently Rachel took ill, and after three weeks of pneumonia lost her brave battle for life.

I have sent this letter to an address she said would in time reach your attention. I do hope it does.

She said on her deathbed that you must not be sad, because at last she and Jimmy will be together.

I now hope to relieve you of any concern for Nicholas. I have already adopted him, and shall do my utmost to see he wants for nothing,

Kindest regards

Lady Arabella Cortonach.'

'Rachel, my dearest sister, you got your rich life, but what a pity you didn't live to enjoy it! Still, I know your last breath would be given to see Nicholas well cared for. Bless you, my sister, sleep peacefully. I shall visit mother's grave for you when I get there.'

In spite of her husband's miraculous rescue and her new-found property, many memories picked up the threads of times past; she ached deeply, and wanted to be alone. The last of her family apart from young Nicholas were lost. 'Why do we come into this world,' she asked the priest, 'if all we do is hurt, then die?'

Clouds were forming in the late afternoon sky. 'Rain's not far off,' he said, putting a hand on her shoulder. 'When it's windy and bright, a woman washes clothes, but not if there's sign of wet weather. Life's a bit like that. We should live with the good and bad, but only remember the best days. You know, my dear, no matter how cloudy life gets, I promise you sunny days are just round the corner.'

Father Flynn said his farewells as she hugged and thanked him. Taking Bruar's hand, she guided him onto the cart. It would take three days to reach Thurso, where she'd sell her horse and cart to whoever gave her a good price. Then, for the final time, they would take the train south to Perth, and from there it was a short journey to the home that her old friend had gifted her.

Soon she was slipping the key of Doctor Mackenzie's house into its lock. For the several weeks that followed, she revelled in cleaning it, inside and out. He'd left a small sum of money, and this allowed a fairly easy winter. The kind folks welcomed them home, and where once doors had been closed to them, the opposite was now the case. Megan and her lost man were greeted with open arms. The ploughmen had no quarrel with her or Bruar. In time they settled into their new life.

Bruar continued to make slow progress, and one night while a wild wind rattled the windows in their frames, he spoke!

It happened without warning. It was the constant battering of wind on the old house that did it. Neither could sleep, such was the intensity of the wind. He was disturbed, and it seemed to agitate him. She pulled bedcovers around them both and sang a soft song. He quietened, then to her utter amazement ran a hand over her head and whispered, as a sliver of moonlight rested on her head, 'Megan has grey hair.'

She threw back the covers and grabbed him by the shoulders; he was smiling from ear to ear.

'That's what you were trying to say at Durness!' She leapt from the bed and dashed across to the dressing table, fumbling with a small oil lamp. She stared into the oval mirror, and there was indeed a very prominent grey-white hair visible among the black.

'Bruar, talk to me—say something, anything!' She lifted a shoe from the floor, held it above her head and asked, 'What's this?' her eyes staring like eggs.

'Put down the shoe, Megan.'

'Oh my dear sweet man, at long last! Mother Earth has heard and answered my prayers.' She dived from the room, threw open the front door, ran into the garden, and danced around her neat flower beds; sprays of rainwater fanning around her bare feet. Such was the joy when she returned to bed, they cried into each other all night long.

From that night Bruar progressed in leaps and bounds. Life took on a gentle serenity. She continued to wander the high hills gathering heather roots and making her pot scourers. He took on work with a shepherd, and showed a wonderful ability for the job. Soon he was able to look after his own flock. With his doggies excitedly circling his feet, the seasons passed in a gentle, harmonious pace.

Children, however, failed to bless the quiet household and many a time Megan would take crocheted mittens to a neighbour's new baby, just to have the excuse to look and hold the tiny infant.

One night, while Bruar had been helping with a farmer's lambing and had been out all night, Megan found sleep difficult. Thinking that she heard him on the doorstep, she wrapped a shawl around her shoulders and opened the door. Half-expecting the dogs to rush past her, she was puzzled to see no one there. She called his name several times and was about to close the door, when she was suddenly startled by a voice. 'Please, missus, don't shut yer door!'

Megan stepped outside and saw a shivering girl, no more than fifteen if she was that, standing by the house. 'Come out of the shadows, lassie, and tell me why you are out at this hour.'

'Missus, ah canna keep it, ah've left it lying in yon wee gairden shed. I ken you'll be good tae it, God bless ye, missus.' The girl reached out to Megan and pushed a torn blanket into her hands. With her sleeve she wiped tears away and said, 'Ah'm a tinker, and faither would kill me. I ca' her Mary.'

At that the girl turned on her heels, and before Megan could utter a word was gone down the road. She wondered if the family was camping in their old site. She wanted to ask who they were, but darkness and the speed of the girl's departure prevented a conversation. Megan felt a sense of déja vu, flashes of visions of herself running off down the road all those years ago. She was about to go back inside the house when a small cry came from behind her in the old garden shed. Her investigation revealed what she had already guessed would be there. Fearing that an infant was lying there in ill-health or worse, she stepped inside. It was dark, but a lamp hung on a nail behind the door. She rushed back to the house and lit the lamp at her fire. Soon she found the tiny parcel curled in a basket covered in bracken—a baby girl, newly born. It took her no time to bring the babe into the warmth of the house and fill it full of warmed milk.

But what to do? Whoever mother was, she certainly wanted no one to know of her child. Megan felt certain, though, that she'd come back when things were better. But she waited and waited, and as one month followed another, the mother never returned.

So into their lives came a daughter who grew strong and single-minded. Her adoptive parents from the beginning told her the truth. It seemed important that she knew of her background. Years passed, and although encouraged to do so, young Mary never left to search for her natural mother. She was content to share her life with clumsy Bruar, even although he stammered and sometimes uttered not a word for months. But when he did find his voice, she marvelled at his tales of Vikings, peat bog monsters, wild waters and high mountains.

The most precious memories of all came from her proud surrogate mother. From her, in winter nights beside a roaring fire, she learned the story of how against insurmountable odds she set off to search for her severely shell-shocked husband, and regardless of fiend or foe, single-handedly brought him home...

One thing moved and haunted Mary—that 'promise'. Megan always felt she might let her man down when he talked about the ancient burial site. So when her death approached before his, she laid it on Mary's shoulders, and asked her, when his time came, if she could fulfil the promise made all those years ago on a bonny windswept hillside.

It was a responsibility she shouldered with pride, and carried out one winter day.

Below the derelict Parbh lighthouse, his remains lie for eternity. Not so his spirit! It dances in the salty sea sprays, gliding among the puffins and seagulls. It holds back hordes of Viking warriors, then sees them blindly descending into the peat bogs of Sutherland. And nearby there's a green-eyed tinker lassie watching with pride.

THE END

POSTSCRIPT

I reflected during many sleepless nights that my storyteller had more insight into her tale than a traveller woman who had just been told it by another. Unable to get free of these restless thoughts, I took a visit to my late friend's lawyer, who held her legal documents. She had left no heir and he agreed to see me. In his presence I viewed the only papers still surviving to say who she really was.

The marriage and death certificates, plus a torn Peddler's Licence, gave familiar information, but there was one more document—a certificate of adoption. Mary had been abandoned as a child and reared by a couple named Margaret and Blair Stewart.

Was Blair none other than Bruar, and was Megan's real name Margaret?

I don't think I want to track down war records or write to the authorities for information about the characters from this story. Something tells me that Mary knew the answers, and that's good enough for me.